MARVEL-V[redacted]

MOON KNIGHT

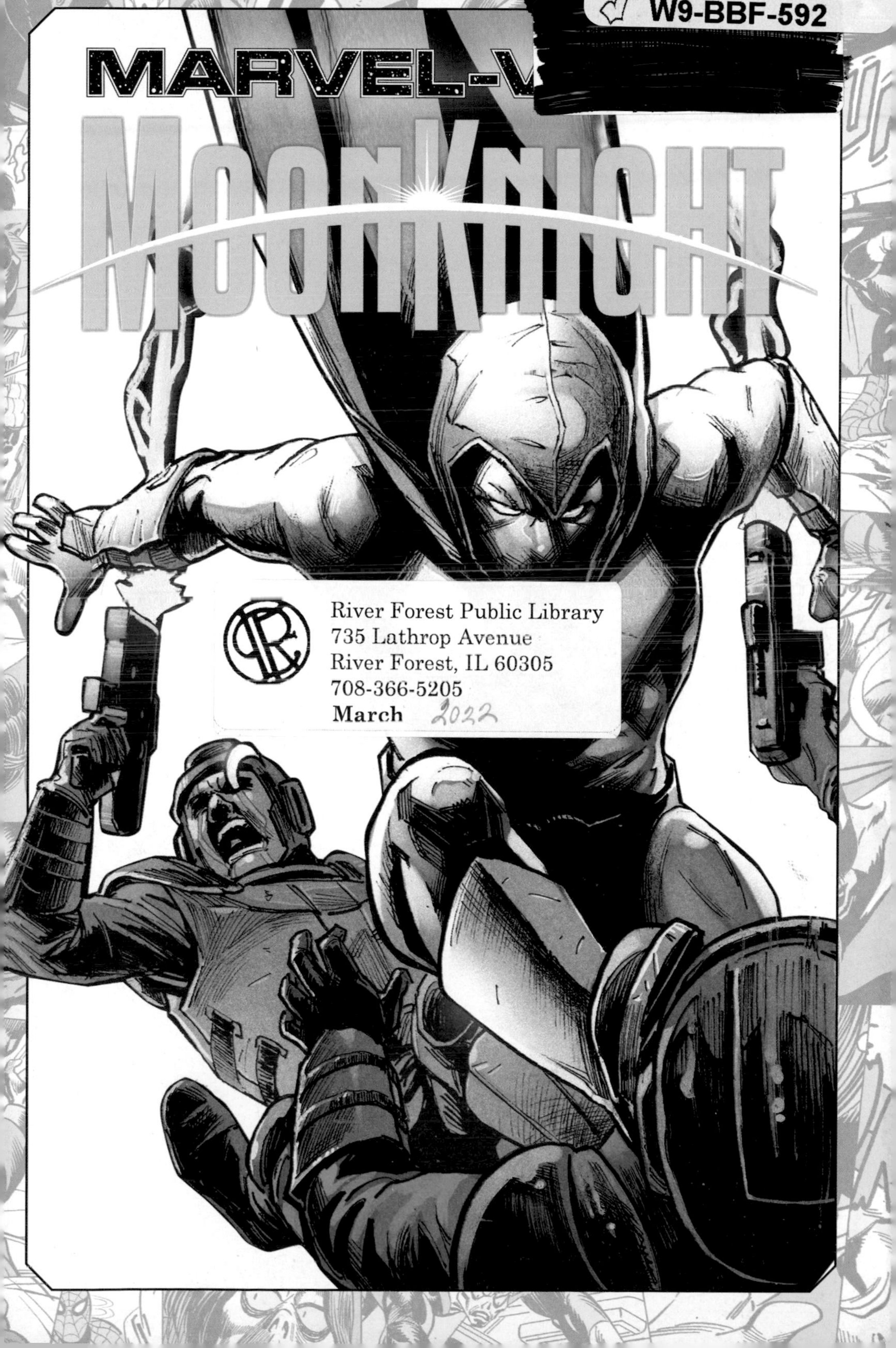

MARVEL-VERSE

MOON KNIGHT

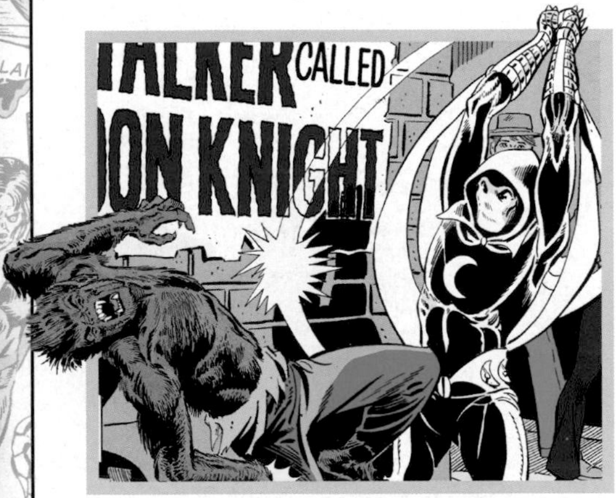
CALLED

WEREWOLF BY NIGHT #32-33

WRITER: **DOUG MOENCH**
PENCILER: **DON PERLIN**
INKER: **HOWIE PERLIN**
COLORISTS: **PHIL RACHELSON & GEORGE ROUSSOS**
LETTERERS: **RAY HOLLOWAY & DEBRA JAMES**
EDITOR: **LEN WEIN**

AMAZING SPIDER-MAN #220

WRITER: **MICHAEL FLEISHER**
ARTIST & LETTERER: **BOB McLEOD**
COLORIST: **BOB SHAREN**
EDITOR: **DENNIS O'NEIL**

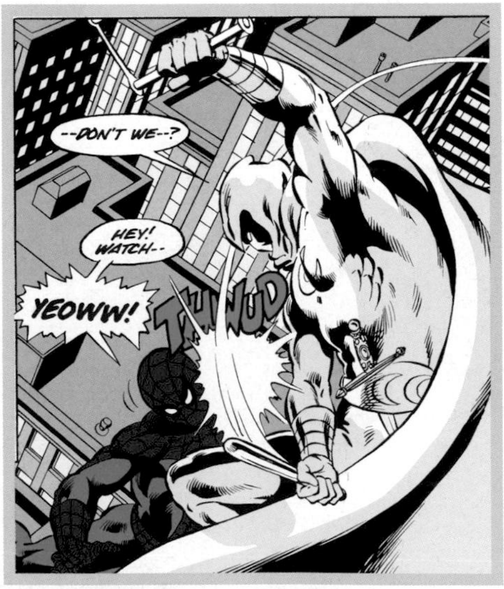
--DON'T WE--?
HEY! WATCH--
YEOWW!

MOON KNIGHT ANNUAL #1

WRITER: **CULLEN BUNN**
ARTISTS: **IBRAHIM MOUSTAFA & MATT HORAK**
COLORIST: **MIKE SPICER**
LETTERER: **VC's JOE SABINO**
COVER ART: **PHILIP TAN & RAIN BEREDO**
EDITOR: **LAUREN AMARO**
EXECUTIVE EDITOR: **TOM BREVOORT**

MOON KNIGHT #13

WRITER: **DOUG MOENCH**
ARTIST: **BILL SIENKIEWICZ**
COLORIST: **CHRISTIE SCHEELE**
LETTERER: **JOE ROSEN**
ASSISTANT EDITOR: **RALPH MACCHIO**
EDITOR: **DENNIS O'NEIL**

COLLECTION EDITOR: **JENNIFER GRÜNWALD** ASSISTANT EDITOR: **DANIEL KIRCHHOFFER**
ASSISTANT MANAGING EDITOR: **MAIA LOY** ASSOCIATE MANAGER, TALENT RELATIONS: **LISA MONTALBANO**
ASSOCIATE MANAGER, DIGITAL ASSETS: **JOE HOCHSTEIN** MASTERWORKS EDITOR: **CORY SEDLMEIER**
VP PRODUCTION & SPECIAL PROJECTS: **JEFF YOUNGQUIST** RESEARCH: **JESS HARROLD**
BOOK DESIGNERS: **STACIE ZUCKER & ADAM DEL RE** WITH **JAY BOWEN**
SVP PRINT, SALES & MARKETING: **DAVID GABRIEL** EDITOR IN CHIEF: **C.B. CEBULSKI**

MARVEL-VERSE: MOON KNIGHT. Contains material originally published in magazine form as WEREWOLF BY NIGHT (1972) #32-33, MOON KNIGHT (1980) #13, MOON KNIGHT ANNUAL (2019) #1 and AMAZING SPIDER-MAN (1963) #220. First printing 2021. ISBN 978-1-302-93392-0. Published by MARVEL WORLDWIDE, INC., a subsidiary of MARVEL ENTERTAINMENT, LLC. OFFICE OF PUBLICATION: 1290 Avenue of the Americas, New York, NY 10104. © 2021 MARVEL No similarity between any of the names, characters, persons, and/or institutions in this book with those of any living or dead person or institution is intended, and any such similarity which may exist is purely coincidental. **Printed in Canada.** KEVIN FEIGE, Chief Creative Officer; DAN BUCKLEY, President, Marvel Entertainment; JOE QUESADA, EVP & Creative Director; DAVID BOGART, Associate Publisher & SVP of Talent Affairs; TOM BREVOORT, VP, Executive Editor; NICK LOWE, Executive Editor, VP of Content, Digital Publishing; DAVID GABRIEL, VP of Print & Digital Publishing; JEFF YOUNGQUIST, VP of Production & Special Projects; ALEX MORALES, Director of Publishing Operations; DAN EDINGTON, Managing Editor; RICKEY PURDIN, Director of Talent Relations; JENNIFER GRÜNWALD, Senior Editor, Special Projects; SUSAN CRESPI, Production Manager; STAN LEE, Chairman Emeritus. For information regarding advertising in Marvel Comics or on Marvel.com, please contact Vit DeBellis, Custom Solutions & Integrated Advertising Manager, at vdebellis@marvel.com. For Marvel subscription inquiries, please call 888-511-5480. **Manufactured between 12/17/2021 and 1/25/2022 by SOLISCO PRINTERS, SCOTT, QC, CANADA.**

10 9 8 7 6 5 4 3 2 1

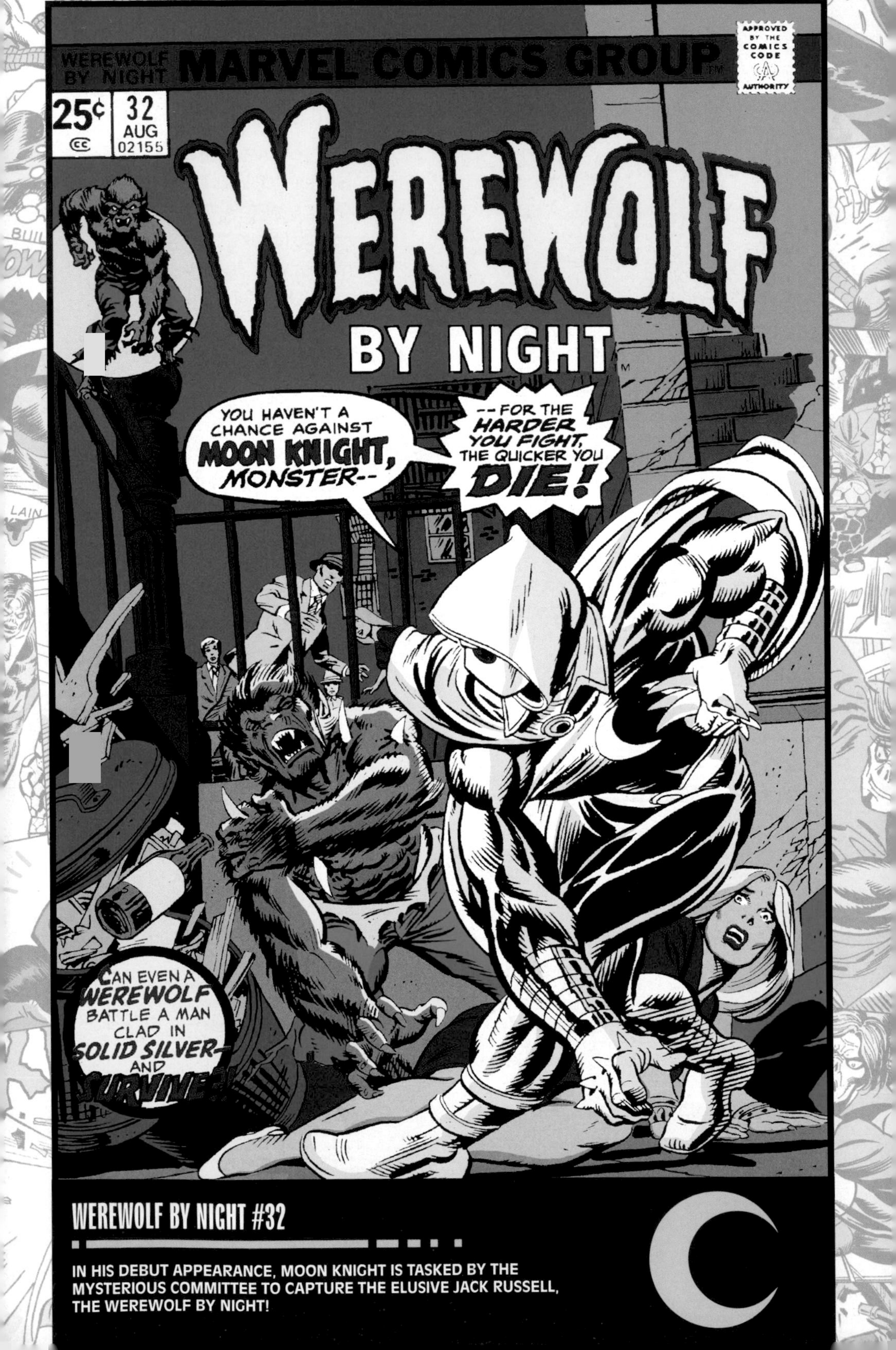
WEREWOLF BY NIGHT
MARVEL COMICS GROUP
APPROVED BY THE COMICS CODE AUTHORITY
25¢
32 AUG 02155
WEREWOLF BY NIGHT
YOU HAVEN'T A CHANCE AGAINST MOON KNIGHT, MONSTER--
--FOR THE HARDER YOU FIGHT, THE QUICKER YOU DIE!
CAN EVEN A WEREWOLF BATTLE A MAN CLAD IN SOLID SILVER— AND SURVIVE!

WEREWOLF BY NIGHT #32

IN HIS DEBUT APPEARANCE, MOON KNIGHT IS TASKED BY THE MYSTERIOUS COMMITTEE TO CAPTURE THE ELUSIVE JACK RUSSELL, THE WEREWOLF BY NIGHT!

The tag's RUSSELL, with a JACK in front of it. The kind of name that fits a normal 19-year-old-dude living out in L.A. — not the kind of name you'd expect to find slapped on a guy who sprouted fangs, pore-to-pore fur, and wolfish howls every time the moon ballooned full. Unless that guy happened to have a father who was cursed by an arcane book called DARKHOLD — and who inherited his father's curse on his 18th birthday.

Stan Lee PRESENTS: WEREWOLF BY NIGHT!™

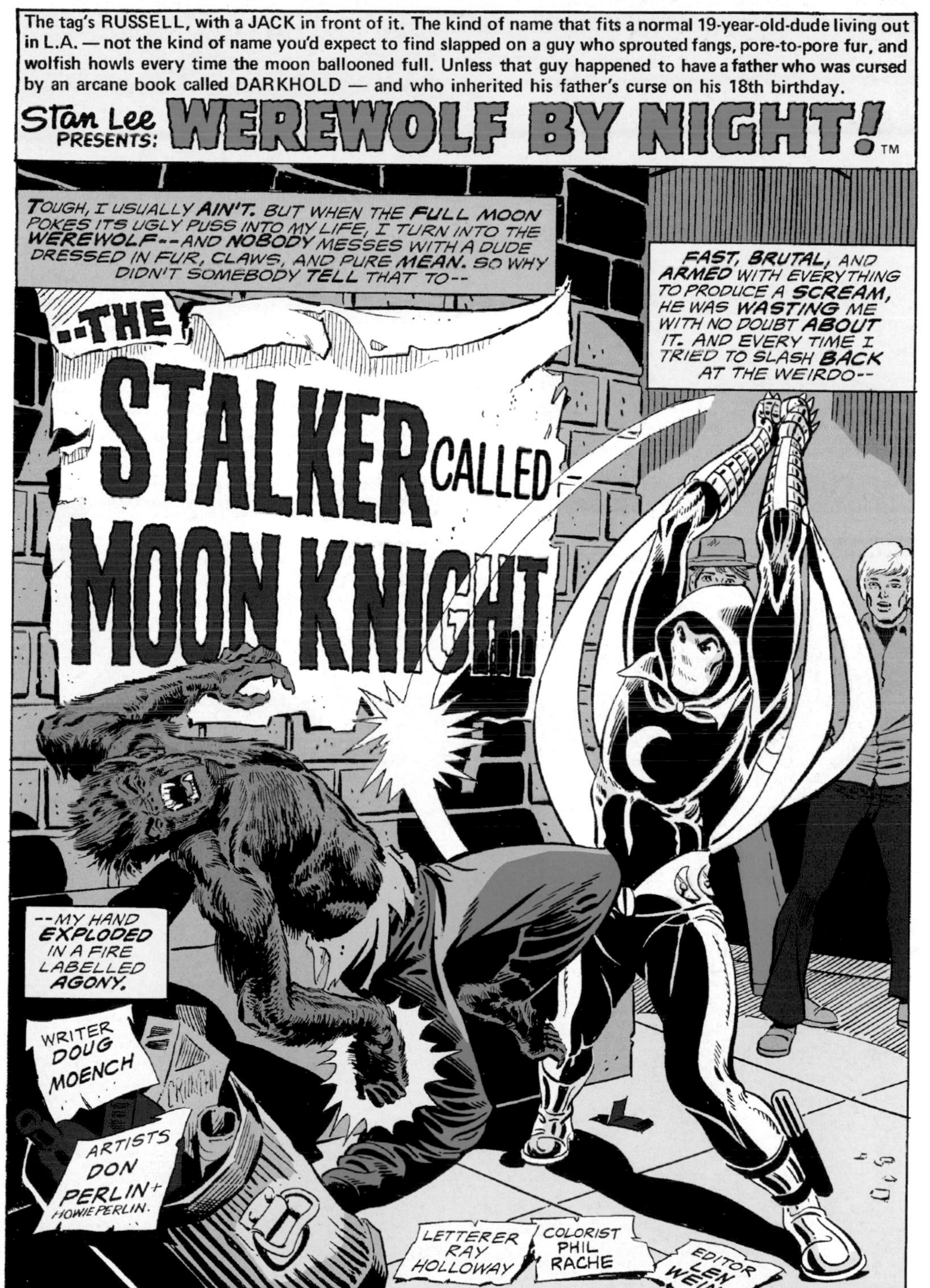

TOUGH, I USUALLY AIN'T. BUT WHEN THE FULL MOON POKES ITS UGLY PUSS INTO MY LIFE, I TURN INTO THE WEREWOLF--AND NOBODY MESSES WITH A DUDE DRESSED IN FUR, CLAWS, AND PURE MEAN. SO WHY DIDN'T SOMEBODY TELL THAT TO--
--THE STALKER CALLED MOON KNIGHT
FAST, BRUTAL, AND ARMED WITH EVERYTHING TO PRODUCE A SCREAM, HE WAS WASTING ME WITH NO DOUBT ABOUT IT. AND EVERY TIME I TRIED TO SLASH BACK AT THE WEIRDO--
--MY HAND EXPLODED IN A FIRE LABELLED AGONY.
WRITER DOUG MOENCH
ARTISTS DON PERLIN + HOWIE PERLIN.
LETTERER RAY HOLLOWAY
COLORIST PHIL RACHE
EDITOR LEN WEIN

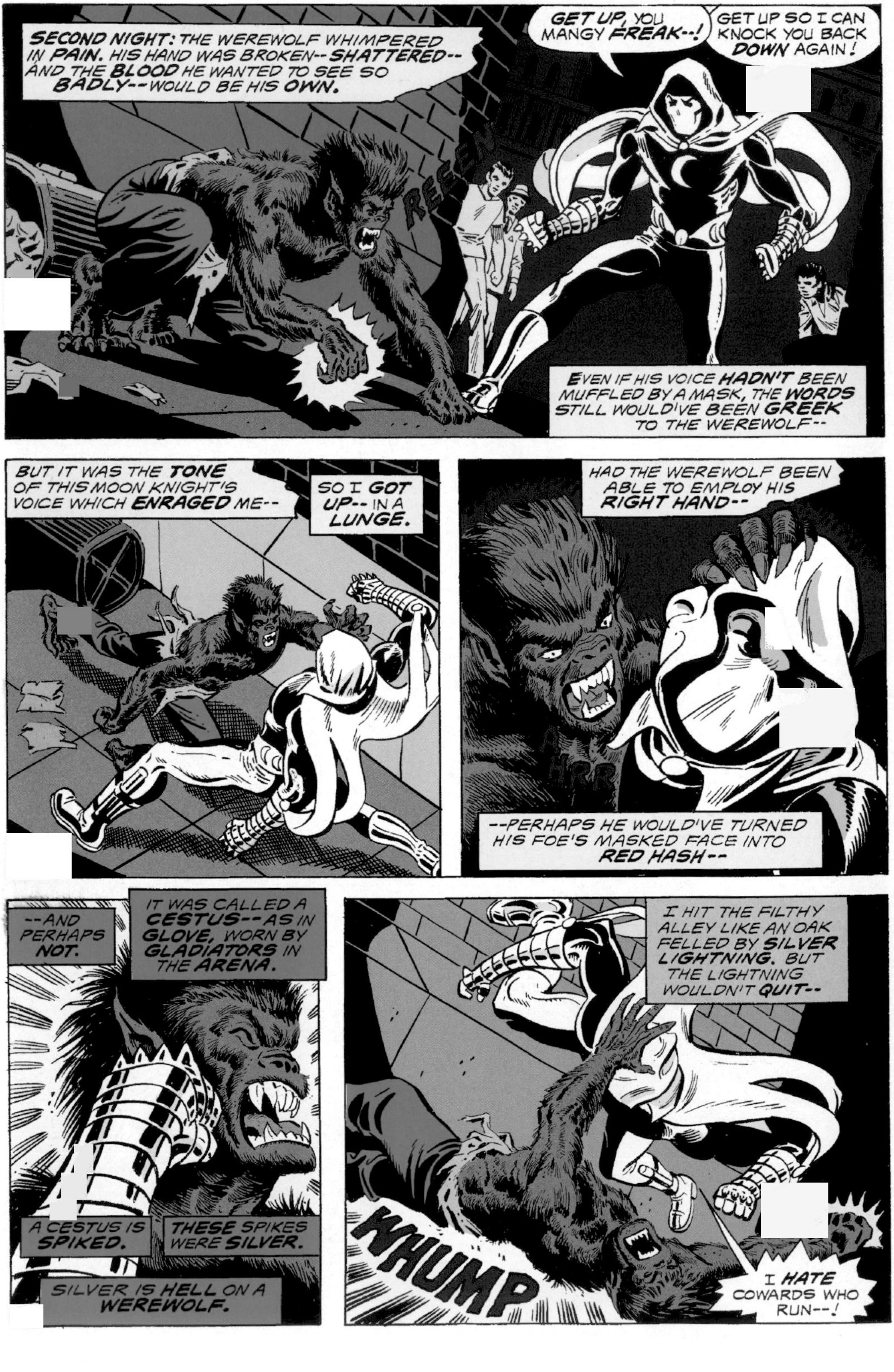
SECOND NIGHT: THE WEREWOLF WHIMPERED IN PAIN. HIS HAND WAS BROKEN-- SHATTERED-- AND THE BLOOD HE WANTED TO SEE SO BADLY-- WOULD BE HIS OWN.
GET UP, YOU MANGY FREAK--!
GET UP SO I CAN KNOCK YOU BACK DOWN AGAIN!
REEE
EVEN IF HIS VOICE HADN'T BEEN MUFFLED BY A MASK, THE WORDS STILL WOULD'VE BEEN GREEK TO THE WEREWOLF--
BUT IT WAS THE TONE OF THIS MOON KNIGHT'S VOICE WHICH ENRAGED ME--
SO I GOT UP-- IN A LUNGE.
HAD THE WEREWOLF BEEN ABLE TO EMPLOY HIS RIGHT HAND--
HRR
--PERHAPS HE WOULD'VE TURNED HIS FOE'S MASKED FACE INTO RED HASH--
--AND PERHAPS NOT.
IT WAS CALLED A CESTUS-- AS IN GLOVE, WORN BY GLADIATORS IN THE ARENA.
A CESTUS IS SPIKED.
THESE SPIKES WERE SILVER.
SILVER IS HELL ON A WEREWOLF.
I HIT THE FILTHY ALLEY LIKE AN OAK FELLED BY SILVER LIGHTNING. BUT THE LIGHTNING WOULDN'T QUIT--
KHUMP
I HATE COWARDS WHO RUN--!

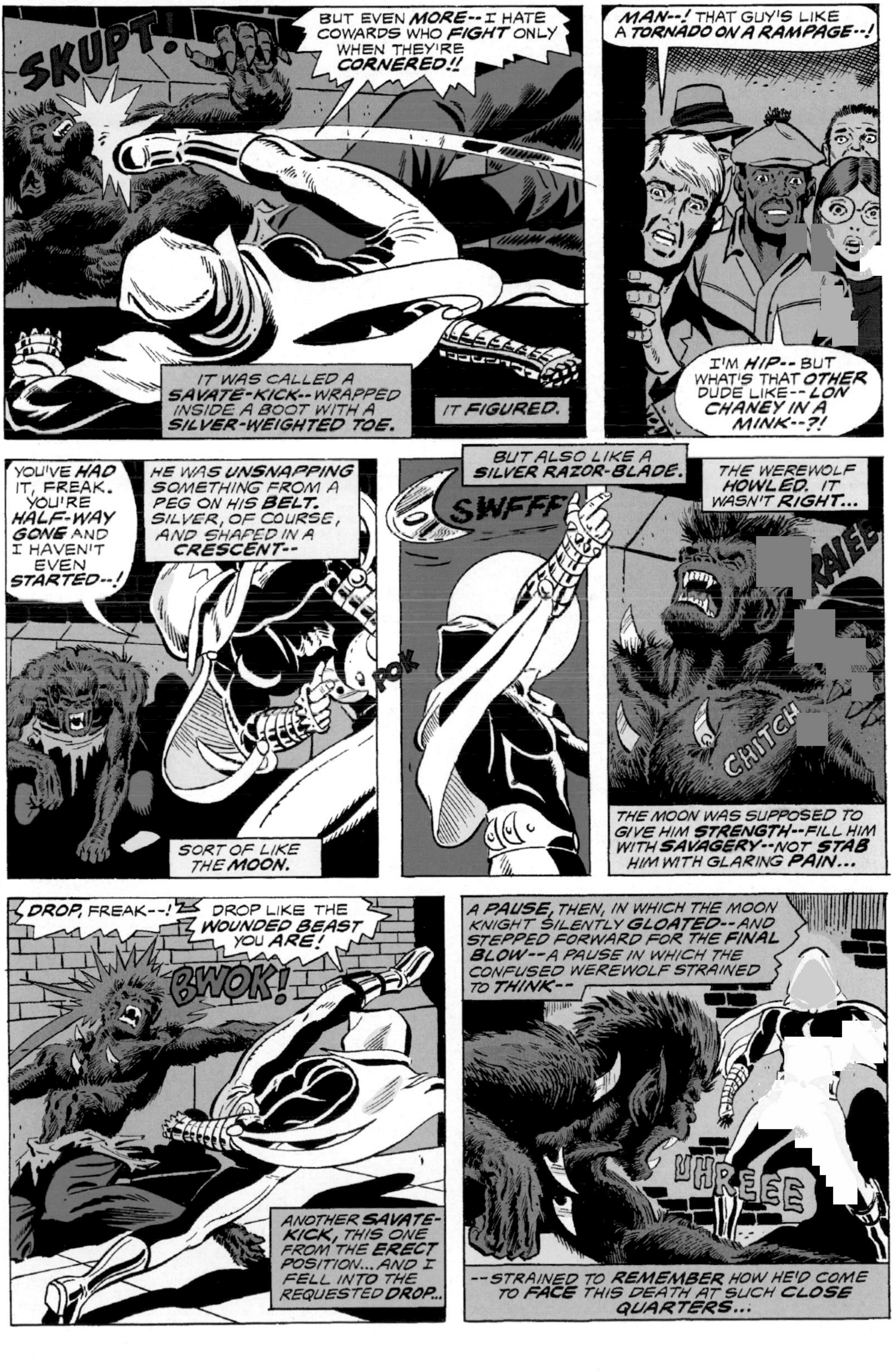
SKUPT!
BUT EVEN MORE-- I HATE COWARDS WHO FIGHT ONLY WHEN THEY'RE CORNERED!!
IT WAS CALLED A SAVATE-KICK--WRAPPED INSIDE A BOOT WITH A SILVER-WEIGHTED TOE.
IT FIGURED.
MAN--! THAT GUY'S LIKE A TORNADO ON A RAMPAGE--!
I'M HIP-- BUT WHAT'S THAT OTHER DUDE LIKE-- LON CHANEY IN A MINK--?!
YOU'VE HAD IT, FREAK. YOU'RE HALF-WAY GONE AND I HAVEN'T EVEN STARTED--!
HE WAS UNSNAPPING SOMETHING FROM A PEG ON HIS BELT. SILVER, OF COURSE, AND SHAPED IN A CRESCENT--
POK
SORT OF LIKE THE MOON.
BUT ALSO LIKE A SILVER RAZOR-BLADE.
SWFFF
THE WEREWOLF HOWLED. IT WASN'T RIGHT...
RAIEE
CHITCH
THE MOON WAS SUPPOSED TO GIVE HIM STRENGTH--FILL HIM WITH SAVAGERY--NOT STAB HIM WITH GLARING PAIN...
DROP, FREAK--!
DROP LIKE THE WOUNDED BEAST YOU ARE!
BWOK!
ANOTHER SAVATE-KICK, THIS ONE FROM THE ERECT POSITION...AND I FELL INTO THE REQUESTED DROP...
A PAUSE, THEN, IN WHICH THE MOON KNIGHT SILENTLY GLOATED--AND STEPPED FORWARD FOR THE FINAL BLOW--A PAUSE IN WHICH THE CONFUSED WEREWOLF STRAINED TO THINK--
UHREEE
--STRAINED TO REMEMBER HOW HE'D COME TO FACE THIS DEATH AT SUCH CLOSE QUARTERS...

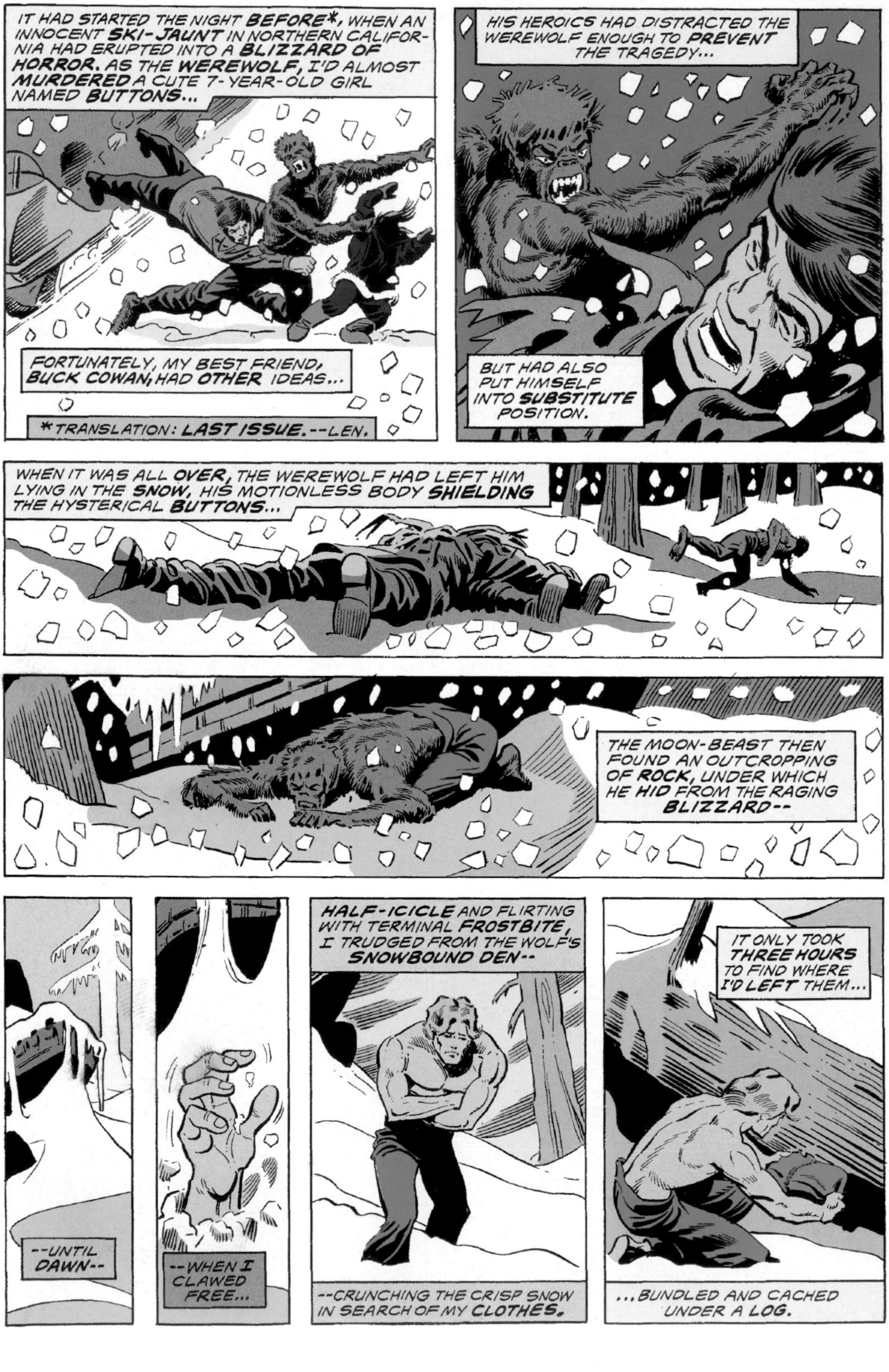
IT HAD STARTED THE NIGHT BEFORE*, WHEN AN INNOCENT SKI-JAUNT IN NORTHERN CALIFORNIA HAD ERUPTED INTO A BLIZZARD OF HORROR. AS THE WEREWOLF, I'D ALMOST MURDERED A CUTE 7-YEAR-OLD GIRL NAMED BUTTONS...
FORTUNATELY, MY BEST FRIEND, BUCK COWAN, HAD OTHER IDEAS...
*TRANSLATION: LAST ISSUE.--LEN.
HIS HEROICS HAD DISTRACTED THE WEREWOLF ENOUGH TO PREVENT THE TRAGEDY...
BUT HAD ALSO PUT HIMSELF INTO SUBSTITUTE POSITION.
WHEN IT WAS ALL OVER, THE WEREWOLF HAD LEFT HIM LYING IN THE SNOW, HIS MOTIONLESS BODY SHIELDING THE HYSTERICAL BUTTONS...
THE MOON-BEAST THEN FOUND AN OUTCROPPING OF ROCK, UNDER WHICH HE HID FROM THE RAGING BLIZZARD--
--UNTIL DAWN--
--WHEN I CLAWED FREE...
HALF-ICICLE AND FLIRTING WITH TERMINAL FROSTBITE, I TRUDGED FROM THE WOLF'S SNOWBOUND DEN--
--CRUNCHING THE CRISP SNOW IN SEARCH OF MY CLOTHES.
IT ONLY TOOK THREE HOURS TO FIND WHERE I'D LEFT THEM...
...BUNDLED AND CACHED UNDER A LOG.

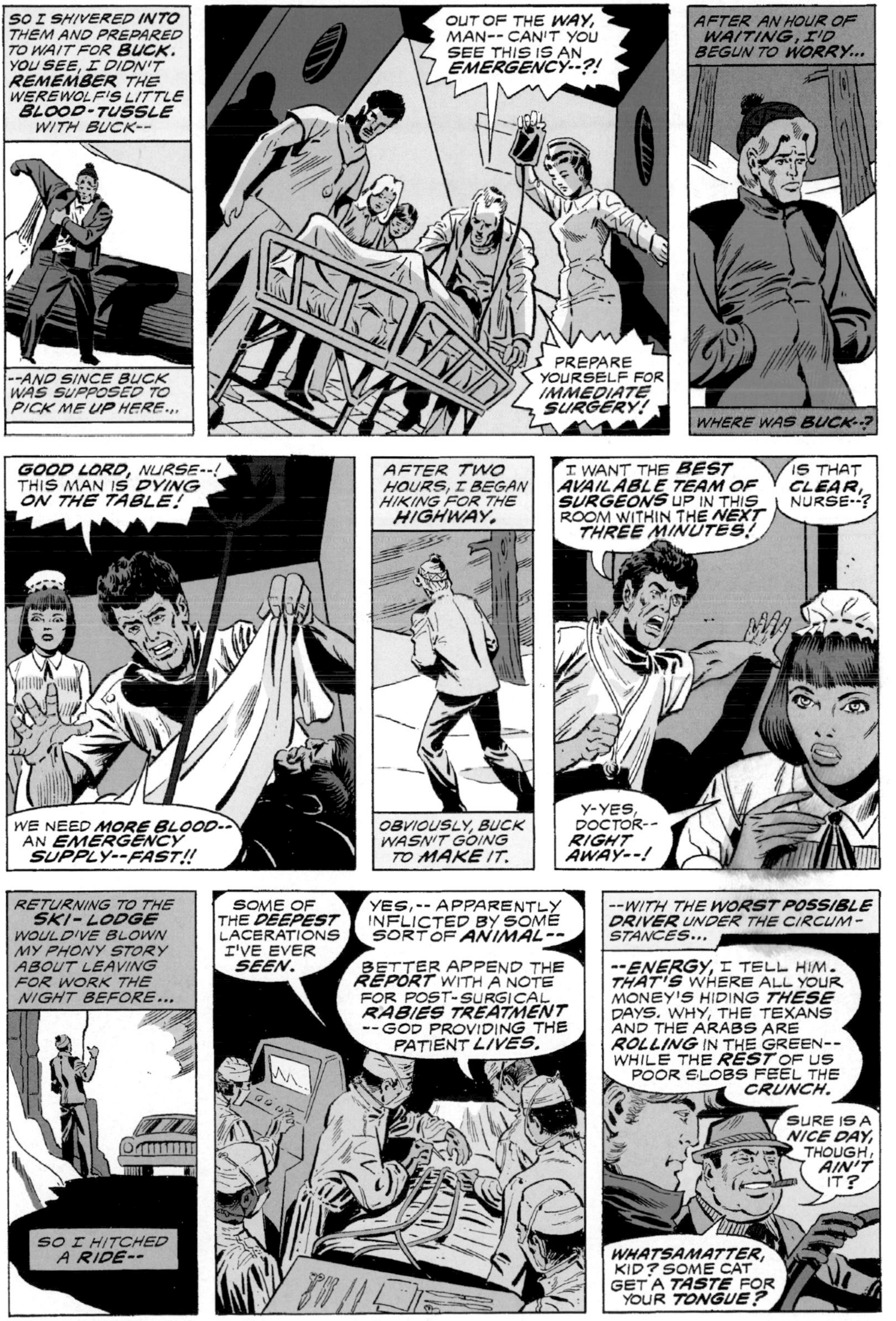
SO I SHIVERED INTO THEM AND PREPARED TO WAIT FOR BUCK. YOU SEE, I DIDN'T REMEMBER THE WEREWOLF'S LITTLE BLOOD-TUSSLE WITH BUCK--
--AND SINCE BUCK WAS SUPPOSED TO PICK ME UP HERE...
OUT OF THE WAY, MAN-- CAN'T YOU SEE THIS IS AN EMERGENCY--?!
PREPARE YOURSELF FOR IMMEDIATE SURGERY!
AFTER AN HOUR OF WAITING, I'D BEGUN TO WORRY...
WHERE WAS BUCK--?
GOOD LORD, NURSE--! THIS MAN IS DYING ON THE TABLE!
WE NEED MORE BLOOD-- AN EMERGENCY SUPPLY--FAST!!
AFTER TWO HOURS, I BEGAN HIKING FOR THE HIGHWAY.
OBVIOUSLY, BUCK WASN'T GOING TO MAKE IT.
I WANT THE BEST AVAILABLE TEAM OF SURGEONS UP IN THIS ROOM WITHIN THE NEXT THREE MINUTES!
IS THAT CLEAR, NURSE--?
Y-YES, DOCTOR-- RIGHT AWAY--!
RETURNING TO THE SKI-LODGE WOULD'VE BLOWN MY PHONY STORY ABOUT LEAVING FOR WORK THE NIGHT BEFORE...
SO I HITCHED A RIDE--
SOME OF THE DEEPEST LACERATIONS I'VE EVER SEEN.
YES,-- APPARENTLY INFLICTED BY SOME SORT OF ANIMAL--
BETTER APPEND THE REPORT WITH A NOTE FOR POST-SURGICAL RABIES TREATMENT --GOD PROVIDING THE PATIENT LIVES.
--WITH THE WORST POSSIBLE DRIVER UNDER THE CIRCUMSTANCES...
--ENERGY, I TELL HIM. THAT'S WHERE ALL YOUR MONEY'S HIDING THESE DAYS. WHY, THE TEXANS AND THE ARABS ARE ROLLING IN THE GREEN-- WHILE THE REST OF US POOR SLOBS FEEL THE CRUNCH.
SURE IS A NICE DAY, THOUGH, AIN'T IT?
WHATSAMATTER, KID? SOME CAT GET A TASTE FOR YOUR TONGUE?

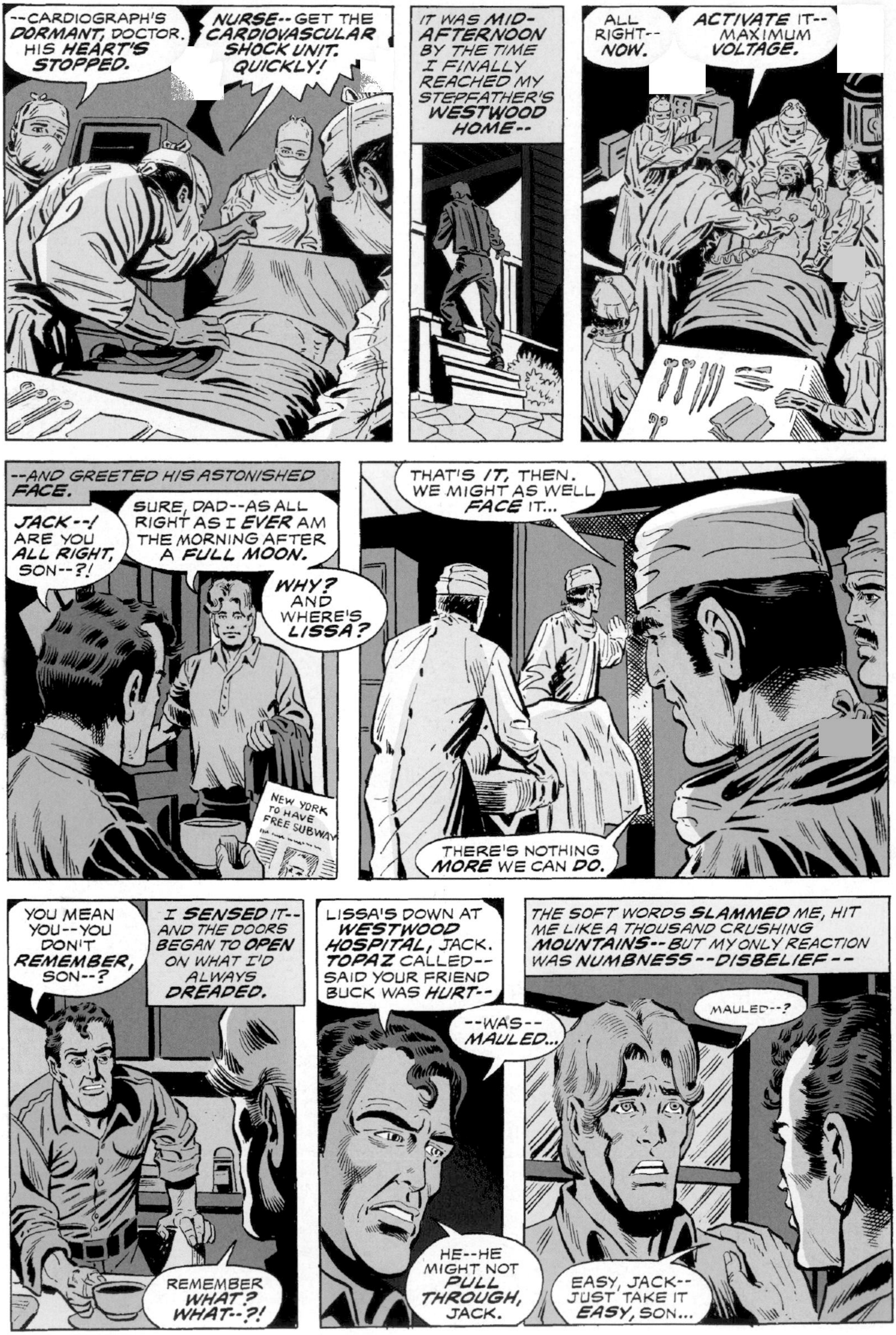
--CARDIOGRAPH'S DORMANT, DOCTOR. HIS HEART'S STOPPED.
NURSE--GET THE CARDIOVASCULAR SHOCK UNIT. QUICKLY!
IT WAS MID-AFTERNOON BY THE TIME I FINALLY REACHED MY STEPFATHER'S WESTWOOD HOME--
ALL RIGHT-- NOW.
ACTIVATE IT-- MAXIMUM VOLTAGE.
--AND GREETED HIS ASTONISHED FACE.
JACK--! ARE YOU ALL RIGHT, SON--?!
SURE, DAD--AS ALL RIGHT AS I EVER AM THE MORNING AFTER A FULL MOON.
WHY? AND WHERE'S LISSA?
NEW YORK TO HAVE FREE SUBWAY
THAT'S IT, THEN. WE MIGHT AS WELL FACE IT...
THERE'S NOTHING MORE WE CAN DO.
YOU MEAN YOU--YOU DON'T REMEMBER, SON--?
I SENSED IT-- AND THE DOORS BEGAN TO OPEN ON WHAT I'D ALWAYS DREADED.
REMEMBER WHAT? WHAT--?!
LISSA'S DOWN AT WESTWOOD HOSPITAL, JACK. TOPAZ CALLED-- SAID YOUR FRIEND BUCK WAS HURT--
--WAS-- MAULED...
HE--HE MIGHT NOT PULL THROUGH, JACK.
THE SOFT WORDS SLAMMED ME, HIT ME LIKE A THOUSAND CRUSHING MOUNTAINS-- BUT MY ONLY REACTION WAS NUMBNESS--DISBELIEF--
MAULED--?
EASY, JACK-- JUST TAKE IT EASY, SON...

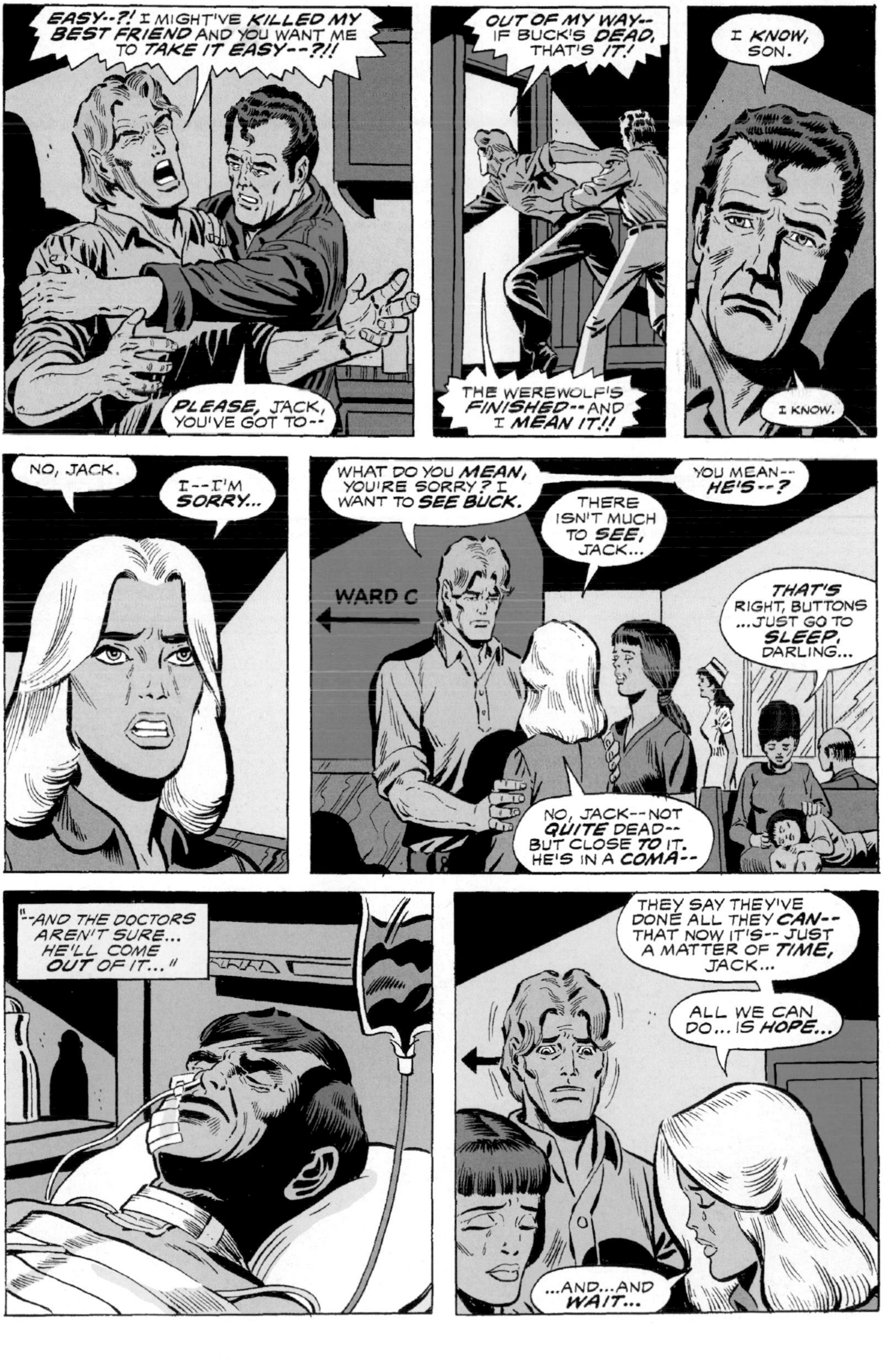
EASY--?! I MIGHT'VE KILLED MY BEST FRIEND AND YOU WANT ME TO TAKE IT EASY--?!!
PLEASE, JACK, YOU'VE GOT TO--
OUT OF MY WAY-- IF BUCK'S DEAD, THAT'S IT!
THE WEREWOLF'S FINISHED--AND I MEAN IT!!
I KNOW, SON.
I KNOW.
NO, JACK.
I--I'M SORRY...
WHAT DO YOU MEAN, YOU'RE SORRY? I WANT TO SEE BUCK.
YOU MEAN-- HE'S--?
THERE ISN'T MUCH TO SEE, JACK...
WARD C
THAT'S RIGHT, BUTTONS ...JUST GO TO SLEEP, DARLING...
NO, JACK--NOT QUITE DEAD-- BUT CLOSE TO IT. HE'S IN A COMA--
"--AND THE DOCTORS AREN'T SURE... HE'LL COME OUT OF IT..."
THEY SAY THEY'VE DONE ALL THEY CAN-- THAT NOW IT'S-- JUST A MATTER OF TIME, JACK...
ALL WE CAN DO... IS HOPE...
...AND...AND WAIT...

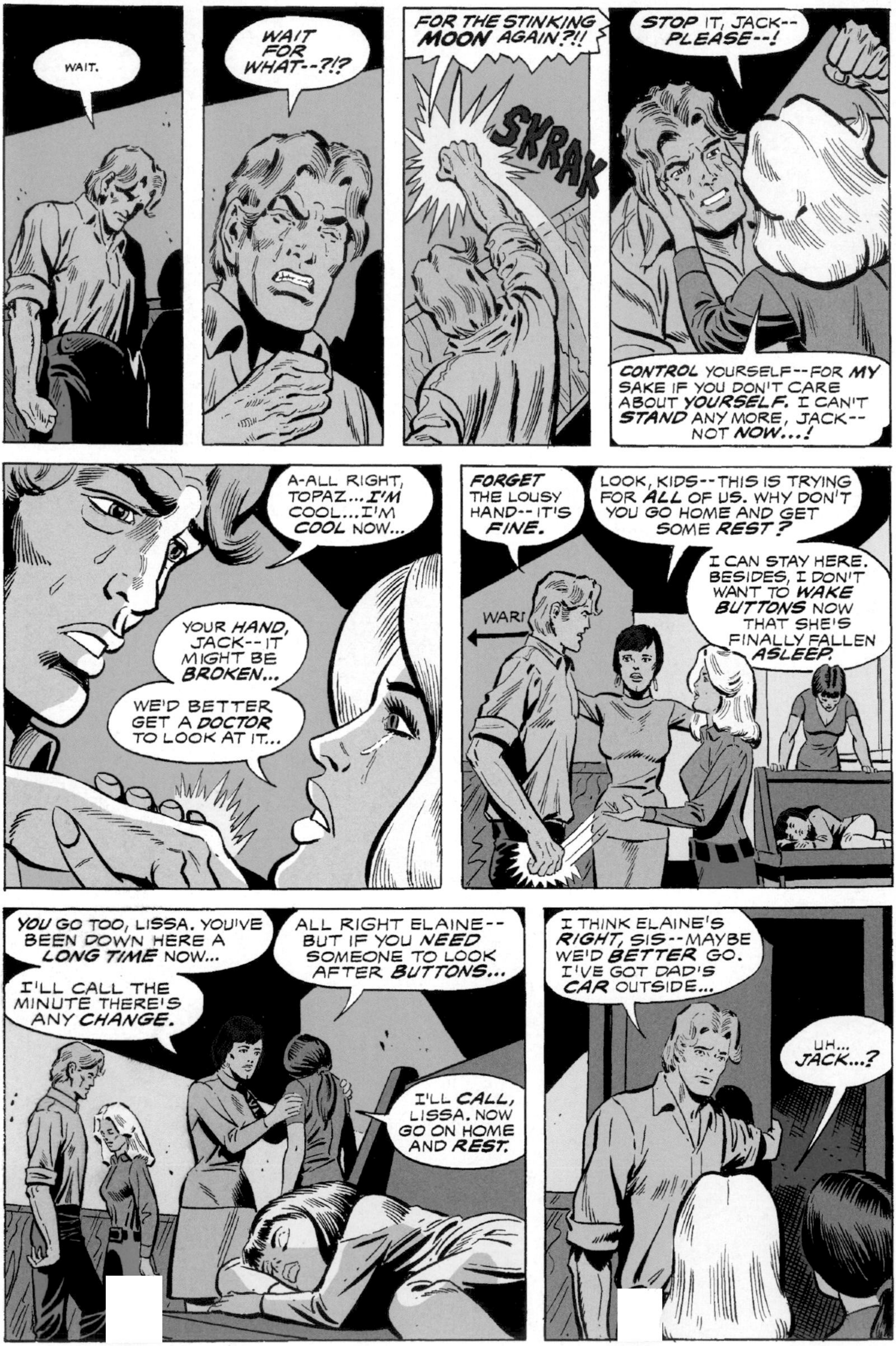
WAIT.
WAIT FOR WHAT--?!?
FOR THE STINKING MOON AGAIN?!!
SKRAK
STOP IT, JACK-- PLEASE--!
CONTROL YOURSELF--FOR MY SAKE IF YOU DON'T CARE ABOUT YOURSELF. I CAN'T STAND ANY MORE, JACK-- NOT NOW...!
A-ALL RIGHT, TOPAZ...I'M COOL...I'M COOL NOW...
YOUR HAND, JACK--IT MIGHT BE BROKEN...
WE'D BETTER GET A DOCTOR TO LOOK AT IT...
FORGET THE LOUSY HAND--IT'S FINE.
WARI
LOOK, KIDS--THIS IS TRYING FOR ALL OF US. WHY DON'T YOU GO HOME AND GET SOME REST?
I CAN STAY HERE. BESIDES, I DON'T WANT TO WAKE BUTTONS NOW THAT SHE'S FINALLY FALLEN ASLEEP.
YOU GO TOO, LISSA. YOU'VE BEEN DOWN HERE A LONG TIME NOW...
I'LL CALL THE MINUTE THERE'S ANY CHANGE.
ALL RIGHT ELAINE-- BUT IF YOU NEED SOMEONE TO LOOK AFTER BUTTONS...
I'LL CALL, LISSA. NOW GO ON HOME AND REST.
I THINK ELAINE'S RIGHT, SIS--MAYBE WE'D BETTER GO. I'VE GOT DAD'S CAR OUTSIDE...
UH... JACK...?

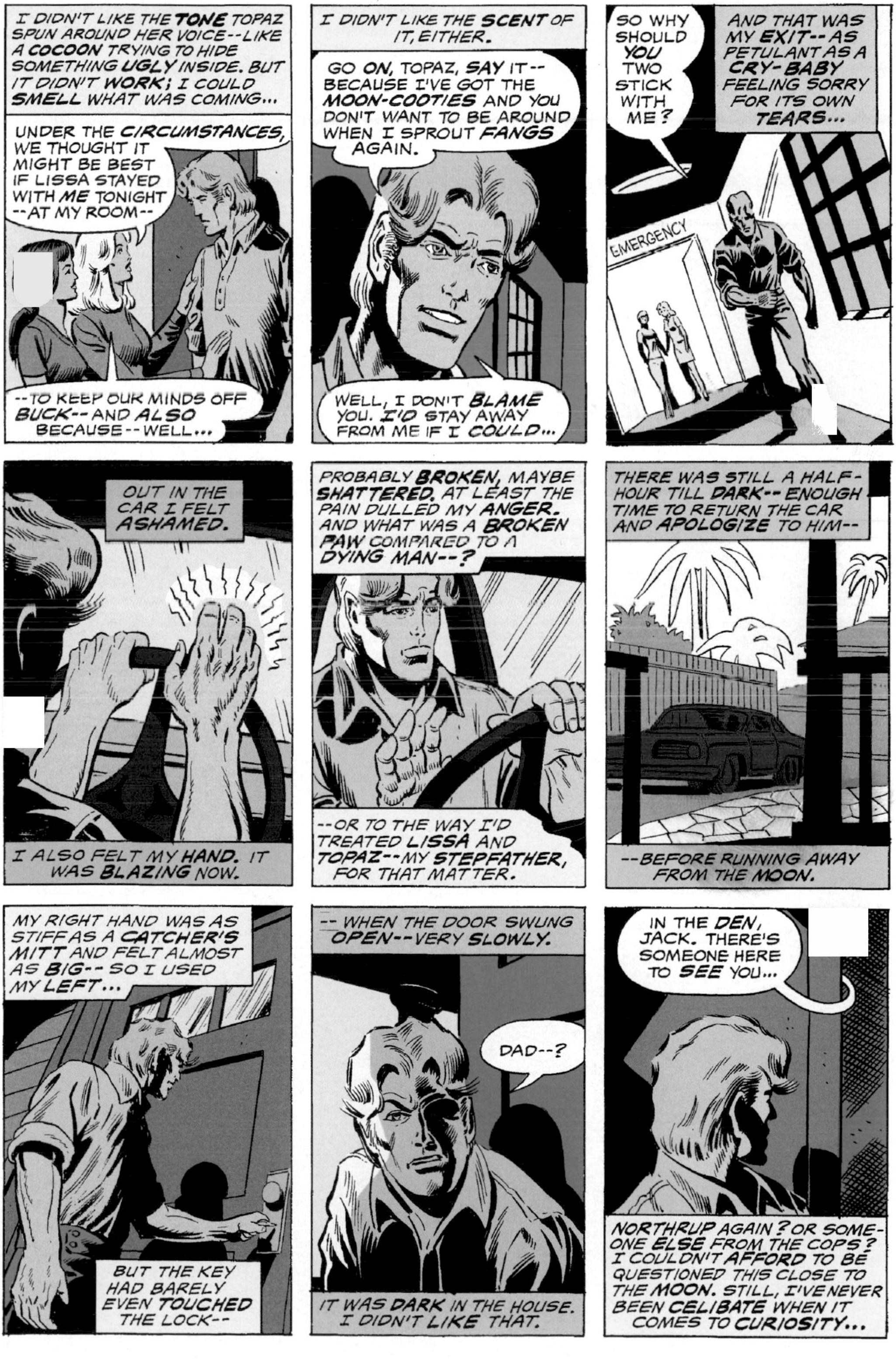
I DIDN'T LIKE THE TONE TOPAZ SPUN AROUND HER VOICE--LIKE A COCOON TRYING TO HIDE SOMETHING UGLY INSIDE. BUT IT DIDN'T WORK; I COULD SMELL WHAT WAS COMING...
UNDER THE CIRCUMSTANCES, WE THOUGHT IT MIGHT BE BEST IF LISSA STAYED WITH ME TONIGHT --AT MY ROOM--
--TO KEEP OUR MINDS OFF BUCK--AND ALSO BECAUSE--WELL...
I DIDN'T LIKE THE SCENT OF IT, EITHER.
GO ON, TOPAZ, SAY IT--BECAUSE I'VE GOT THE MOON-COOTIES AND YOU DON'T WANT TO BE AROUND WHEN I SPROUT FANGS AGAIN.
WELL, I DON'T BLAME YOU. I'D STAY AWAY FROM ME IF I COULD...
SO WHY SHOULD YOU TWO STICK WITH ME?
AND THAT WAS MY EXIT--AS PETULANT AS A CRY-BABY FEELING SORRY FOR ITS OWN TEARS...
EMERGENCY
OUT IN THE CAR I FELT ASHAMED.
I ALSO FELT MY HAND. IT WAS BLAZING NOW.
PROBABLY BROKEN, MAYBE SHATTERED. AT LEAST THE PAIN DULLED MY ANGER. AND WHAT WAS A BROKEN PAW COMPARED TO A DYING MAN--?
--OR TO THE WAY I'D TREATED LISSA AND TOPAZ--MY STEPFATHER, FOR THAT MATTER.
THERE WAS STILL A HALF-HOUR TILL DARK--ENOUGH TIME TO RETURN THE CAR AND APOLOGIZE TO HIM--
--BEFORE RUNNING AWAY FROM THE MOON.
MY RIGHT HAND WAS AS STIFF AS A CATCHER'S MITT AND FELT ALMOST AS BIG--SO I USED MY LEFT...
BUT THE KEY HAD BARELY EVEN TOUCHED THE LOCK--
--WHEN THE DOOR SWUNG OPEN--VERY SLOWLY.
DAD--?
IT WAS DARK IN THE HOUSE. I DIDN'T LIKE THAT.
IN THE DEN, JACK. THERE'S SOMEONE HERE TO SEE YOU...
NORTHRUP AGAIN? OR SOMEONE ELSE FROM THE COPS? I COULDN'T AFFORD TO BE QUESTIONED THIS CLOSE TO THE MOON. STILL, I'VE NEVER BEEN CELIBATE WHEN IT COMES TO CURIOSITY...

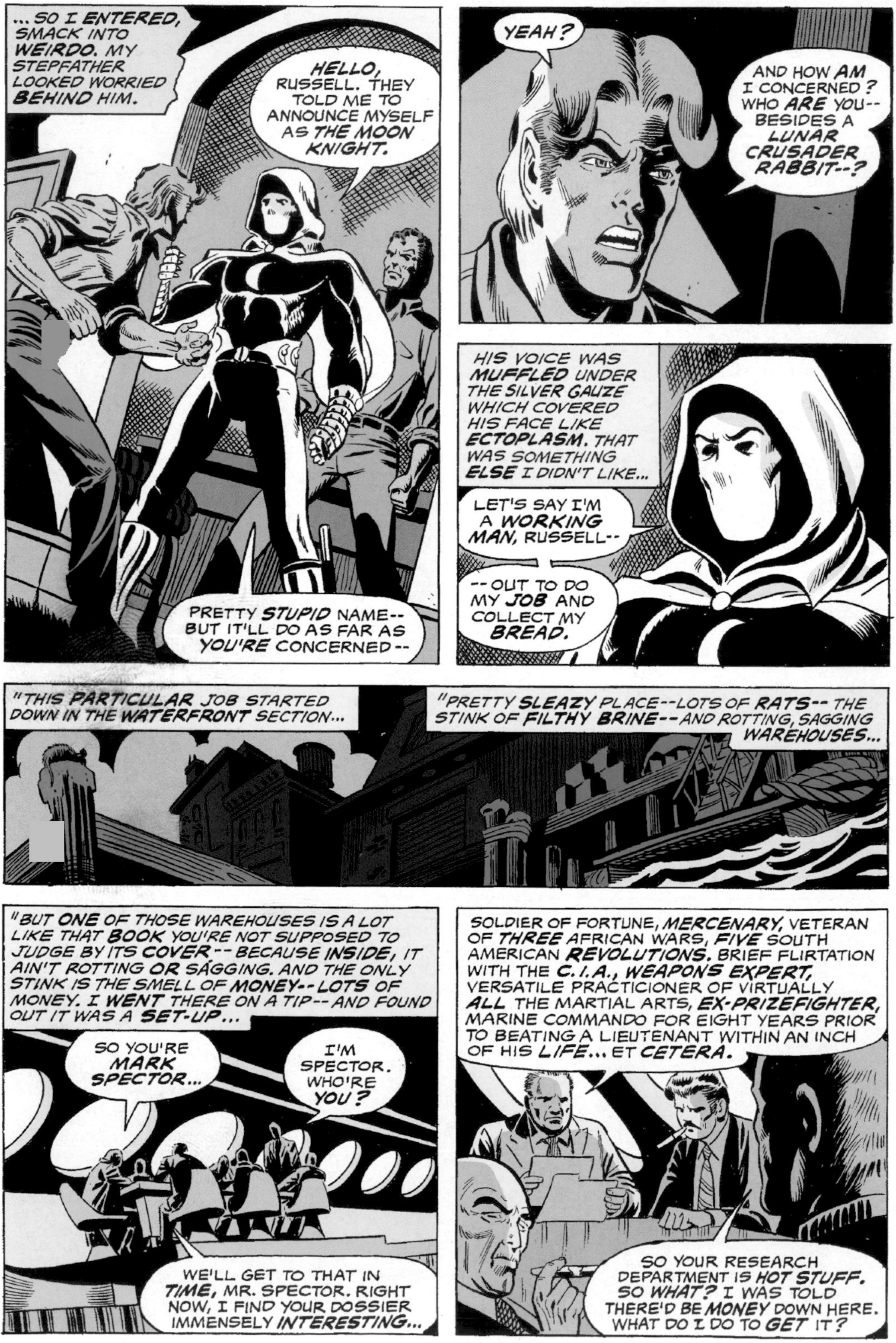
...SO I ENTERED, SMACK INTO WEIRDO. MY STEPFATHER LOOKED WORRIED BEHIND HIM.
HELLO, RUSSELL. THEY TOLD ME TO ANNOUNCE MYSELF AS THE MOON KNIGHT.
PRETTY STUPID NAME--BUT IT'LL DO AS FAR AS YOU'RE CONCERNED--
YEAH?
AND HOW AM I CONCERNED? WHO ARE YOU--BESIDES A LUNAR CRUSADER RABBIT--?
HIS VOICE WAS MUFFLED UNDER THE SILVER GAUZE WHICH COVERED HIS FACE LIKE ECTOPLASM. THAT WAS SOMETHING ELSE I DIDN'T LIKE...
LET'S SAY I'M A WORKING MAN, RUSSELL--
--OUT TO DO MY JOB AND COLLECT MY BREAD.
"THIS PARTICULAR JOB STARTED DOWN IN THE WATERFRONT SECTION...
"PRETTY SLEAZY PLACE--LOTS OF RATS--THE STINK OF FILTHY BRINE--AND ROTTING, SAGGING WAREHOUSES...
"BUT ONE OF THOSE WAREHOUSES IS A LOT LIKE THAT BOOK YOU'RE NOT SUPPOSED TO JUDGE BY ITS COVER--BECAUSE INSIDE, IT AIN'T ROTTING OR SAGGING. AND THE ONLY STINK IS THE SMELL OF MONEY--LOTS OF MONEY. I WENT THERE ON A TIP--AND FOUND OUT IT WAS A SET-UP...
SO YOU'RE MARK SPECTOR...
I'M SPECTOR. WHO'RE YOU?
WE'LL GET TO THAT IN TIME, MR. SPECTOR. RIGHT NOW, I FIND YOUR DOSSIER IMMENSELY INTERESTING...
SOLDIER OF FORTUNE, MERCENARY, VETERAN OF THREE AFRICAN WARS, FIVE SOUTH AMERICAN REVOLUTIONS. BRIEF FLIRTATION WITH THE C.I.A., WEAPONS EXPERT, VERSATILE PRACTICIONER OF VIRTUALLY ALL THE MARTIAL ARTS, EX-PRIZEFIGHTER, MARINE COMMANDO FOR EIGHT YEARS PRIOR TO BEATING A LIEUTENANT WITHIN AN INCH OF HIS LIFE... ET CETERA.
SO YOUR RESEARCH DEPARTMENT IS HOT STUFF. SO WHAT? I WAS TOLD THERE'D BE MONEY DOWN HERE. WHAT DO I DO TO GET IT?

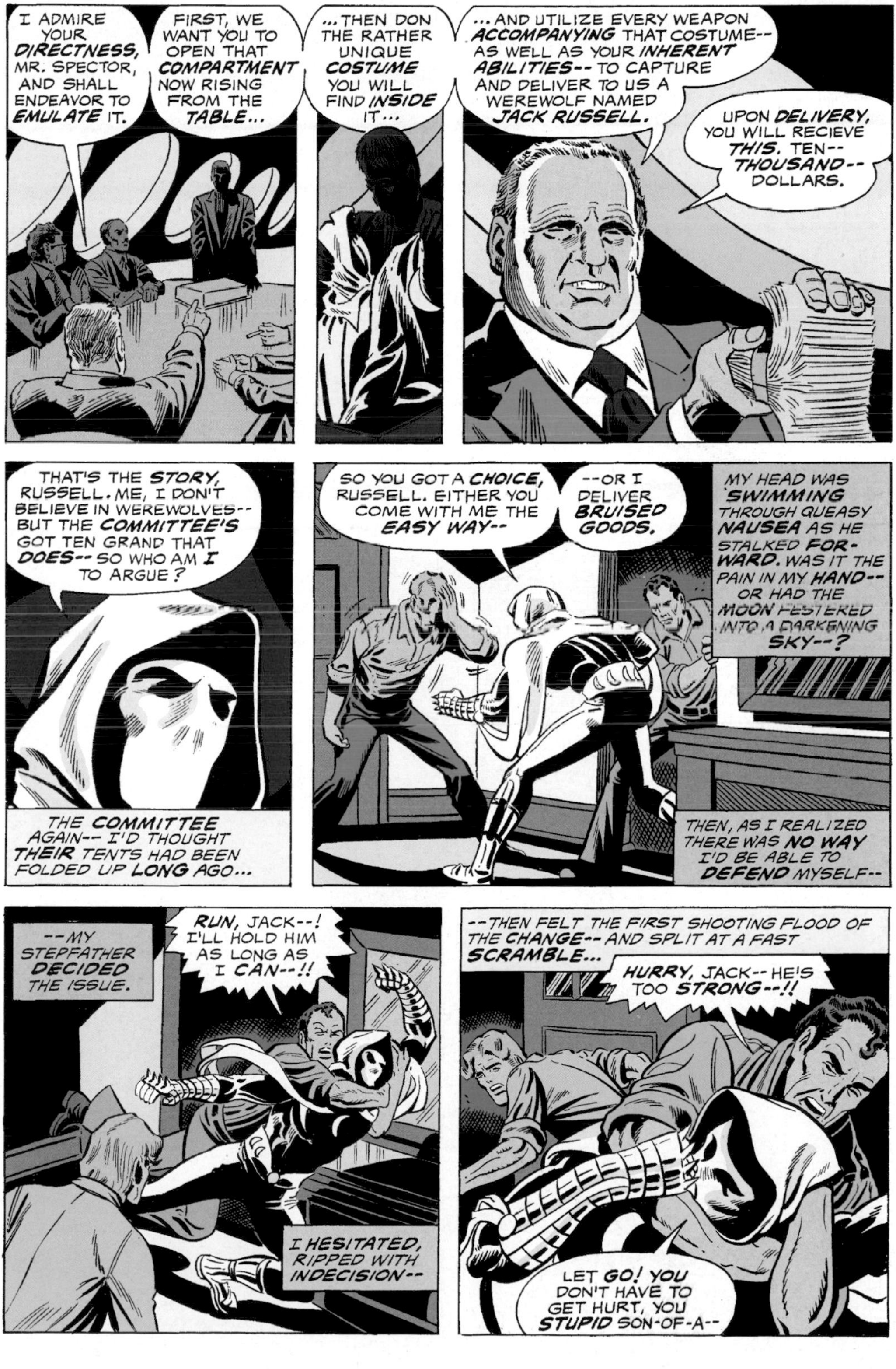
I ADMIRE YOUR DIRECTNESS, MR. SPECTOR, AND SHALL ENDEAVOR TO EMULATE IT.
FIRST, WE WANT YOU TO OPEN THAT COMPARTMENT NOW RISING FROM THE TABLE...
...THEN DON THE RATHER UNIQUE COSTUME YOU WILL FIND INSIDE IT...
...AND UTILIZE EVERY WEAPON ACCOMPANYING THAT COSTUME-- AS WELL AS YOUR INHERENT ABILITIES-- TO CAPTURE AND DELIVER TO US A WEREWOLF NAMED JACK RUSSELL.
UPON DELIVERY, YOU WILL RECIEVE THIS. TEN-- THOUSAND-- DOLLARS.
THAT'S THE STORY, RUSSELL. ME, I DON'T BELIEVE IN WEREWOLVES-- BUT THE COMMITTEE'S GOT TEN GRAND THAT DOES-- SO WHO AM I TO ARGUE?
THE COMMITTEE AGAIN-- I'D THOUGHT THEIR TENTS HAD BEEN FOLDED UP LONG AGO...
SO YOU GOT A CHOICE, RUSSELL. EITHER YOU COME WITH ME THE EASY WAY--
--OR I DELIVER BRUISED GOODS.
MY HEAD WAS SWIMMING THROUGH QUEASY NAUSEA AS HE STALKED FOR-WARD. WAS IT THE PAIN IN MY HAND-- OR HAD THE MOON FESTERED INTO A DARKENING SKY--?
THEN, AS I REALIZED THERE WAS NO WAY I'D BE ABLE TO DEFEND MYSELF--
--MY STEPFATHER DECIDED THE ISSUE.
RUN, JACK--! I'LL HOLD HIM AS LONG AS I CAN--!!
I HESITATED, RIPPED WITH INDECISION--
--THEN FELT THE FIRST SHOOTING FLOOD OF THE CHANGE-- AND SPLIT AT A FAST SCRAMBLE...
HURRY, JACK-- HE'S TOO STRONG--!!
LET GO! YOU DON'T HAVE TO GET HURT, YOU STUPID SON-OF-A--

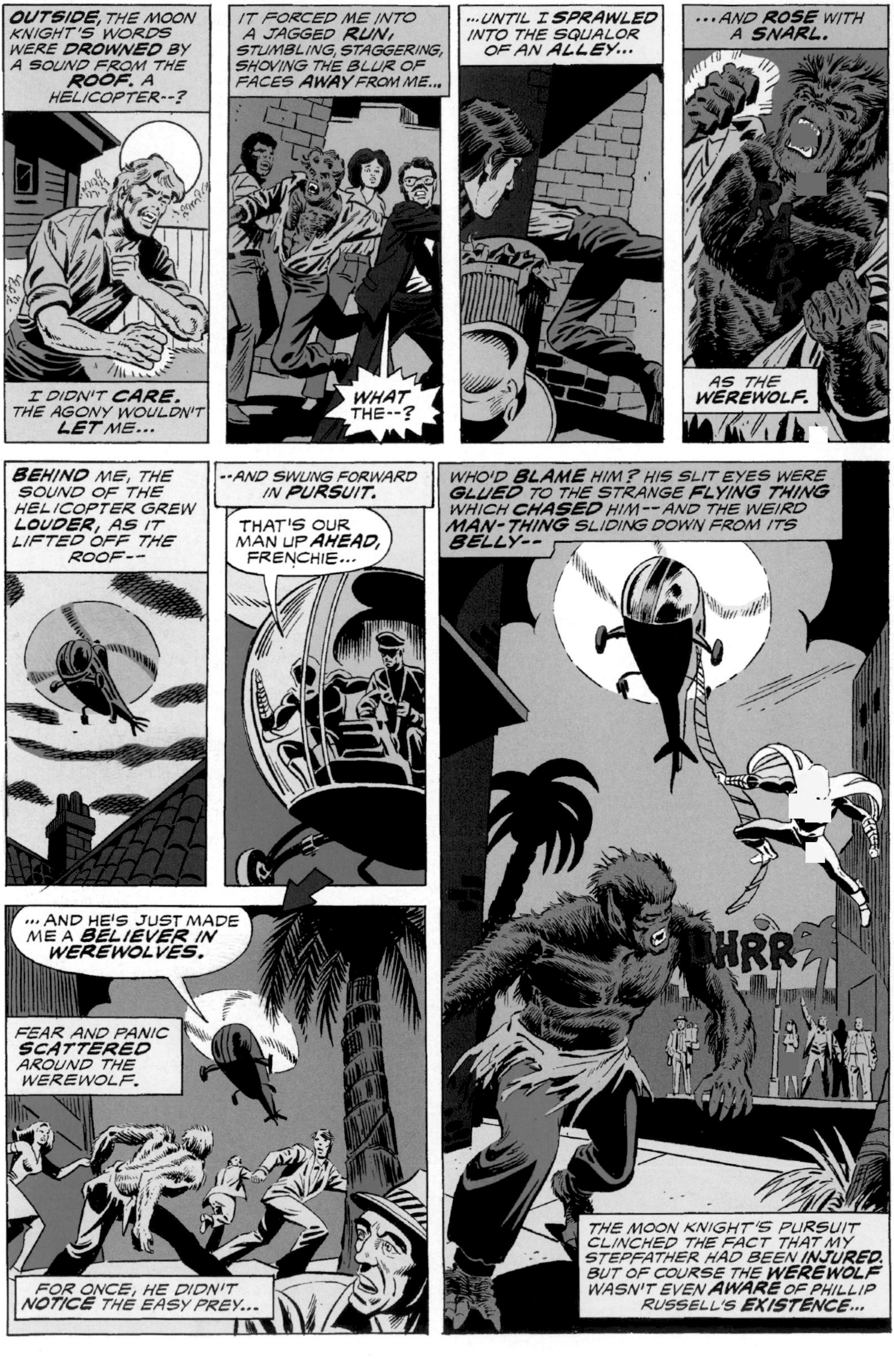

OUTSIDE, THE MOON KNIGHT'S WORDS WERE DROWNED BY A SOUND FROM THE ROOF. A HELICOPTER--?
I DIDN'T CARE. THE AGONY WOULDN'T LET ME...
IT FORCED ME INTO A JAGGED RUN, STUMBLING, STAGGERING, SHOVING THE BLUR OF FACES AWAY FROM ME...
WHAT THE--?
...UNTIL I SPRAWLED INTO THE SQUALOR OF AN ALLEY...
...AND ROSE WITH A SNARL.
RARR
AS THE WEREWOLF.
BEHIND ME, THE SOUND OF THE HELICOPTER GREW LOUDER, AS IT LIFTED OFF THE ROOF--
--AND SWUNG FORWARD IN PURSUIT.
THAT'S OUR MAN UP AHEAD, FRENCHIE...
WHO'D BLAME HIM? HIS SLIT EYES WERE GLUED TO THE STRANGE FLYING THING WHICH CHASED HIM--AND THE WEIRD MAN-THING SLIDING DOWN FROM ITS BELLY--
...AND HE'S JUST MADE ME A BELIEVER IN WEREWOLVES.
FEAR AND PANIC SCATTERED AROUND THE WEREWOLF.
FOR ONCE, HE DIDN'T NOTICE THE EASY PREY...
UHRR
THE MOON KNIGHT'S PURSUIT CLINCHED THE FACT THAT MY STEPFATHER HAD BEEN INJURED. BUT OF COURSE THE WEREWOLF WASN'T EVEN AWARE OF PHILLIP RUSSELL'S EXISTENCE...

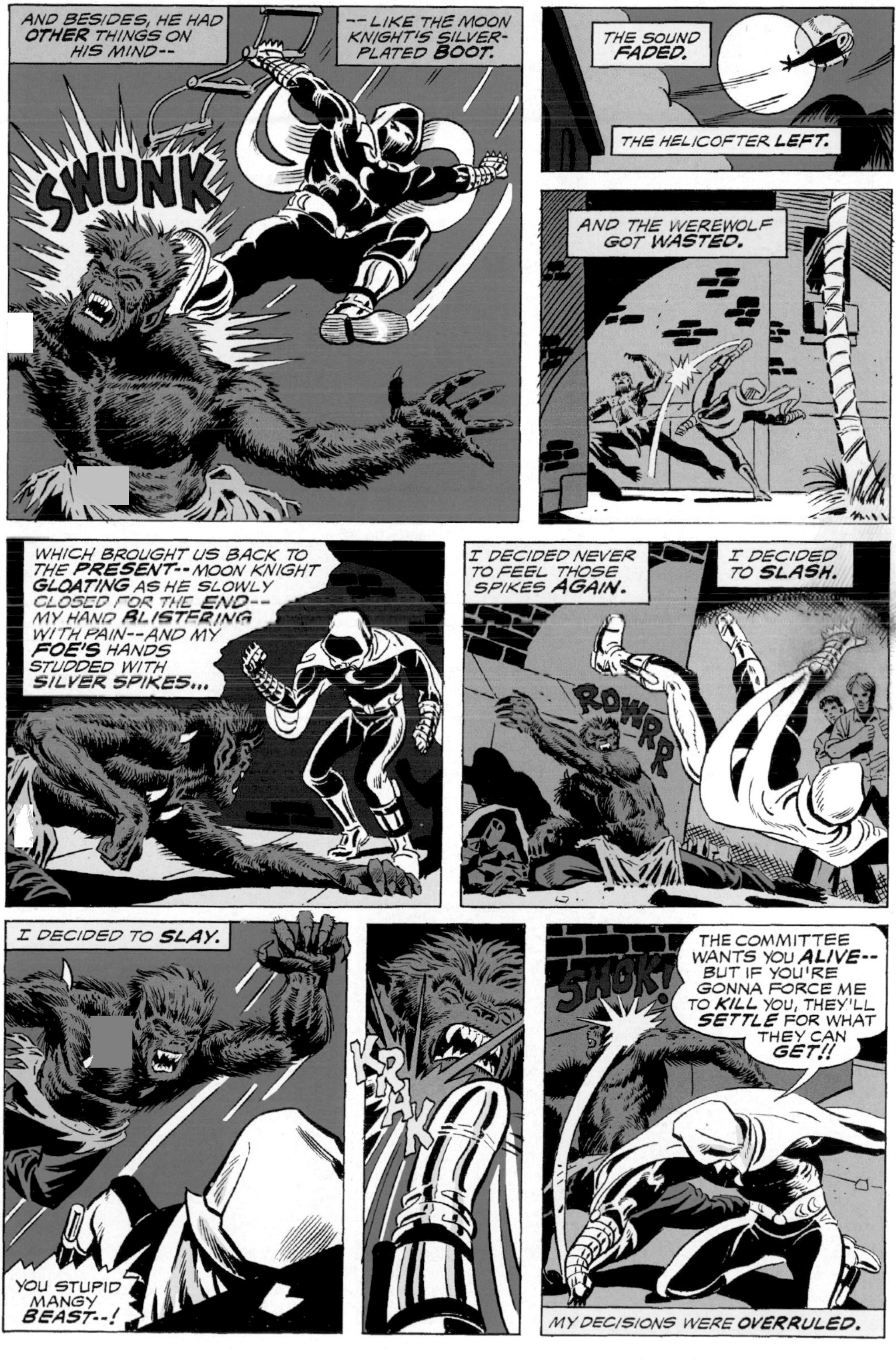

AND BESIDES, HE HAD OTHER THINGS ON HIS MIND--
--LIKE THE MOON KNIGHT'S SILVER-PLATED BOOT.
SWUNK
THE SOUND FADED.
THE HELICOFTER LEFT.
AND THE WEREWOLF GOT WASTED.
WHICH BROUGHT US BACK TO THE PRESENT--MOON KNIGHT GLOATING AS HE SLOWLY CLOSED FOR THE END--MY HAND BLISTERING WITH PAIN--AND MY FOE'S HANDS STUDDED WITH SILVER SPIKES...
I DECIDED NEVER TO FEEL THOSE SPIKES AGAIN.
I DECIDED TO SLASH.
ROWRR
I DECIDED TO SLAY.
YOU STUPID MANGY BEAST--!
KRAK
SHOK!
THE COMMITTEE WANTS YOU ALIVE--BUT IF YOU'RE GONNA FORCE ME TO KILL YOU, THEY'LL SETTLE FOR WHAT THEY CAN GET!!
MY DECISIONS WERE OVERRULED.

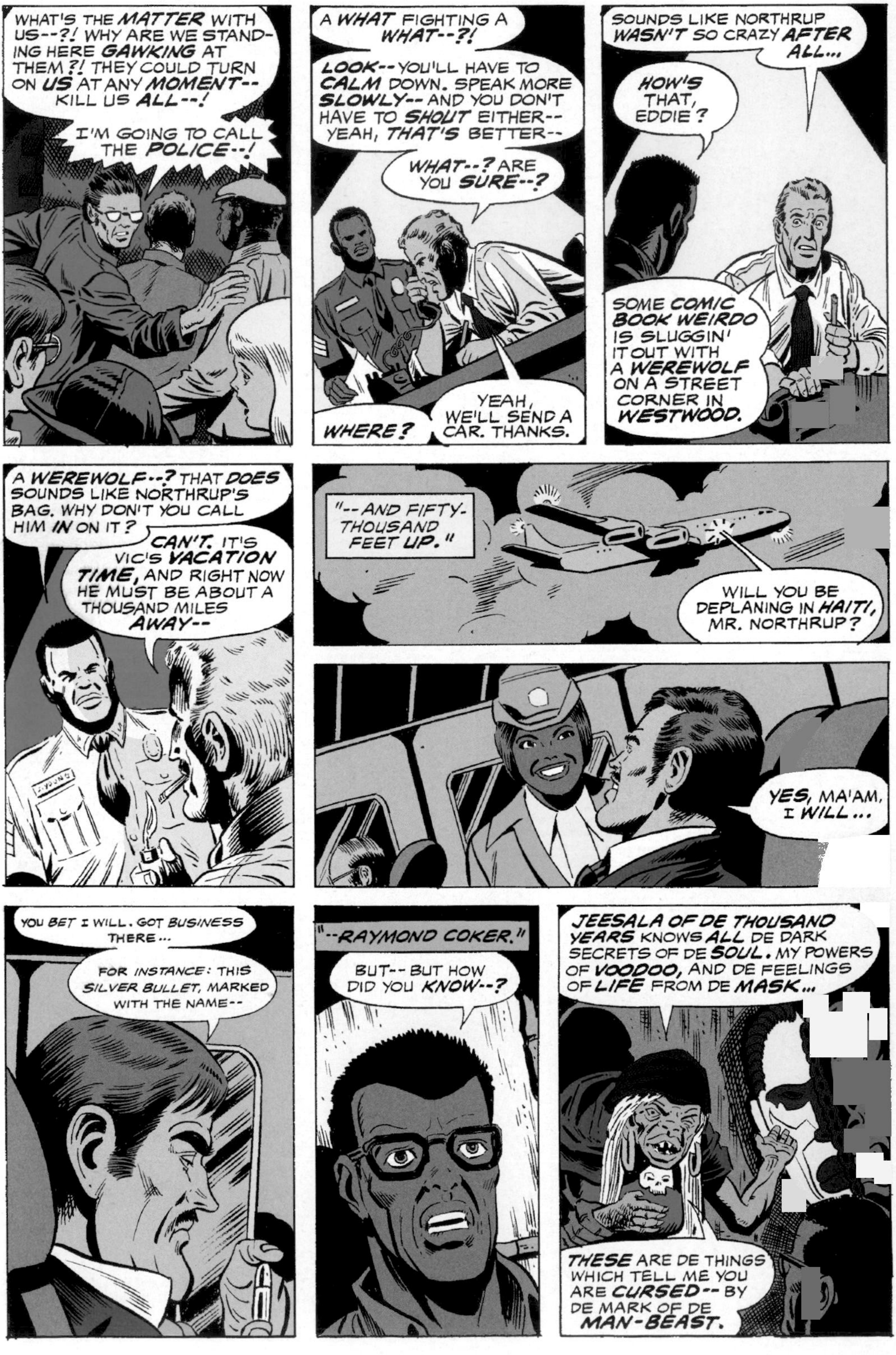
WHAT'S THE MATTER WITH US--?! WHY ARE WE STANDING HERE GAWKING AT THEM?! THEY COULD TURN ON US AT ANY MOMENT-- KILL US ALL--!
I'M GOING TO CALL THE POLICE--!
A WHAT FIGHTING A WHAT--?!
LOOK-- YOU'LL HAVE TO CALM DOWN. SPEAK MORE SLOWLY-- AND YOU DON'T HAVE TO SHOUT EITHER-- YEAH, THAT'S BETTER--
WHAT--? ARE YOU SURE--?
WHERE?
YEAH, WE'LL SEND A CAR. THANKS.
SOUNDS LIKE NORTHRUP WASN'T SO CRAZY AFTER ALL...
HOW'S THAT, EDDIE?
SOME COMIC BOOK WEIRDO IS SLUGGIN' IT OUT WITH A WEREWOLF ON A STREET CORNER IN WESTWOOD.
A WEREWOLF--? THAT DOES SOUNDS LIKE NORTHRUP'S BAG. WHY DON'T YOU CALL HIM IN ON IT?
CAN'T. IT'S VIC'S VACATION TIME, AND RIGHT NOW HE MUST BE ABOUT A THOUSAND MILES AWAY--
"--AND FIFTY-THOUSAND FEET UP."
WILL YOU BE DEPLANING IN HAITI, MR. NORTHRUP?
YES, MA'AM, I WILL...
YOU BET I WILL. GOT BUSINESS THERE...
FOR INSTANCE: THIS SILVER BULLET, MARKED WITH THE NAME--
"--RAYMOND COKER."
BUT-- BUT HOW DID YOU KNOW--?
JEESALA OF DE THOUSAND YEARS KNOWS ALL DE DARK SECRETS OF DE SOUL. MY POWERS OF VOODOO, AND DE FEELINGS OF LIFE FROM DE MASK...
THESE ARE DE THINGS WHICH TELL ME YOU ARE CURSED-- BY DE MARK OF DE MAN-BEAST.

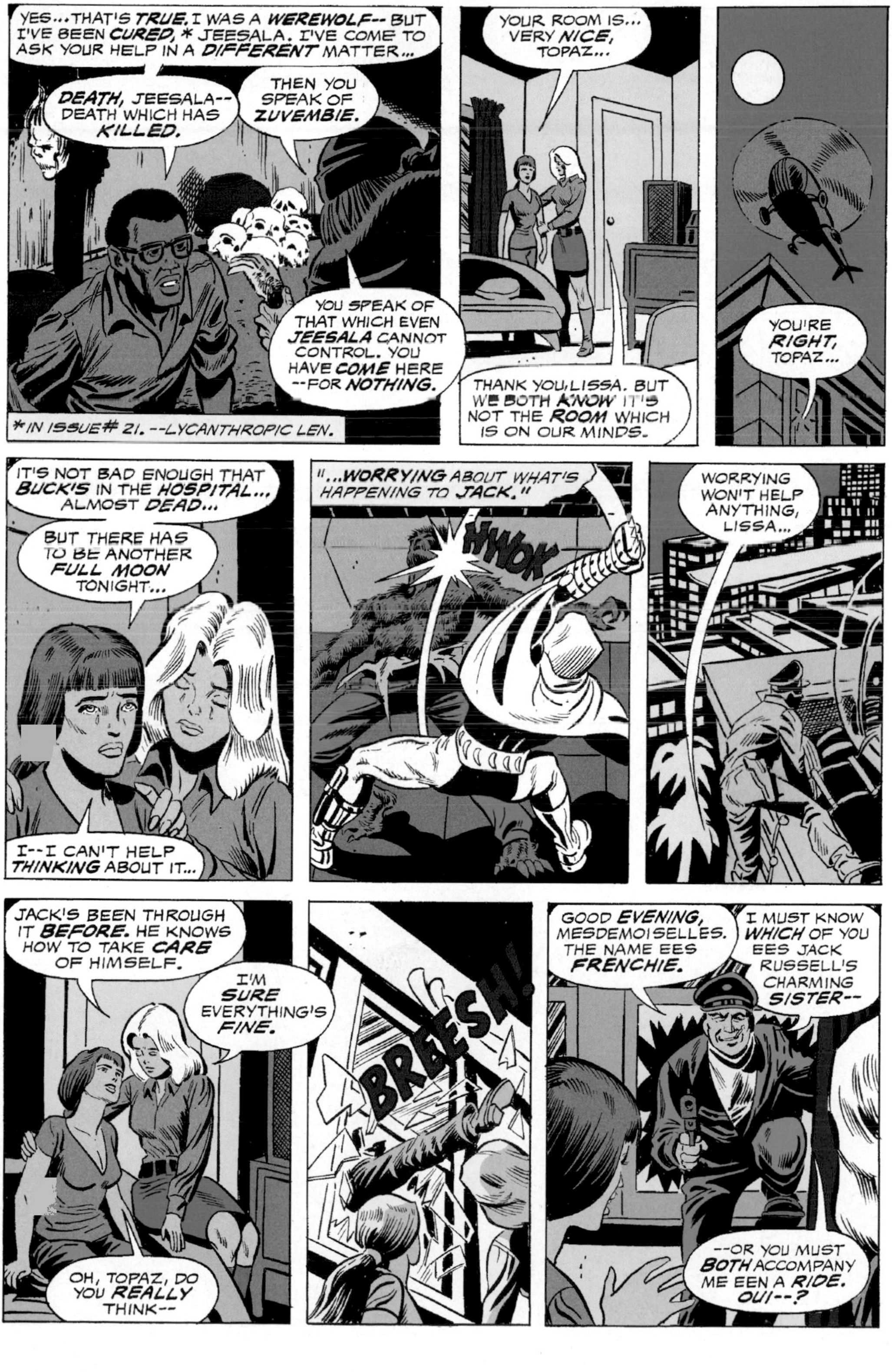
YES...THAT'S TRUE. I WAS A WEREWOLF-- BUT I'VE BEEN CURED,* JEESALA. I'VE COME TO ASK YOUR HELP IN A DIFFERENT MATTER...
DEATH, JEESALA-- DEATH WHICH HAS KILLED.
THEN YOU SPEAK OF ZUVEMBIE.
YOU SPEAK OF THAT WHICH EVEN JEESALA CANNOT CONTROL. YOU HAVE COME HERE --FOR NOTHING.
*IN ISSUE# 21. --LYCANTHROPIC LEN.
YOUR ROOM IS... VERY NICE, TOPAZ...
THANK YOU, LISSA. BUT WE BOTH KNOW IT'S NOT THE ROOM WHICH IS ON OUR MINDS.
YOU'RE RIGHT, TOPAZ...
IT'S NOT BAD ENOUGH THAT BUCK'S IN THE HOSPITAL... ALMOST DEAD...
BUT THERE HAS TO BE ANOTHER FULL MOON TONIGHT...
I--I CAN'T HELP THINKING ABOUT IT...
"...WORRYING ABOUT WHAT'S HAPPENING TO JACK."
HWOK
WORRYING WON'T HELP ANYTHING, LISSA...
JACK'S BEEN THROUGH IT BEFORE. HE KNOWS HOW TO TAKE CARE OF HIMSELF.
I'M SURE EVERYTHING'S FINE.
OH, TOPAZ, DO YOU REALLY THINK--
BREESH!
GOOD EVENING, MESDEMOISELLES. THE NAME EES FRENCHIE.
I MUST KNOW WHICH OF YOU EES JACK RUSSELL'S CHARMING SISTER--
--OR YOU MUST BOTH ACCOMPANY ME EEN A RIDE. OUI--?

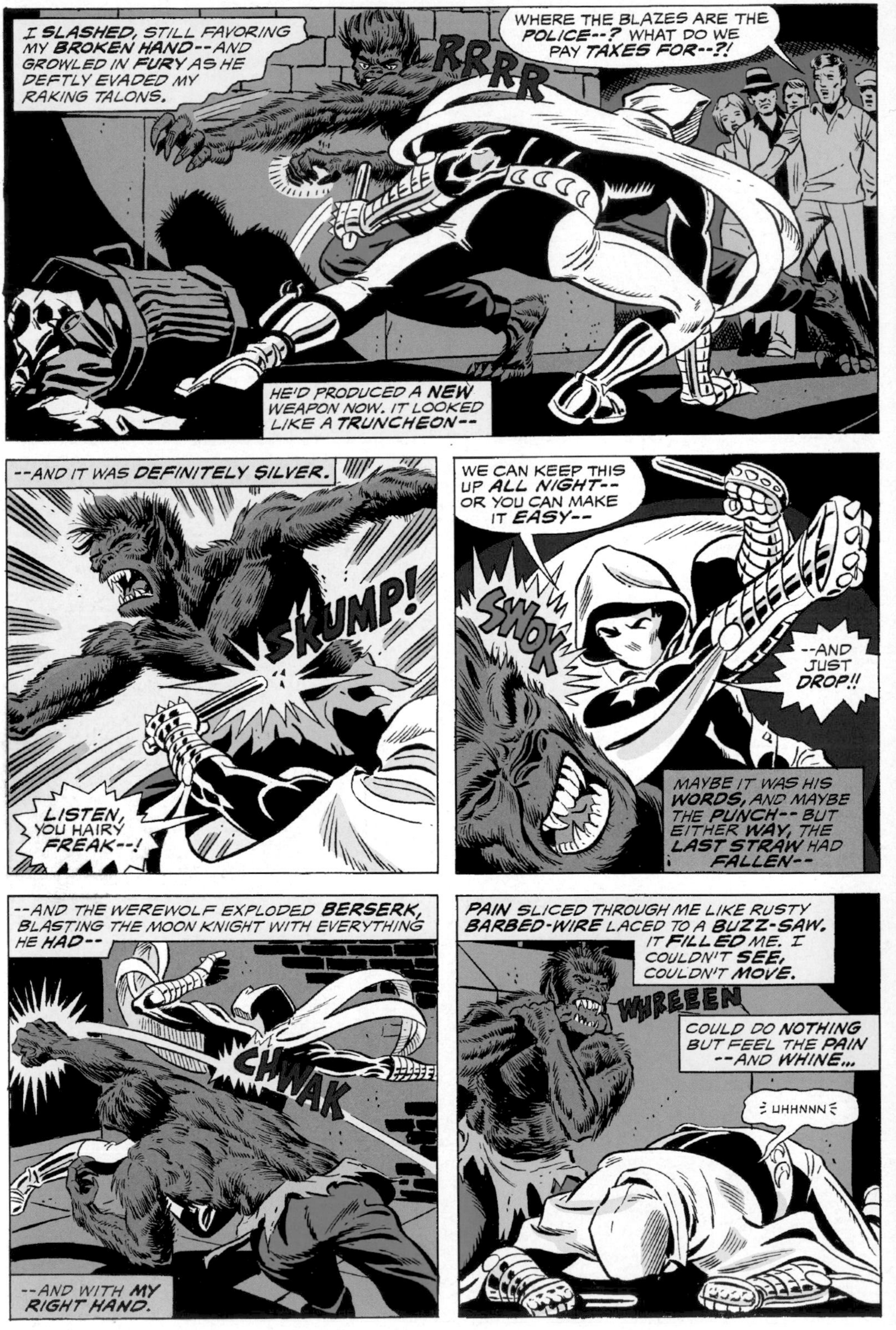
I SLASHED, STILL FAVORING MY BROKEN HAND--AND GROWLED IN FURY AS HE DEFTLY EVADED MY RAKING TALONS.
RRRRR
WHERE THE BLAZES ARE THE POLICE--? WHAT DO WE PAY TAXES FOR--?!
HE'D PRODUCED A NEW WEAPON NOW. IT LOOKED LIKE A TRUNCHEON--
--AND IT WAS DEFINITELY SILVER.
SKUMP!
LISTEN, YOU HAIRY FREAK--!
WE CAN KEEP THIS UP ALL NIGHT--OR YOU CAN MAKE IT EASY--
SWOK
--AND JUST DROP!!
MAYBE IT WAS HIS WORDS, AND MAYBE THE PUNCH--BUT EITHER WAY, THE LAST STRAW HAD FALLEN--
--AND THE WEREWOLF EXPLODED BERSERK, BLASTING THE MOON KNIGHT WITH EVERYTHING HE HAD--
CHWAK
--AND WITH MY RIGHT HAND.
PAIN SLICED THROUGH ME LIKE RUSTY BARBED-WIRE LACED TO A BUZZ-SAW. IT FILLED ME. I COULDN'T SEE, COULDN'T MOVE.
WHREEEN
COULD DO NOTHING BUT FEEL THE PAIN --AND WHINE...
UHHNNN

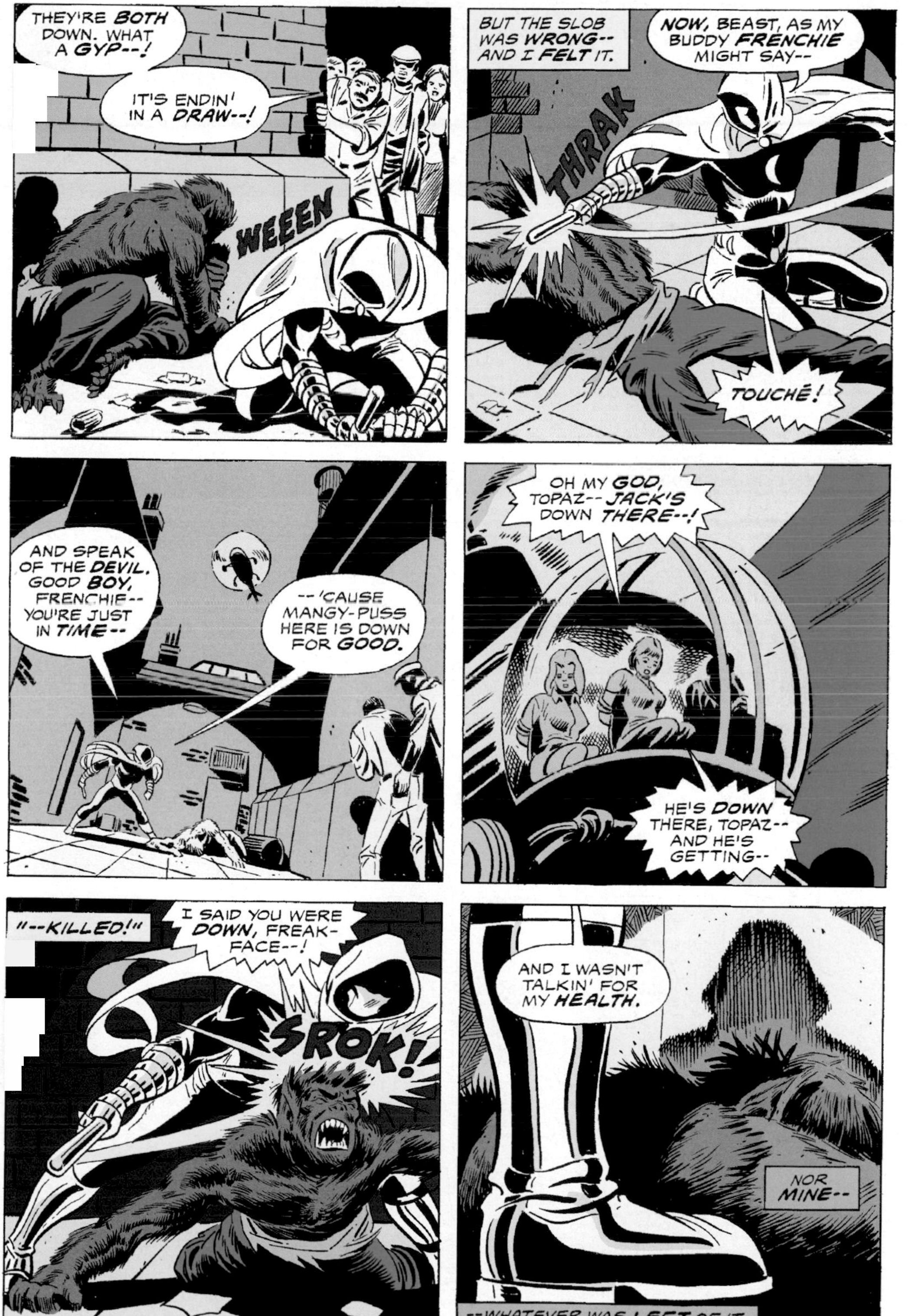

THEY'RE BOTH DOWN. WHAT A GYP--!
IT'S ENDIN' IN A DRAW--!
WEEEN
BUT THE SLOB WAS WRONG-- AND I FELT IT.
NOW, BEAST, AS MY BUDDY FRENCHIE MIGHT SAY--
THRAK
TOUCHÉ!
AND SPEAK OF THE DEVIL. GOOD BOY, FRENCHIE-- YOU'RE JUST IN TIME--
--'CAUSE MANGY-PUSS HERE IS DOWN FOR GOOD.
OH MY GOD, TOPAZ-- JACK'S DOWN THERE--!
HE'S DOWN THERE, TOPAZ-- AND HE'S GETTING--
"--KILLED!"
I SAID YOU WERE DOWN, FREAK-FACE--!
SROK!
AND I WASN'T TALKIN' FOR MY HEALTH.
NOR MINE--
--WHATEVER WAS LEFT OF IT.

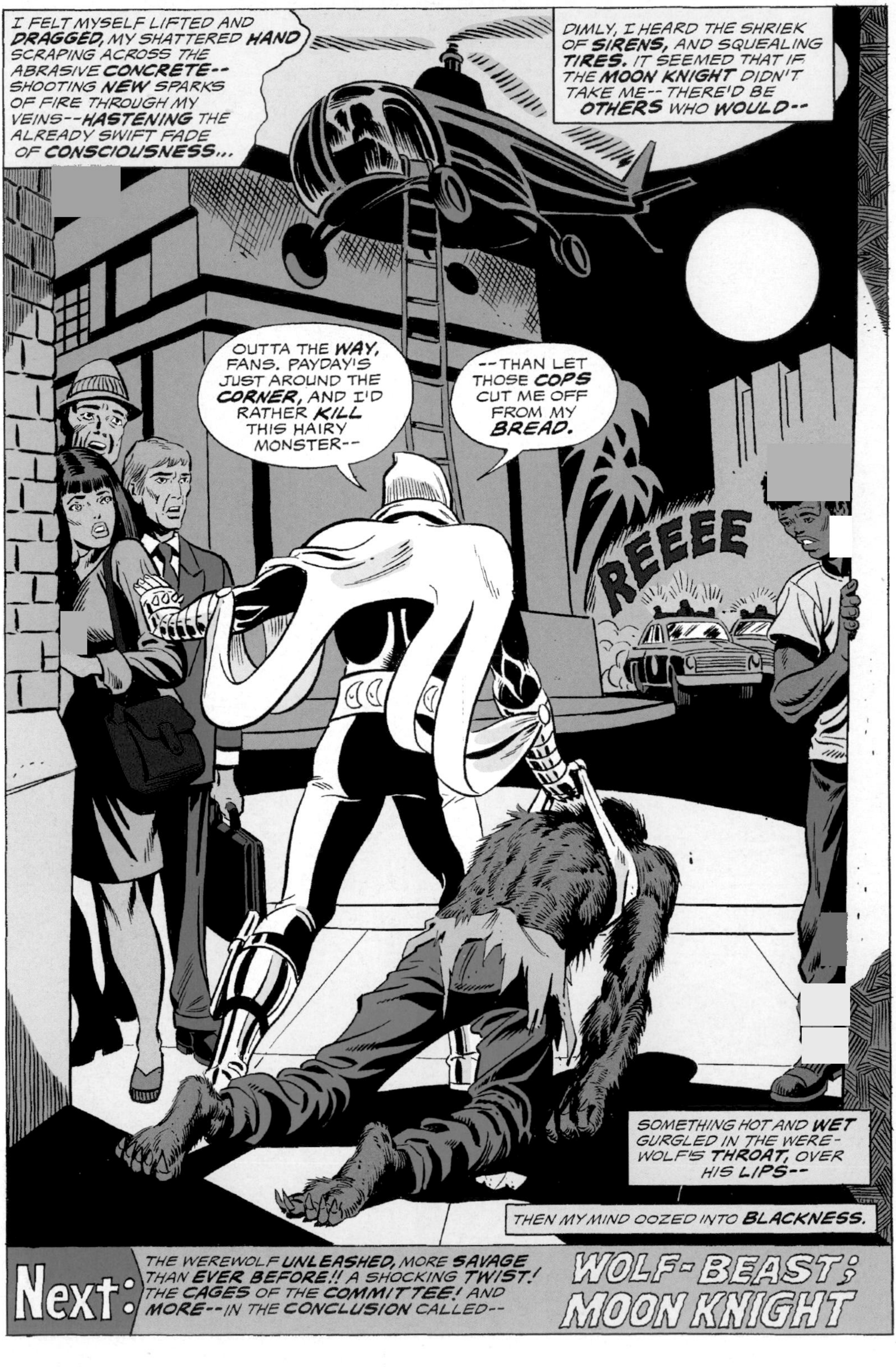
I FELT MYSELF LIFTED AND DRAGGED, MY SHATTERED HAND SCRAPING ACROSS THE ABRASIVE CONCRETE-- SHOOTING NEW SPARKS OF FIRE THROUGH MY VEINS--HASTENING THE ALREADY SWIFT FADE OF CONSCIOUSNESS...
DIMLY, I HEARD THE SHRIEK OF SIRENS, AND SQUEALING TIRES. IT SEEMED THAT IF THE MOON KNIGHT DIDN'T TAKE ME-- THERE'D BE OTHERS WHO WOULD--
OUTTA THE WAY, FANS. PAYDAY'S JUST AROUND THE CORNER, AND I'D RATHER KILL THIS HAIRY MONSTER--
--THAN LET THOSE COPS CUT ME OFF FROM MY BREAD.
REEEEE
SOMETHING HOT AND WET GURGLED IN THE WERE-WOLF'S THROAT, OVER HIS LIPS--
THEN MY MIND OOZED INTO BLACKNESS.
Next: THE WEREWOLF UNLEASHED, MORE SAVAGE THAN EVER BEFORE!! A SHOCKING TWIST! THE CAGES OF THE COMMITTEE! AND MORE--IN THE CONCLUSION CALLED--
WOLF-BEAST; MOON KNIGHT

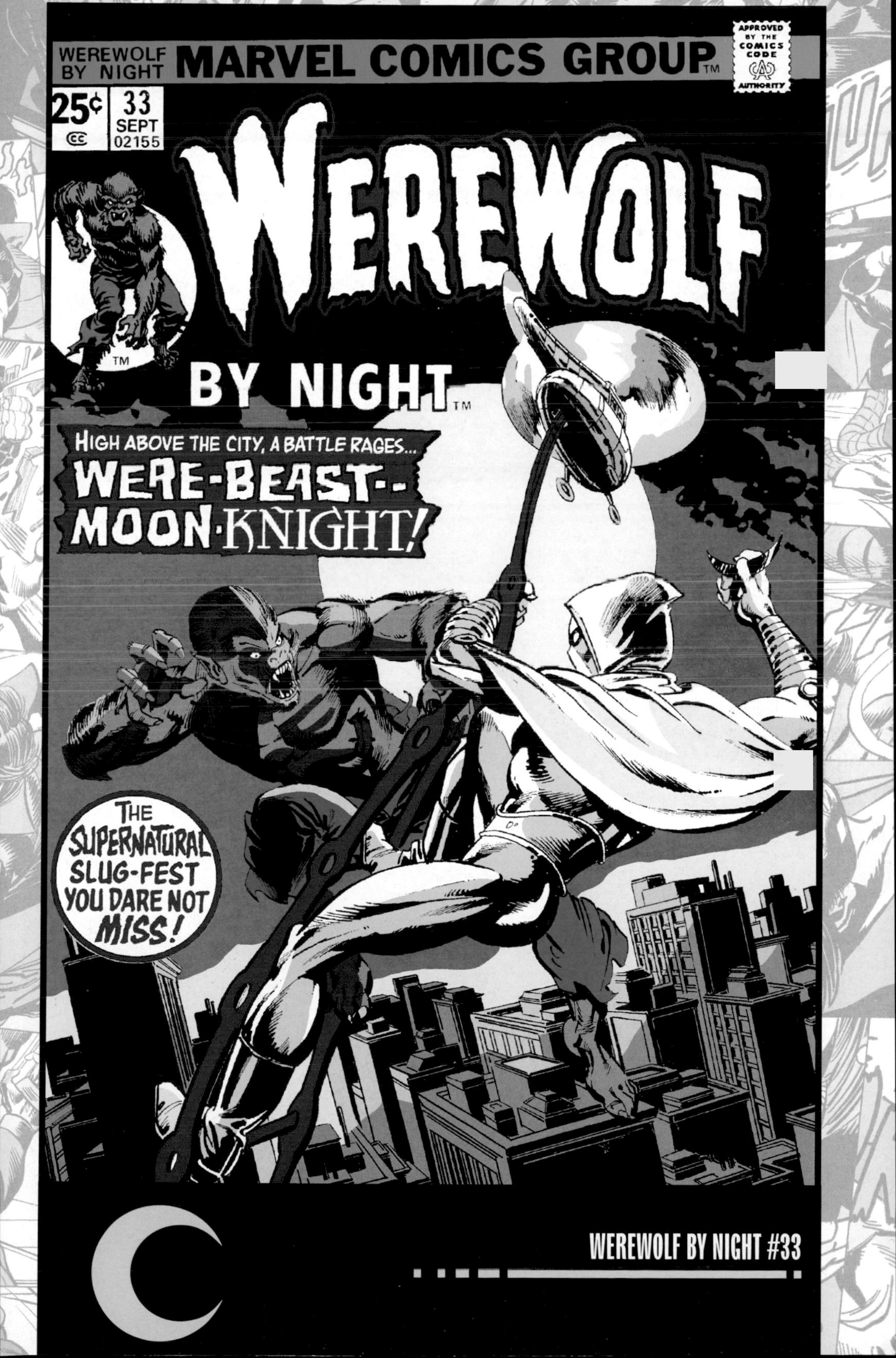
WEREWOLF BY NIGHT
MARVEL COMICS GROUP
APPROVED BY THE COMICS CODE AUTHORITY
25¢
33
SEPT
02155
WEREWOLF
BY NIGHT
HIGH ABOVE THE CITY, A BATTLE RAGES...
WERE-BEAST--
MOON·KNIGHT!
THE SUPERNATURAL SLUG-FEST YOU DARE NOT MISS!

WEREWOLF BY NIGHT #33

The tag's RUSSELL, with a JACK in front of it. The kind of name that fits a normal 19-year-old-dude living out in L.A. — not the kind of name you'd expect to find slapped on a guy who sprouted fangs, pore-to-pore fur, and wolfish howls every time the moon ballooned full. Unless that guy happened to have a father who was cursed by an arcane book called DARKHOLD — and who inherited his father's curse on his 18th birthday.

Stan Lee PRESENTS: WEREWOLF BY NIGHT!™

WOLF-BEAST vs. MOON KNIGHT
THE SECOND NIGHT: WAS ALMOST DRIED OF DARKNESS AND READY TO BE DRENCHED WITH DAWN. I WAS STILL THE WEREWOLF, BUT THE WEREWOLF WAS OUT OF IT-- AND THE MOON KNIGHT HAD HIM.*
BUT IT SEEMED THE SPOOK ON MY BACK WASN'T ENOUGH. JUST BEFORE HE'D BEATEN ME INTO A BLACKED-OUT PULP, I'D HEARD SIRENS SHRIEKING... WHICH MEANT THERE WERE OTHERS SCRAMBLING TO GET BOTH OF US...
ALL RIGHT, YOU TWO-- HOLD IT!!
THIS IS THE POLICE! TELL YOUR PILOT TO STOP-- OR WE'LL FIRE!!
DOUG MOENCH STORY
DON PERLIN + HOWIE PERLIN ART
DEBRA JAMES LETTERING
GEORGE ROUSSOS COLORING
LEN WEIN EDITOR
*FOR THE FULL STORY OF THE WEREWOLF'S CAPTURE AT THE HANDS OF THE RELENTLESS MOON KNIGHT, SEE LAST ISSUE.--LEN.

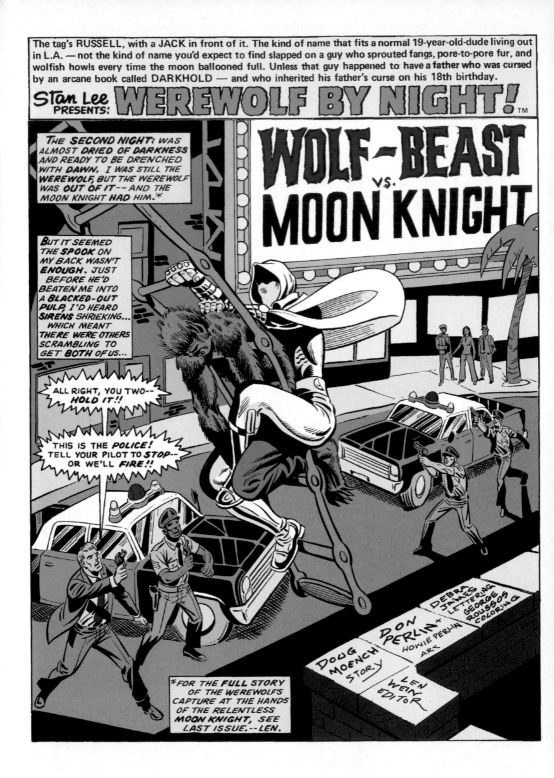

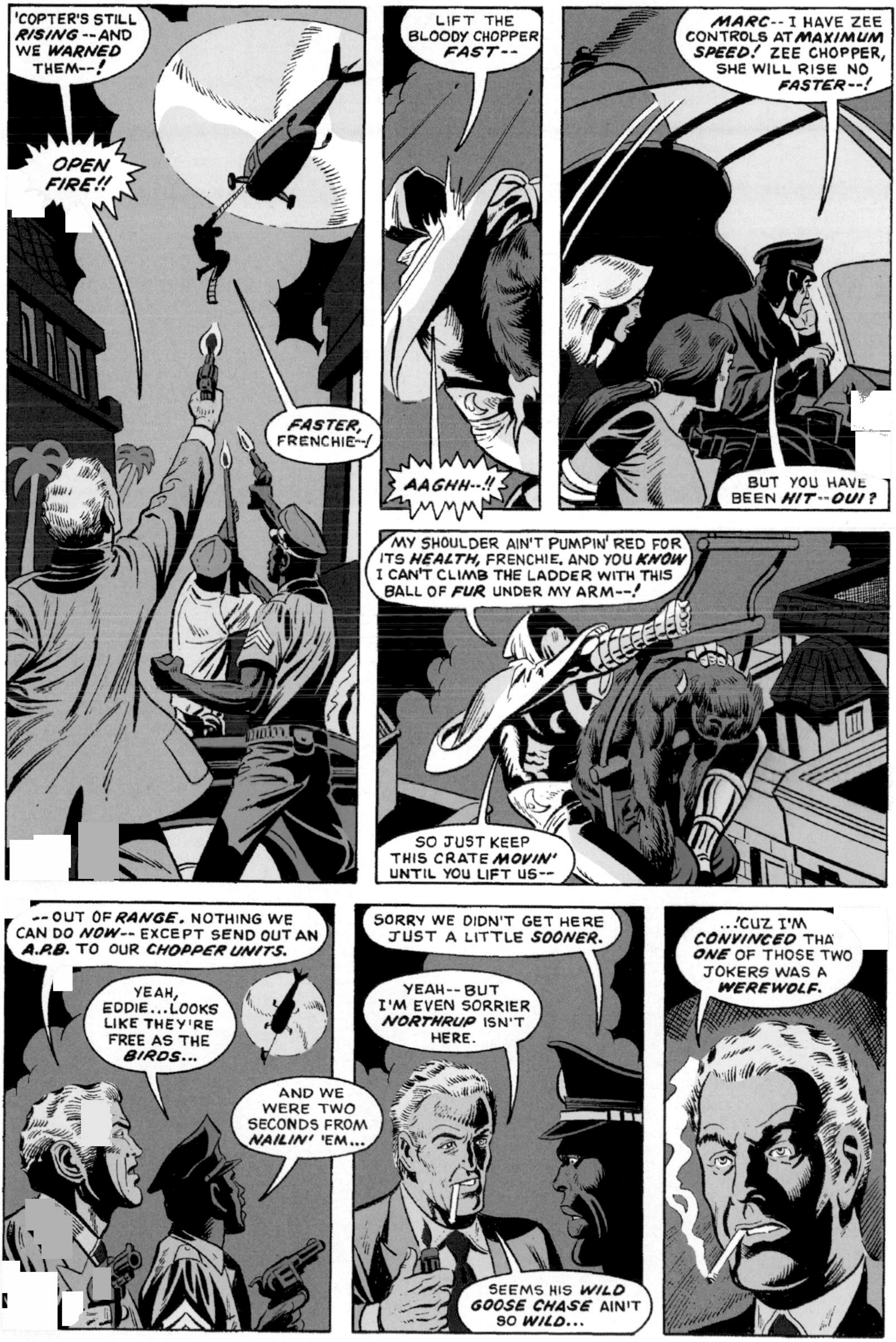

'COPTER'S STILL RISING--AND WE WARNED THEM--!
OPEN FIRE!!
FASTER, FRENCHIE--!
LIFT THE BLOODY CHOPPER FAST--
AAGHH--!!
MARC--I HAVE ZEE CONTROLS AT MAXIMUM SPEED! ZEE CHOPPER, SHE WILL RISE NO FASTER--!
BUT YOU HAVE BEEN HIT--OUI?
MY SHOULDER AIN'T PUMPIN' RED FOR ITS HEALTH, FRENCHIE. AND YOU KNOW I CAN'T CLIMB THE LADDER WITH THIS BALL OF FUR UNDER MY ARM--!
SO JUST KEEP THIS CRATE MOVIN' UNTIL YOU LIFT US--
--OUT OF RANGE. NOTHING WE CAN DO NOW--EXCEPT SEND OUT AN A.P.B. TO OUR CHOPPER UNITS.
YEAH, EDDIE...LOOKS LIKE THEY'RE FREE AS THE BIRDS...
AND WE WERE TWO SECONDS FROM NAILIN' 'EM...
SORRY WE DIDN'T GET HERE JUST A LITTLE SOONER.
YEAH--BUT I'M EVEN SORRIER NORTHRUP ISN'T HERE.
SEEMS HIS WILD GOOSE CHASE AIN'T SO WILD...
...'CUZ I'M CONVINCED THA ONE OF THOSE TWO JOKERS WAS A WEREWOLF.

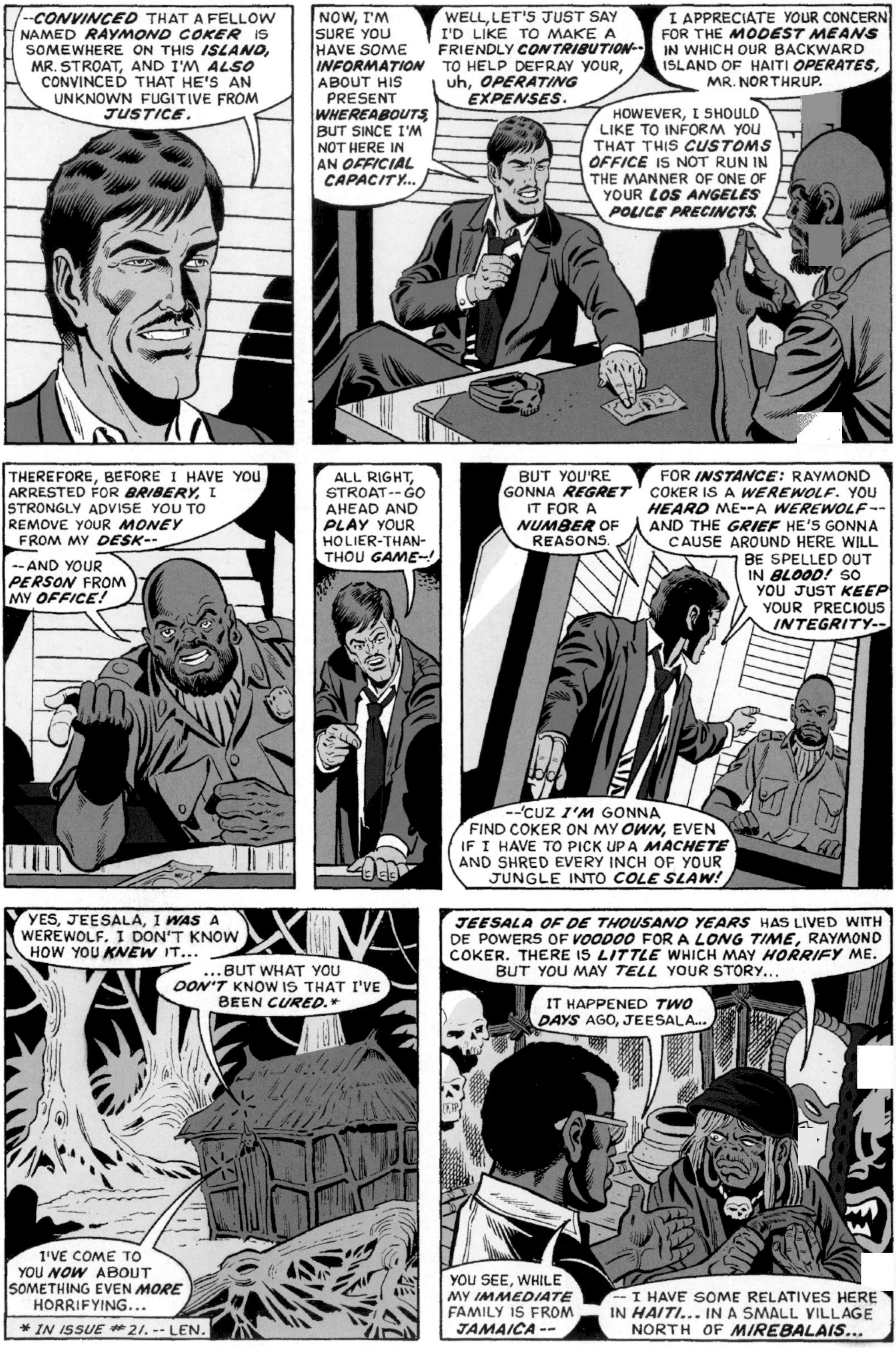
--CONVINCED THAT A FELLOW NAMED RAYMOND COKER IS SOMEWHERE ON THIS ISLAND, MR. STROAT, AND I'M ALSO CONVINCED THAT HE'S AN UNKNOWN FUGITIVE FROM JUSTICE.
NOW, I'M SURE YOU HAVE SOME INFORMATION ABOUT HIS PRESENT WHEREABOUTS, BUT SINCE I'M NOT HERE IN AN OFFICIAL CAPACITY...
WELL, LET'S JUST SAY I'D LIKE TO MAKE A FRIENDLY CONTRIBUTION-- TO HELP DEFRAY YOUR, uh, OPERATING EXPENSES.
I APPRECIATE YOUR CONCERN FOR THE MODEST MEANS IN WHICH OUR BACKWARD ISLAND OF HAITI OPERATES, MR. NORTHRUP.
HOWEVER, I SHOULD LIKE TO INFORM YOU THAT THIS CUSTOMS OFFICE IS NOT RUN IN THE MANNER OF ONE OF YOUR LOS ANGELES POLICE PRECINCTS.
THEREFORE, BEFORE I HAVE YOU ARRESTED FOR BRIBERY, I STRONGLY ADVISE YOU TO REMOVE YOUR MONEY FROM MY DESK--
--AND YOUR PERSON FROM MY OFFICE!
ALL RIGHT, STROAT--GO AHEAD AND PLAY YOUR HOLIER-THAN-THOU GAME--!
BUT YOU'RE GONNA REGRET IT FOR A NUMBER OF REASONS.
FOR INSTANCE: RAYMOND COKER IS A WEREWOLF. YOU HEARD ME--A WEREWOLF-- AND THE GRIEF HE'S GONNA CAUSE AROUND HERE WILL BE SPELLED OUT IN BLOOD! SO YOU JUST KEEP YOUR PRECIOUS INTEGRITY--
--'CUZ I'M GONNA FIND COKER ON MY OWN, EVEN IF I HAVE TO PICK UP A MACHETE AND SHRED EVERY INCH OF YOUR JUNGLE INTO COLE SLAW!
YES, JEESALA, I WAS A WEREWOLF. I DON'T KNOW HOW YOU KNEW IT...
...BUT WHAT YOU DON'T KNOW IS THAT I'VE BEEN CURED.*
I'VE COME TO YOU NOW ABOUT SOMETHING EVEN MORE HORRIFYING...
* IN ISSUE #21. -- LEN.
JEESALA OF DE THOUSAND YEARS HAS LIVED WITH DE POWERS OF VOODOO FOR A LONG TIME, RAYMOND COKER. THERE IS LITTLE WHICH MAY HORRIFY ME. BUT YOU MAY TELL YOUR STORY...
IT HAPPENED TWO DAYS AGO, JEESALA...
YOU SEE, WHILE MY IMMEDIATE FAMILY IS FROM JAMAICA--
--I HAVE SOME RELATIVES HERE IN HAITI... IN A SMALL VILLAGE NORTH OF MIREBALAIS...

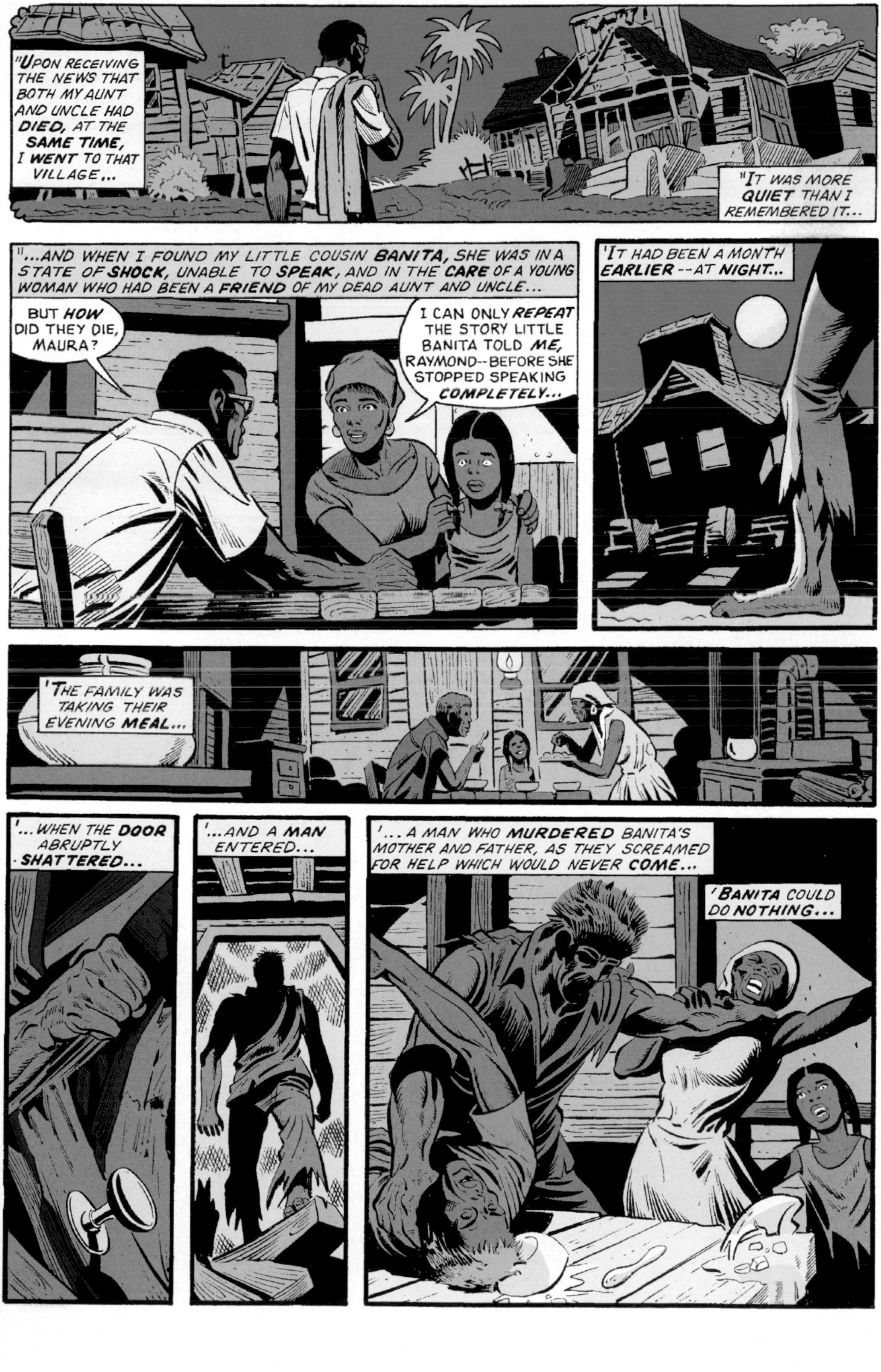
"UPON RECEIVING THE NEWS THAT BOTH MY AUNT AND UNCLE HAD DIED, AT THE SAME TIME, I WENT TO THAT VILLAGE...
"IT WAS MORE QUIET THAN I REMEMBERED IT...
"...AND WHEN I FOUND MY LITTLE COUSIN BANITA, SHE WAS IN A STATE OF SHOCK, UNABLE TO SPEAK, AND IN THE CARE OF A YOUNG WOMAN WHO HAD BEEN A FRIEND OF MY DEAD AUNT AND UNCLE...
BUT HOW DID THEY DIE, MAURA?
I CAN ONLY REPEAT THE STORY LITTLE BANITA TOLD ME, RAYMOND--BEFORE SHE STOPPED SPEAKING COMPLETELY...
'IT HAD BEEN A MONTH EARLIER--AT NIGHT...
'THE FAMILY WAS TAKING THEIR EVENING MEAL...
'...WHEN THE DOOR ABRUPTLY SHATTERED...
'...AND A MAN ENTERED...
'...A MAN WHO MURDERED BANITA'S MOTHER AND FATHER, AS THEY SCREAMED FOR HELP WHICH WOULD NEVER COME...
'BANITA COULD DO NOTHING...

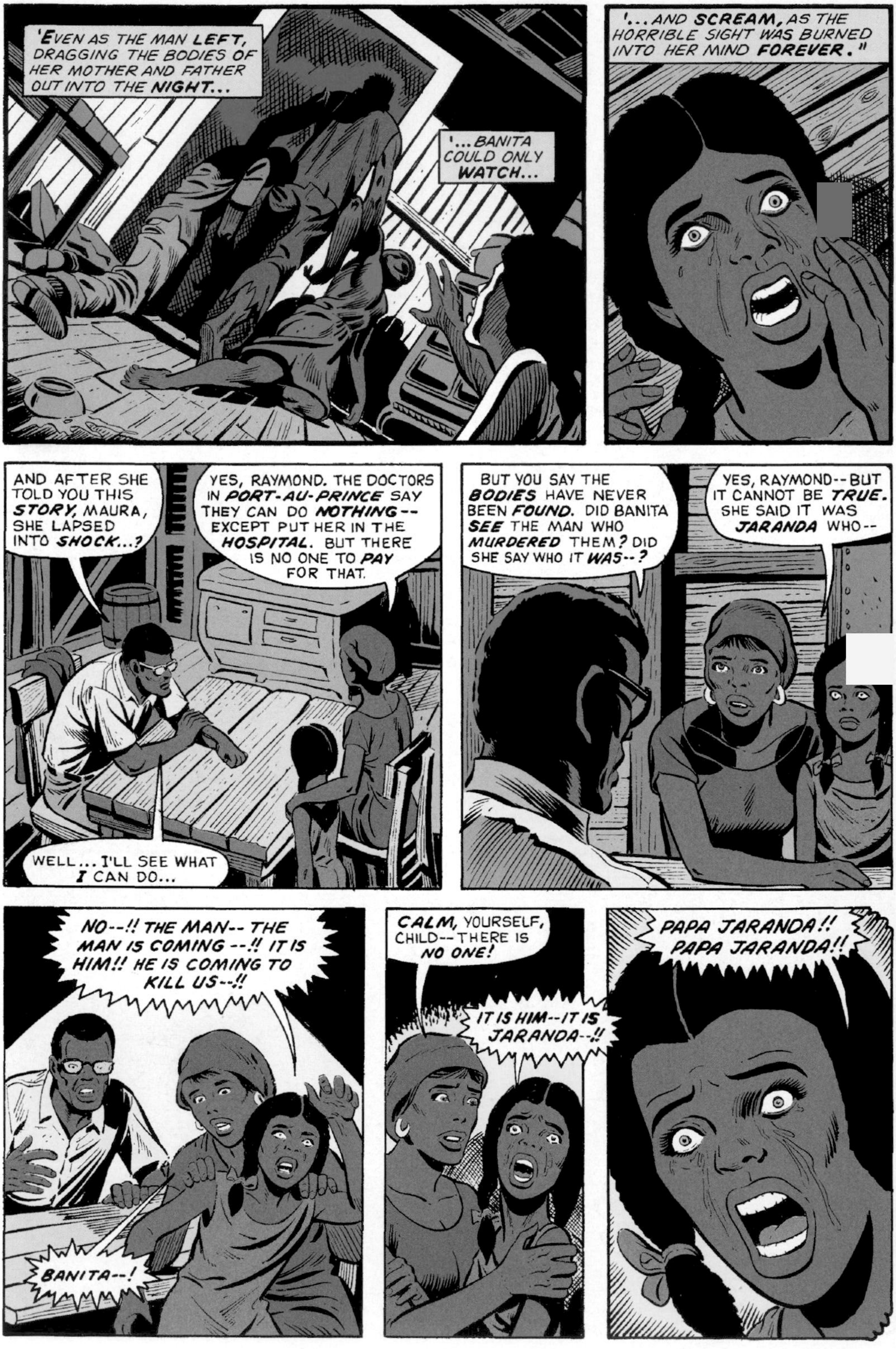
'EVEN AS THE MAN LEFT, DRAGGING THE BODIES OF HER MOTHER AND FATHER OUT INTO THE NIGHT...
'...BANITA COULD ONLY WATCH...
'...AND SCREAM, AS THE HORRIBLE SIGHT WAS BURNED INTO HER MIND FOREVER."
AND AFTER SHE TOLD YOU THIS STORY, MAURA, SHE LAPSED INTO SHOCK...?
YES, RAYMOND. THE DOCTORS IN PORT-AU-PRINCE SAY THEY CAN DO NOTHING-- EXCEPT PUT HER IN THE HOSPITAL. BUT THERE IS NO ONE TO PAY FOR THAT.
WELL... I'LL SEE WHAT I CAN DO...
BUT YOU SAY THE BODIES HAVE NEVER BEEN FOUND. DID BANITA SEE THE MAN WHO MURDERED THEM? DID SHE SAY WHO IT WAS--?
YES, RAYMOND--BUT IT CANNOT BE TRUE. SHE SAID IT WAS JARANDA WHO--
NO--!! THE MAN-- THE MAN IS COMING--!! IT IS HIM!! HE IS COMING TO KILL US--!!
BANITA--!
CALM, YOURSELF, CHILD-- THERE IS NO ONE!
IT IS HIM--IT IS JARANDA--!!
PAPA JARANDA!! PAPA JARANDA!!

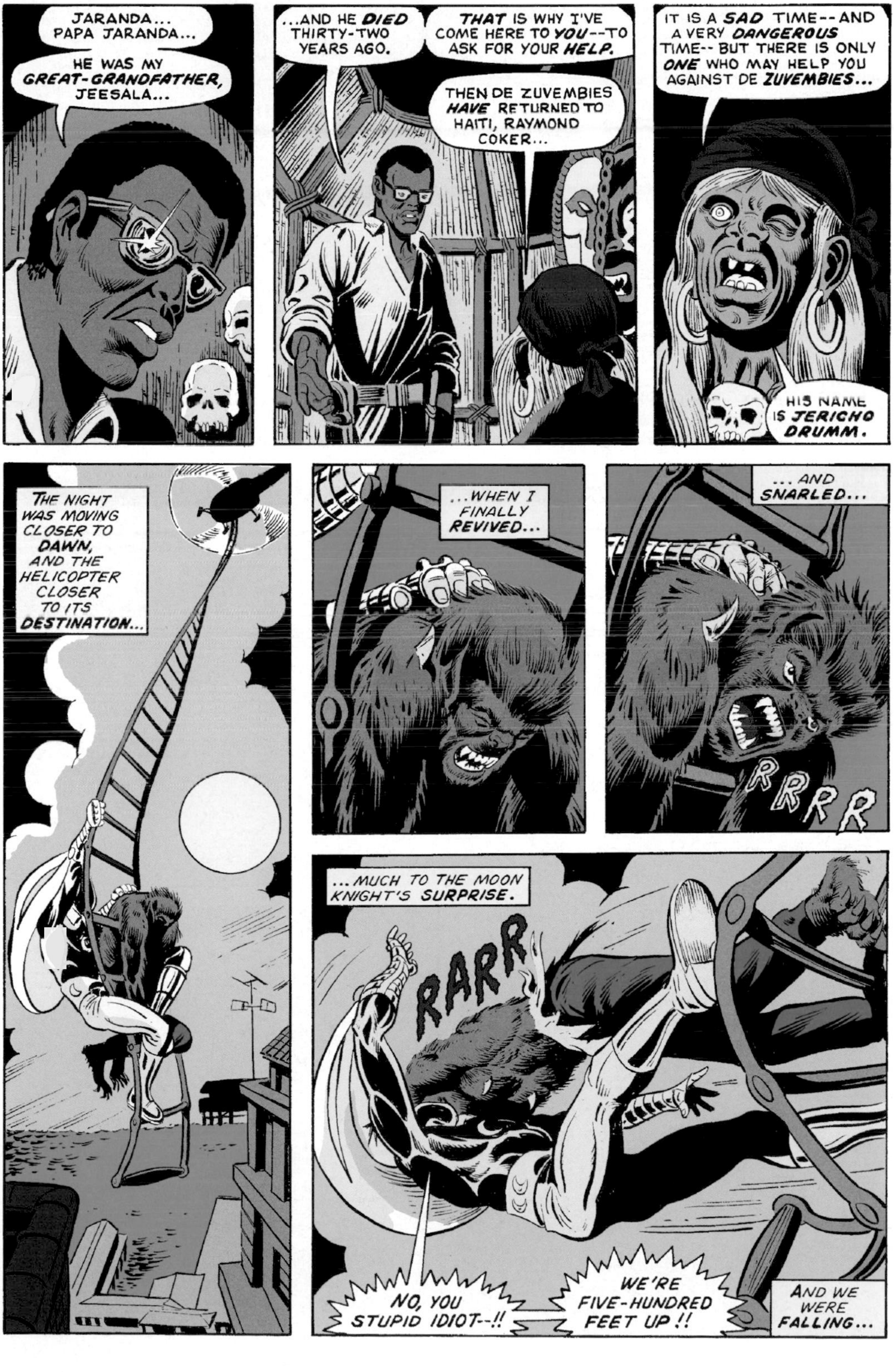
JARANDA... PAPA JARANDA...
HE WAS MY GREAT-GRANDFATHER, JEESALA...
...AND HE DIED THIRTY-TWO YEARS AGO.
THAT IS WHY I'VE COME HERE TO YOU--TO ASK FOR YOUR HELP.
THEN DE ZUVEMBIES HAVE RETURNED TO HAITI, RAYMOND COKER...
IT IS A SAD TIME--AND A VERY DANGEROUS TIME--BUT THERE IS ONLY ONE WHO MAY HELP YOU AGAINST DE ZUVEMBIES...
HIS NAME IS JERICHO DRUMM.
THE NIGHT WAS MOVING CLOSER TO DAWN, AND THE HELICOPTER CLOSER TO ITS DESTINATION...
...WHEN I FINALLY REVIVED...
...AND SNARLED...
RRRRR
...MUCH TO THE MOON KNIGHT'S SURPRISE.
RARR
NO, YOU STUPID IDIOT--!!
WE'RE FIVE-HUNDRED FEET UP!!
AND WE WERE FALLING...

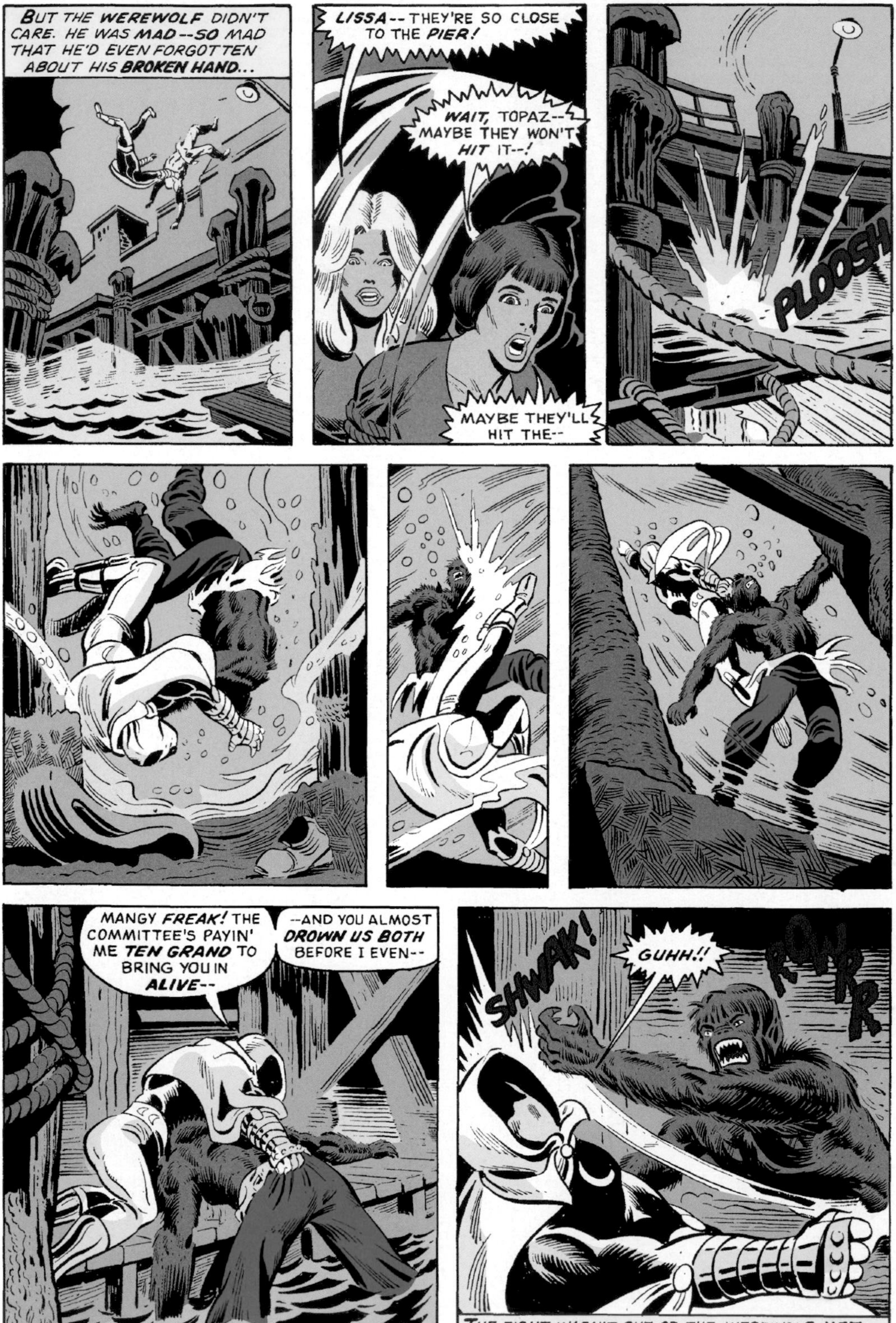

BUT THE WEREWOLF DIDN'T CARE. HE WAS MAD--SO MAD THAT HE'D EVEN FORGOTTEN ABOUT HIS BROKEN HAND...
LISSA--THEY'RE SO CLOSE TO THE PIER!
WAIT, TOPAZ--MAYBE THEY WON'T HIT IT--!
MAYBE THEY'LL HIT THE--
PLOOSH
MANGY FREAK! THE COMMITTEE'S PAYIN' ME TEN GRAND TO BRING YOU IN ALIVE--
--AND YOU ALMOST DROWN US BOTH BEFORE I EVEN--
SHWAK!
GUHH!!
ROWRR
THE FIGHT WASN'T OUT OF THE WEREWOLF YET...

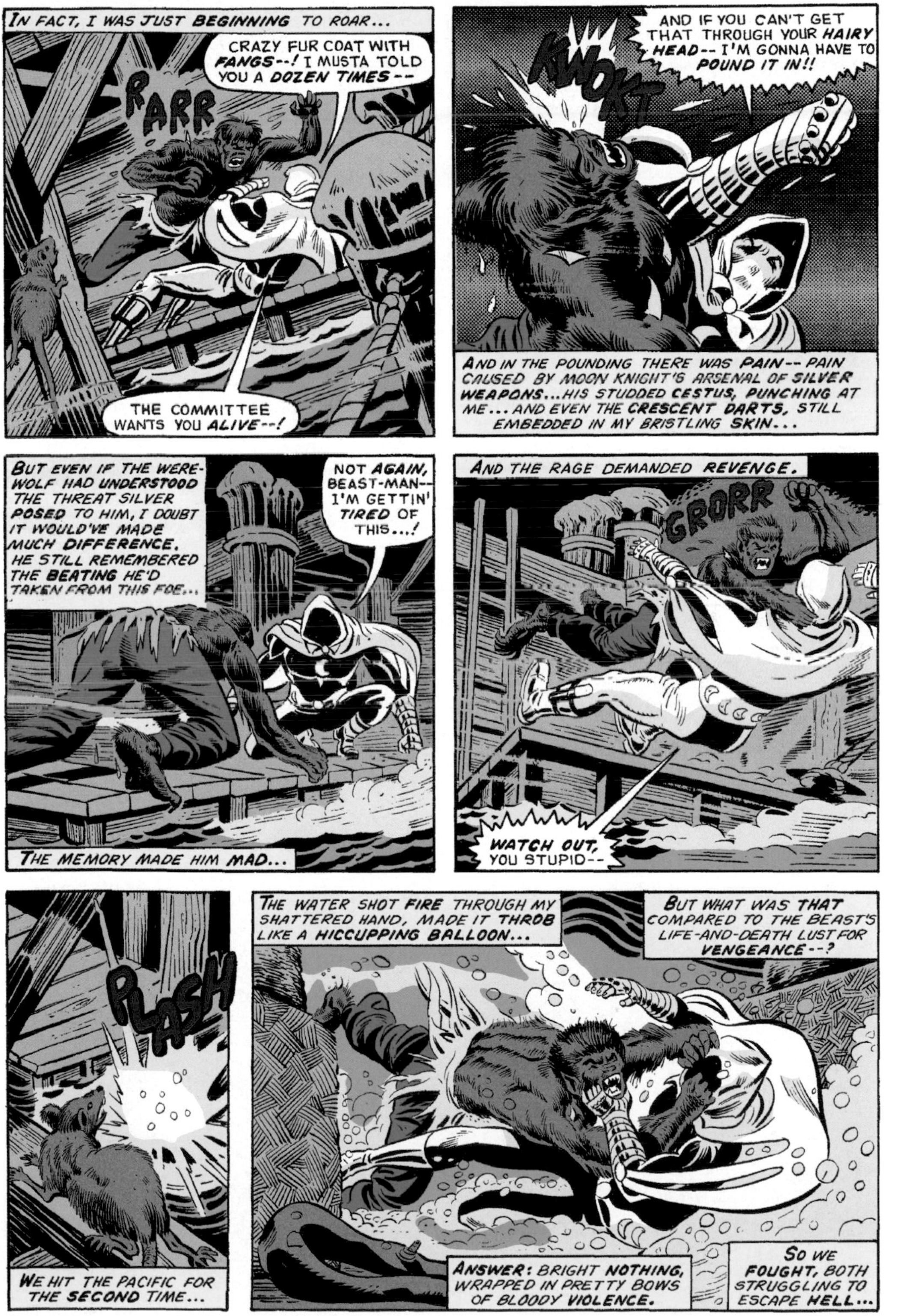

IN FACT, I WAS JUST BEGINNING TO ROAR...
RARR
CRAZY FUR COAT WITH FANGS--! I MUSTA TOLD YOU A DOZEN TIMES--
THE COMMITTEE WANTS YOU ALIVE--!
KWOKT
AND IF YOU CAN'T GET THAT THROUGH YOUR HAIRY HEAD-- I'M GONNA HAVE TO POUND IT IN!!
AND IN THE POUNDING THERE WAS PAIN-- PAIN CAUSED BY MOON KNIGHT'S ARSENAL OF SILVER WEAPONS...HIS STUDDED CESTUS, PUNCHING AT ME... AND EVEN THE CRESCENT DARTS, STILL EMBEDDED IN MY BRISTLING SKIN...
BUT EVEN IF THE WEREWOLF HAD UNDERSTOOD THE THREAT SILVER POSED TO HIM, I DOUBT IT WOULD'VE MADE MUCH DIFFERENCE. HE STILL REMEMBERED THE BEATING HE'D TAKEN FROM THIS FOE...
NOT AGAIN, BEAST-MAN-- I'M GETTIN' TIRED OF THIS...!
THE MEMORY MADE HIM MAD...
AND THE RAGE DEMANDED REVENGE.
GRORR
WATCH OUT, YOU STUPID--
PLASH
WE HIT THE PACIFIC FOR THE SECOND TIME...
THE WATER SHOT FIRE THROUGH MY SHATTERED HAND, MADE IT THROB LIKE A HICCUPPING BALLOON...
BUT WHAT WAS THAT COMPARED TO THE BEAST'S LIFE-AND-DEATH LUST FOR VENGEANCE--?
ANSWER: BRIGHT NOTHING, WRAPPED IN PRETTY BOWS OF BLOODY VIOLENCE.
SO WE FOUGHT, BOTH STRUGGLING TO ESCAPE HELL...

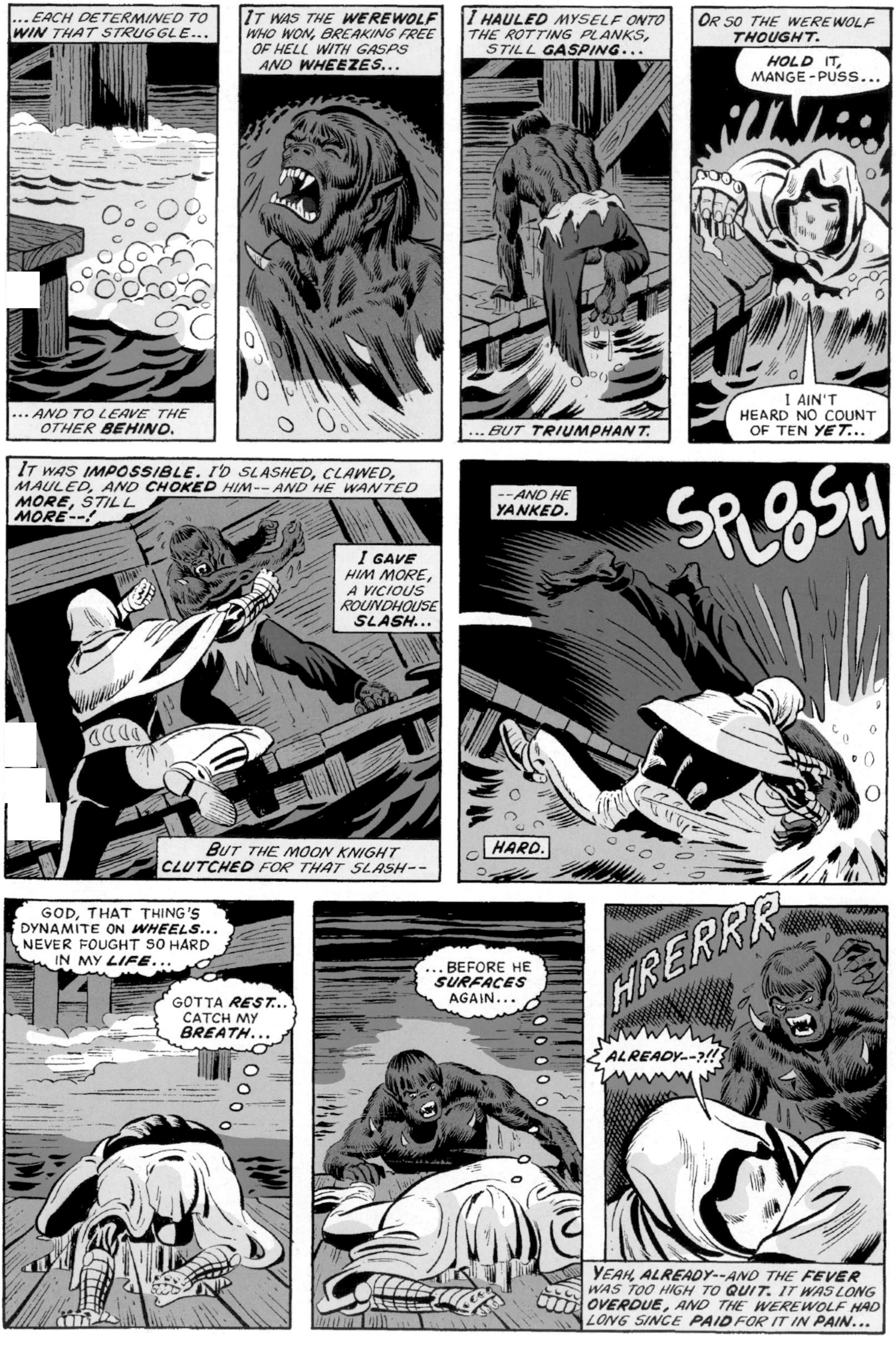
...EACH DETERMINED TO WIN THAT STRUGGLE...
...AND TO LEAVE THE OTHER BEHIND.
IT WAS THE WEREWOLF WHO WON, BREAKING FREE OF HELL WITH GASPS AND WHEEZES...
I HAULED MYSELF ONTO THE ROTTING PLANKS, STILL GASPING...
...BUT TRIUMPHANT.
OR SO THE WEREWOLF THOUGHT.
HOLD IT, MANGE-PUSS...
I AIN'T HEARD NO COUNT OF TEN YET...
IT WAS IMPOSSIBLE. I'D SLASHED, CLAWED, MAULED, AND CHOKED HIM-- AND HE WANTED MORE, STILL MORE--!
I GAVE HIM MORE, A VICIOUS ROUNDHOUSE SLASH...
BUT THE MOON KNIGHT CLUTCHED FOR THAT SLASH--
--AND HE YANKED.
SPLOSH
HARD.
GOD, THAT THING'S DYNAMITE ON WHEELS... NEVER FOUGHT SO HARD IN MY LIFE...
GOTTA REST... CATCH MY BREATH...
...BEFORE HE SURFACES AGAIN...
HRERRR
ALREADY--?!!
YEAH, ALREADY--AND THE FEVER WAS TOO HIGH TO QUIT. IT WAS LONG OVERDUE, AND THE WEREWOLF HAD LONG SINCE PAID FOR IT IN PAIN...

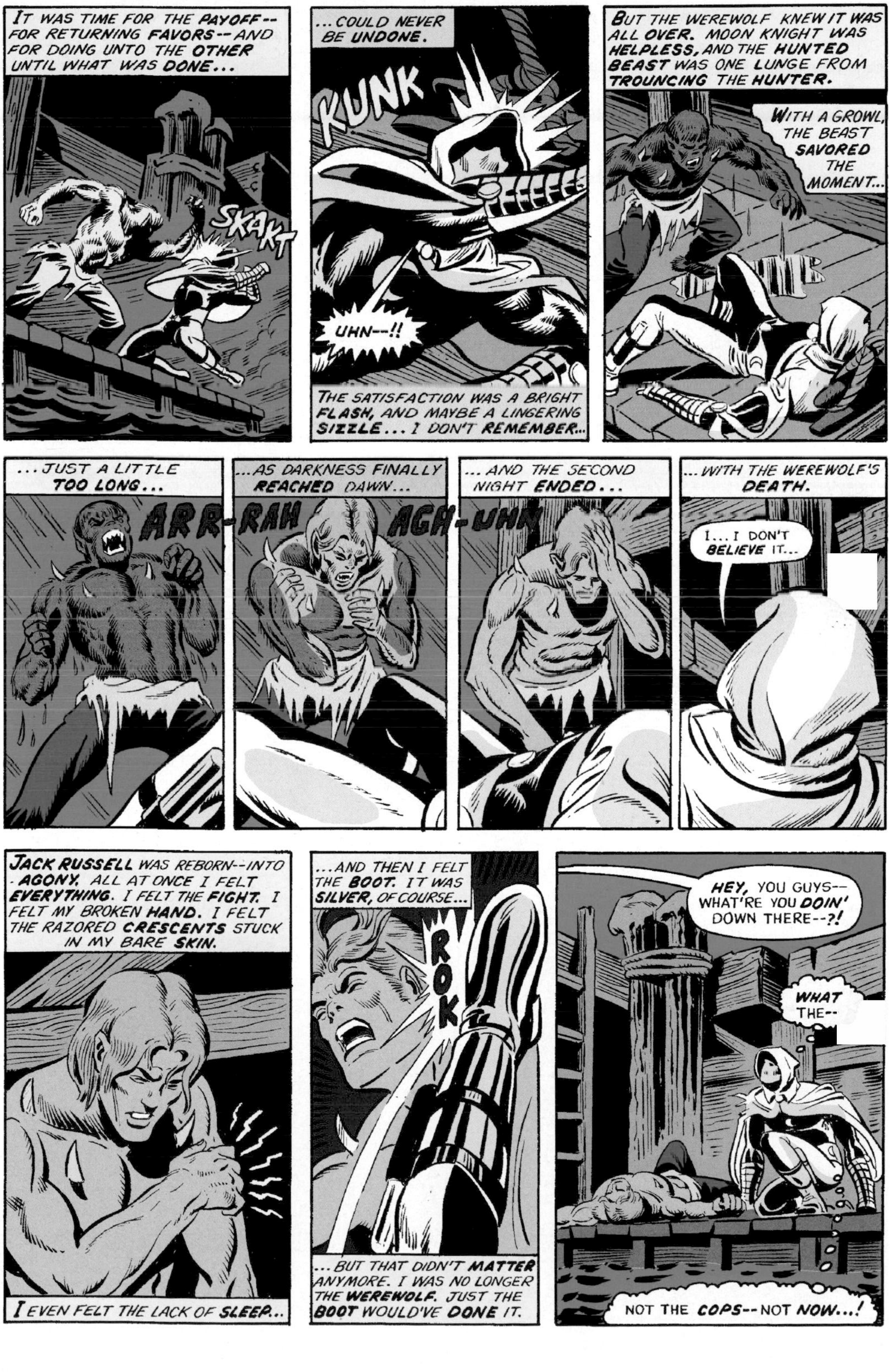
IT WAS TIME FOR THE PAYOFF--FOR RETURNING FAVORS--AND FOR DOING UNTO THE OTHER UNTIL WHAT WAS DONE...
SKAKT
...COULD NEVER BE UNDONE.
KUNK
UHN--!!
THE SATISFACTION WAS A BRIGHT FLASH, AND MAYBE A LINGERING SIZZLE... I DON'T REMEMBER...
BUT THE WEREWOLF KNEW IT WAS ALL OVER. MOON KNIGHT WAS HELPLESS, AND THE HUNTED BEAST WAS ONE LUNGE FROM TROUNCING THE HUNTER.
WITH A GROWL, THE BEAST SAVORED THE MOMENT...
...JUST A LITTLE TOO LONG...
ARR-RAH
...AS DARKNESS FINALLY REACHED DAWN...
AGH-UHN
...AND THE SECOND NIGHT ENDED...
...WITH THE WEREWOLF'S DEATH.
I... I DON'T BELIEVE IT...
JACK RUSSELL WAS REBORN--INTO AGONY. ALL AT ONCE I FELT EVERYTHING. I FELT THE FIGHT. I FELT MY BROKEN HAND. I FELT THE RAZORED CRESCENTS STUCK IN MY BARE SKIN.
I EVEN FELT THE LACK OF SLEEP...
...AND THEN I FELT THE BOOT. IT WAS SILVER, OF COURSE...
ROK
...BUT THAT DIDN'T MATTER ANYMORE. I WAS NO LONGER THE WEREWOLF. JUST THE BOOT WOULD'VE DONE IT.
HEY, YOU GUYS--WHAT'RE YOU DOIN' DOWN THERE--?!
WHAT THE--
NOT THE COPS--NOT NOW...!

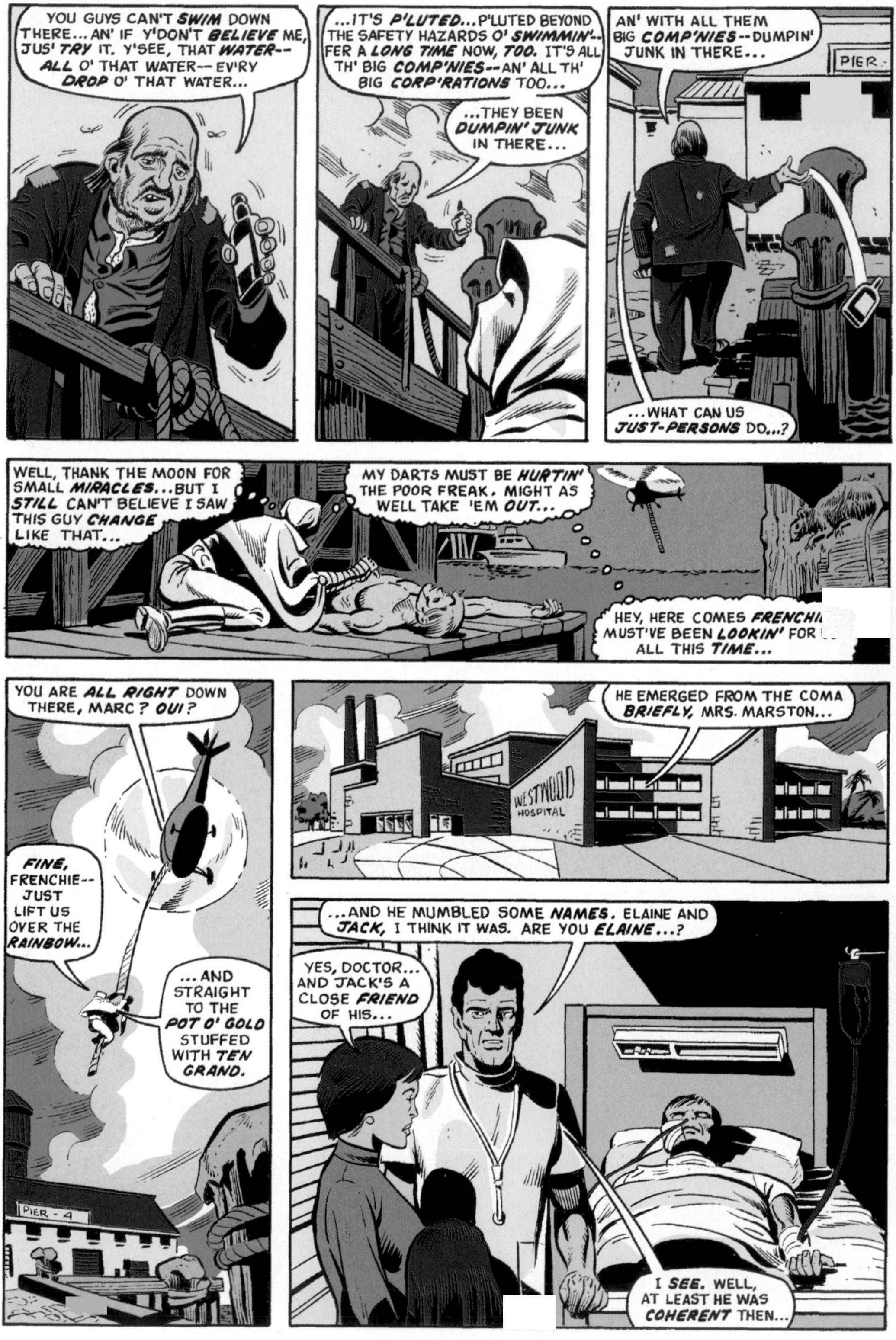
YOU GUYS CAN'T SWIM DOWN THERE... AN' IF Y'DON'T BELIEVE ME, JUS' TRY IT. Y'SEE, THAT WATER-- ALL O' THAT WATER-- EV'RY DROP O' THAT WATER...
...IT'S P'LUTED... P'LUTED BEYOND THE SAFETY HAZARDS O' SWIMMIN'-- FER A LONG TIME NOW, TOO. IT'S ALL TH' BIG COMP'NIES-- AN' ALL TH' BIG CORP'RATIONS TOO...
...THEY BEEN DUMPIN' JUNK IN THERE...
AN' WITH ALL THEM BIG COMP'NIES-- DUMPIN' JUNK IN THERE...
PIER
...WHAT CAN US JUST-PERSONS DO...?
WELL, THANK THE MOON FOR SMALL MIRACLES... BUT I STILL CAN'T BELIEVE I SAW THIS GUY CHANGE LIKE THAT...
MY DARTS MUST BE HURTIN' THE POOR FREAK. MIGHT AS WELL TAKE 'EM OUT...
HEY, HERE COMES FRENCHI
MUST'VE BEEN LOOKIN' FOR
ALL THIS TIME...
YOU ARE ALL RIGHT DOWN THERE, MARC? OUI?
FINE, FRENCHIE-- JUST LIFT US OVER THE RAINBOW...
...AND STRAIGHT TO THE POT O' GOLD STUFFED WITH TEN GRAND.
PIER - 4
HE EMERGED FROM THE COMA BRIEFLY, MRS. MARSTON...
WESTWOOD HOSPITAL
...AND HE MUMBLED SOME NAMES. ELAINE AND JACK, I THINK IT WAS. ARE YOU ELAINE...?
YES, DOCTOR... AND JACK'S A CLOSE FRIEND OF HIS...
I SEE. WELL, AT LEAST HE WAS COHERENT THEN...

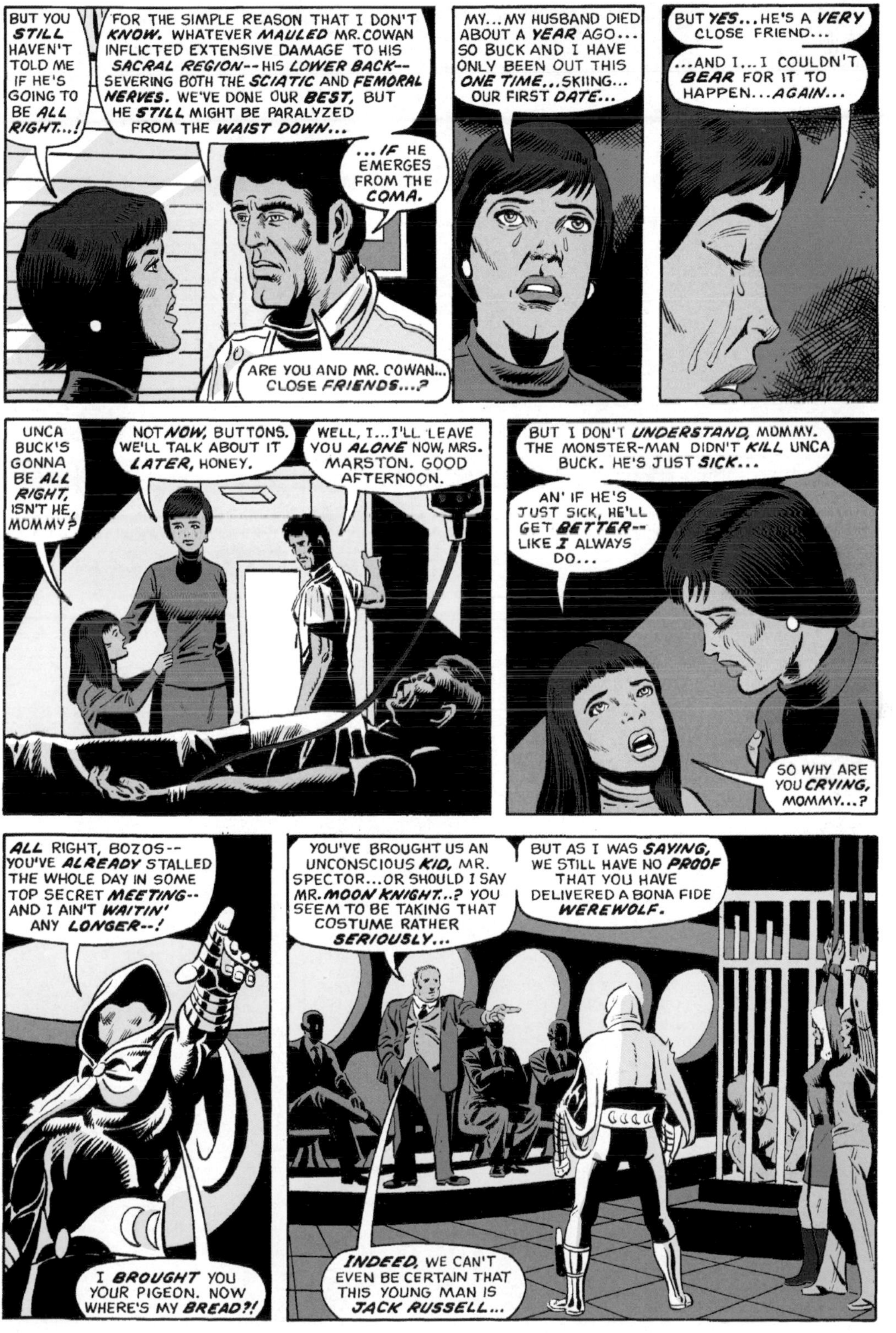

BUT YOU STILL HAVEN'T TOLD ME IF HE'S GOING TO BE ALL RIGHT...!
FOR THE SIMPLE REASON THAT I DON'T KNOW. WHATEVER MAULED MR. COWAN INFLICTED EXTENSIVE DAMAGE TO HIS SACRAL REGION--HIS LOWER BACK--SEVERING BOTH THE SCIATIC AND FEMORAL NERVES. WE'VE DONE OUR BEST, BUT HE STILL MIGHT BE PARALYZED FROM THE WAIST DOWN...
...IF HE EMERGES FROM THE COMA.
ARE YOU AND MR. COWAN... CLOSE FRIENDS...?
MY... MY HUSBAND DIED ABOUT A YEAR AGO... SO BUCK AND I HAVE ONLY BEEN OUT THIS ONE TIME... SKIING... OUR FIRST DATE...
BUT YES... HE'S A VERY CLOSE FRIEND...
...AND I... I COULDN'T BEAR FOR IT TO HAPPEN... AGAIN...
UNCA BUCK'S GONNA BE ALL RIGHT, ISN'T HE, MOMMY?
NOT NOW, BUTTONS. WE'LL TALK ABOUT IT LATER, HONEY.
WELL, I... I'LL LEAVE YOU ALONE NOW, MRS. MARSTON. GOOD AFTERNOON.
BUT I DON'T UNDERSTAND, MOMMY. THE MONSTER-MAN DIDN'T KILL UNCA BUCK. HE'S JUST SICK...
AN' IF HE'S JUST SICK, HE'LL GET BETTER--LIKE I ALWAYS DO...
SO WHY ARE YOU CRYING, MOMMY...?
ALL RIGHT, BOZOS--YOU'VE ALREADY STALLED THE WHOLE DAY IN SOME TOP SECRET MEETING--AND I AIN'T WAITIN' ANY LONGER--!
I BROUGHT YOU YOUR PIGEON. NOW WHERE'S MY BREAD?!
YOU'VE BROUGHT US AN UNCONSCIOUS KID, MR. SPECTOR... OR SHOULD I SAY MR. MOON KNIGHT...? YOU SEEM TO BE TAKING THAT COSTUME RATHER SERIOUSLY...
BUT AS I WAS SAYING, WE STILL HAVE NO PROOF THAT YOU HAVE DELIVERED A BONA FIDE WEREWOLF.
INDEED, WE CAN'T EVEN BE CERTAIN THAT THIS YOUNG MAN IS JACK RUSSELL...

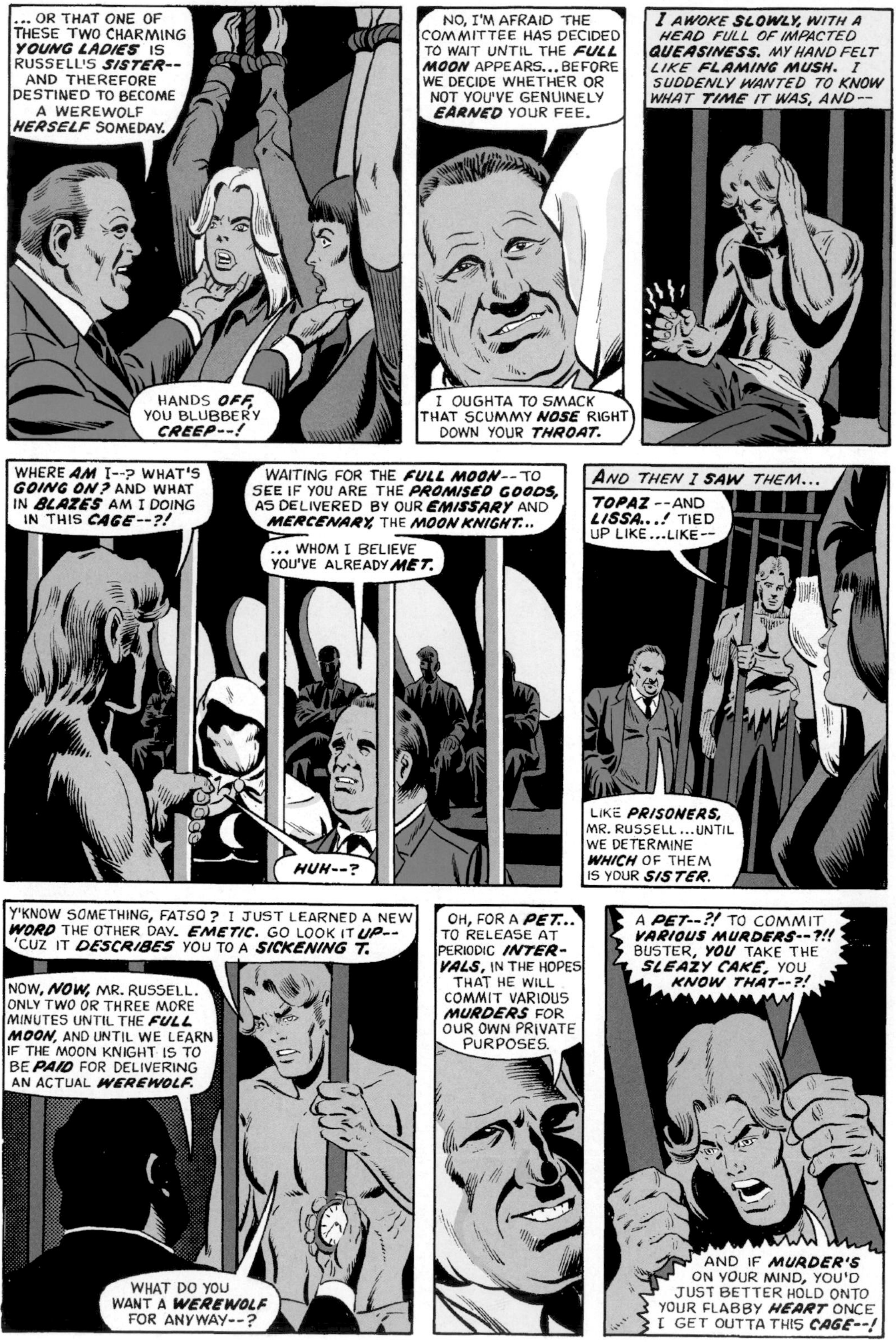
...OR THAT ONE OF THESE TWO CHARMING YOUNG LADIES IS RUSSELL'S SISTER-- AND THEREFORE DESTINED TO BECOME A WEREWOLF HERSELF SOMEDAY.
HANDS OFF, YOU BLUBBERY CREEP--!
NO, I'M AFRAID THE COMMITTEE HAS DECIDED TO WAIT UNTIL THE FULL MOON APPEARS... BEFORE WE DECIDE WHETHER OR NOT YOU'VE GENUINELY EARNED YOUR FEE.
I OUGHTA TO SMACK THAT SCUMMY NOSE RIGHT DOWN YOUR THROAT.
I AWOKE SLOWLY, WITH A HEAD FULL OF IMPACTED QUEASINESS. MY HAND FELT LIKE FLAMING MUSH. I SUDDENLY WANTED TO KNOW WHAT TIME IT WAS, AND--
WHERE AM I--? WHAT'S GOING ON? AND WHAT IN BLAZES AM I DOING IN THIS CAGE--?!
WAITING FOR THE FULL MOON-- TO SEE IF YOU ARE THE PROMISED GOODS, AS DELIVERED BY OUR EMISSARY AND MERCENARY, THE MOON KNIGHT...
...WHOM I BELIEVE YOU'VE ALREADY MET.
HUH--?
AND THEN I SAW THEM...
TOPAZ --AND LISSA...! TIED UP LIKE...LIKE--
LIKE PRISONERS, MR. RUSSELL...UNTIL WE DETERMINE WHICH OF THEM IS YOUR SISTER.
Y'KNOW SOMETHING, FATSO? I JUST LEARNED A NEW WORD THE OTHER DAY. EMETIC. GO LOOK IT UP-- 'CUZ IT DESCRIBES YOU TO A SICKENING T.
NOW, NOW, MR. RUSSELL. ONLY TWO OR THREE MORE MINUTES UNTIL THE FULL MOON, AND UNTIL WE LEARN IF THE MOON KNIGHT IS TO BE PAID FOR DELIVERING AN ACTUAL WEREWOLF.
WHAT DO YOU WANT A WEREWOLF FOR ANYWAY--?
OH, FOR A PET... TO RELEASE AT PERIODIC INTERVALS, IN THE HOPES THAT HE WILL COMMIT VARIOUS MURDERS FOR OUR OWN PRIVATE PURPOSES.
A PET--?! TO COMMIT VARIOUS MURDERS--?!! BUSTER, YOU TAKE THE SLEAZY CAKE, YOU KNOW THAT--?!
AND IF MURDER'S ON YOUR MIND, YOU'D JUST BETTER HOLD ONTO YOUR FLABBY HEART ONCE I GET OUTTA THIS CAGE--!

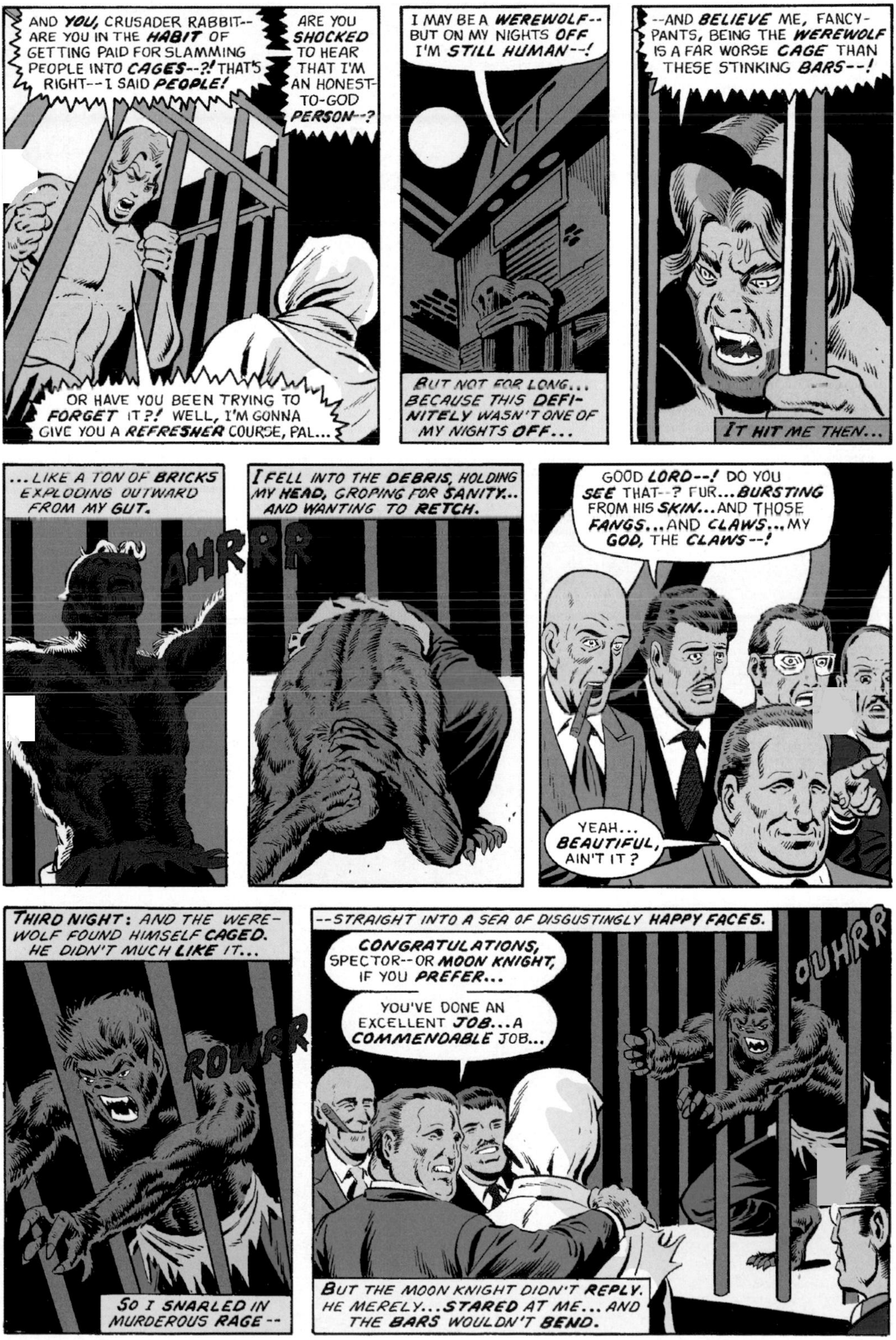
AND YOU, CRUSADER RABBIT-- ARE YOU IN THE HABIT OF GETTING PAID FOR SLAMMING PEOPLE INTO CAGES--?! THAT'S RIGHT--I SAID PEOPLE!
ARE YOU SHOCKED TO HEAR THAT I'M AN HONEST-TO-GOD PERSON--?
OR HAVE YOU BEEN TRYING TO FORGET IT?! WELL, I'M GONNA GIVE YOU A REFRESHER COURSE, PAL...
I MAY BE A WEREWOLF-- BUT ON MY NIGHTS OFF I'M STILL HUMAN--!
BUT NOT FOR LONG... BECAUSE THIS DEFINITELY WASN'T ONE OF MY NIGHTS OFF...
--AND BELIEVE ME, FANCY-PANTS, BEING THE WEREWOLF IS A FAR WORSE CAGE THAN THESE STINKING BARS--!
IT HIT ME THEN...
...LIKE A TON OF BRICKS EXPLODING OUTWARD FROM MY GUT.
AHRRRR
I FELL INTO THE DEBRIS, HOLDING MY HEAD, GROPING FOR SANITY... AND WANTING TO RETCH.
GOOD LORD--! DO YOU SEE THAT--? FUR...BURSTING FROM HIS SKIN...AND THOSE FANGS...AND CLAWS...MY GOD, THE CLAWS--!
YEAH... BEAUTIFUL, AIN'T IT?
THIRD NIGHT: AND THE WEREWOLF FOUND HIMSELF CAGED. HE DIDN'T MUCH LIKE IT...
ROWRR
SO I SNARLED IN MURDEROUS RAGE--
--STRAIGHT INTO A SEA OF DISGUSTINGLY HAPPY FACES.
CONGRATULATIONS, SPECTOR--OR MOON KNIGHT, IF YOU PREFER...
YOU'VE DONE AN EXCELLENT JOB...A COMMENDABLE JOB...
OUHRR
BUT THE MOON KNIGHT DIDN'T REPLY. HE MERELY...STARED AT ME... AND THE BARS WOULDN'T BEND.

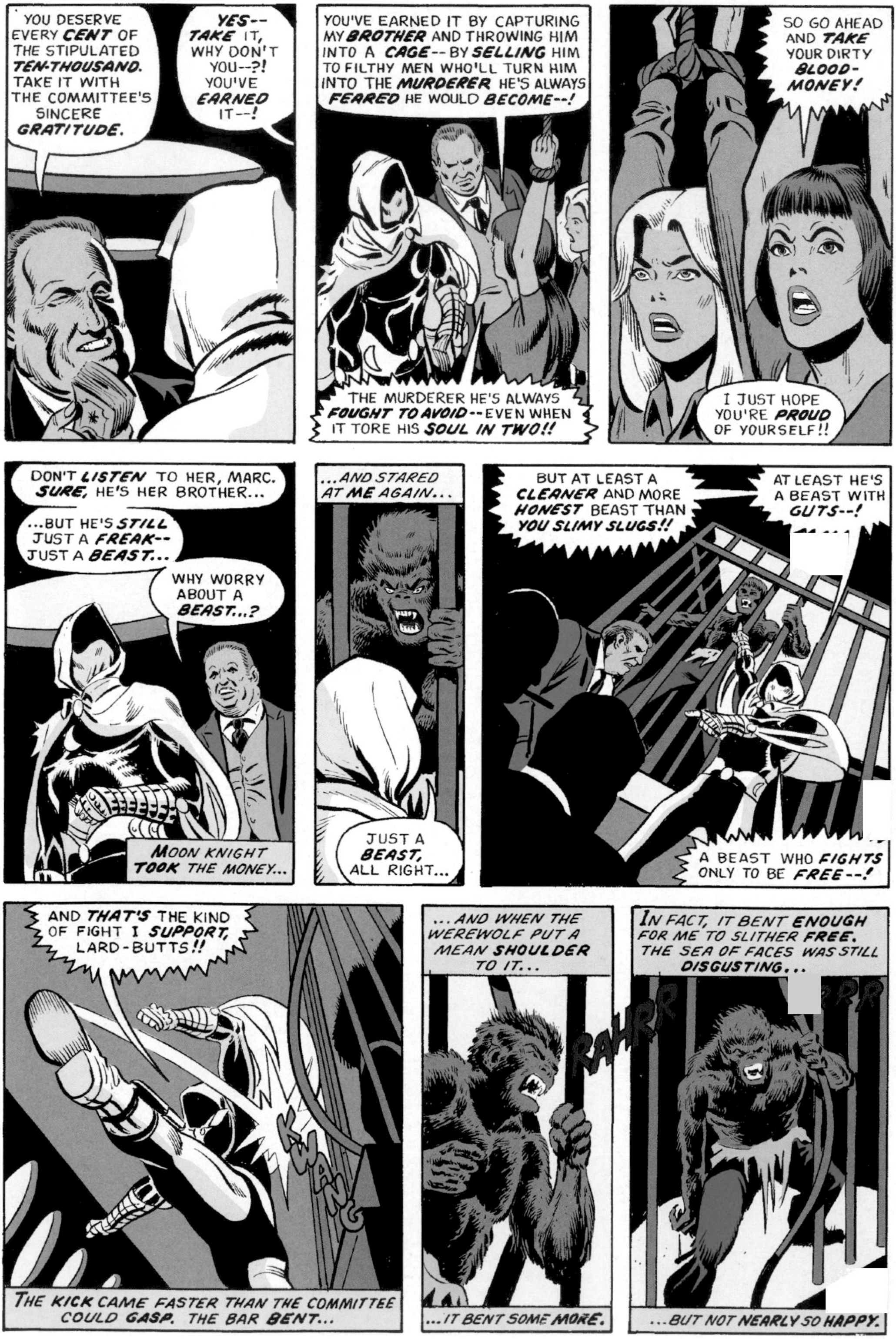

YOU DESERVE EVERY CENT OF THE STIPULATED TEN-THOUSAND. TAKE IT WITH THE COMMITTEE'S SINCERE GRATITUDE.
YES-- TAKE IT, WHY DON'T YOU--?! YOU'VE EARNED IT--!
YOU'VE EARNED IT BY CAPTURING MY BROTHER AND THROWING HIM INTO A CAGE--BY SELLING HIM TO FILTHY MEN WHO'LL TURN HIM INTO THE MURDERER HE'S ALWAYS FEARED HE WOULD BECOME--!
THE MURDERER HE'S ALWAYS FOUGHT TO AVOID--EVEN WHEN IT TORE HIS SOUL IN TWO!!
SO GO AHEAD AND TAKE YOUR DIRTY BLOOD-MONEY!
I JUST HOPE YOU'RE PROUD OF YOURSELF!!
DON'T LISTEN TO HER, MARC. SURE, HE'S HER BROTHER...
...BUT HE'S STILL JUST A FREAK-- JUST A BEAST...
WHY WORRY ABOUT A BEAST...?
MOON KNIGHT TOOK THE MONEY...
...AND STARED AT ME AGAIN...
JUST A BEAST, ALL RIGHT...
BUT AT LEAST A CLEANER AND MORE HONEST BEAST THAN YOU SLIMY SLUGS!!
AT LEAST HE'S A BEAST WITH GUTS--!
A BEAST WHO FIGHTS ONLY TO BE FREE--!
AND THAT'S THE KIND OF FIGHT I SUPPORT, LARD-BUTTS!!
KWANG
THE KICK CAME FASTER THAN THE COMMITTEE COULD GASP. THE BAR BENT...
...AND WHEN THE WEREWOLF PUT A MEAN SHOULDER TO IT...
RAHRR
...IT BENT SOME MORE.
IN FACT, IT BENT ENOUGH FOR ME TO SLITHER FREE. THE SEA OF FACES WAS STILL DISGUSTING...
...BUT NOT NEARLY SO HAPPY.

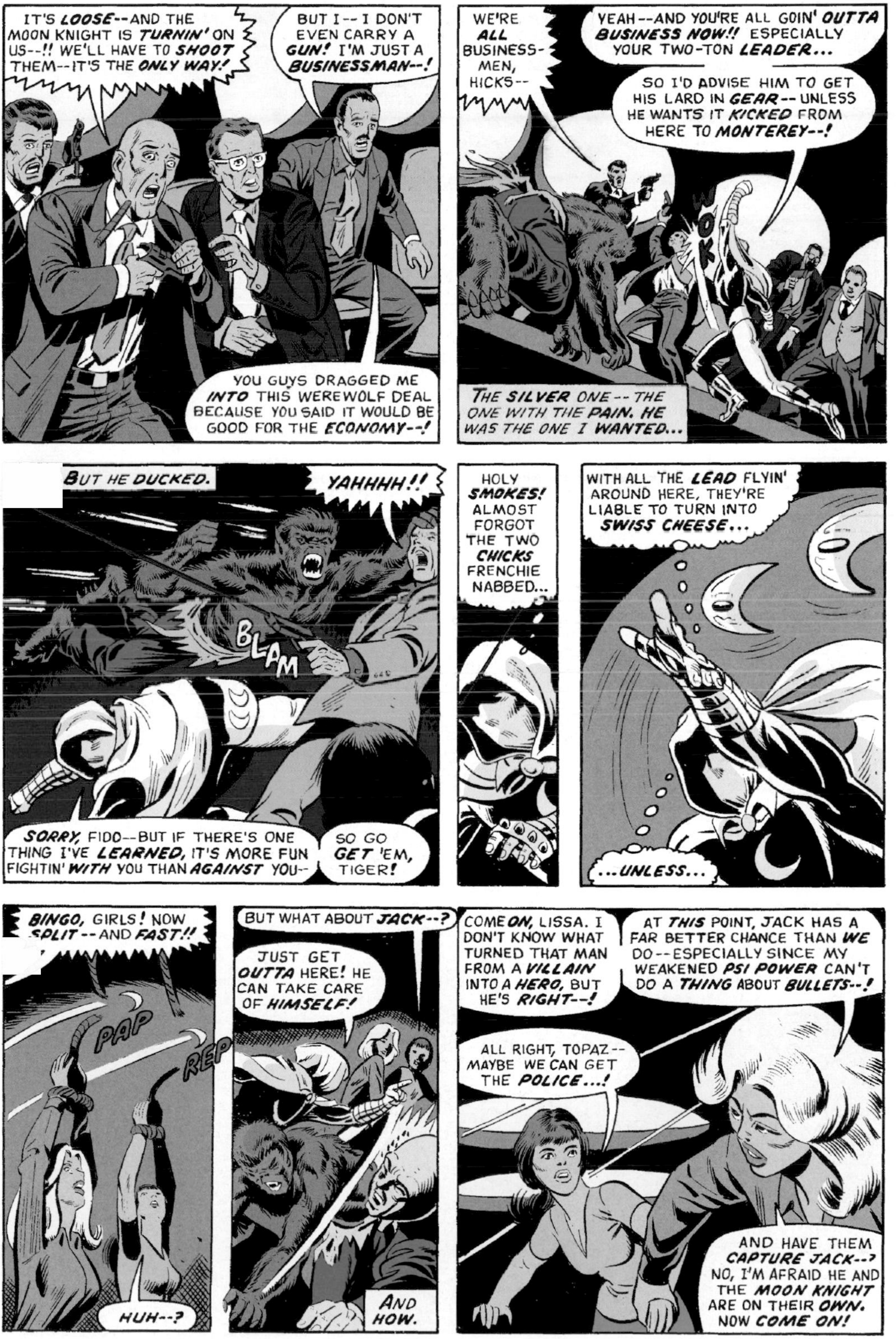
IT'S LOOSE--AND THE MOON KNIGHT IS TURNIN' ON US--!! WE'LL HAVE TO SHOOT THEM--IT'S THE ONLY WAY!
BUT I--I DON'T EVEN CARRY A GUN! I'M JUST A BUSINESSMAN--!
YOU GUYS DRAGGED ME INTO THIS WEREWOLF DEAL BECAUSE YOU SAID IT WOULD BE GOOD FOR THE ECONOMY--!
WE'RE ALL BUSINESSMEN, HICKS--
YEAH--AND YOU'RE ALL GOIN' OUTTA BUSINESS NOW!! ESPECIALLY YOUR TWO-TON LEADER...
SO I'D ADVISE HIM TO GET HIS LARD IN GEAR--UNLESS HE WANTS IT KICKED FROM HERE TO MONTEREY--!
THE SILVER ONE--THE ONE WITH THE PAIN. HE WAS THE ONE I WANTED...
BUT HE DUCKED.
YAHHHH!!
BLAM
SORRY, FIDO--BUT IF THERE'S ONE THING I'VE LEARNED, IT'S MORE FUN FIGHTIN' WITH YOU THAN AGAINST YOU--
SO GO GET 'EM, TIGER!
HOLY SMOKES! ALMOST FORGOT THE TWO CHICKS FRENCHIE NABBED...
WITH ALL THE LEAD FLYIN' AROUND HERE, THEY'RE LIABLE TO TURN INTO SWISS CHEESE...
...UNLESS...
BINGO, GIRLS! NOW SPLIT--AND FAST!!
PAP
REP
HUH--?
BUT WHAT ABOUT JACK--?
JUST GET OUTTA HERE! HE CAN TAKE CARE OF HIMSELF!
AND HOW.
COME ON, LISSA. I DON'T KNOW WHAT TURNED THAT MAN FROM A VILLAIN INTO A HERO, BUT HE'S RIGHT--!
AT THIS POINT, JACK HAS A FAR BETTER CHANCE THAN WE DO--ESPECIALLY SINCE MY WEAKENED PSI POWER CAN'T DO A THING ABOUT BULLETS--!
ALL RIGHT, TOPAZ--MAYBE WE CAN GET THE POLICE...!
AND HAVE THEM CAPTURE JACK--? NO, I'M AFRAID HE AND THE MOON KNIGHT ARE ON THEIR OWN. NOW COME ON!

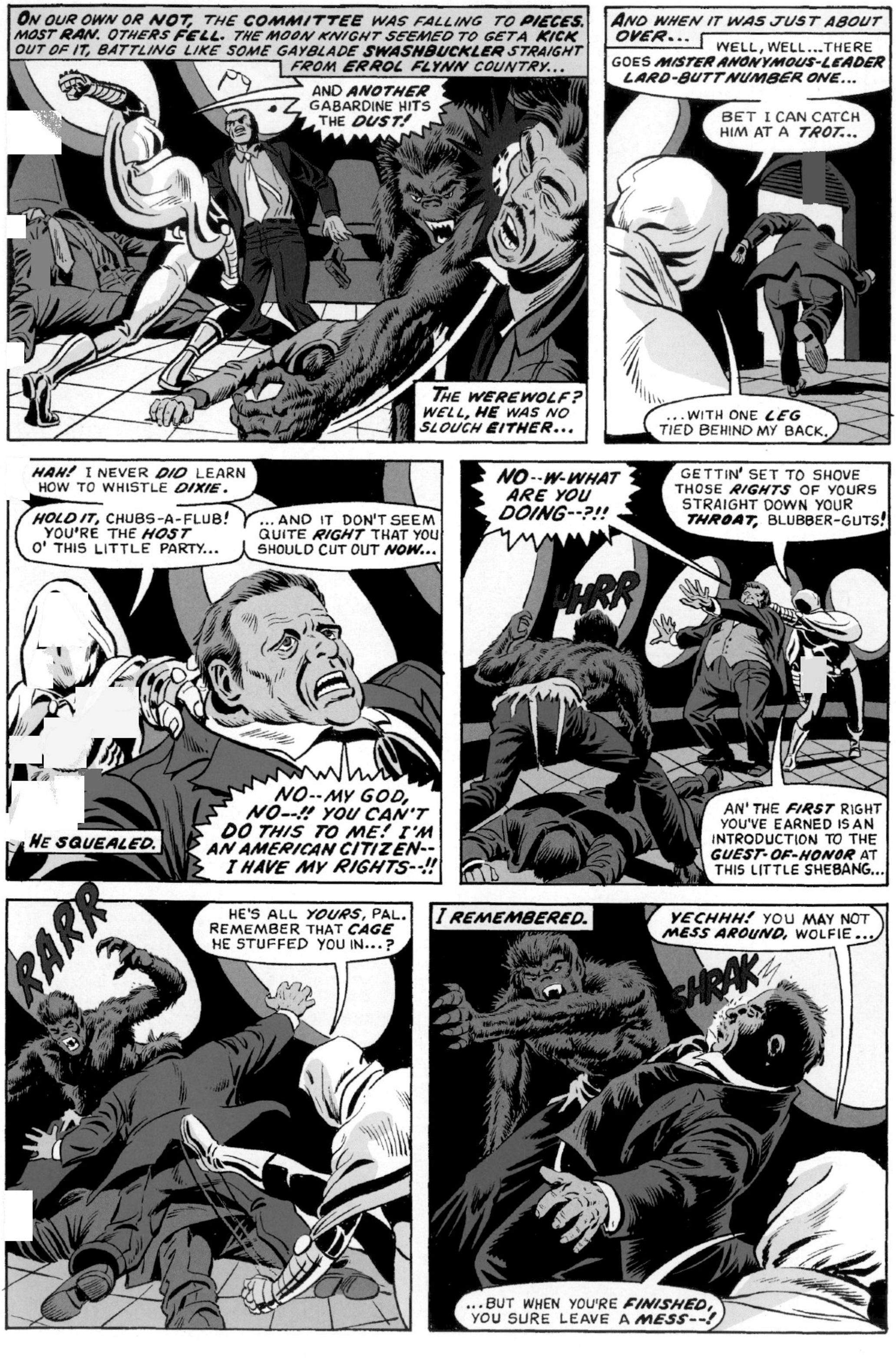
ON OUR OWN OR NOT, THE COMMITTEE WAS FALLING TO PIECES. MOST RAN. OTHERS FELL. THE MOON KNIGHT SEEMED TO GET A KICK OUT OF IT, BATTLING LIKE SOME GAYBLADE SWASHBUCKLER STRAIGHT FROM ERROL FLYNN COUNTRY...
AND ANOTHER GABARDINE HITS THE DUST!
THE WEREWOLF? WELL, HE WAS NO SLOUCH EITHER...
AND WHEN IT WAS JUST ABOUT OVER...
WELL, WELL...THERE GOES MISTER ANONYMOUS-LEADER LARD-BUTT NUMBER ONE...
BET I CAN CATCH HIM AT A TROT...
...WITH ONE LEG TIED BEHIND MY BACK.
HAH! I NEVER DID LEARN HOW TO WHISTLE DIXIE.
HOLD IT, CHUBS-A-FLUB! YOU'RE THE HOST O' THIS LITTLE PARTY...
...AND IT DON'T SEEM QUITE RIGHT THAT YOU SHOULD CUT OUT NOW...
NO--MY GOD, NO--!! YOU CAN'T DO THIS TO ME! I'M AN AMERICAN CITIZEN--I HAVE MY RIGHTS--!!
HE SQUEALED.
NO--W-WHAT ARE YOU DOING--?!!
GETTIN' SET TO SHOVE THOSE RIGHTS OF YOURS STRAIGHT DOWN YOUR THROAT, BLUBBER-GUTS!
UHRR
AN' THE FIRST RIGHT YOU'VE EARNED IS AN INTRODUCTION TO THE GUEST-OF-HONOR AT THIS LITTLE SHEBANG...
RARR
HE'S ALL YOURS, PAL. REMEMBER THAT CAGE HE STUFFED YOU IN...?
I REMEMBERED.
YECHHH! YOU MAY NOT MESS AROUND, WOLFIE...
SHRAK
...BUT WHEN YOU'RE FINISHED, YOU SURE LEAVE A MESS--!

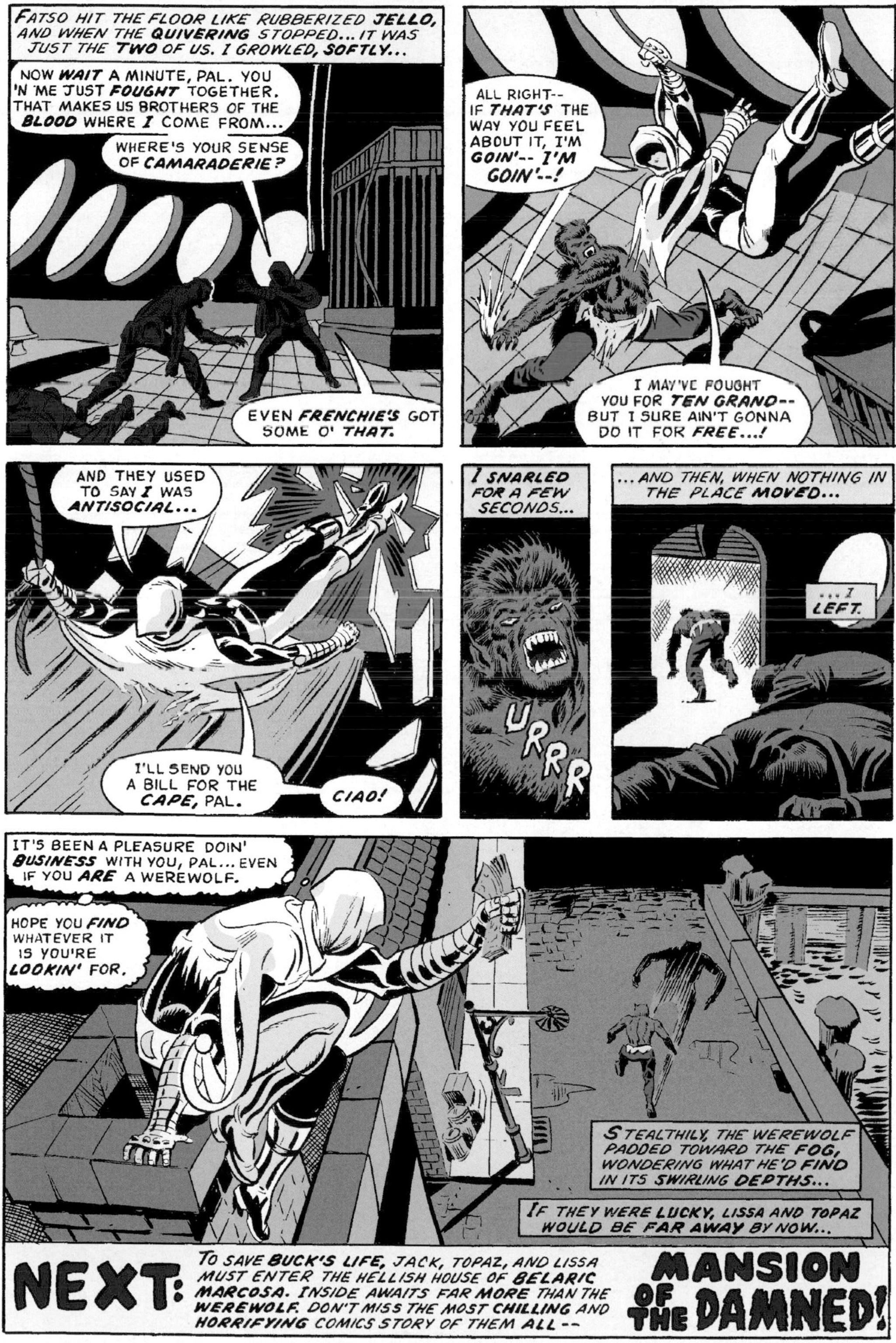
FATSO HIT THE FLOOR LIKE RUBBERIZED JELLO, AND WHEN THE QUIVERING STOPPED... IT WAS JUST THE TWO OF US. I GROWLED, SOFTLY...
NOW WAIT A MINUTE, PAL. YOU 'N ME JUST FOUGHT TOGETHER. THAT MAKES US BROTHERS OF THE BLOOD WHERE I COME FROM...
WHERE'S YOUR SENSE OF CAMARADERIE?
EVEN FRENCHIE'S GOT SOME O' THAT.
ALL RIGHT-- IF THAT'S THE WAY YOU FEEL ABOUT IT, I'M GOIN'-- I'M GOIN'--!
I MAY'VE FOUGHT YOU FOR TEN GRAND-- BUT I SURE AIN'T GONNA DO IT FOR FREE...!
AND THEY USED TO SAY I WAS ANTISOCIAL...
I'LL SEND YOU A BILL FOR THE CAPE, PAL.
CIAO!
I SNARLED FOR A FEW SECONDS...
URRR
...AND THEN, WHEN NOTHING IN THE PLACE MOVED...
...I LEFT.
IT'S BEEN A PLEASURE DOIN' BUSINESS WITH YOU, PAL... EVEN IF YOU ARE A WEREWOLF.
HOPE YOU FIND WHATEVER IT IS YOU'RE LOOKIN' FOR.
STEALTHILY, THE WEREWOLF PADDED TOWARD THE FOG, WONDERING WHAT HE'D FIND IN ITS SWIRLING DEPTHS...
IF THEY WERE LUCKY, LISSA AND TOPAZ WOULD BE FAR AWAY BY NOW...
NEXT:
TO SAVE BUCK'S LIFE, JACK, TOPAZ, AND LISSA MUST ENTER THE HELLISH HOUSE OF BELARIC MARCOSA. INSIDE AWAITS FAR MORE THAN THE WEREWOLF. DON'T MISS THE MOST CHILLING AND HORRIFYING COMICS STORY OF THEM ALL --
MANSION OF THE DAMNED!

50¢
220
SEPT
02457
MARVEL COMICS GROUP
APPROVED BY THE COMICS CODE AUTHORITY
A COFFIN FOR...
the AMAZING SPIDER-MAN
©1981 MARVEL COMICS GROUP
BOB LAYTON
GHOST STARRING...
THE MACABRE
MOON KNIGHT

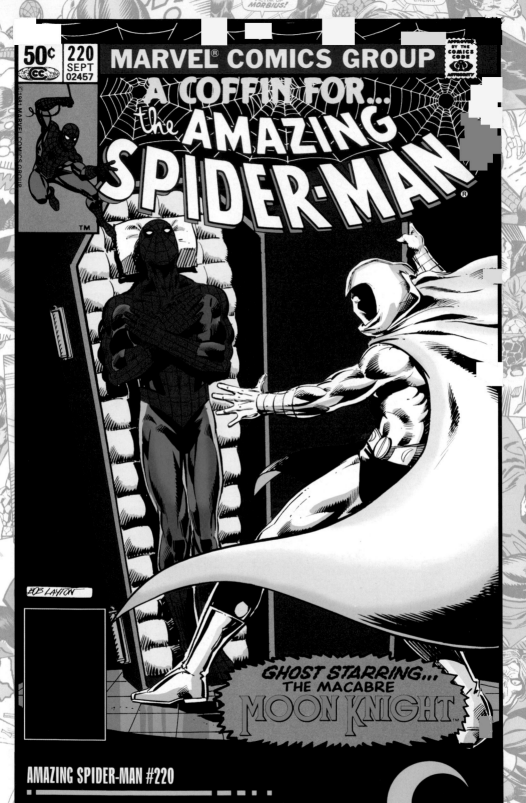

AMAZING SPIDER-MAN #220

MOON KNIGHT AND SPIDER-MAN ARE CAUGHT IN THE CROSSFIRE OF A VILLAINOUS COMPETITION TO ENTER THE RANKS OF NEW YORK CITY'S CRIMINAL UNDERWORLD!

Stan Lee PRESENTS: THE AMAZING SPIDER-MAN®

MICHAEL FLEISHER Script | BOB McLEOD Art and Lettering | BOB SHAREN Coloring | DENNY O'NEIL Editor | JIM SHOOTER Editor-in-Chief

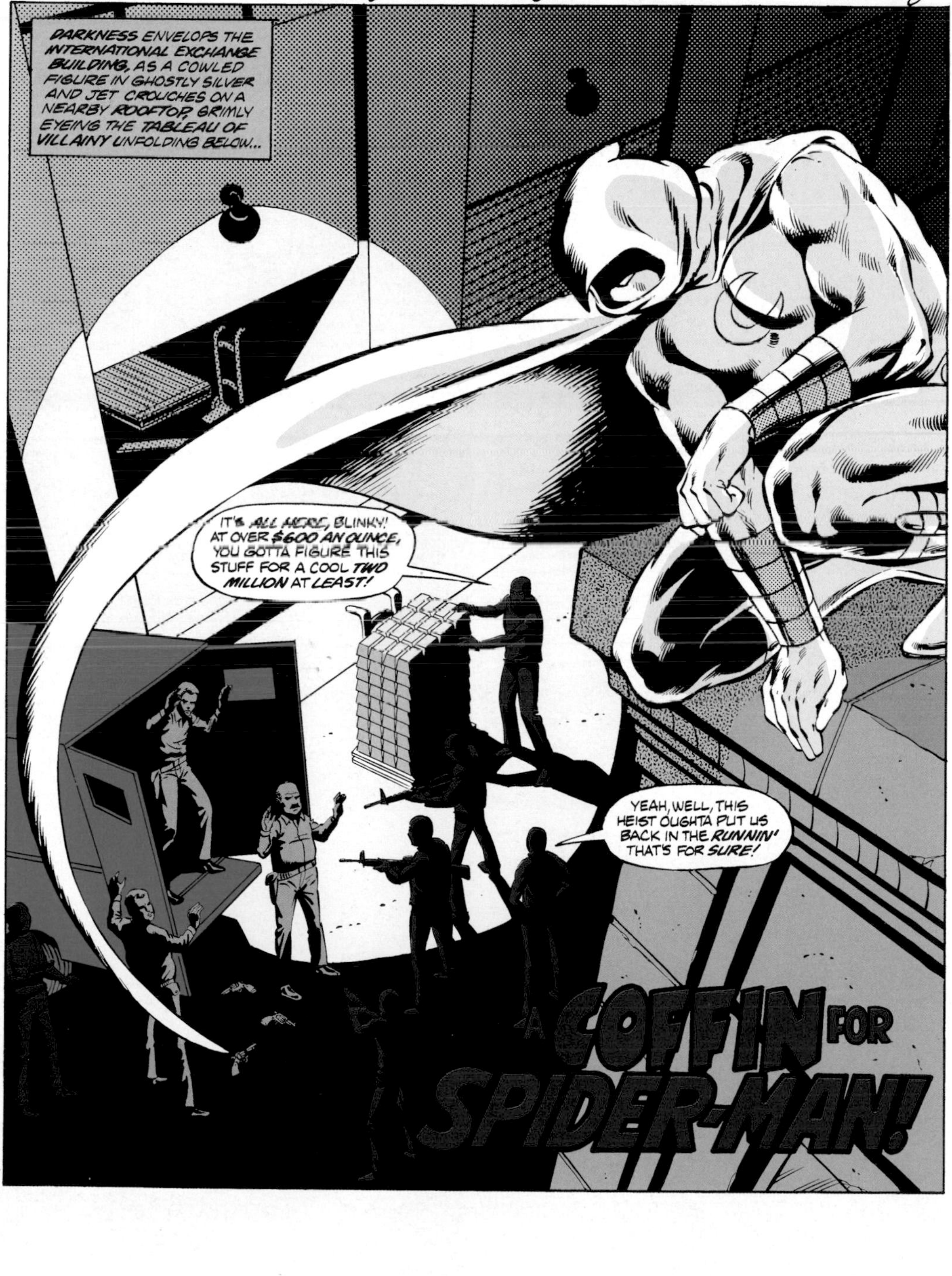
DARKNESS ENVELOPS THE INTERNATIONAL EXCHANGE BUILDING, AS A COWLED FIGURE IN GHOSTLY SILVER AND JET CROUCHES ON A NEARBY ROOFTOP, GRIMLY EYEING THE TABLEAU OF VILLAINY UNFOLDING BELOW...
IT'S ALL HERE, BLINKY! AT OVER $600 AN OUNCE, YOU GOTTA FIGURE THIS STUFF FOR A COOL TWO MILLION AT LEAST!
YEAH, WELL, THIS HEIST OUGHTA PUT US BACK IN THE RUNNIN' THAT'S FOR SURE!
A COFFIN FOR SPIDER-MAN!

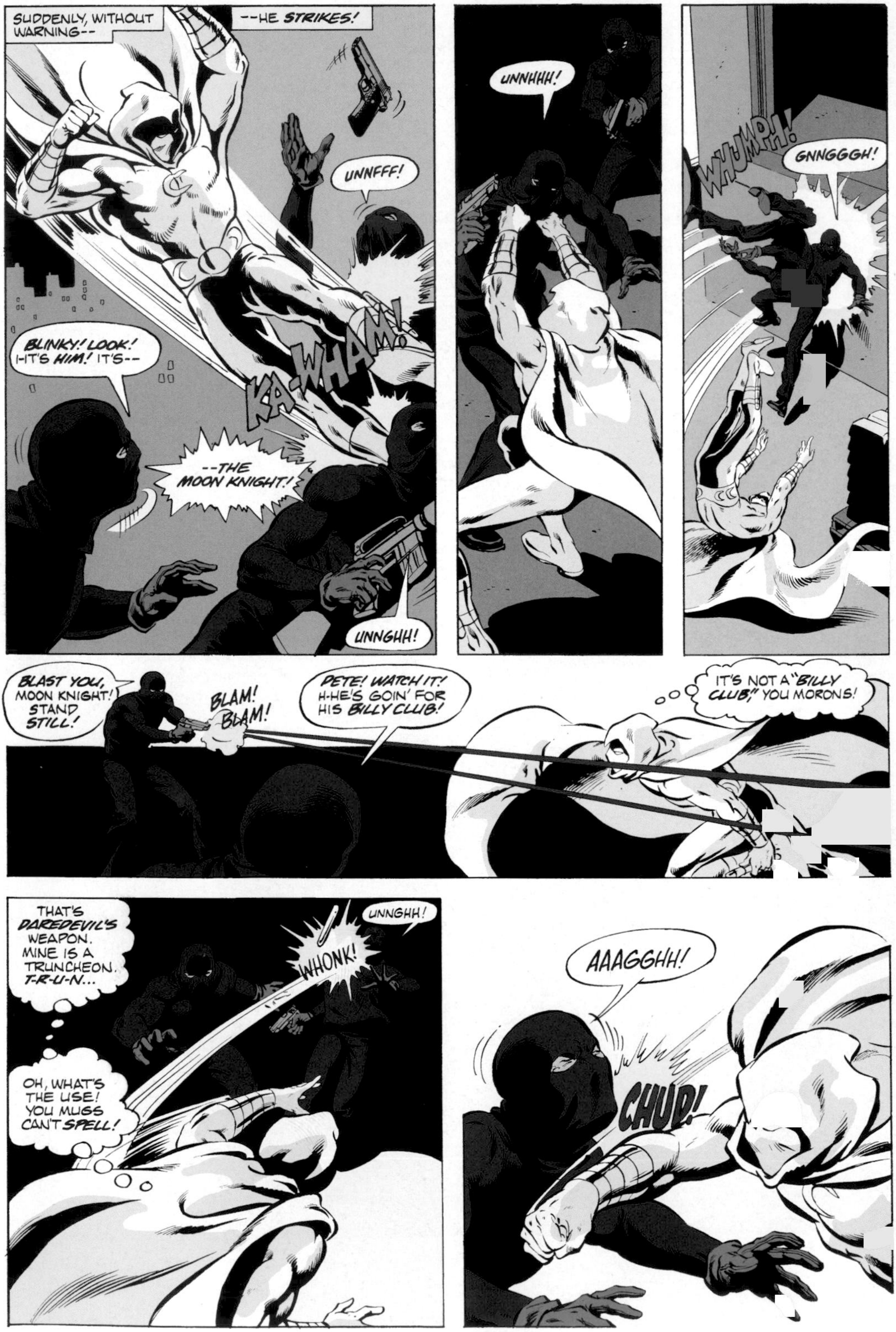

SUDDENLY, WITHOUT WARNING--
--HE STRIKES!
UNNFFF!
BLINKY! LOOK! I-IT'S HIM! IT'S--
KA-WHAM!
--THE MOON KNIGHT!
UNNGHH!
UNNHHH!
WHUMPH!
GNNGGGH!
BLAST YOU, MOON KNIGHT! STAND STILL!
BLAM! BLAM!
PETE! WATCH IT! H-HE'S GOIN' FOR HIS BILLY CLUB!
IT'S NOT A "BILLY CLUB," YOU MORONS!
THAT'S DAREDEVIL'S WEAPON. MINE IS A TRUNCHEON. T-R-U-N...
WHONK!
UNNGHH!
OH, WHAT'S THE USE! YOU MUGS CAN'T SPELL!
AAAGGHH!
CHUD!

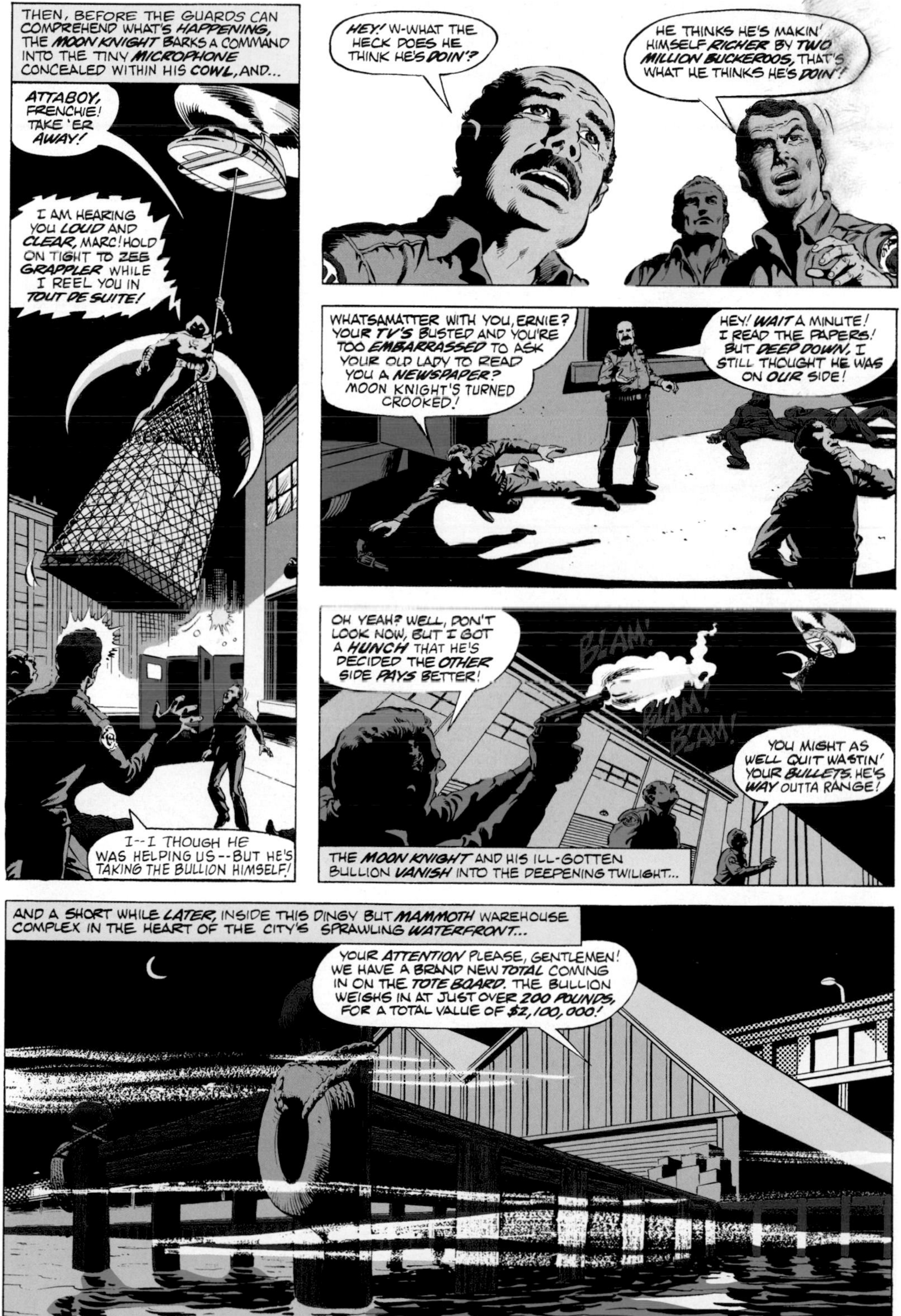

THEN, BEFORE THE GUARDS CAN COMPREHEND WHAT'S HAPPENING, THE MOON KNIGHT BARKS A COMMAND INTO THE TINY MICROPHONE CONCEALED WITHIN HIS COWL, AND...
ATTABOY, FRENCHIE! TAKE 'ER AWAY!
I AM HEARING YOU LOUD AND CLEAR, MARC! HOLD ON TIGHT TO ZEE GRAPPLER WHILE I REEL YOU IN TOUT DE SUITE!
I--I THOUGH HE WAS HELPING US--BUT HE'S TAKING THE BULLION HIMSELF!
HEY! W-WHAT THE HECK DOES HE THINK HE'S DOIN'?
HE THINKS HE'S MAKIN' HIMSELF RICHER BY TWO MILLION BUCKEROOS, THAT'S WHAT HE THINKS HE'S DOIN'!
WHATSAMATTER WITH YOU, ERNIE? YOUR TV'S BUSTED AND YOU'RE TOO EMBARRASSED TO ASK YOUR OLD LADY TO READ YOU A NEWSPAPER? MOON KNIGHT'S TURNED CROOKED!
HEY! WAIT A MINUTE! I READ THE PAPERS! BUT DEEP DOWN, I STILL THOUGHT HE WAS ON OUR SIDE!
OH YEAH? WELL, DON'T LOOK NOW, BUT I GOT A HUNCH THAT HE'S DECIDED THE OTHER SIDE PAYS BETTER!
BLAM!
BLAM!
BLAM!
YOU MIGHT AS WELL QUIT WASTIN' YOUR BULLETS. HE'S WAY OUTTA RANGE!
THE MOON KNIGHT AND HIS ILL-GOTTEN BULLION VANISH INTO THE DEEPENING TWILIGHT...
AND A SHORT WHILE LATER, INSIDE THIS DINGY BUT MAMMOTH WAREHOUSE COMPLEX IN THE HEART OF THE CITY'S SPRAWLING WATERFRONT...
YOUR ATTENTION PLEASE, GENTLEMEN! WE HAVE A BRAND NEW TOTAL COMING IN ON THE TOTE BOARD. THE BULLION WEIGHS IN AT JUST OVER 200 POUNDS, FOR A TOTAL VALUE OF $2,100,000!

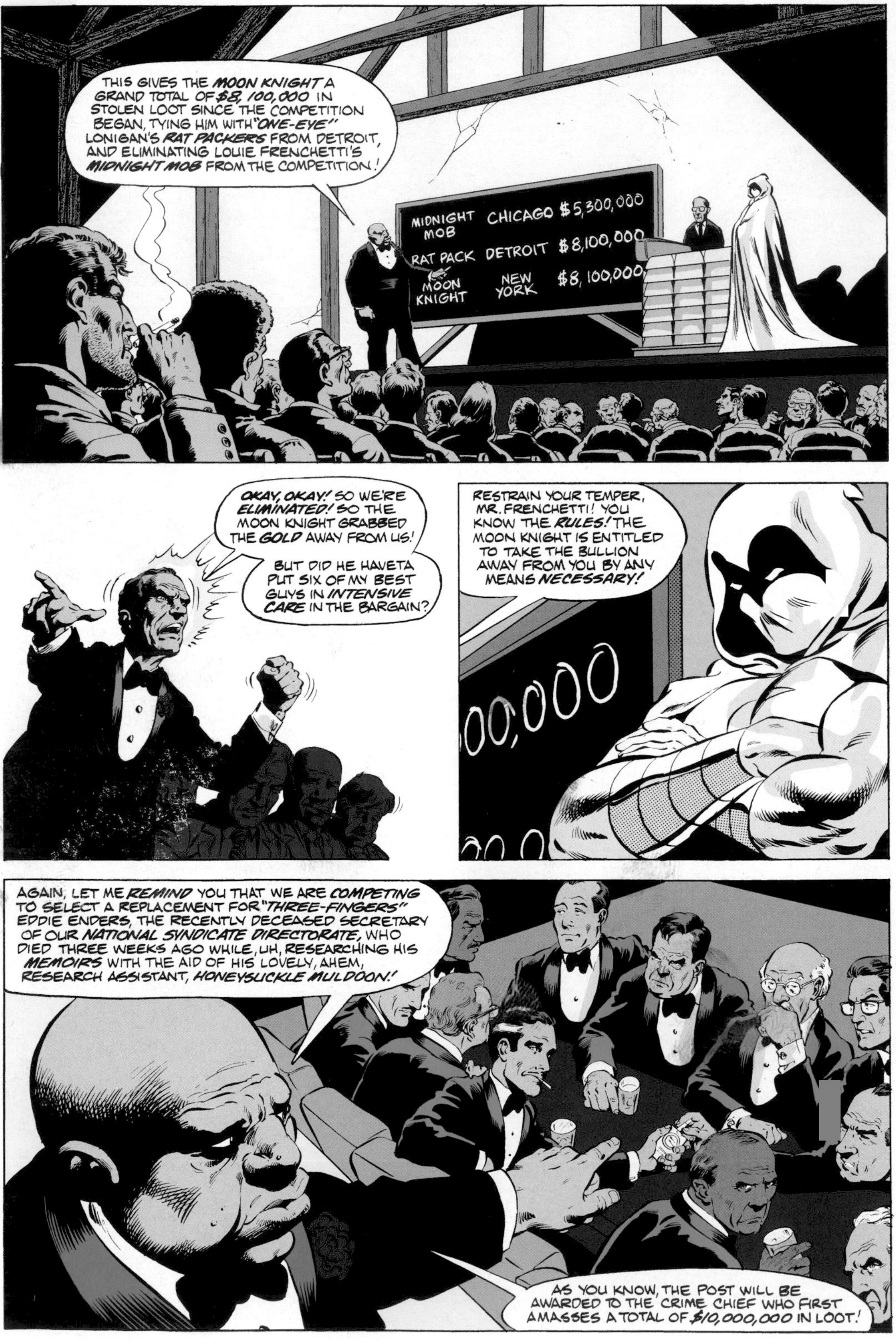
THIS GIVES THE MOON KNIGHT A GRAND TOTAL OF $8,100,000 IN STOLEN LOOT SINCE THE COMPETITION BEGAN, TYING HIM WITH "ONE-EYE" LONIGAN'S RAT PACKERS FROM DETROIT, AND ELIMINATING LOUIE FRENCHETTI'S MIDNIGHT MOB FROM THE COMPETITION!
MIDNIGHT MOB CHICAGO $5,300,000
RAT PACK DETROIT $8,100,000
MOON KNIGHT NEW YORK $8,100,000
OKAY, OKAY! SO WE'RE ELIMINATED! SO THE MOON KNIGHT GRABBED THE GOLD AWAY FROM US!
BUT DID HE HAVETA PUT SIX OF MY BEST GUYS IN INTENSIVE CARE IN THE BARGAIN?
RESTRAIN YOUR TEMPER, MR. FRENCHETTI! YOU KNOW THE RULES! THE MOON KNIGHT IS ENTITLED TO TAKE THE BULLION AWAY FROM YOU BY ANY MEANS NECESSARY!
AGAIN, LET ME REMIND YOU THAT WE ARE COMPETING TO SELECT A REPLACEMENT FOR "THREE-FINGERS" EDDIE ENDERS, THE RECENTLY DECEASED SECRETARY OF OUR NATIONAL SYNDICATE DIRECTORATE, WHO DIED THREE WEEKS AGO WHILE, UH, RESEARCHING HIS MEMOIRS WITH THE AID OF HIS LOVELY, AHEM, RESEARCH ASSISTANT, HONEYSUCKLE MULDOON!
AS YOU KNOW, THE POST WILL BE AWARDED TO THE CRIME CHIEF WHO FIRST AMASSES A TOTAL OF $10,000,000 IN LOOT!

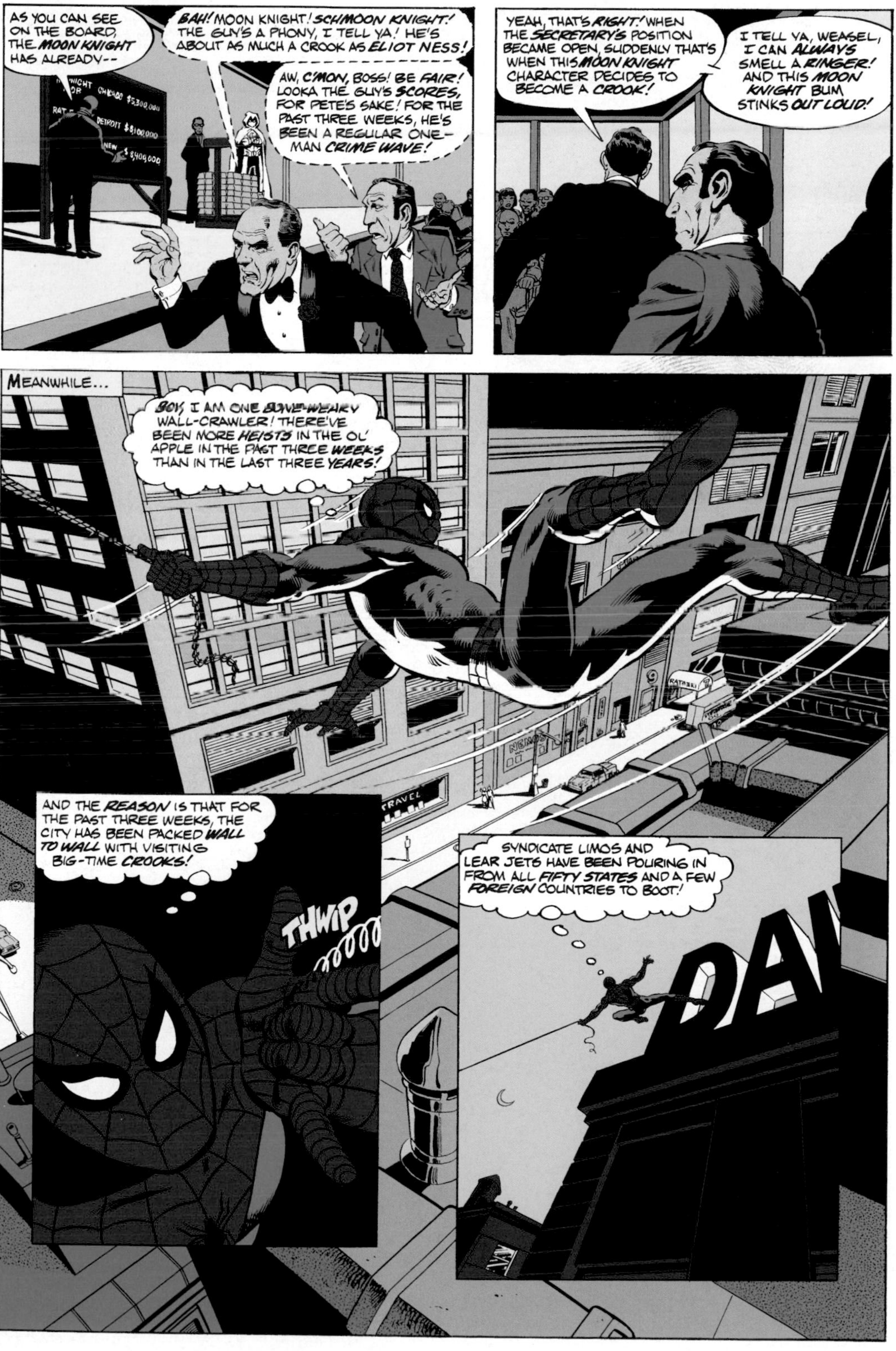

AS YOU CAN SEE ON THE BOARD, THE MOON KNIGHT HAS ALREADY--
BAH! MOON KNIGHT! SCHMOON KNIGHT! THE GUY'S A PHONY, I TELL YA! HE'S ABOUT AS MUCH A CROOK AS ELIOT NESS!
AW, C'MON, BOSS! BE FAIR! LOOKA THE GUY'S SCORES, FOR PETE'S SAKE! FOR THE PAST THREE WEEKS, HE'S BEEN A REGULAR ONE-MAN CRIME WAVE!
CHICAGO $5,300,000
DETROIT $8,100,000
$8,400,000
YEAH, THAT'S RIGHT! WHEN THE SECRETARY'S POSITION BECAME OPEN, SUDDENLY THAT'S WHEN THIS MOON KNIGHT CHARACTER DECIDES TO BECOME A CROOK!
I TELL YA, WEASEL, I CAN ALWAYS SMELL A RINGER! AND THIS MOON KNIGHT BUM STINKS OUT LOUD!
MEANWHILE...
BOY, I AM ONE BONE-WEARY WALL-CRAWLER! THERE'VE BEEN MORE HEISTS IN THE OL' APPLE IN THE PAST THREE WEEKS THAN IN THE LAST THREE YEARS!
TRAVEL
AND THE REASON IS THAT FOR THE PAST THREE WEEKS, THE CITY HAS BEEN PACKED WALL TO WALL WITH VISITING BIG-TIME CROOKS!
THWIP
SYNDICATE LIMOS AND LEAR JETS HAVE BEEN POURING IN FROM ALL FIFTY STATES AND A FEW FOREIGN COUNTRIES TO BOOT!

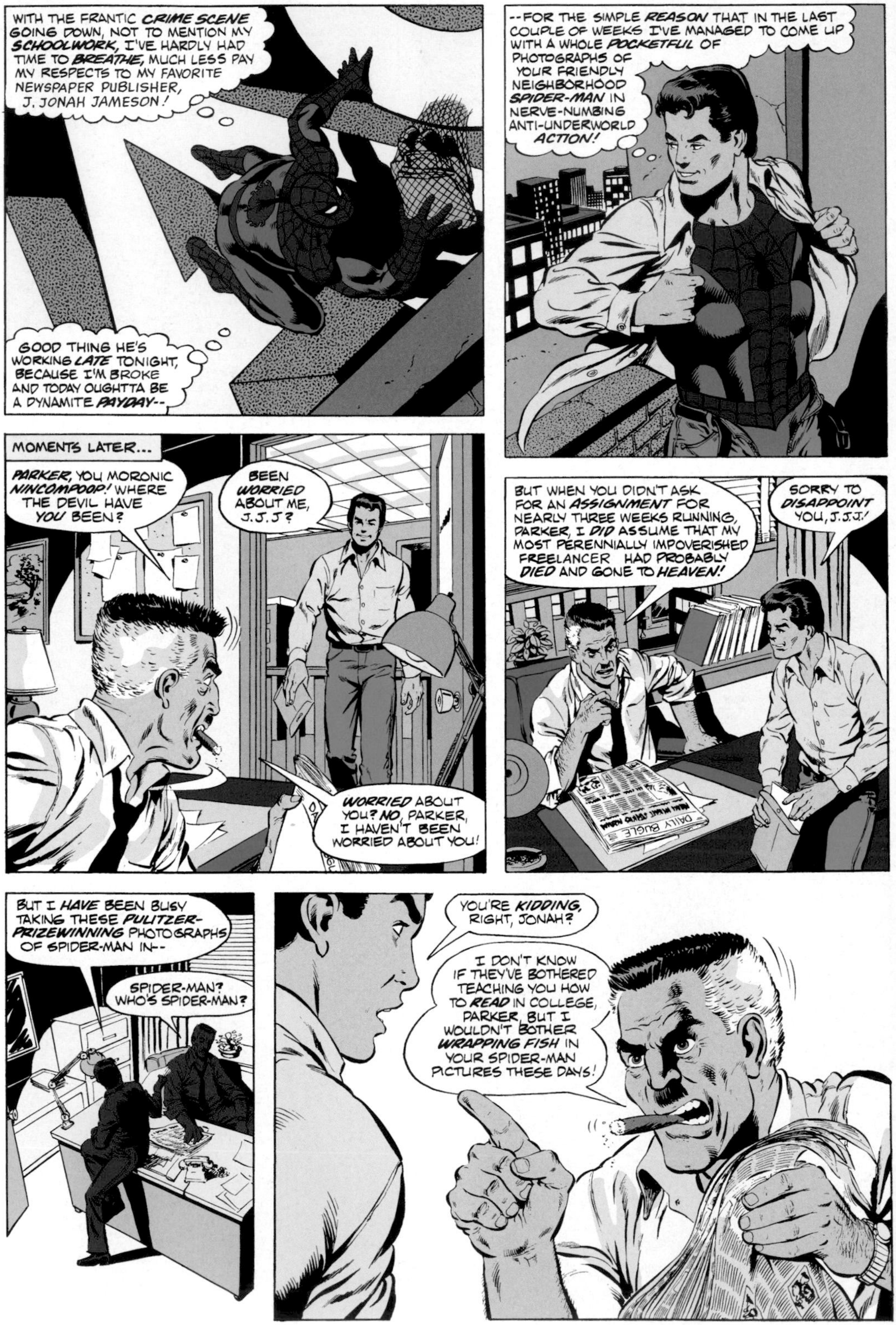
WITH THE FRANTIC CRIME SCENE GOING DOWN, NOT TO MENTION MY SCHOOLWORK, I'VE HARDLY HAD TIME TO BREATHE, MUCH LESS PAY MY RESPECTS TO MY FAVORITE NEWSPAPER PUBLISHER, J. JONAH JAMESON!
GOOD THING HE'S WORKING LATE TONIGHT, BECAUSE I'M BROKE AND TODAY OUGHTTA BE A DYNAMITE PAYDAY--
--FOR THE SIMPLE REASON THAT IN THE LAST COUPLE OF WEEKS I'VE MANAGED TO COME UP WITH A WHOLE POCKETFUL OF PHOTOGRAPHS OF YOUR FRIENDLY NEIGHBORHOOD SPIDER-MAN IN NERVE-NUMBING ANTI-UNDERWORLD ACTION!
MOMENTS LATER...
PARKER, YOU MORONIC NINCOMPOOP! WHERE THE DEVIL HAVE YOU BEEN?
BEEN WORRIED ABOUT ME, J.J.J?
WORRIED ABOUT YOU? NO, PARKER, I HAVEN'T BEEN WORRIED ABOUT YOU!
BUT WHEN YOU DIDN'T ASK FOR AN ASSIGNMENT FOR NEARLY THREE WEEKS RUNNING, PARKER, I DID ASSUME THAT MY MOST PERENNIALLY IMPOVERISHED FREELANCER HAD PROBABLY DIED AND GONE TO HEAVEN!
SORRY TO DISAPPOINT YOU, J.J.J.!
DAILY BUGLE
BUT I HAVE BEEN BUSY TAKING THESE PULITZER-PRIZEWINNING PHOTOGRAPHS OF SPIDER-MAN IN--
SPIDER-MAN? WHO'S SPIDER-MAN?
YOU'RE KIDDING, RIGHT, JONAH?
I DON'T KNOW IF THEY'VE BOTHERED TEACHING YOU HOW TO READ IN COLLEGE, PARKER, BUT I WOULDN'T BOTHER WRAPPING FISH IN YOUR SPIDER-MAN PICTURES THESE DAYS!

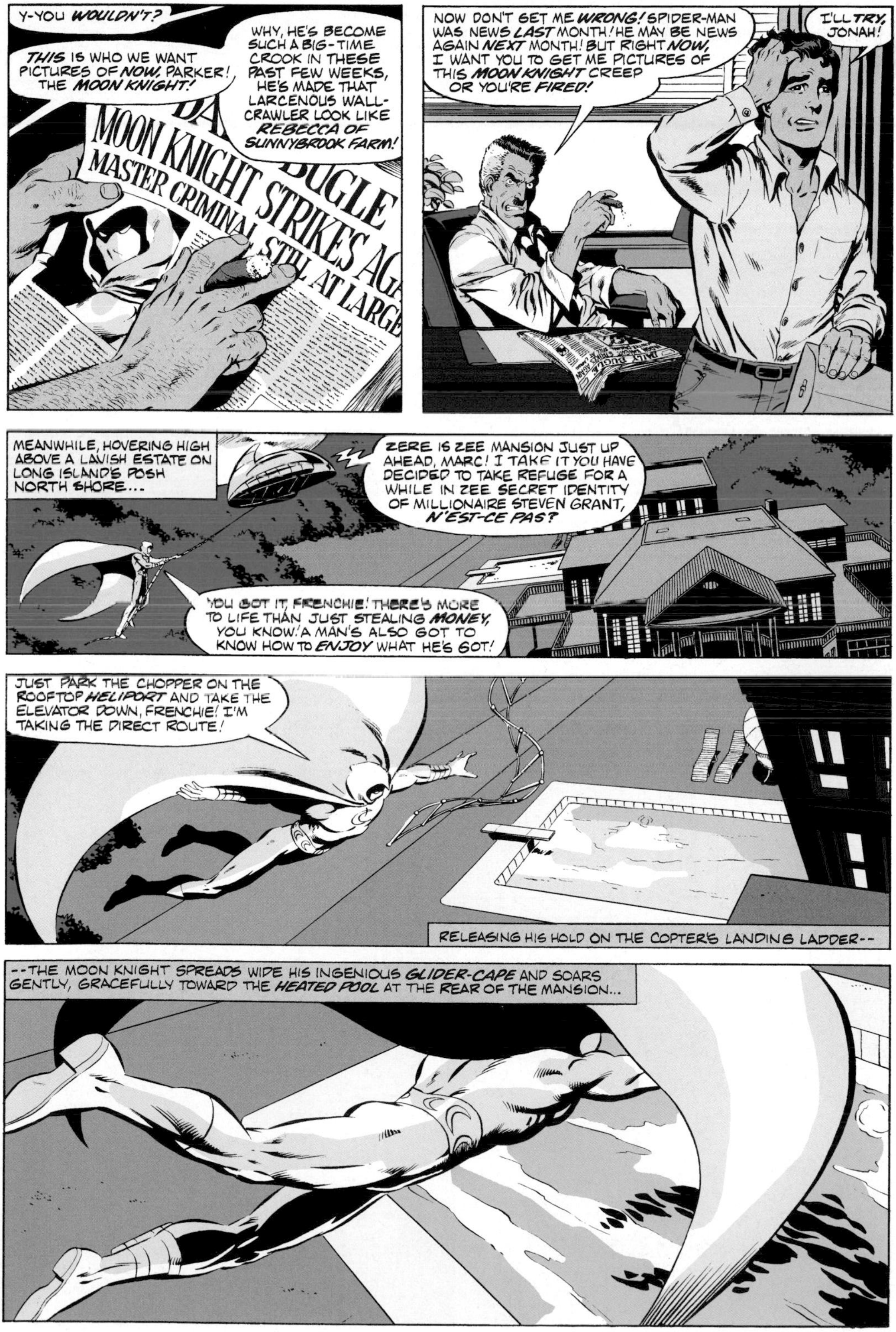
Y-YOU WOULDN'T?
THIS IS WHO WE WANT PICTURES OF NOW, PARKER! THE MOON KNIGHT!
WHY, HE'S BECOME SUCH A BIG-TIME CROOK IN THESE PAST FEW WEEKS, HE'S MADE THAT LARCENOUS WALL-CRAWLER LOOK LIKE REBECCA OF SUNNYBROOK FARM!
BUGLE
MOON KNIGHT STRIKES AG
MASTER CRIMINAL STILL AT LARGE
NOW DON'T GET ME WRONG! SPIDER-MAN WAS NEWS LAST MONTH! HE MAY BE NEWS AGAIN NEXT MONTH! BUT RIGHT NOW, I WANT YOU TO GET ME PICTURES OF THIS MOON KNIGHT CREEP OR YOU'RE FIRED!
I'LL TRY, JONAH!
MEANWHILE, HOVERING HIGH ABOVE A LAVISH ESTATE ON LONG ISLAND'S POSH NORTH SHORE...
ZERE IS ZEE MANSION JUST UP AHEAD, MARC! I TAKE IT YOU HAVE DECIDED TO TAKE REFUGE FOR A WHILE IN ZEE SECRET IDENTITY OF MILLIONAIRE STEVEN GRANT, N'EST-CE PAS?
YOU GOT IT, FRENCHIE! THERE'S MORE TO LIFE THAN JUST STEALING MONEY, YOU KNOW! A MAN'S ALSO GOT TO KNOW HOW TO ENJOY WHAT HE'S GOT!
JUST PARK THE CHOPPER ON THE ROOFTOP HELIPORT AND TAKE THE ELEVATOR DOWN, FRENCHIE! I'M TAKING THE DIRECT ROUTE!
RELEASING HIS HOLD ON THE COPTER'S LANDING LADDER--
--THE MOON KNIGHT SPREADS WIDE HIS INGENIOUS GLIDER-CAPE AND SOARS GENTLY, GRACEFULLY TOWARD THE HEATED POOL AT THE REAR OF THE MANSION...

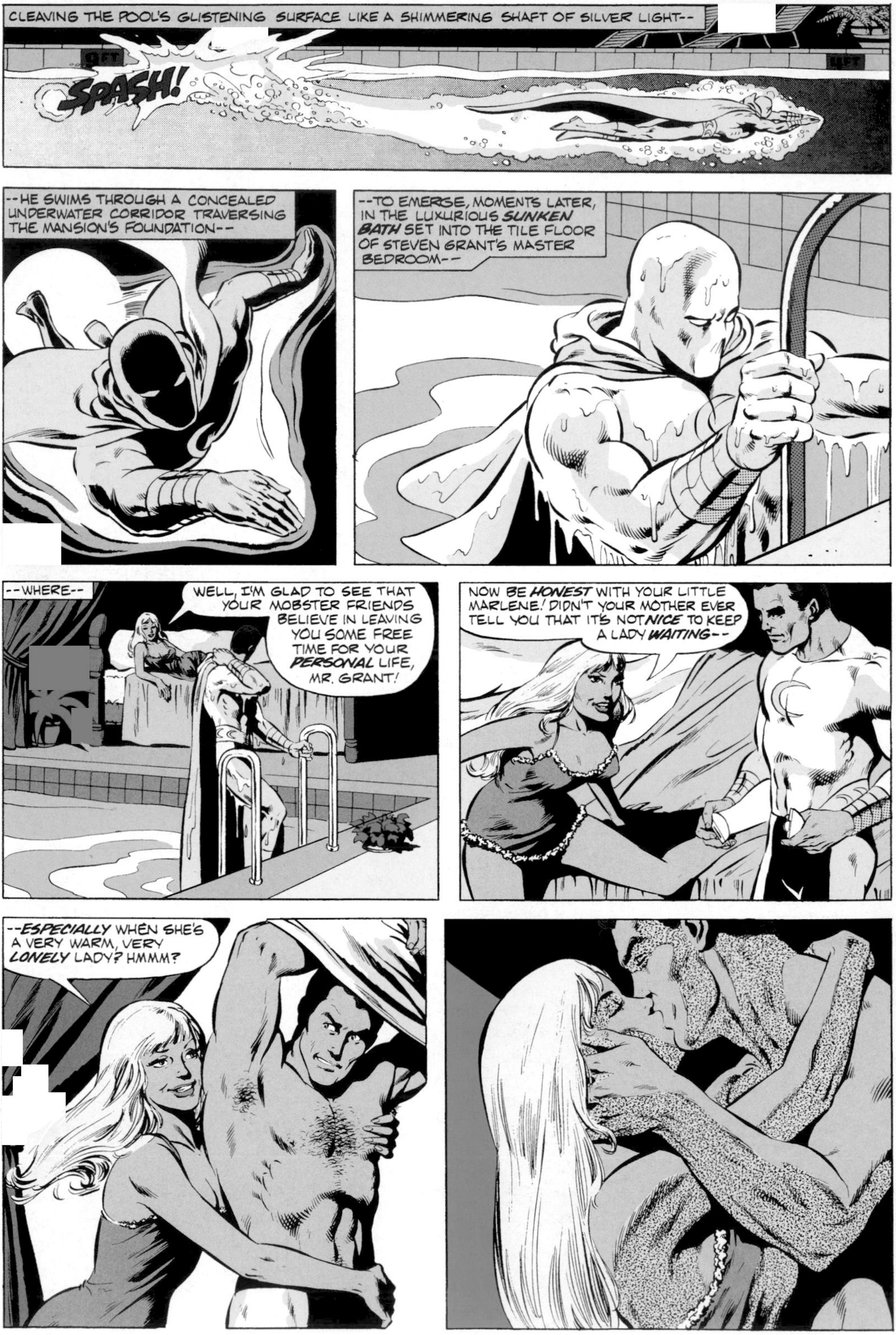

CLEAVING THE POOL'S GLISTENING SURFACE LIKE A SHIMMERING SHAFT OF SILVER LIGHT--
SPASH!
--HE SWIMS THROUGH A CONCEALED UNDERWATER CORRIDOR TRAVERSING THE MANSION'S FOUNDATION--
--TO EMERGE, MOMENTS LATER, IN THE LUXURIOUS SUNKEN BATH SET INTO THE TILE FLOOR OF STEVEN GRANT'S MASTER BEDROOM--
--WHERE--
WELL, I'M GLAD TO SEE THAT YOUR MOBSTER FRIENDS BELIEVE IN LEAVING YOU SOME FREE TIME FOR YOUR PERSONAL LIFE, MR. GRANT!
NOW BE HONEST WITH YOUR LITTLE MARLENE! DIDN'T YOUR MOTHER EVER TELL YOU THAT IT'S NOT NICE TO KEEP A LADY WAITING--
--ESPECIALLY WHEN SHE'S A VERY WARM, VERY LONELY LADY? HMMM?

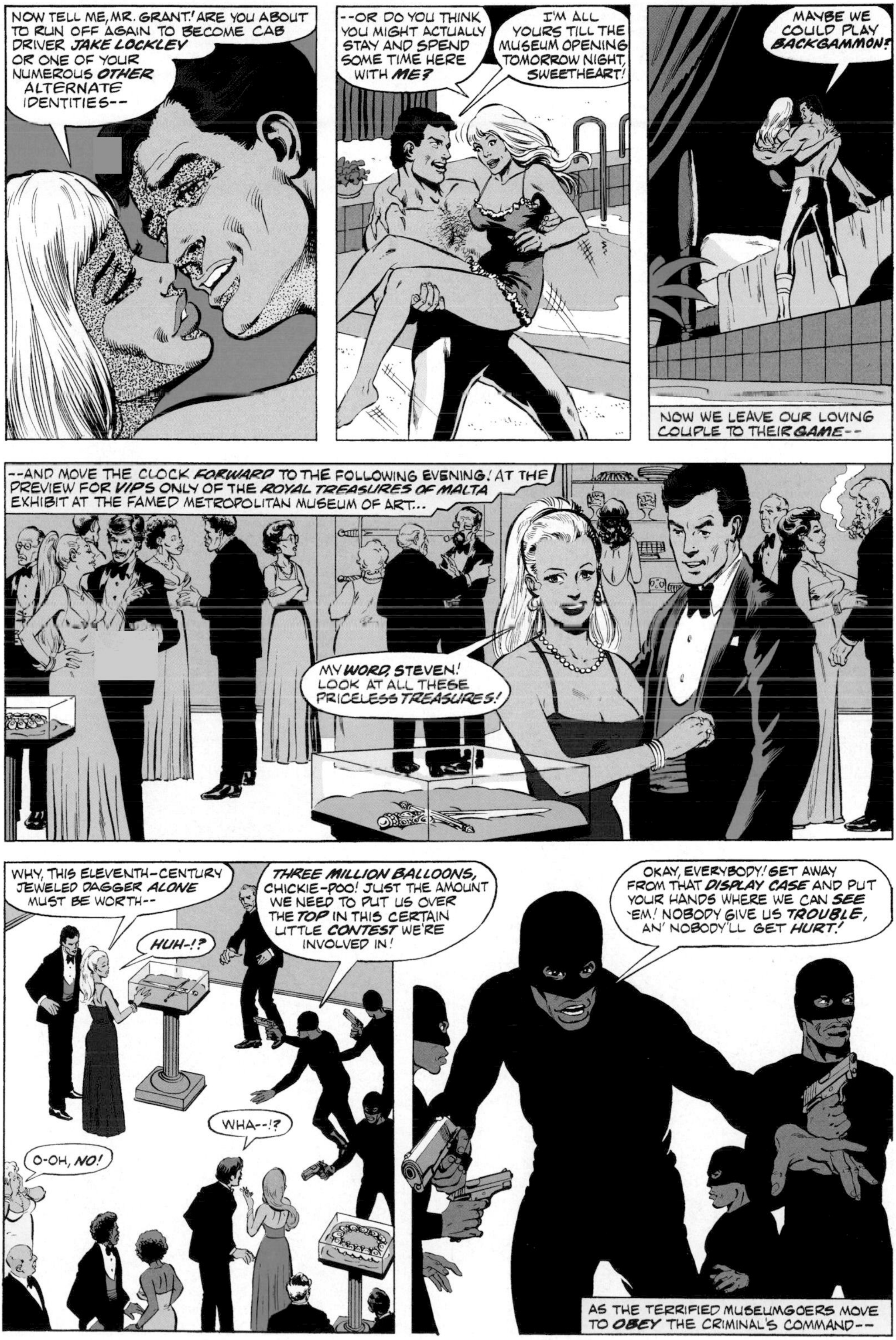
NOW TELL ME, MR. GRANT! ARE YOU ABOUT TO RUN OFF AGAIN TO BECOME CAB DRIVER JAKE LOCKLEY OR ONE OF YOUR NUMEROUS OTHER ALTERNATE IDENTITIES--
--OR DO YOU THINK YOU MIGHT ACTUALLY STAY AND SPEND SOME TIME HERE WITH ME?
I'M ALL YOURS TILL THE MUSEUM OPENING TOMORROW NIGHT, SWEETHEART!
MAYBE WE COULD PLAY BACKGAMMON!
NOW WE LEAVE OUR LOVING COUPLE TO THEIR GAME--
--AND MOVE THE CLOCK FORWARD TO THE FOLLOWING EVENING! AT THE PREVIEW FOR VIPS ONLY OF THE ROYAL TREASURES OF MALTA EXHIBIT AT THE FAMED METROPOLITAN MUSEUM OF ART...
MY WORD, STEVEN! LOOK AT ALL THESE PRICELESS TREASURES!
WHY, THIS ELEVENTH-CENTURY JEWELED DAGGER ALONE MUST BE WORTH--
THREE MILLION BALLOONS, CHICKIE-POO! JUST THE AMOUNT WE NEED TO PUT US OVER THE TOP IN THIS CERTAIN LITTLE CONTEST WE'RE INVOLVED IN!
HUH-!?
WHA--!?
O-OH, NO!
OKAY, EVERYBODY! GET AWAY FROM THAT DISPLAY CASE AND PUT YOUR HANDS WHERE WE CAN SEE 'EM! NOBODY GIVE US TROUBLE, AN' NOBODY'LL GET HURT!
AS THE TERRIFIED MUSEUMGOERS MOVE TO OBEY THE CRIMINAL'S COMMAND--

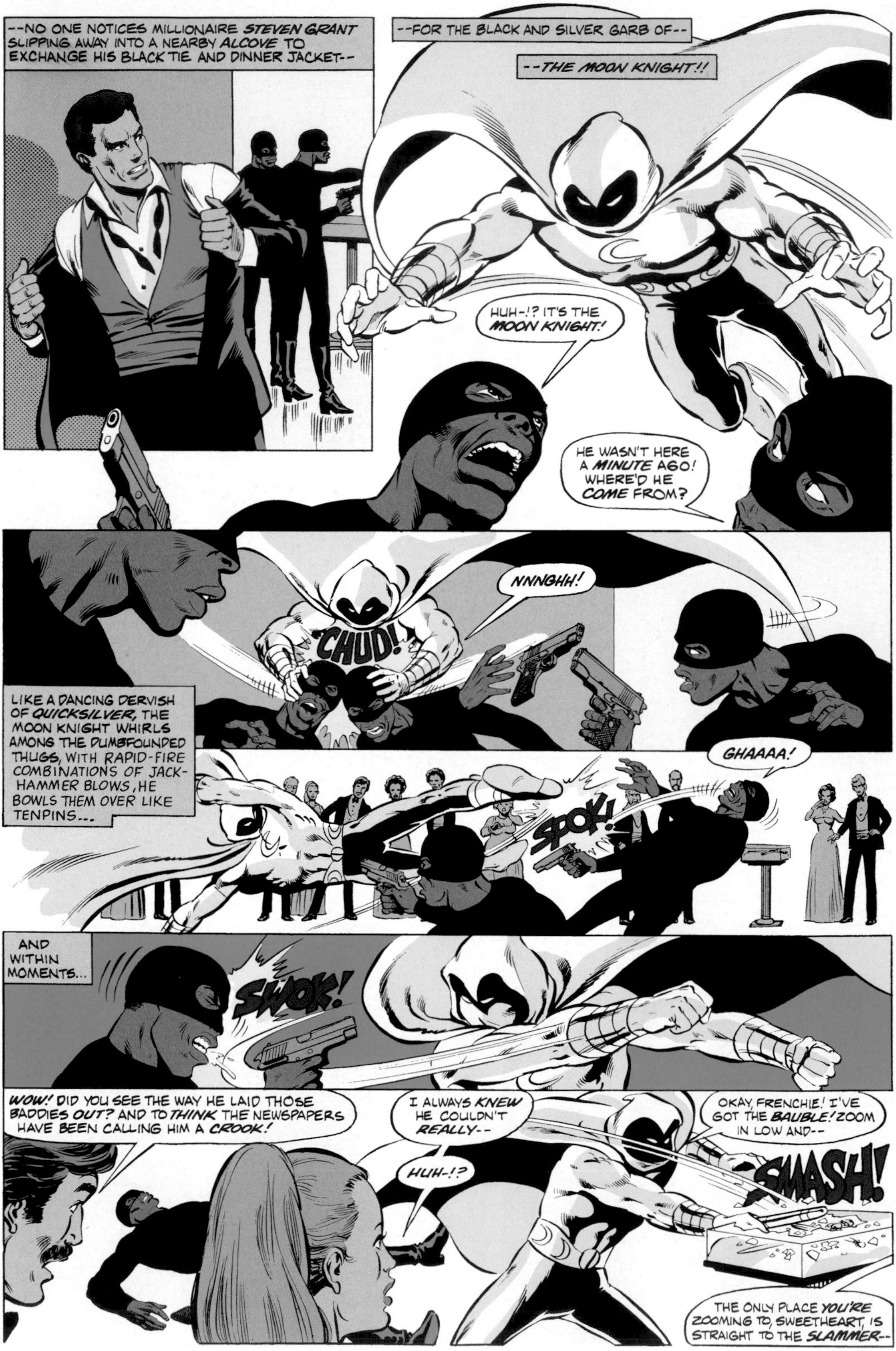

--NO ONE NOTICES MILLIONAIRE STEVEN GRANT SLIPPING AWAY INTO A NEARBY ALCOVE TO EXCHANGE HIS BLACK TIE AND DINNER JACKET--
--FOR THE BLACK AND SILVER GARB OF--
--THE MOON KNIGHT!!
HUH-!? IT'S THE MOON KNIGHT!
HE WASN'T HERE A MINUTE AGO! WHERE'D HE COME FROM?
NNNGHH!
CHUD!
LIKE A DANCING DERVISH OF QUICKSILVER, THE MOON KNIGHT WHIRLS AMONG THE DUMBFOUNDED THUGS, WITH RAPID-FIRE COMBINATIONS OF JACK-HAMMER BLOWS, HE BOWLS THEM OVER LIKE TENPINS...
GHAAAA!
SPOK!
AND WITHIN MOMENTS...
SWOK!
WOW! DID YOU SEE THE WAY HE LAID THOSE BADDIES OUT? AND TO THINK THE NEWSPAPERS HAVE BEEN CALLING HIM A CROOK!
I ALWAYS KNEW HE COULDN'T REALLY--
HUH-!?
OKAY, FRENCHIE! I'VE GOT THE BAUBLE! ZOOM IN LOW AND--
SMASH!
THE ONLY PLACE YOU'RE ZOOMING TO, SWEETHEART, IS STRAIGHT TO THE SLAMMER--

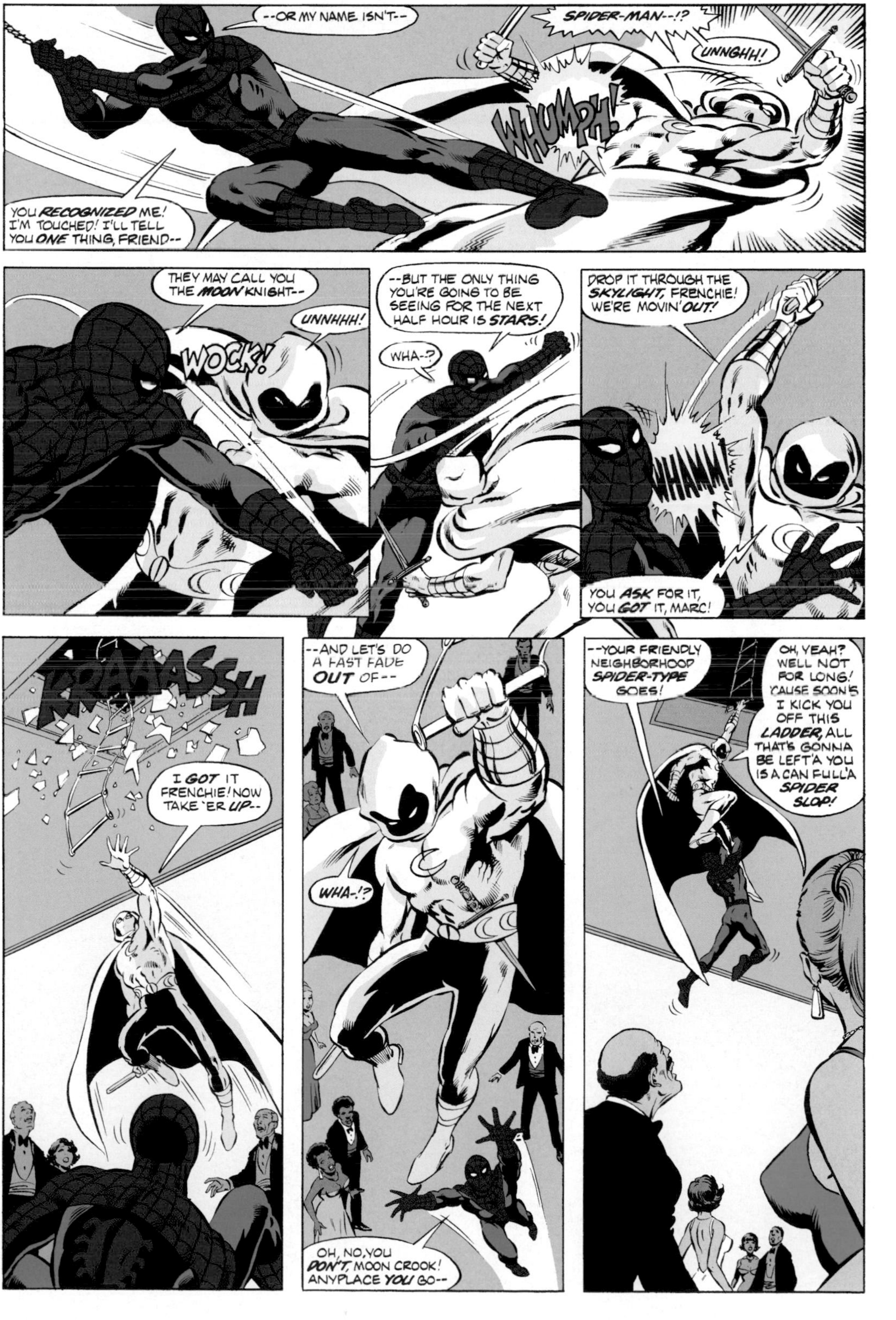
--OR MY NAME ISN'T--
SPIDER-MAN--!?
UNNGHH!
WHUMPH!
YOU RECOGNIZED ME! I'M TOUCHED! I'LL TELL YOU ONE THING, FRIEND--
THEY MAY CALL YOU THE MOON KNIGHT--
UNNHHH!
WOCK!
--BUT THE ONLY THING YOU'RE GOING TO BE SEEING FOR THE NEXT HALF HOUR IS STARS!
WHA-?
DROP IT THROUGH THE SKYLIGHT, FRENCHIE! WE'RE MOVIN' OUT!
WHAM
YOU ASK FOR IT, YOU GOT IT, MARC!
KRAAASSH
I GOT IT FRENCHIE! NOW TAKE 'ER UP--
--AND LET'S DO A FAST FADE OUT OF--
WHA-!?
OH, NO, YOU DON'T, MOON CROOK! ANYPLACE YOU GO--
--YOUR FRIENDLY NEIGHBORHOOD SPIDER-TYPE GOES!
OH, YEAH? WELL NOT FOR LONG! 'CAUSE SOON'S I KICK YOU OFF THIS LADDER, ALL THAT'S GONNA BE LEFT'A YOU IS A CAN FULL'A SPIDER SLOP!

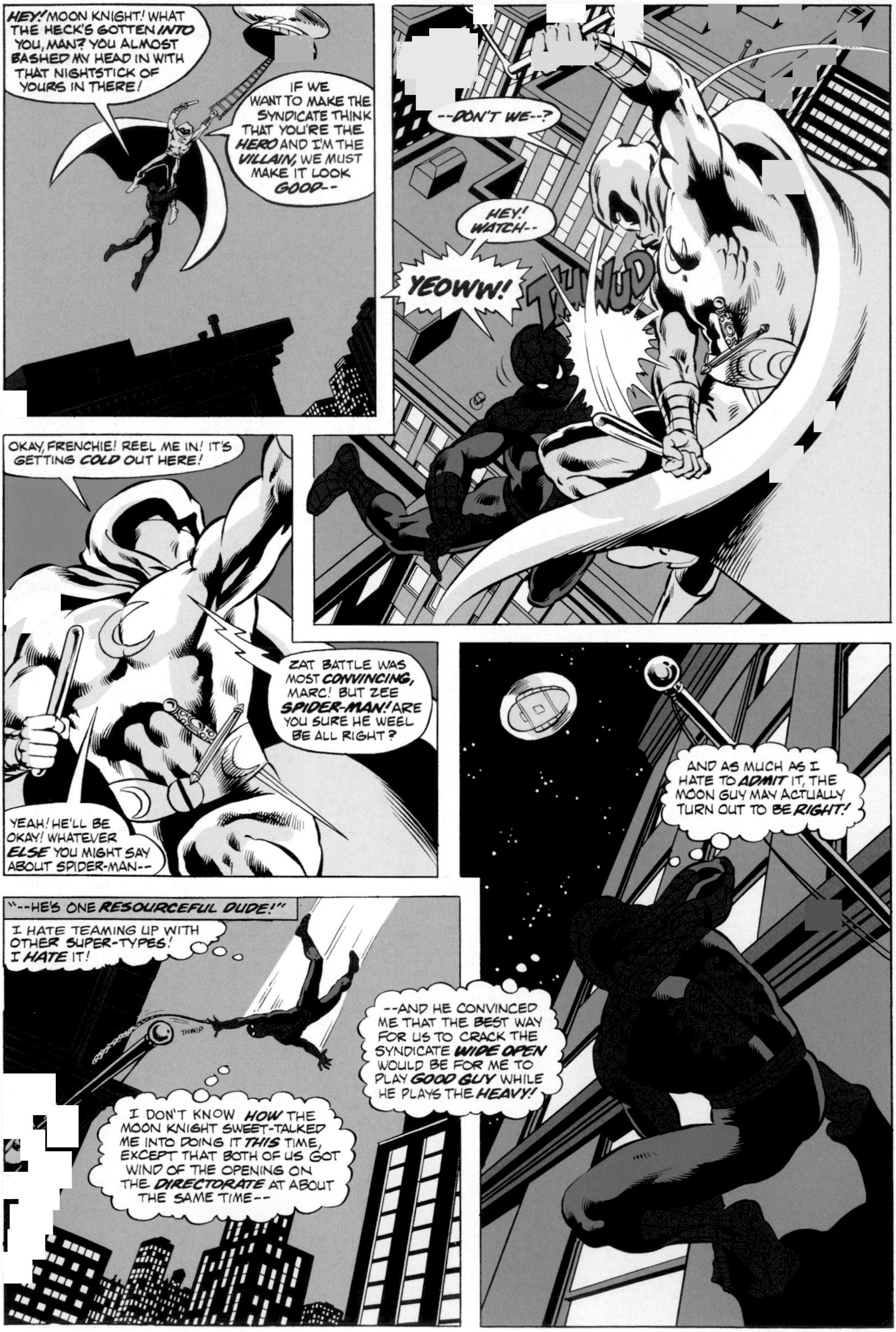
HEY! MOON KNIGHT! WHAT THE HECK'S GOTTEN INTO YOU, MAN? YOU ALMOST BASHED MY HEAD IN WITH THAT NIGHTSTICK OF YOURS IN THERE!
IF WE WANT TO MAKE THE SYNDICATE THINK THAT YOU'RE THE HERO AND I'M THE VILLAIN, WE MUST MAKE IT LOOK GOOD--
--DON'T WE--?
HEY! WATCH--
YEOWW!
THWUD
OKAY, FRENCHIE! REEL ME IN! IT'S GETTING COLD OUT HERE!
ZAT BATTLE WAS MOST CONVINCING, MARC! BUT ZEE SPIDER-MAN! ARE YOU SURE HE WEEL BE ALL RIGHT?
YEAH! HE'LL BE OKAY! WHATEVER ELSE YOU MIGHT SAY ABOUT SPIDER-MAN--
"--HE'S ONE RESOURCEFUL DUDE!"
I HATE TEAMING UP WITH OTHER SUPER-TYPES! I HATE IT!
THWIP
I DON'T KNOW HOW THE MOON KNIGHT SWEET-TALKED ME INTO DOING IT THIS TIME, EXCEPT THAT BOTH OF US GOT WIND OF THE OPENING ON THE DIRECTORATE AT ABOUT THE SAME TIME--
--AND HE CONVINCED ME THAT THE BEST WAY FOR US TO CRACK THE SYNDICATE WIDE OPEN WOULD BE FOR ME TO PLAY GOOD GUY WHILE HE PLAYS THE HEAVY!
AND AS MUCH AS I HATE TO ADMIT IT, THE MOON GUY MAY ACTUALLY TURN OUT TO BE RIGHT!

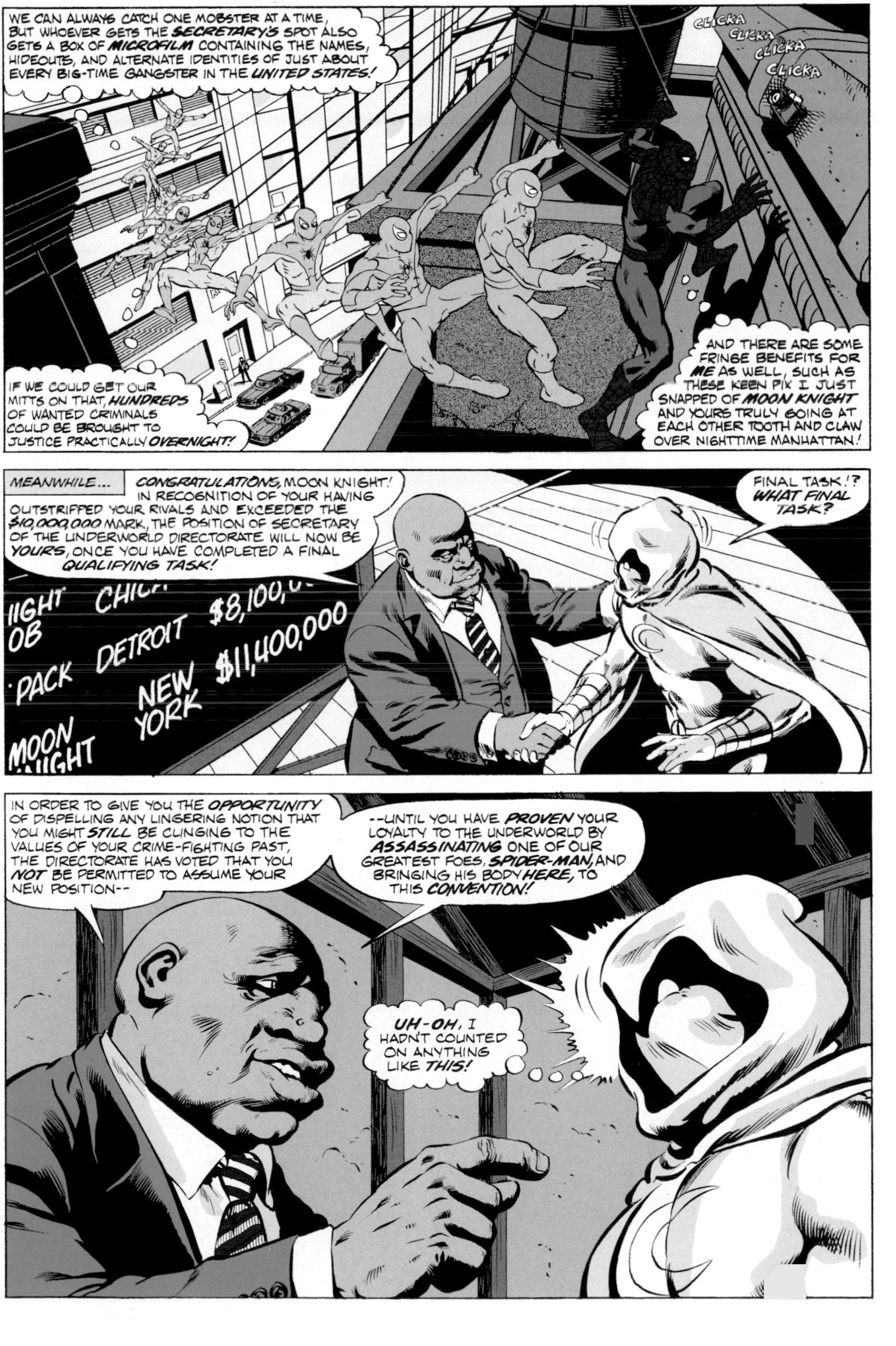
WE CAN ALWAYS CATCH ONE MOBSTER AT A TIME, BUT WHOEVER GETS THE SECRETARY'S SPOT ALSO GETS A BOX OF MICROFILM CONTAINING THE NAMES, HIDEOUTS, AND ALTERNATE IDENTITIES OF JUST ABOUT EVERY BIG-TIME GANGSTER IN THE UNITED STATES!
CLICKA CLICKA CLICKA CLICKA
IF WE COULD GET OUR MITTS ON THAT, HUNDREDS OF WANTED CRIMINALS COULD BE BROUGHT TO JUSTICE PRACTICALLY OVERNIGHT!
AND THERE ARE SOME FRINGE BENEFITS FOR ME AS WELL, SUCH AS THESE KEEN PIX I JUST SNAPPED OF MOON KNIGHT AND YOURS TRULY GOING AT EACH OTHER TOOTH AND CLAW OVER NIGHTTIME MANHATTAN!
MEANWHILE...
CONGRATULATIONS, MOON KNIGHT! IN RECOGNITION OF YOUR HAVING OUTSTRIPPED YOUR RIVALS AND EXCEEDED THE $10,000,000 MARK, THE POSITION OF SECRETARY OF THE UNDERWORLD DIRECTORATE WILL NOW BE YOURS, ONCE YOU HAVE COMPLETED A FINAL QUALIFYING TASK!
FINAL TASK!? WHAT FINAL TASK?
DETROIT $8,100,
NEW YORK $11,400,000
IN ORDER TO GIVE YOU THE OPPORTUNITY OF DISPELLING ANY LINGERING NOTION THAT YOU MIGHT STILL BE CLINGING TO THE VALUES OF YOUR CRIME-FIGHTING PAST, THE DIRECTORATE HAS VOTED THAT YOU NOT BE PERMITTED TO ASSUME YOUR NEW POSITION--
--UNTIL YOU HAVE PROVEN YOUR LOYALTY TO THE UNDERWORLD BY ASSASSINATING ONE OF OUR GREATEST FOES, SPIDER-MAN, AND BRINGING HIS BODY HERE, TO THIS CONVENTION!
UH-OH, I HADN'T COUNTED ON ANYTHING LIKE THIS!

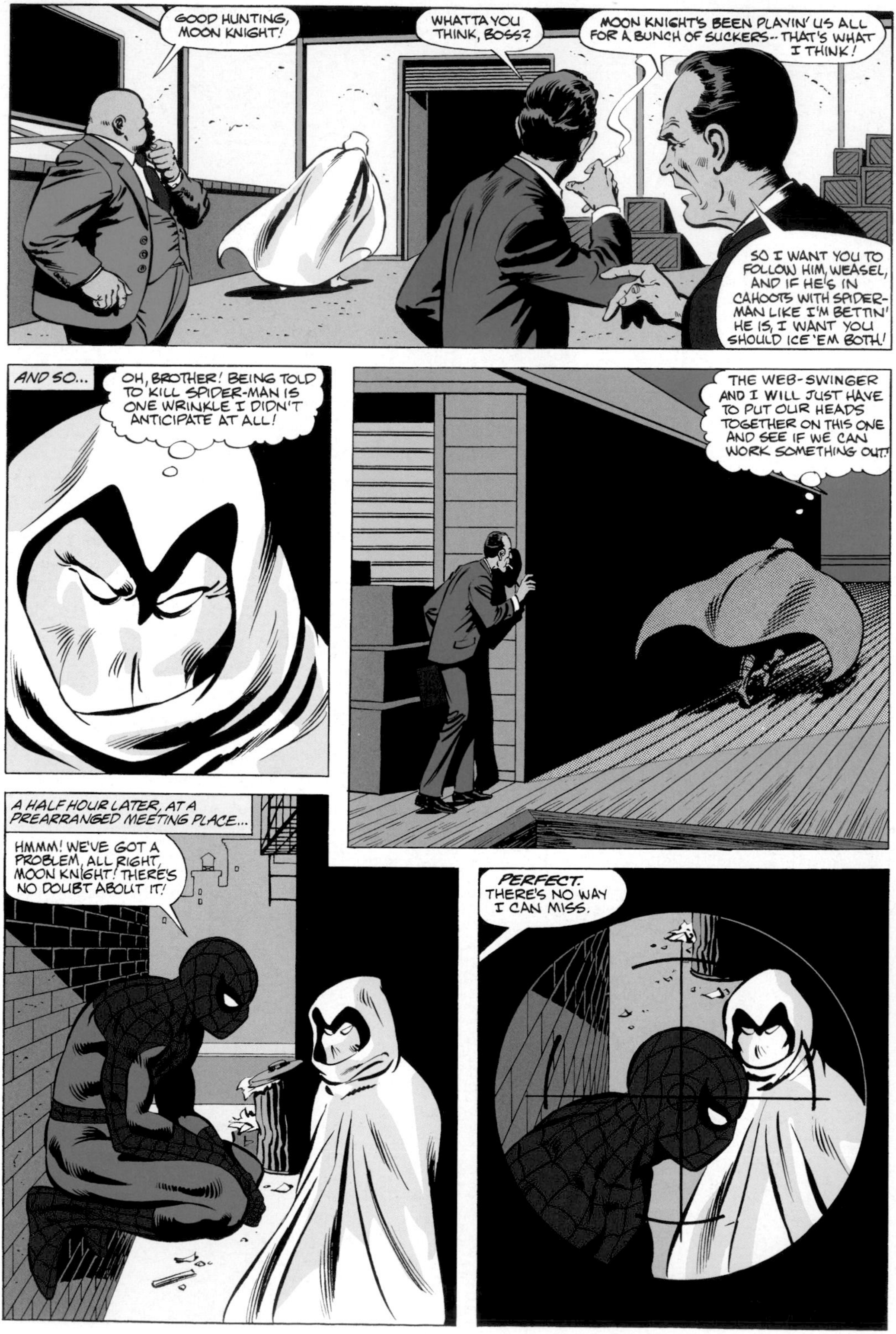
GOOD HUNTING, MOON KNIGHT!
WHATTA YOU THINK, BOSS?
MOON KNIGHT'S BEEN PLAYIN' US ALL FOR A BUNCH OF SUCKERS-- THAT'S WHAT I THINK!
SO I WANT YOU TO FOLLOW HIM, WEASEL, AND IF HE'S IN CAHOOTS WITH SPIDER-MAN LIKE I'M BETTIN' HE IS, I WANT YOU SHOULD ICE 'EM BOTH!
AND SO...
OH, BROTHER! BEING TOLD TO KILL SPIDER-MAN IS ONE WRINKLE I DIDN'T ANTICIPATE AT ALL!
THE WEB-SWINGER AND I WILL JUST HAVE TO PUT OUR HEADS TOGETHER ON THIS ONE AND SEE IF WE CAN WORK SOMETHING OUT!
A HALF HOUR LATER, AT A PREARRANGED MEETING PLACE...
HMMM! WE'VE GOT A PROBLEM, ALL RIGHT, MOON KNIGHT! THERE'S NO DOUBT ABOUT IT!
PERFECT. THERE'S NO WAY I CAN MISS.

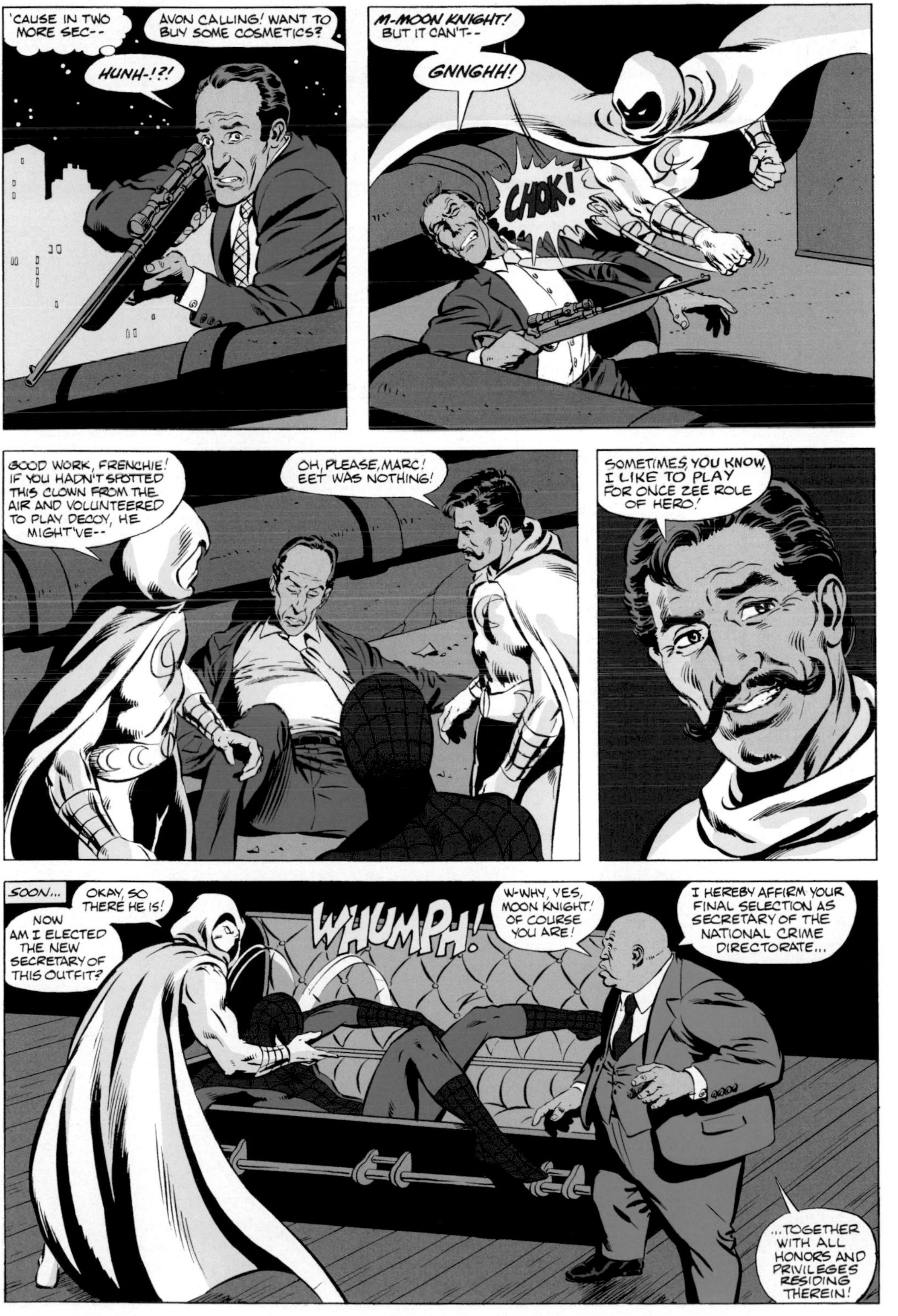
'CAUSE IN TWO MORE SEC--
AVON CALLING! WANT TO BUY SOME COSMETICS?
HUNH-!?!
M-MOON KNIGHT! BUT IT CAN'T--
GNNGHH!
CHOK!
GOOD WORK, FRENCHIE! IF YOU HADN'T SPOTTED THIS CLOWN FROM THE AIR AND VOLUNTEERED TO PLAY DECOY, HE MIGHT'VE--
OH, PLEASE, MARC! EET WAS NOTHING!
SOMETIMES, YOU KNOW, I LIKE TO PLAY FOR ONCE ZEE ROLE OF HERO!
SOON...
OKAY, SO THERE HE IS!
NOW AM I ELECTED THE NEW SECRETARY OF THIS OUTFIT?
WHUMPH!
W-WHY, YES, MOON KNIGHT! OF COURSE YOU ARE!
I HEREBY AFFIRM YOUR FINAL SELECTION AS SECRETARY OF THE NATIONAL CRIME DIRECTORATE...
...TOGETHER WITH ALL HONORS AND PRIVILEGES RESIDING THEREIN!

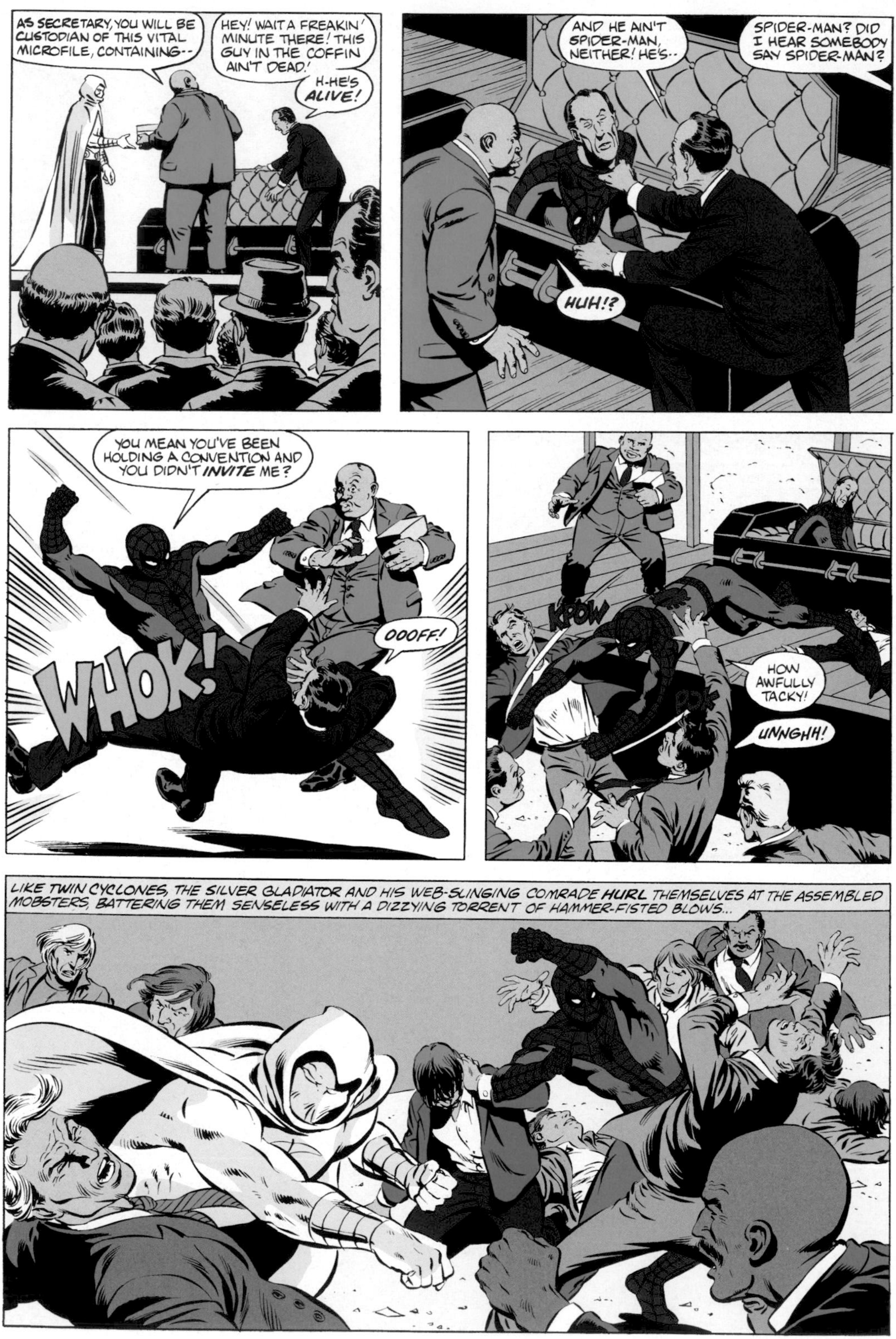
AS SECRETARY, YOU WILL BE CUSTODIAN OF THIS VITAL MICROFILE, CONTAINING--
HEY! WAIT A FREAKIN' MINUTE THERE! THIS GUY IN THE COFFIN AIN'T DEAD!
H-HE'S ALIVE!
AND HE AIN'T SPIDER-MAN, NEITHER! HE'S..
SPIDER-MAN? DID I HEAR SOMEBODY SAY SPIDER-MAN?
HUH!?
YOU MEAN YOU'VE BEEN HOLDING A CONVENTION AND YOU DIDN'T INVITE ME?
WHOK!
OOOFF!
KPOW
HOW AWFULLY TACKY!
UNNGHH!
LIKE TWIN CYCLONES, THE SILVER GLADIATOR AND HIS WEB-SLINGING COMRADE HURL THEMSELVES AT THE ASSEMBLED MOBSTERS, BATTERING THEM SENSELESS WITH A DIZZYING TORRENT OF HAMMER-FISTED BLOWS...

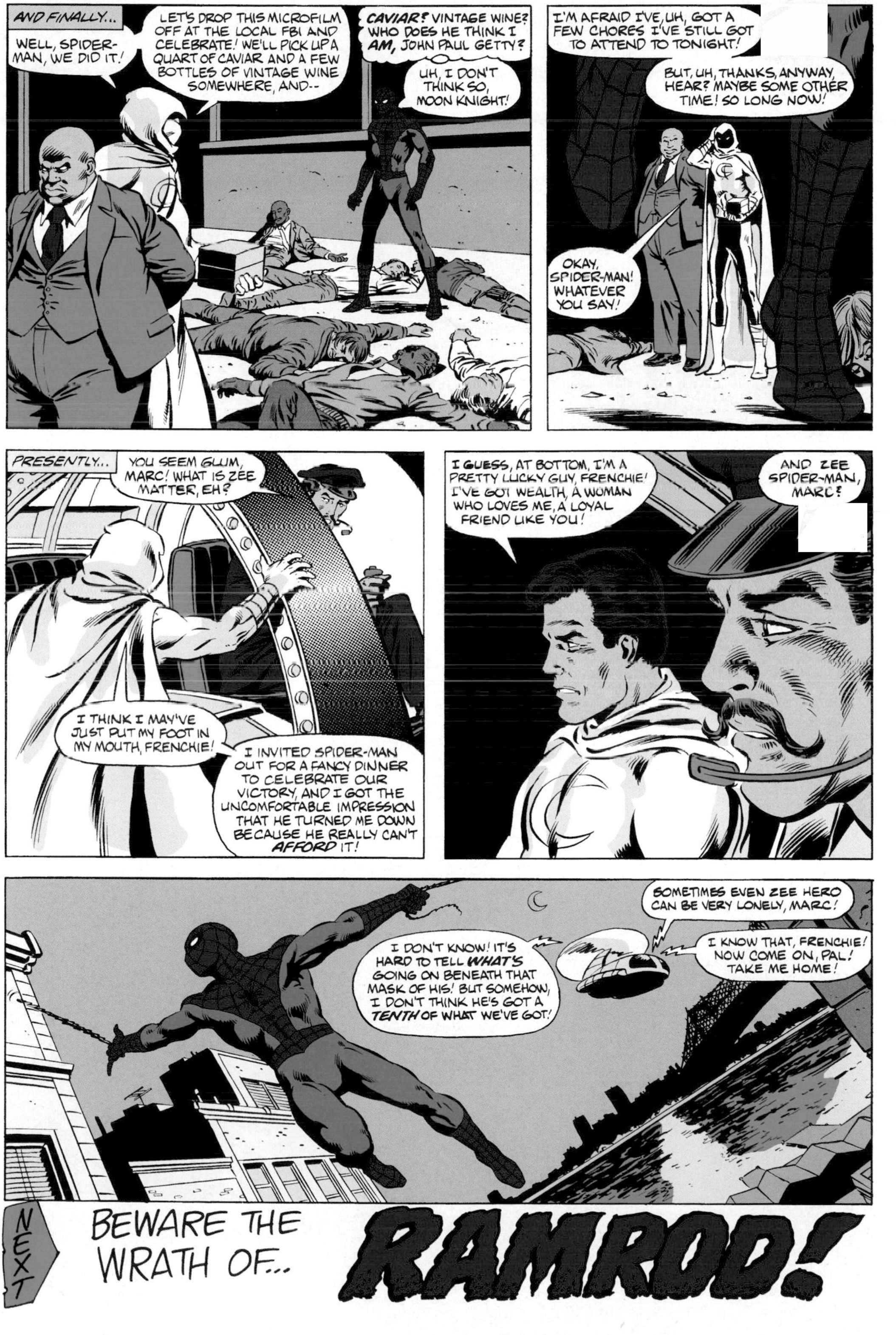
AND FINALLY...
WELL, SPIDER-MAN, WE DID IT!
LET'S DROP THIS MICROFILM OFF AT THE LOCAL FBI AND CELEBRATE! WE'LL PICK UP A QUART OF CAVIAR AND A FEW BOTTLES OF VINTAGE WINE SOMEWHERE, AND--
CAVIAR? VINTAGE WINE? WHO DOES HE THINK I AM, JOHN PAUL GETTY?
UH, I DON'T THINK SO, MOON KNIGHT!
I'M AFRAID I'VE, UH, GOT A FEW CHORES I'VE STILL GOT TO ATTEND TO TONIGHT!
BUT, UH, THANKS, ANYWAY, HEAR? MAYBE SOME OTHER TIME! SO LONG NOW!
OKAY, SPIDER-MAN! WHATEVER YOU SAY!
PRESENTLY...
YOU SEEM GLUM, MARC! WHAT IS ZÉE MATTER, EH?
I THINK I MAY'VE JUST PUT MY FOOT IN MY MOUTH, FRENCHIE!
I INVITED SPIDER-MAN OUT FOR A FANCY DINNER TO CELEBRATE OUR VICTORY, AND I GOT THE UNCOMFORTABLE IMPRESSION THAT HE TURNED ME DOWN BECAUSE HE REALLY CAN'T AFFORD IT!
I GUESS, AT BOTTOM, I'M A PRETTY LUCKY GUY, FRENCHIE! I'VE GOT WEALTH, A WOMAN WHO LOVES ME, A LOYAL FRIEND LIKE YOU!
AND ZEE SPIDER-MAN, MARC?
I DON'T KNOW! IT'S HARD TO TELL WHAT'S GOING ON BENEATH THAT MASK OF HIS! BUT SOMEHOW, I DON'T THINK HE'S GOT A TENTH OF WHAT WE'VE GOT!
SOMETIMES EVEN ZEE HERO CAN BE VERY LONELY, MARC!
I KNOW THAT, FRENCHIE! NOW COME ON, PAL! TAKE ME HOME!
NEXT
BEWARE THE WRATH OF... RAMROD!

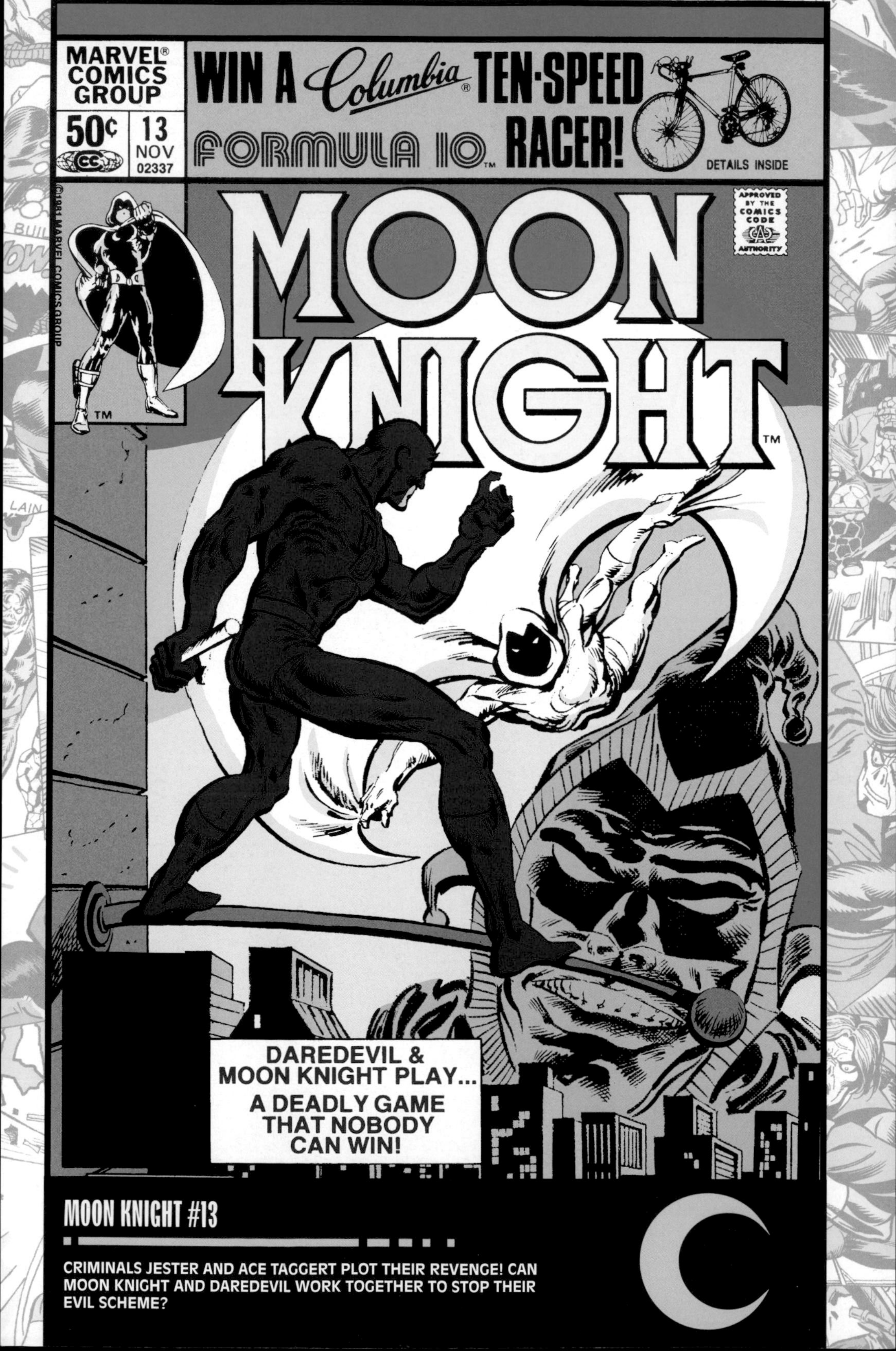
MARVEL® COMICS GROUP
50¢
13 NOV 02337
WIN A Columbia® TEN-SPEED
FORMULA 10™ RACER!
DETAILS INSIDE
MOON KNIGHT™
APPROVED BY THE COMICS CODE AUTHORITY
©1981 MARVEL COMICS GROUP
TM
DAREDEVIL & MOON KNIGHT PLAY...
A DEADLY GAME THAT NOBODY CAN WIN!

MOON KNIGHT #13

CRIMINALS JESTER AND ACE TAGGERT PLOT THEIR REVENGE! CAN MOON KNIGHT AND DAREDEVIL WORK TOGETHER TO STOP THEIR EVIL SCHEME?

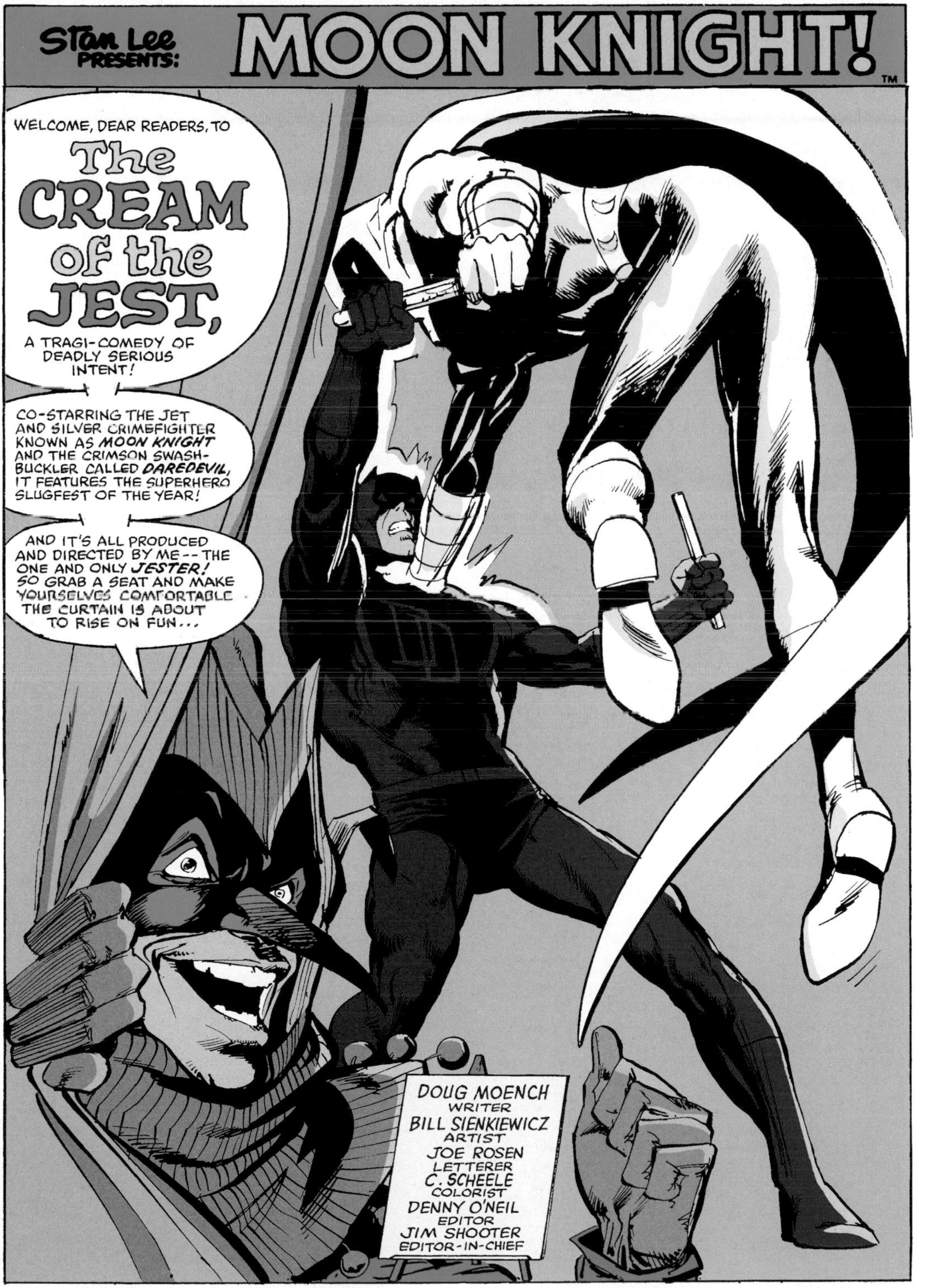
Stan Lee PRESENTS:
MOON KNIGHT!™
WELCOME, DEAR READERS, TO The CREAM of the JEST, A TRAGI-COMEDY OF DEADLY SERIOUS INTENT!
CO-STARRING THE JET AND SILVER CRIMEFIGHTER KNOWN AS MOON KNIGHT AND THE CRIMSON SWASH-BUCKLER CALLED DAREDEVIL, IT FEATURES THE SUPERHERO SLUGFEST OF THE YEAR!
AND IT'S ALL PRODUCED AND DIRECTED BY ME -- THE ONE AND ONLY JESTER! SO GRAB A SEAT AND MAKE YOURSELVES COMFORTABLE THE CURTAIN IS ABOUT TO RISE ON FUN...
DOUG MOENCH WRITER
BILL SIENKIEWICZ ARTIST
JOE ROSEN LETTERER
C. SCHEELE COLORIST
DENNY O'NEIL EDITOR
JIM SHOOTER EDITOR-IN-CHIEF

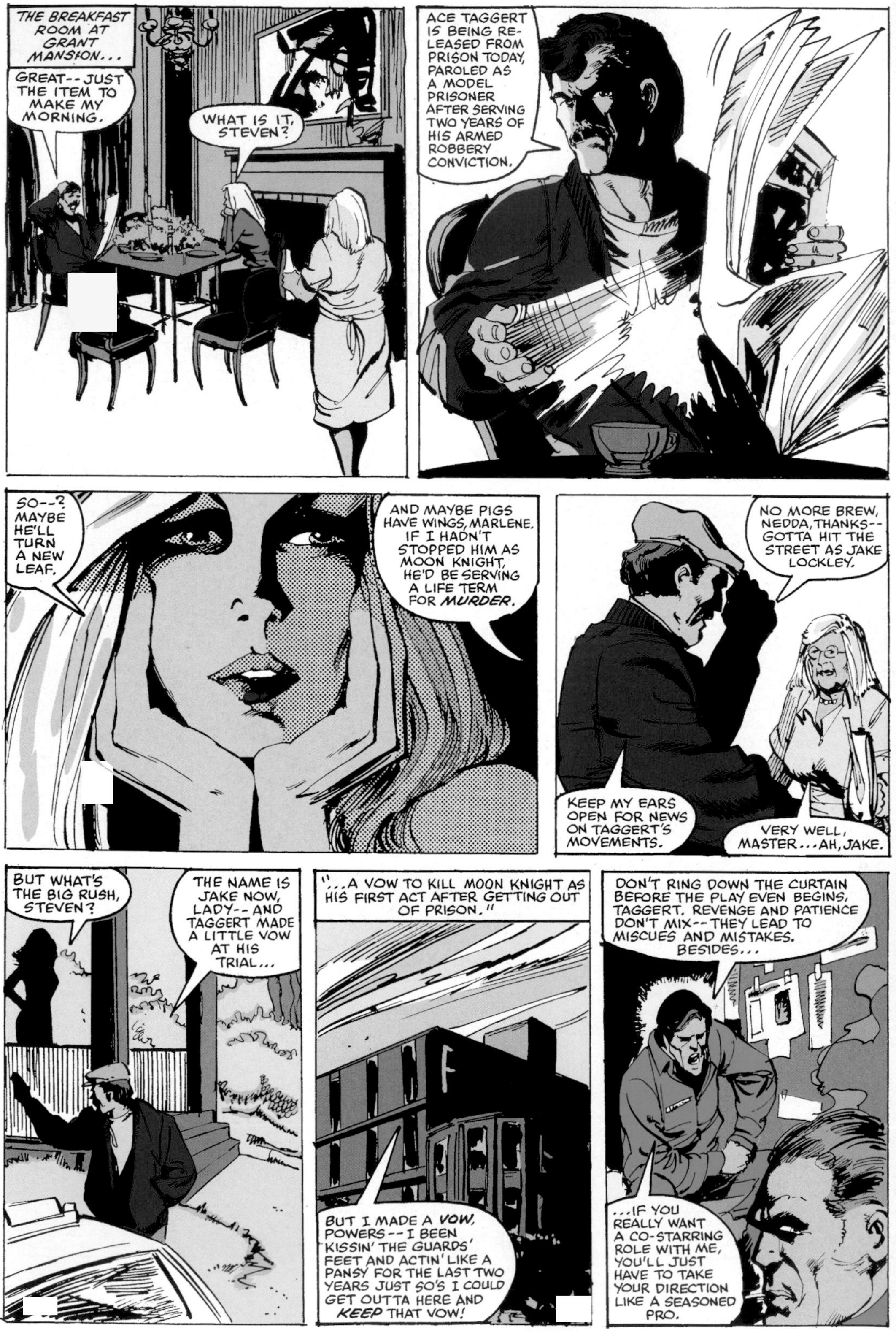
THE BREAKFAST ROOM AT GRANT MANSION...
GREAT--JUST THE ITEM TO MAKE MY MORNING.
WHAT IS IT, STEVEN?
ACE TAGGERT IS BEING RE-LEASED FROM PRISON TODAY, PAROLED AS A MODEL PRISONER AFTER SERVING TWO YEARS OF HIS ARMED ROBBERY CONVICTION.
SO--? MAYBE HE'LL TURN A NEW LEAF.
AND MAYBE PIGS HAVE WINGS, MARLENE. IF I HADN'T STOPPED HIM AS MOON KNIGHT, HE'D BE SERVING A LIFE TERM FOR MURDER.
NO MORE BREW, NEDDA, THANKS--GOTTA HIT THE STREET AS JAKE LOCKLEY.
KEEP MY EARS OPEN FOR NEWS ON TAGGERT'S MOVEMENTS.
VERY WELL, MASTER...AH, JAKE.
BUT WHAT'S THE BIG RUSH, STEVEN?
THE NAME IS JAKE NOW, LADY--AND TAGGERT MADE A LITTLE VOW AT HIS TRIAL...
"...A VOW TO KILL MOON KNIGHT AS HIS FIRST ACT AFTER GETTING OUT OF PRISON."
BUT I MADE A VOW, POWERS--I BEEN KISSIN' THE GUARDS' FEET AND ACTIN' LIKE A PANSY FOR THE LAST TWO YEARS JUST SO'S I COULD GET OUTTA HERE AND KEEP THAT VOW!
DON'T RING DOWN THE CURTAIN BEFORE THE PLAY EVEN BEGINS, TAGGERT. REVENGE AND PATIENCE DON'T MIX--THEY LEAD TO MISCUES AND MISTAKES. BESIDES...
...IF YOU REALLY WANT A CO-STARRING ROLE WITH ME, YOU'LL JUST HAVE TO TAKE YOUR DIRECTION LIKE A SEASONED PRO.

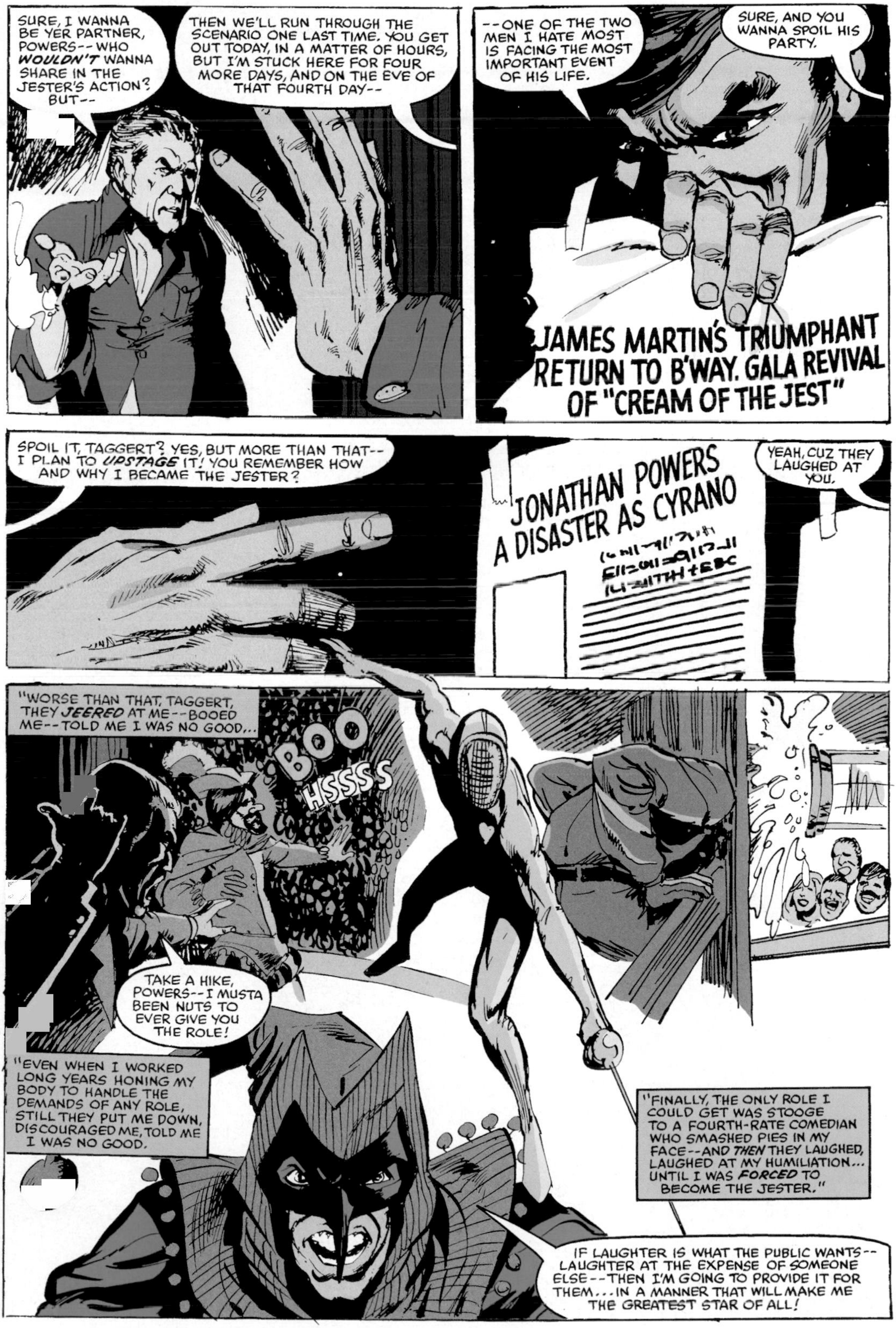
SURE, I WANNA BE YER PARTNER, POWERS--WHO WOULDN'T WANNA SHARE IN THE JESTER'S ACTION? BUT--
THEN WE'LL RUN THROUGH THE SCENARIO ONE LAST TIME. YOU GET OUT TODAY, IN A MATTER OF HOURS, BUT I'M STUCK HERE FOR FOUR MORE DAYS, AND ON THE EVE OF THAT FOURTH DAY--
--ONE OF THE TWO MEN I HATE MOST IS FACING THE MOST IMPORTANT EVENT OF HIS LIFE.
SURE, AND YOU WANNA SPOIL HIS PARTY.
JAMES MARTIN'S TRIUMPHANT RETURN TO B'WAY. GALA REVIVAL OF "CREAM OF THE JEST"
SPOIL IT, TAGGERT? YES, BUT MORE THAN THAT--I PLAN TO UPSTAGE IT! YOU REMEMBER HOW AND WHY I BECAME THE JESTER?
JONATHAN POWERS A DISASTER AS CYRANO
YEAH, CUZ THEY LAUGHED AT YOU.
"WORSE THAN THAT, TAGGERT, THEY JEERED AT ME--BOOED ME--TOLD ME I WAS NO GOOD...
BOO
HSSSS
TAKE A HIKE, POWERS--I MUSTA BEEN NUTS TO EVER GIVE YOU THE ROLE!
"EVEN WHEN I WORKED LONG YEARS HONING MY BODY TO HANDLE THE DEMANDS OF ANY ROLE, STILL THEY PUT ME DOWN, DISCOURAGED ME, TOLD ME I WAS NO GOOD.
"FINALLY, THE ONLY ROLE I COULD GET WAS STOOGE TO A FOURTH-RATE COMEDIAN WHO SMASHED PIES IN MY FACE--AND THEN THEY LAUGHED, LAUGHED AT MY HUMILIATION... UNTIL I WAS FORCED TO BECOME THE JESTER."
IF LAUGHTER IS WHAT THE PUBLIC WANTS--LAUGHTER AT THE EXPENSE OF SOMEONE ELSE--THEN I'M GOING TO PROVIDE IT FOR THEM... IN A MANNER THAT WILL MAKE ME THE GREATEST STAR OF ALL!

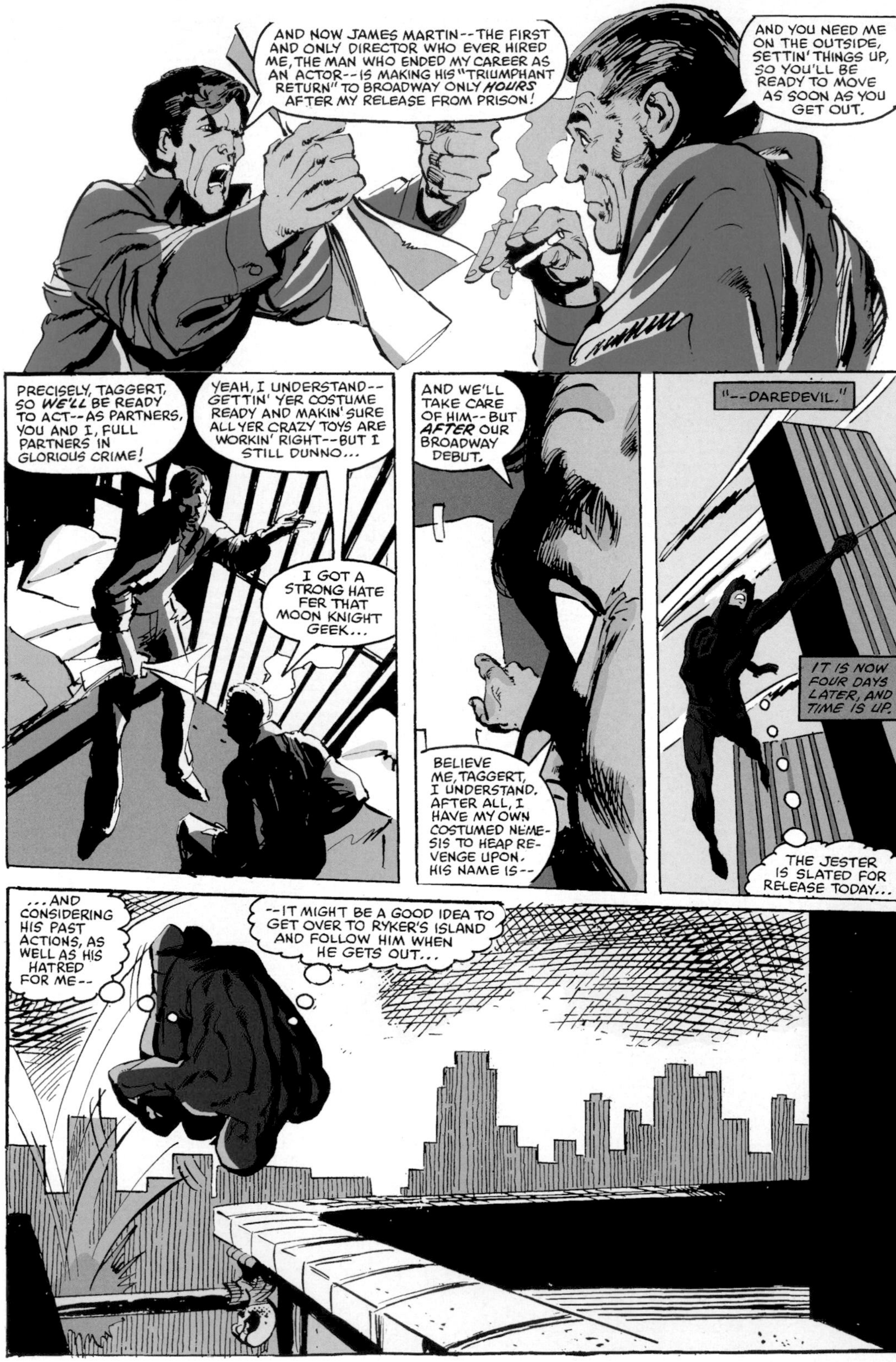
AND NOW JAMES MARTIN--THE FIRST AND ONLY DIRECTOR WHO EVER HIRED ME, THE MAN WHO ENDED MY CAREER AS AN ACTOR--IS MAKING HIS "TRIUMPHANT RETURN" TO BROADWAY ONLY HOURS AFTER MY RELEASE FROM PRISON!
AND YOU NEED ME ON THE OUTSIDE, SETTIN' THINGS UP, SO YOU'LL BE READY TO MOVE AS SOON AS YOU GET OUT.
PRECISELY, TAGGERT, SO WE'LL BE READY TO ACT--AS PARTNERS, YOU AND I, FULL PARTNERS IN GLORIOUS CRIME!
YEAH, I UNDERSTAND--GETTIN' YER COSTUME READY AND MAKIN' SURE ALL YER CRAZY TOYS ARE WORKIN' RIGHT--BUT I STILL DUNNO...
I GOT A STRONG HATE FER THAT MOON KNIGHT GEEK...
AND WE'LL TAKE CARE OF HIM--BUT AFTER OUR BROADWAY DEBUT.
BELIEVE ME, TAGGERT, I UNDERSTAND. AFTER ALL, I HAVE MY OWN COSTUMED NEMESIS TO HEAP REVENGE UPON. HIS NAME IS--
"--DAREDEVIL."
IT IS NOW FOUR DAYS LATER, AND TIME IS UP.
THE JESTER IS SLATED FOR RELEASE TODAY...
...AND CONSIDERING HIS PAST ACTIONS, AS WELL AS HIS HATRED FOR ME--
--IT MIGHT BE A GOOD IDEA TO GET OVER TO RYKER'S ISLAND AND FOLLOW HIM WHEN HE GETS OUT...

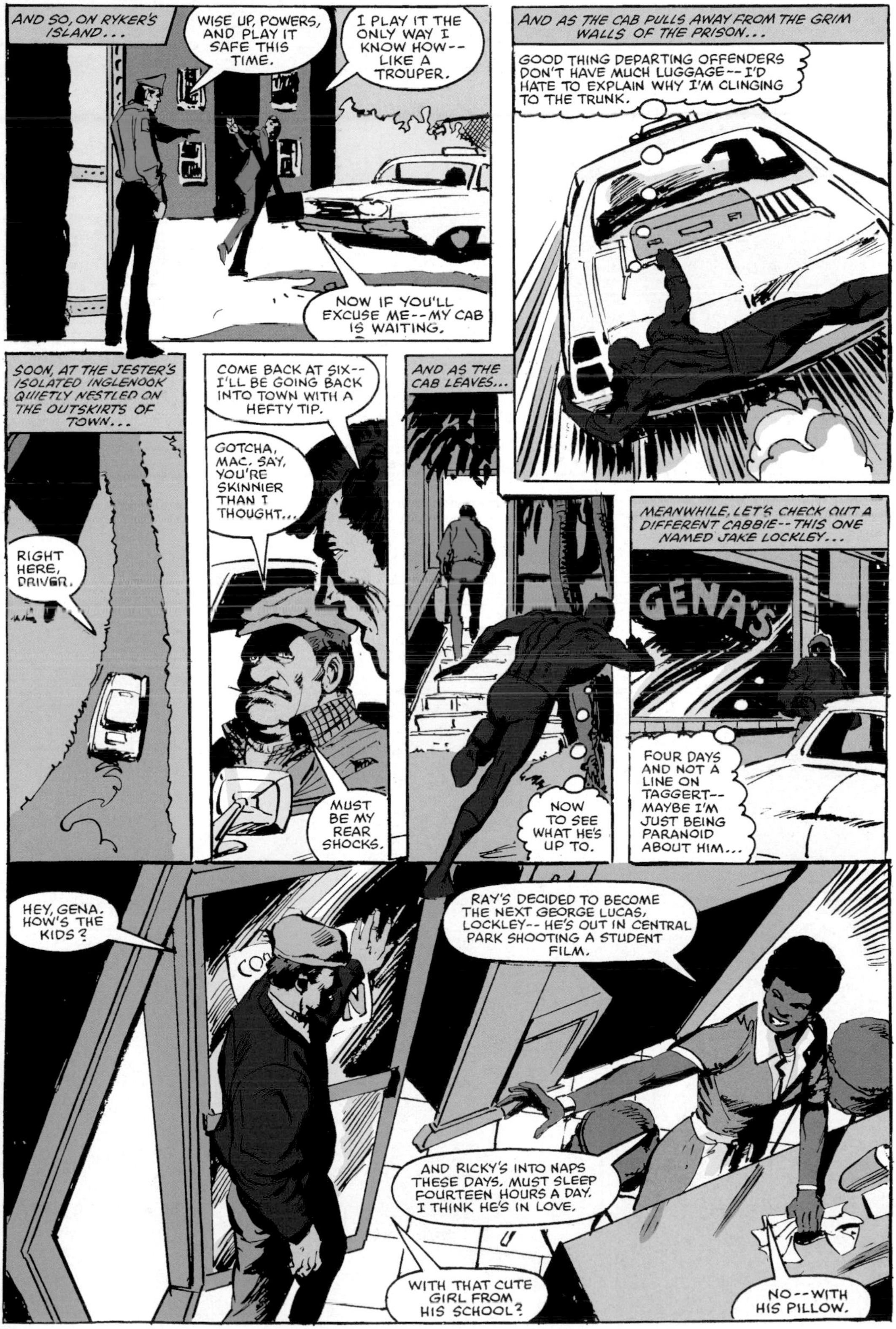
AND SO, ON RYKER'S ISLAND...
WISE UP, POWERS, AND PLAY IT SAFE THIS TIME.
I PLAY IT THE ONLY WAY I KNOW HOW--LIKE A TROUPER.
NOW IF YOU'LL EXCUSE ME--MY CAB IS WAITING.
AND AS THE CAB PULLS AWAY FROM THE GRIM WALLS OF THE PRISON...
GOOD THING DEPARTING OFFENDERS DON'T HAVE MUCH LUGGAGE--I'D HATE TO EXPLAIN WHY I'M CLINGING TO THE TRUNK.
SOON, AT THE JESTER'S ISOLATED INGLENOOK QUIETLY NESTLED ON THE OUTSKIRTS OF TOWN...
RIGHT HERE, DRIVER.
COME BACK AT SIX--I'LL BE GOING BACK INTO TOWN WITH A HEFTY TIP.
GOTCHA, MAC. SAY, YOU'RE SKINNIER THAN I THOUGHT...
MUST BE MY REAR SHOCKS.
AND AS THE CAB LEAVES...
NOW TO SEE WHAT HE'S UP TO.
MEANWHILE, LET'S CHECK OUT A DIFFERENT CABBIE--THIS ONE NAMED JAKE LOCKLEY...
GENA'S
FOUR DAYS AND NOT A LINE ON TAGGERT--MAYBE I'M JUST BEING PARANOID ABOUT HIM...
HEY, GENA. HOW'S THE KIDS?
RAY'S DECIDED TO BECOME THE NEXT GEORGE LUCAS, LOCKLEY--HE'S OUT IN CENTRAL PARK SHOOTING A STUDENT FILM.
AND RICKY'S INTO NAPS THESE DAYS. MUST SLEEP FOURTEEN HOURS A DAY. I THINK HE'S IN LOVE.
WITH THAT CUTE GIRL FROM HIS SCHOOL?
NO--WITH HIS PILLOW.

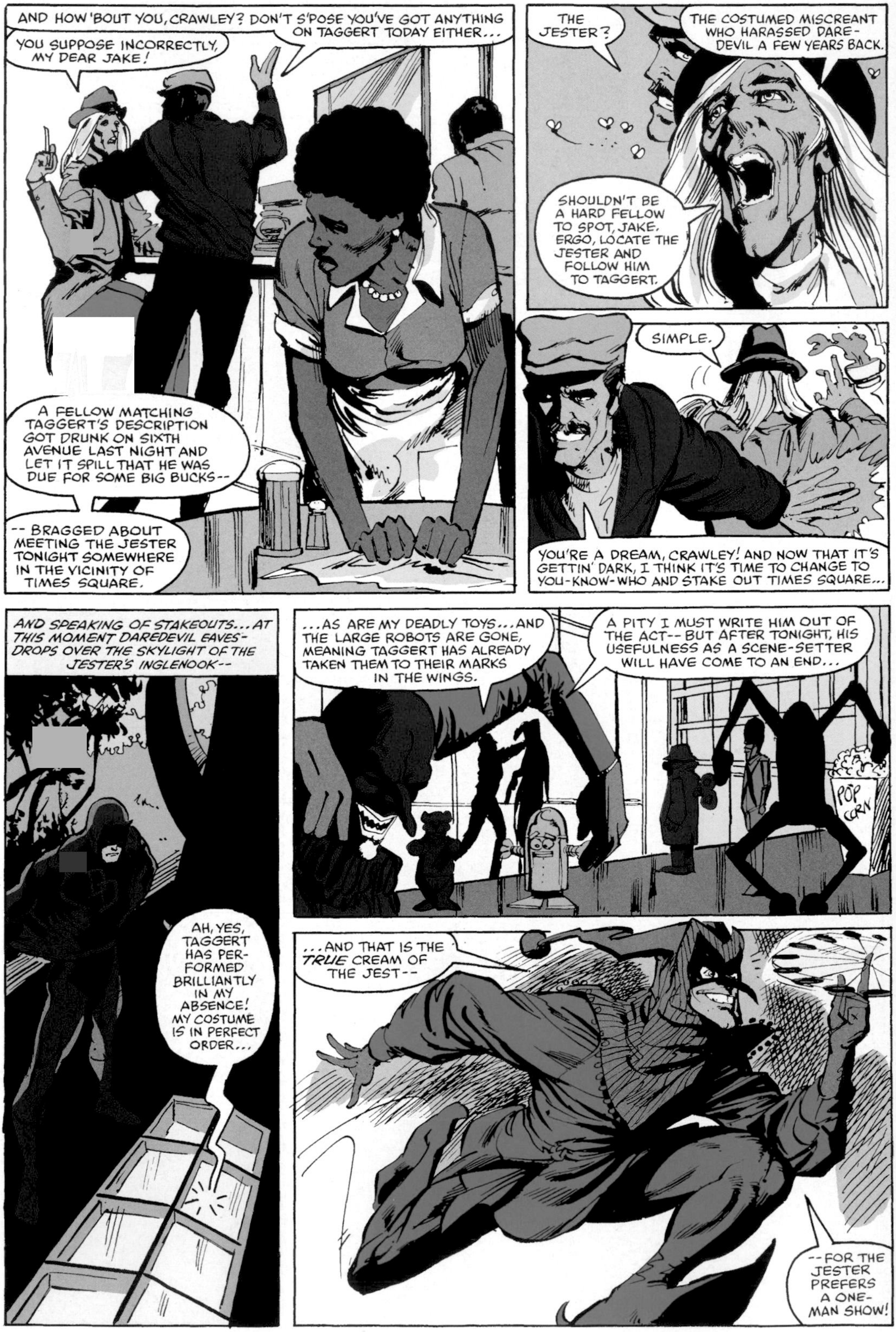
AND HOW 'BOUT YOU, CRAWLEY? DON'T S'POSE YOU'VE GOT ANYTHING ON TAGGERT TODAY EITHER...
YOU SUPPOSE INCORRECTLY, MY DEAR JAKE!
A FELLOW MATCHING TAGGERT'S DESCRIPTION GOT DRUNK ON SIXTH AVENUE LAST NIGHT AND LET IT SPILL THAT HE WAS DUE FOR SOME BIG BUCKS--
-- BRAGGED ABOUT MEETING THE JESTER TONIGHT SOMEWHERE IN THE VICINITY OF TIMES SQUARE.
THE JESTER?
THE COSTUMED MISCREANT WHO HARASSED DARE-DEVIL A FEW YEARS BACK.
SHOULDN'T BE A HARD FELLOW TO SPOT, JAKE. ERGO, LOCATE THE JESTER AND FOLLOW HIM TO TAGGERT.
SIMPLE.
YOU'RE A DREAM, CRAWLEY! AND NOW THAT IT'S GETTIN' DARK, I THINK IT'S TIME TO CHANGE TO YOU-KNOW-WHO AND STAKE OUT TIMES SQUARE...
AND SPEAKING OF STAKEOUTS... AT THIS MOMENT DAREDEVIL EAVES-DROPS OVER THE SKYLIGHT OF THE JESTER'S INGLENOOK--
AH, YES, TAGGERT HAS PER-FORMED BRILLIANTLY IN MY ABSENCE! MY COSTUME IS IN PERFECT ORDER...
...AS ARE MY DEADLY TOYS... AND THE LARGE ROBOTS ARE GONE, MEANING TAGGERT HAS ALREADY TAKEN THEM TO THEIR MARKS IN THE WINGS.
A PITY I MUST WRITE HIM OUT OF THE ACT-- BUT AFTER TONIGHT, HIS USEFULNESS AS A SCENE-SETTER WILL HAVE COME TO AN END...
POP CORN
...AND THAT IS THE TRUE CREAM OF THE JEST--
--FOR THE JESTER PREFERS A ONE-MAN SHOW!

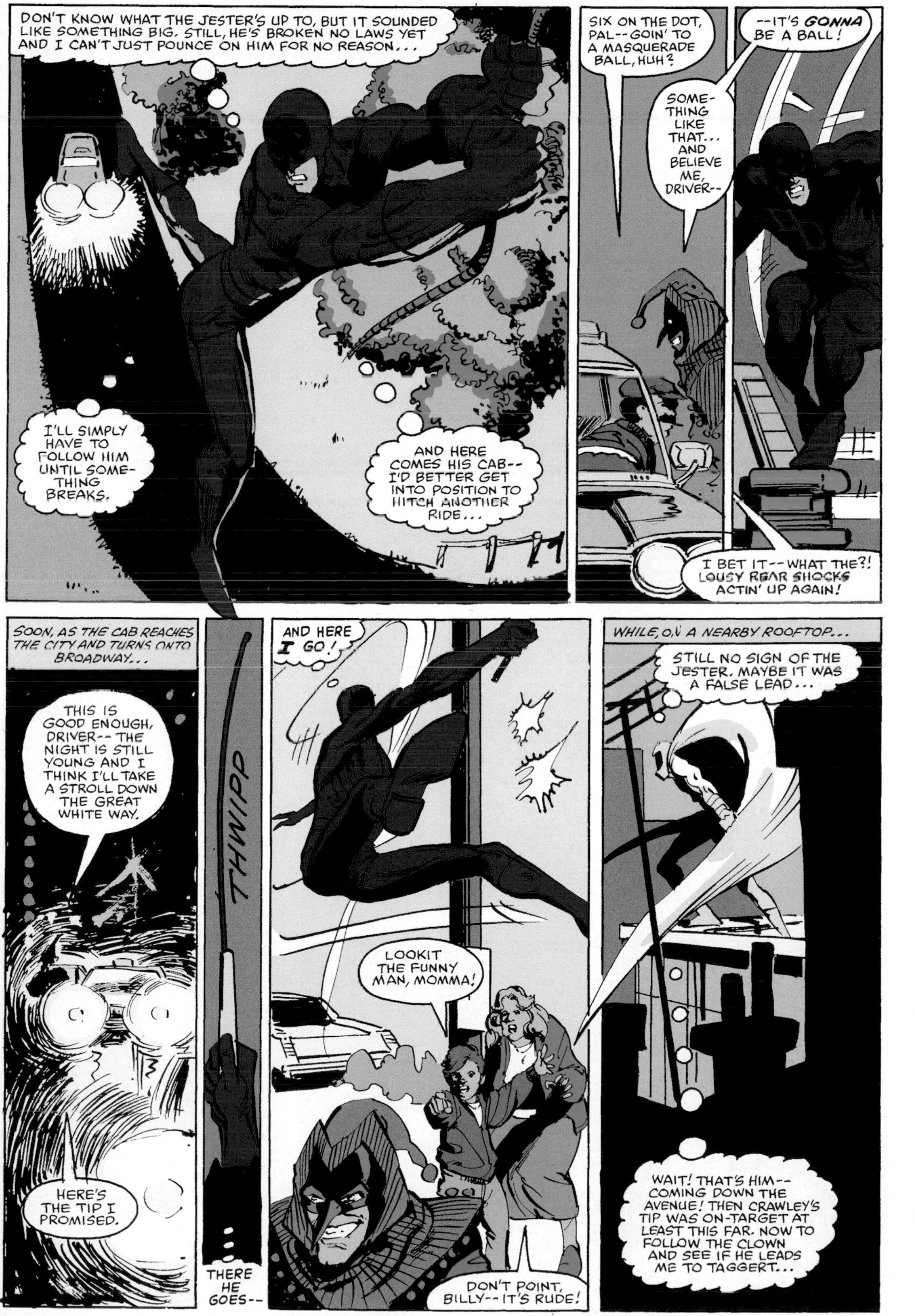
DON'T KNOW WHAT THE JESTER'S UP TO, BUT IT SOUNDED LIKE SOMETHING BIG. STILL, HE'S BROKEN NO LAWS YET AND I CAN'T JUST POUNCE ON HIM FOR NO REASON...
I'LL SIMPLY HAVE TO FOLLOW HIM UNTIL SOMETHING BREAKS.
AND HERE COMES HIS CAB-- I'D BETTER GET INTO POSITION TO HITCH ANOTHER RIDE...
SIX ON THE DOT, PAL--GOIN' TO A MASQUERADE BALL, HUH?
SOMETHING LIKE THAT... AND BELIEVE ME, DRIVER--
--IT'S GONNA BE A BALL!
I BET IT--WHAT THE?! LOUSY REAR SHOCKS ACTIN' UP AGAIN!
SOON, AS THE CAB REACHES THE CITY AND TURNS ONTO BROADWAY...
THIS IS GOOD ENOUGH, DRIVER-- THE NIGHT IS STILL YOUNG AND I THINK I'LL TAKE A STROLL DOWN THE GREAT WHITE WAY.
HERE'S THE TIP I PROMISED.
THWIPP
THERE HE GOES--
AND HERE I GO!
LOOKIT THE FUNNY MAN, MOMMA!
DON'T POINT, BILLY--IT'S RUDE!
WHILE, ON A NEARBY ROOFTOP...
STILL NO SIGN OF THE JESTER. MAYBE IT WAS A FALSE LEAD...
WAIT! THAT'S HIM-- COMING DOWN THE AVENUE! THEN CRAWLEY'S TIP WAS ON-TARGET AT LEAST THIS FAR. NOW TO FOLLOW THE CLOWN AND SEE IF HE LEADS ME TO TAGGERT...

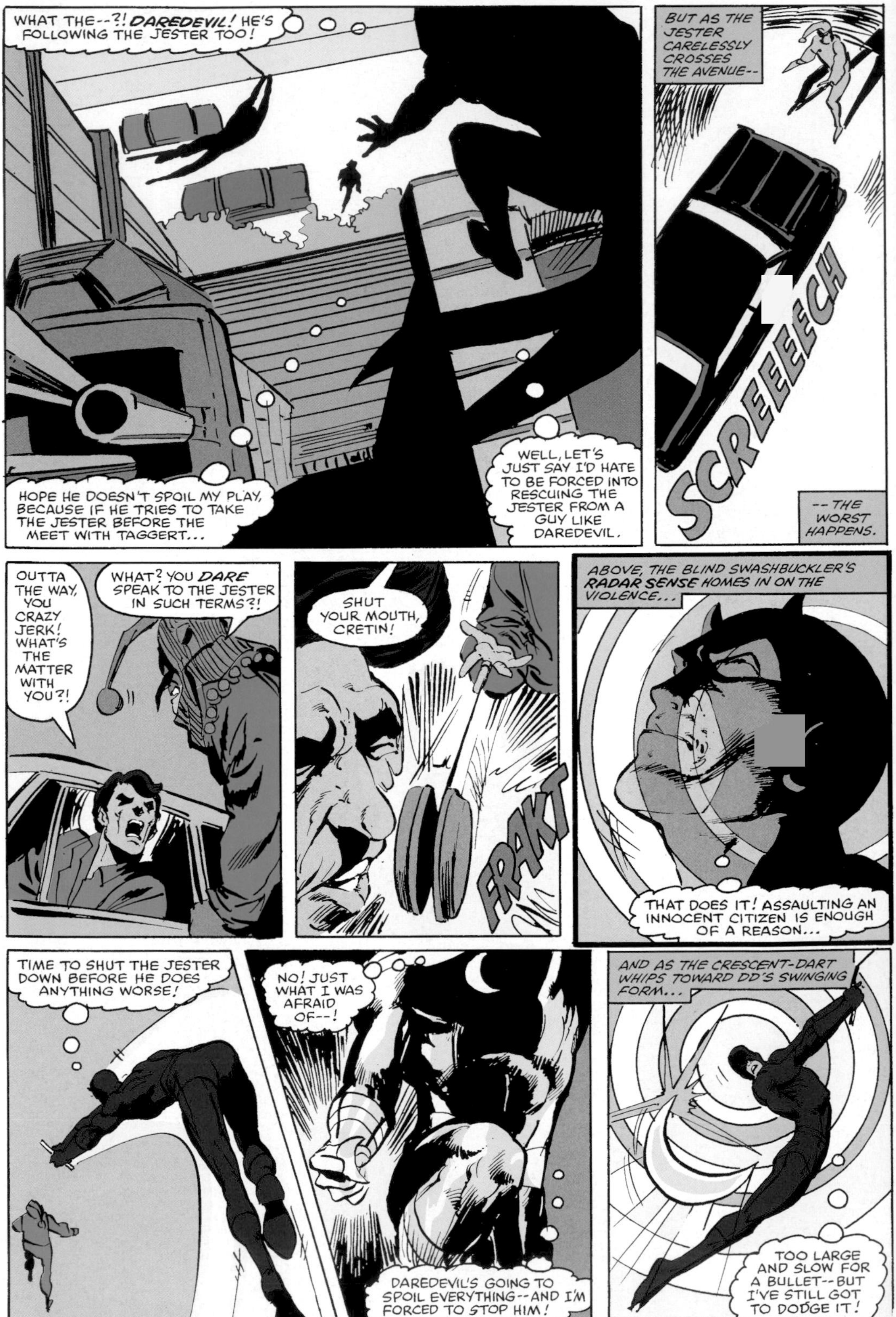

WHAT THE--?! DAREDEVIL! HE'S FOLLOWING THE JESTER TOO!
HOPE HE DOESN'T SPOIL MY PLAY, BECAUSE IF HE TRIES TO TAKE THE JESTER BEFORE THE MEET WITH TAGGERT...
WELL, LET'S JUST SAY I'D HATE TO BE FORCED INTO RESCUING THE JESTER FROM A GUY LIKE DAREDEVIL.
BUT AS THE JESTER CARELESSLY CROSSES THE AVENUE--
SCREEEECH
--THE WORST HAPPENS.
OUTTA THE WAY, YOU CRAZY JERK! WHAT'S THE MATTER WITH YOU?!
WHAT? YOU DARE SPEAK TO THE JESTER IN SUCH TERMS?!
SHUT YOUR MOUTH, CRETIN!
FRAKT
ABOVE, THE BLIND SWASHBUCKLER'S RADAR SENSE HOMES IN ON THE VIOLENCE...
THAT DOES IT! ASSAULTING AN INNOCENT CITIZEN IS ENOUGH OF A REASON...
TIME TO SHUT THE JESTER DOWN BEFORE HE DOES ANYTHING WORSE!
NO! JUST WHAT I WAS AFRAID OF--!
DAREDEVIL'S GOING TO SPOIL EVERYTHING--AND I'M FORCED TO STOP HIM!
AND AS THE CRESCENT-DART WHIPS TOWARD DD'S SWINGING FORM...
TOO LARGE AND SLOW FOR A BULLET--BUT I'VE STILL GOT TO DODGE IT!

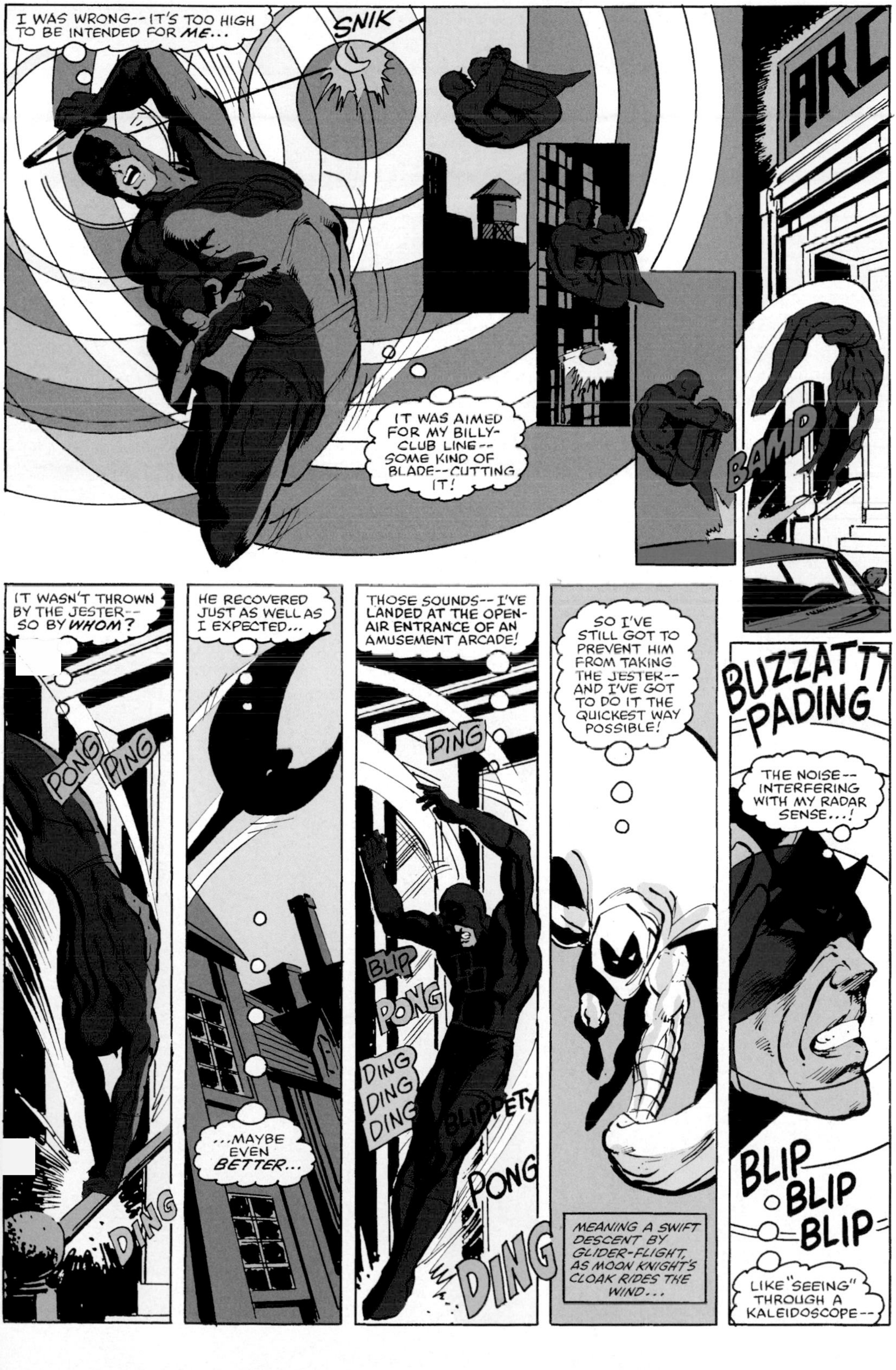

I WAS WRONG--IT'S TOO HIGH TO BE INTENDED FOR *ME*...
SNIK
IT WAS AIMED FOR MY BILLY-CLUB LINE--SOME KIND OF BLADE--CUTTING IT!
ARC
BAMP
IT WASN'T THROWN BY THE JESTER--SO BY *WHOM*?
PONG
PING
DING
HE RECOVERED JUST AS WELL AS I EXPECTED...
...MAYBE EVEN *BETTER*...
THOSE SOUNDS--I'VE LANDED AT THE OPEN-AIR ENTRANCE OF AN AMUSEMENT ARCADE!
PING
BLIP
PONG
DING
DING
DING
BLIPPETY
PONG
DING
SO I'VE STILL GOT TO PREVENT HIM FROM TAKING THE JESTER--AND I'VE GOT TO DO IT THE QUICKEST WAY POSSIBLE!
MEANING A SWIFT DESCENT BY GLIDER-FLIGHT, AS MOON KNIGHT'S CLOAK RIDES THE WIND...
BUZZATT PADING
THE NOISE--INTERFERING WITH MY RADAR SENSE...!
BLIP
BLIP
BLIP
LIKE "SEEING" THROUGH A KALEIDOSCOPE--

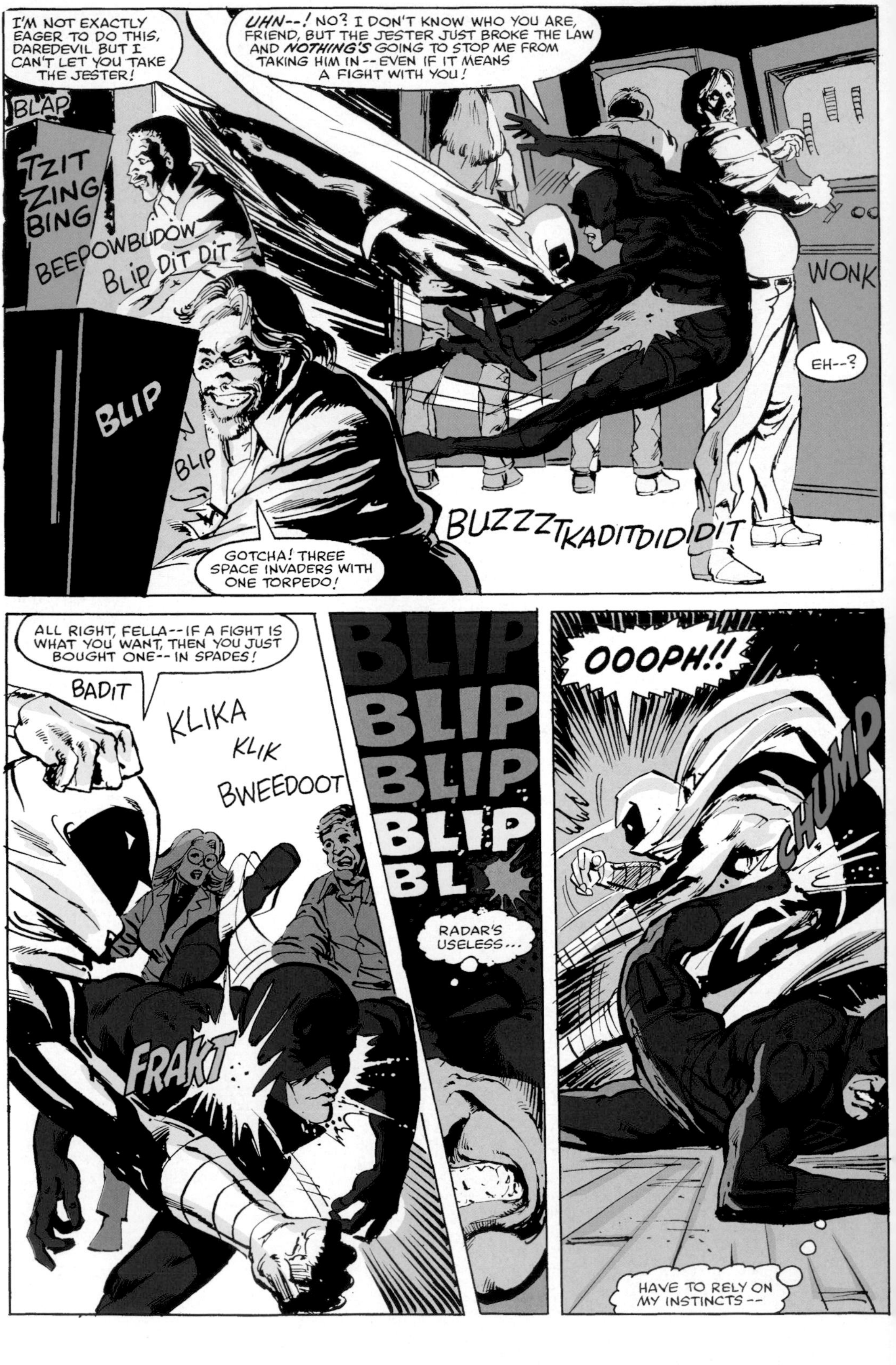
I'M NOT EXACTLY EAGER TO DO THIS, DAREDEVIL BUT I CAN'T LET YOU TAKE THE JESTER!
UHN--! NO? I DON'T KNOW WHO YOU ARE, FRIEND, BUT THE JESTER JUST BROKE THE LAW AND NOTHING'S GOING TO STOP ME FROM TAKING HIM IN -- EVEN IF IT MEANS A FIGHT WITH YOU!
BLAP
TZIT ZING BING
BEEPOWBUDOW
BLIP DIT DIT
WONK
EH--?
BLIP
BLIP
BUZZZT KADITDIDIDIT
GOTCHA! THREE SPACE INVADERS WITH ONE TORPEDO!
ALL RIGHT, FELLA-- IF A FIGHT IS WHAT YOU WANT, THEN YOU JUST BOUGHT ONE-- IN SPADES!
BADIT
KLIKA
KLIK
BWEEDOOT
FRAKT
BLIP BLIP BLIP BLIP BL
RADAR'S USELESS...
OOOPH!!
CHUMP
HAVE TO RELY ON MY INSTINCTS --

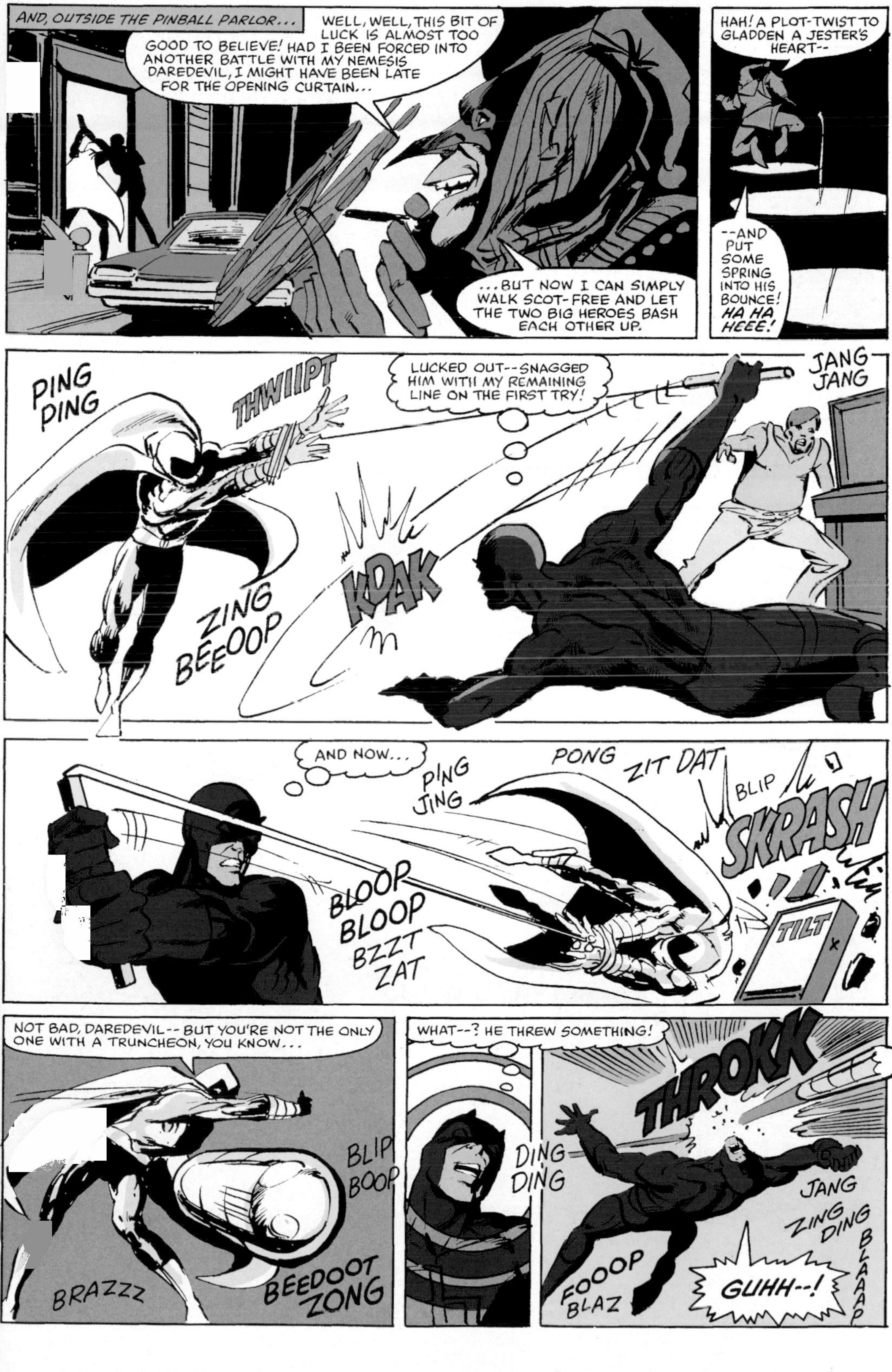

AND, OUTSIDE THE PINBALL PARLOR...
WELL, WELL, THIS BIT OF LUCK IS ALMOST TOO GOOD TO BELIEVE! HAD I BEEN FORCED INTO ANOTHER BATTLE WITH MY NEMESIS DAREDEVIL, I MIGHT HAVE BEEN LATE FOR THE OPENING CURTAIN...
...BUT NOW I CAN SIMPLY WALK SCOT-FREE AND LET THE TWO BIG HEROES BASH EACH OTHER UP.
HAH! A PLOT-TWIST TO GLADDEN A JESTER'S HEART--
--AND PUT SOME SPRING INTO HIS BOUNCE! HA HA HEEE!
PING PING
THWIIPT
LUCKED OUT--SNAGGED HIM WITH MY REMAINING LINE ON THE FIRST TRY!
JANG JANG
KDAK
ZING BEEEOOP
AND NOW...
PING JING
PONG
ZIT DAT
BLIP
SKRASH
BLOOP BLOOP BZZT ZAT
TILT
NOT BAD, DAREDEVIL--BUT YOU'RE NOT THE ONLY ONE WITH A TRUNCHEON, YOU KNOW...
BLIP BOOP
BRAZZZ
BEEDOOT ZONG
WHAT--? HE THREW SOMETHING!
DING DING
THROKK
JANG
ZING DING
BLAAAP
FOOOP BLAZ
GUHH--!

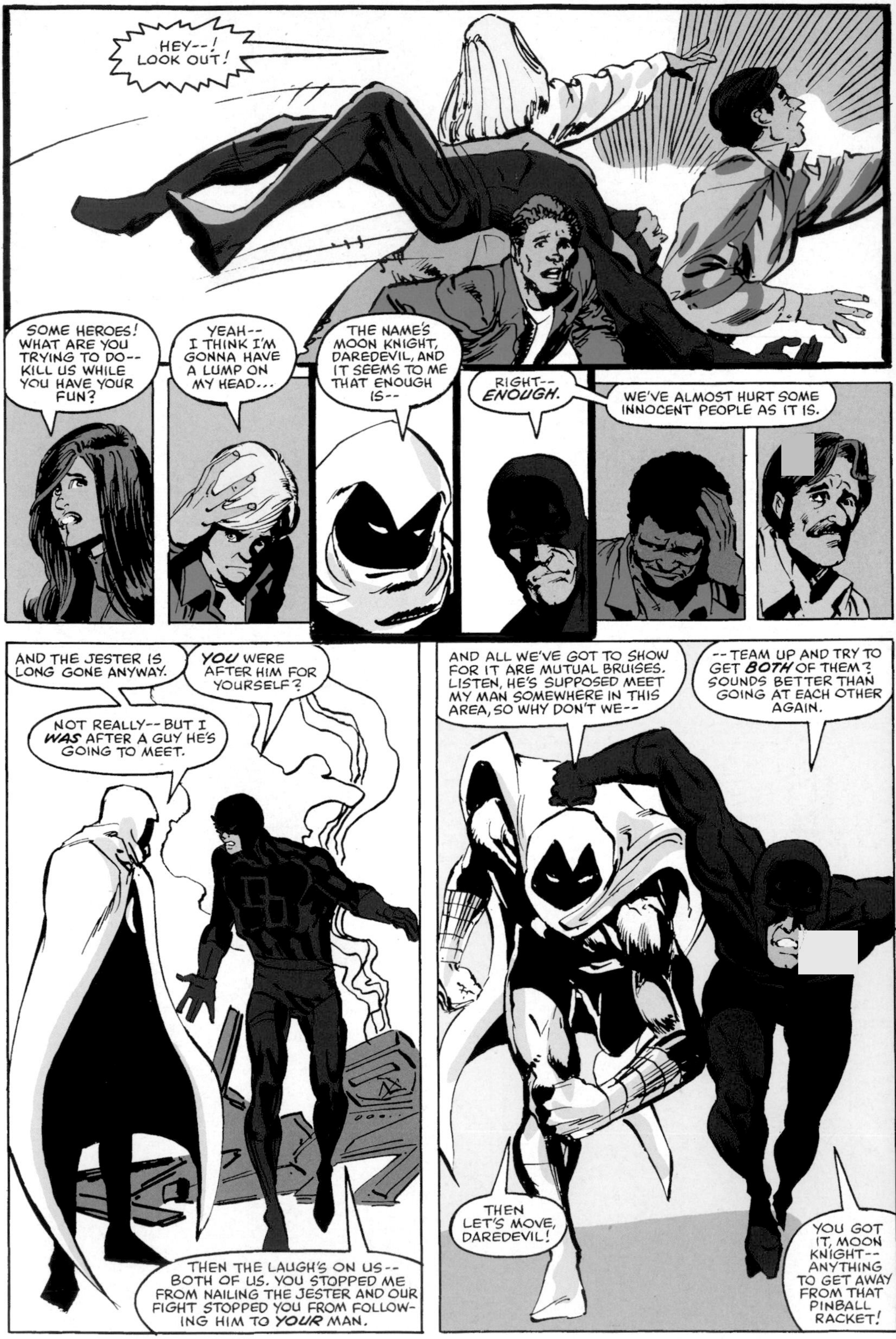
HEY--! LOOK OUT!
SOME HEROES! WHAT ARE YOU TRYING TO DO-- KILL US WHILE YOU HAVE YOUR FUN?
YEAH-- I THINK I'M GONNA HAVE A LUMP ON MY HEAD...
THE NAME'S MOON KNIGHT, DAREDEVIL, AND IT SEEMS TO ME THAT ENOUGH IS--
RIGHT-- ENOUGH.
WE'VE ALMOST HURT SOME INNOCENT PEOPLE AS IT IS.
AND THE JESTER IS LONG GONE ANYWAY.
YOU WERE AFTER HIM FOR YOURSELF?
NOT REALLY-- BUT I WAS AFTER A GUY HE'S GOING TO MEET.
THEN THE LAUGH'S ON US-- BOTH OF US. YOU STOPPED ME FROM NAILING THE JESTER AND OUR FIGHT STOPPED YOU FROM FOLLOWING HIM TO YOUR MAN.
AND ALL WE'VE GOT TO SHOW FOR IT ARE MUTUAL BRUISES. LISTEN, HE'S SUPPOSED MEET MY MAN SOMEWHERE IN THIS AREA, SO WHY DON'T WE--
--TEAM UP AND TRY TO GET BOTH OF THEM? SOUNDS BETTER THAN GOING AT EACH OTHER AGAIN.
THEN LET'S MOVE, DAREDEVIL!
YOU GOT IT, MOON KNIGHT-- ANYTHING TO GET AWAY FROM THAT PINBALL RACKET!

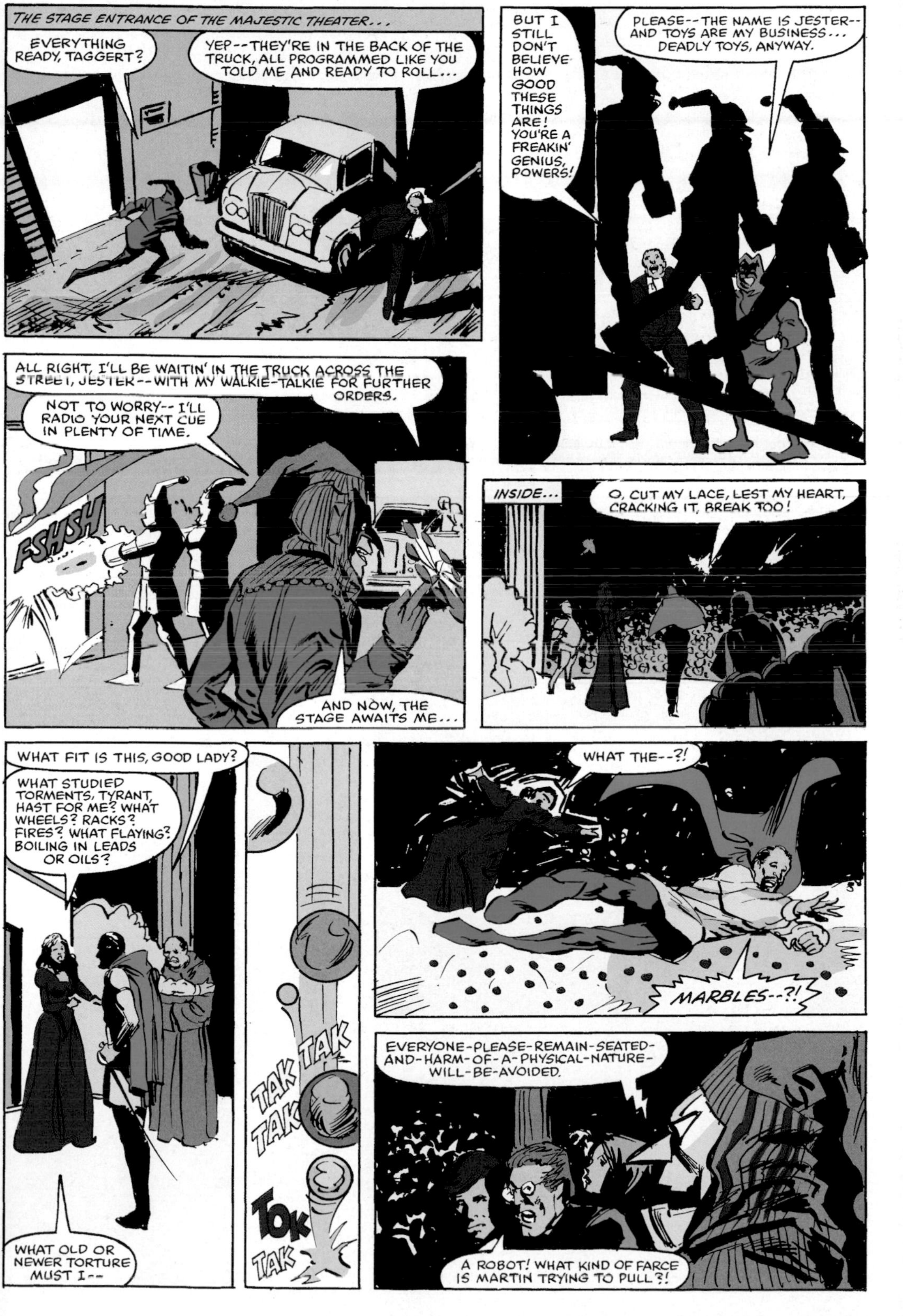
THE STAGE ENTRANCE OF THE MAJESTIC THEATER...
EVERYTHING READY, TAGGERT?
YEP--THEY'RE IN THE BACK OF THE TRUCK, ALL PROGRAMMED LIKE YOU TOLD ME AND READY TO ROLL...
BUT I STILL DON'T BELIEVE HOW GOOD THESE THINGS ARE! YOU'RE A FREAKIN' GENIUS, POWERS!
PLEASE--THE NAME IS JESTER--AND TOYS ARE MY BUSINESS... DEADLY TOYS, ANYWAY.
ALL RIGHT, I'LL BE WAITIN' IN THE TRUCK ACROSS THE STREET, JESTER--WITH MY WALKIE-TALKIE FOR FURTHER ORDERS.
NOT TO WORRY-- I'LL RADIO YOUR NEXT CUE IN PLENTY OF TIME.
FSHSH
AND NOW, THE STAGE AWAITS ME...
INSIDE...
O, CUT MY LACE, LEST MY HEART, CRACKING IT, BREAK TOO!
WHAT FIT IS THIS, GOOD LADY?
WHAT STUDIED TORMENTS, TYRANT, HAST FOR ME? WHAT WHEELS? RACKS? FIRES? WHAT FLAYING? BOILING IN LEADS OR OILS?
WHAT OLD OR NEWER TORTURE MUST I--
TAK TAK
TAK TAK
TOK
TAK
WHAT THE--?!
MARBLES--?!
EVERYONE-PLEASE-REMAIN-SEATED-AND-HARM-OF-A-PHYSICAL-NATURE-WILL-BE-AVOIDED.
A ROBOT! WHAT KIND OF FARCE IS MARTIN TRYING TO PULL?!

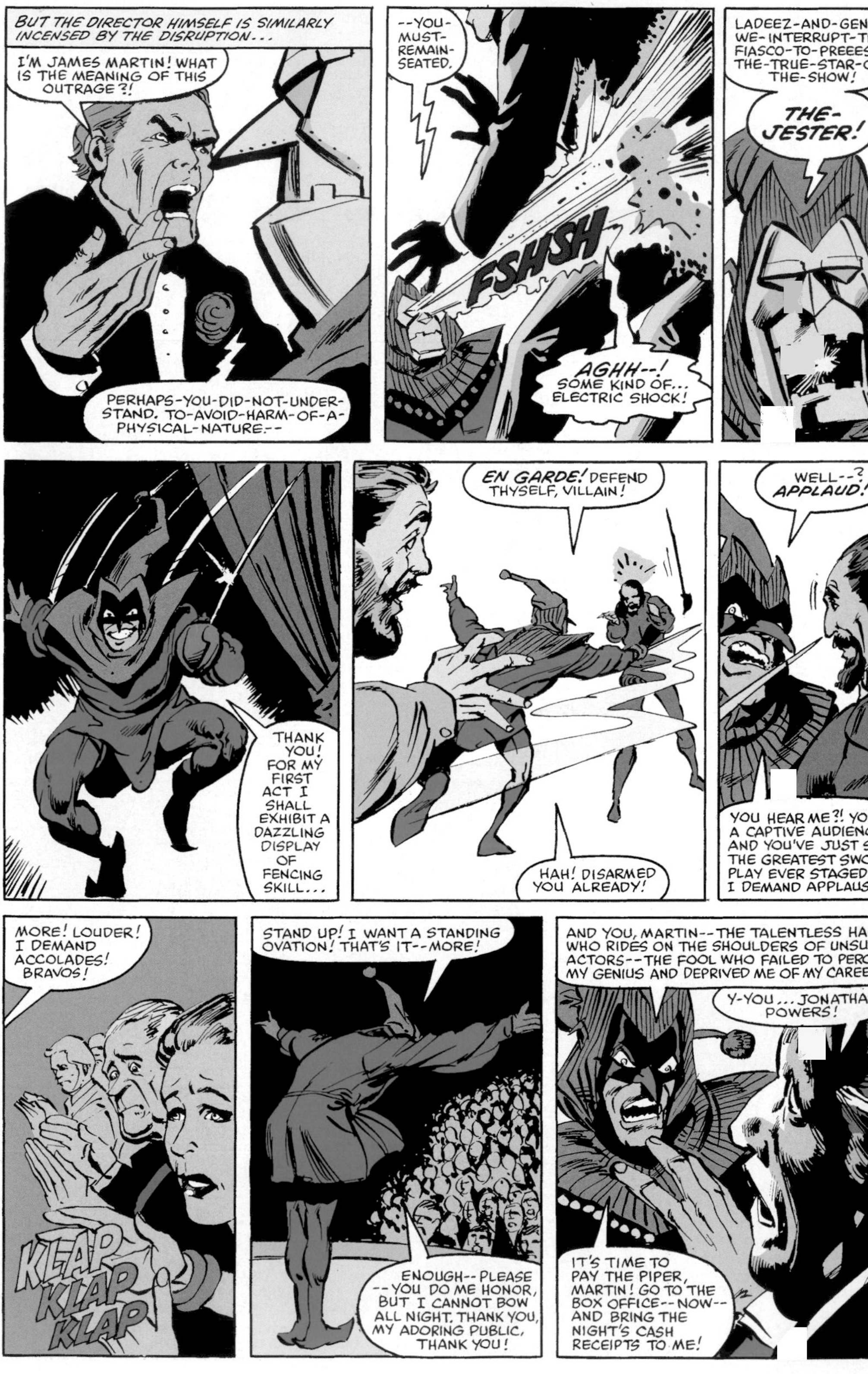
BUT THE DIRECTOR HIMSELF IS SIMILARLY INCENSED BY THE DISRUPTION...
I'M JAMES MARTIN! WHAT IS THE MEANING OF THIS OUTRAGE?!
PERHAPS-YOU-DID-NOT-UNDER-STAND. TO-AVOID-HARM-OF-A-PHYSICAL-NATURE--
--YOU-MUST-REMAIN-SEATED.
FSHSH
AGHH--! SOME KIND OF... ELECTRIC SHOCK!
LADEEZ-AND-GENMUN-WE-INTERRUPT-THIS-FIASCO-TO-PREEESENT-THE-TRUE-STAR-OF-THE-SHOW!
THE-JESTER!
THANK YOU! FOR MY FIRST ACT I SHALL EXHIBIT A DAZZLING DISPLAY OF FENCING SKILL...
EN GARDE! DEFEND THYSELF, VILLAIN!
HAH! DISARMED YOU ALREADY!
WELL--? APPLAUD!
YOU HEAR ME?! YOU'RE A CAPTIVE AUDIENCE AND YOU'VE JUST SEEN THE GREATEST SWORD-PLAY EVER STAGED! I DEMAND APPLAUSE!
MORE! LOUDER! I DEMAND ACCOLADES! BRAVOS!
KLAP KLAP KLAP
STAND UP! I WANT A STANDING OVATION! THAT'S IT--MORE!
ENOUGH--PLEASE--YOU DO ME HONOR, BUT I CANNOT BOW ALL NIGHT. THANK YOU, MY ADORING PUBLIC, THANK YOU!
AND YOU, MARTIN--THE TALENTLESS HACK WHO RIDES ON THE SHOULDERS OF UNSUNG ACTORS--THE FOOL WHO FAILED TO PERCEIVE MY GENIUS AND DEPRIVED ME OF MY CAREER--!
Y-YOU... JONATHAN POWERS!
IT'S TIME TO PAY THE PIPER, MARTIN! GO TO THE BOX OFFICE--NOW--AND BRING THE NIGHT'S CASH RECEIPTS TO ME!

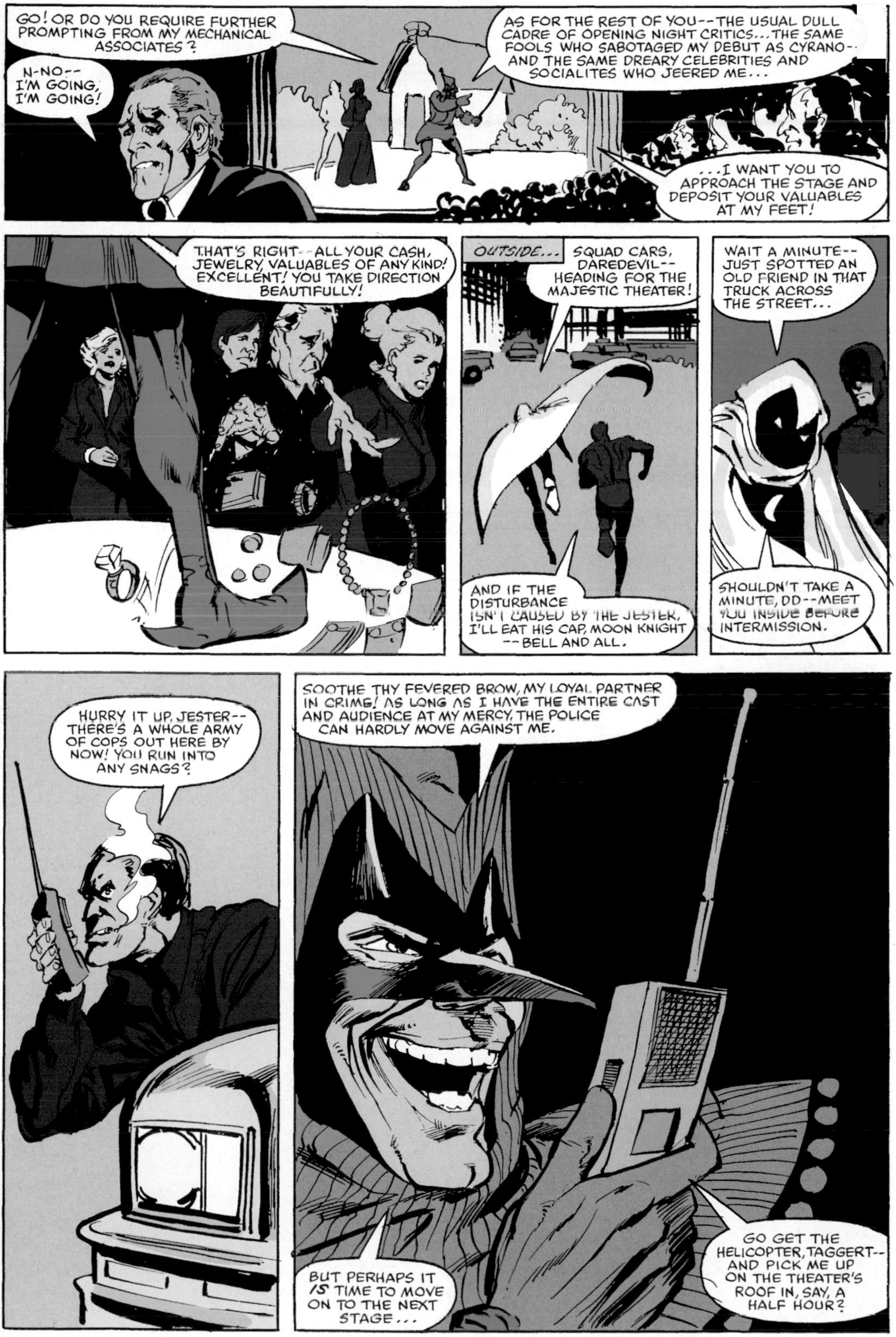
GO! OR DO YOU REQUIRE FURTHER PROMPTING FROM MY MECHANICAL ASSOCIATES?
N-NO-- I'M GOING, I'M GOING!
AS FOR THE REST OF YOU--THE USUAL DULL CADRE OF OPENING NIGHT CRITICS... THE SAME FOOLS WHO SABOTAGED MY DEBUT AS CYRANO-- AND THE SAME DREARY CELEBRITIES AND SOCIALITES WHO JEERED ME...
...I WANT YOU TO APPROACH THE STAGE AND DEPOSIT YOUR VALUABLES AT MY FEET!
THAT'S RIGHT--ALL YOUR CASH, JEWELRY, VALUABLES OF ANY KIND! EXCELLENT! YOU TAKE DIRECTION BEAUTIFULLY!
OUTSIDE...
SQUAD CARS, DAREDEVIL-- HEADING FOR THE MAJESTIC THEATER!
AND IF THE DISTURBANCE ISN'T CAUSED BY THE JESTER, I'LL EAT HIS CAP, MOON KNIGHT --BELL AND ALL.
WAIT A MINUTE-- JUST SPOTTED AN OLD FRIEND IN THAT TRUCK ACROSS THE STREET...
SHOULDN'T TAKE A MINUTE, DD--MEET YOU INSIDE BEFORE INTERMISSION.
HURRY IT UP, JESTER-- THERE'S A WHOLE ARMY OF COPS OUT HERE BY NOW! YOU RUN INTO ANY SNAGS?
SOOTHE THY FEVERED BROW, MY LOYAL PARTNER IN CRIME! AS LONG AS I HAVE THE ENTIRE CAST AND AUDIENCE AT MY MERCY, THE POLICE CAN HARDLY MOVE AGAINST ME.
BUT PERHAPS IT IS TIME TO MOVE ON TO THE NEXT STAGE...
GO GET THE HELICOPTER, TAGGERT-- AND PICK ME UP ON THE THEATER'S ROOF IN, SAY, A HALF HOUR?

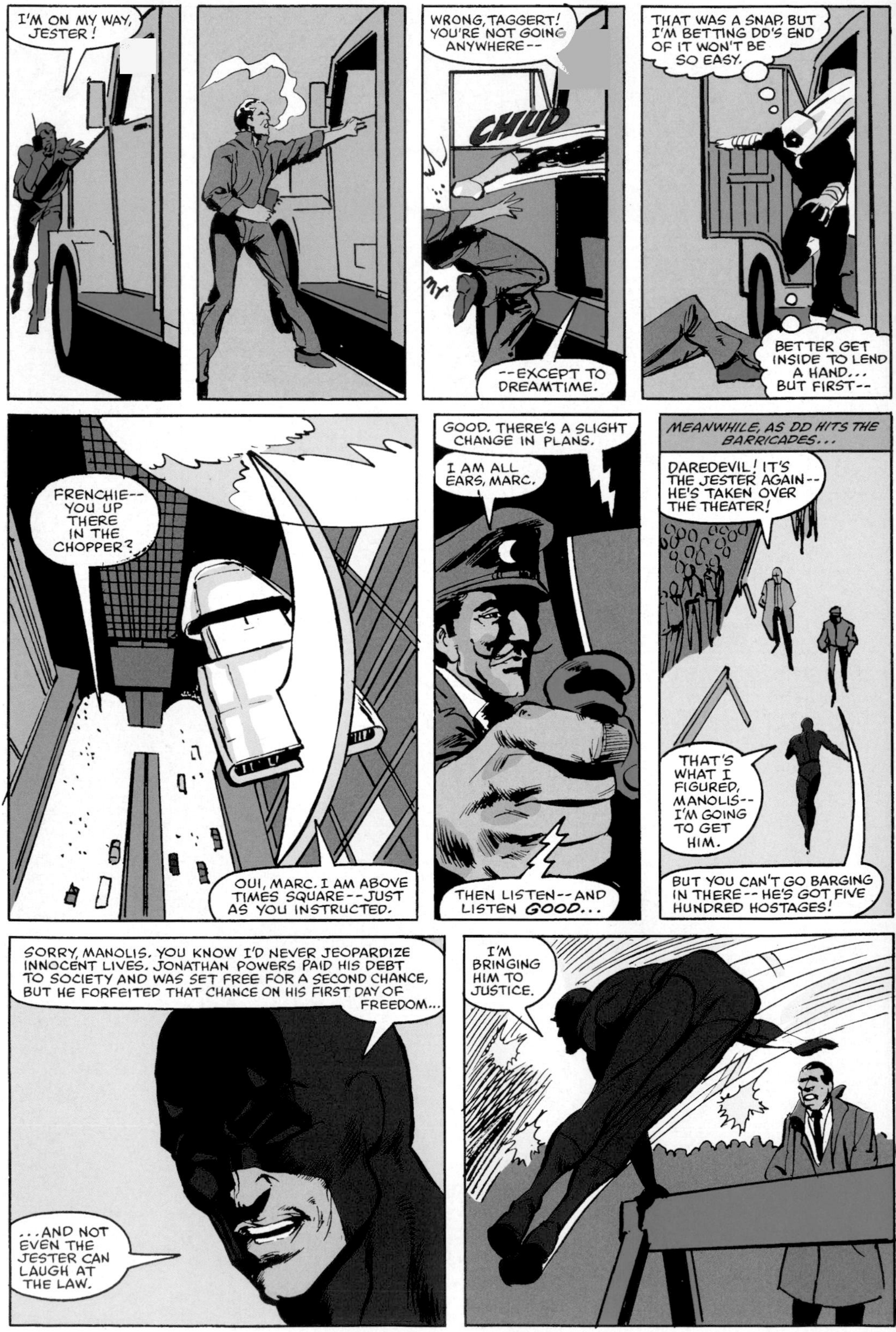
I'M ON MY WAY, JESTER!
WRONG, TAGGERT! YOU'RE NOT GOING ANYWHERE--
CHUD
--EXCEPT TO DREAMTIME.
THAT WAS A SNAP, BUT I'M BETTING DD'S END OF IT WON'T BE SO EASY.
BETTER GET INSIDE TO LEND A HAND... BUT FIRST--
FRENCHIE-- YOU UP THERE IN THE CHOPPER?
OUI, MARC. I AM ABOVE TIMES SQUARE--JUST AS YOU INSTRUCTED.
GOOD. THERE'S A SLIGHT CHANGE IN PLANS.
I AM ALL EARS, MARC.
THEN LISTEN--AND LISTEN GOOD...
MEANWHILE, AS DD HITS THE BARRICADES...
DAREDEVIL! IT'S THE JESTER AGAIN-- HE'S TAKEN OVER THE THEATER!
THAT'S WHAT I FIGURED, MANOLIS-- I'M GOING TO GET HIM.
BUT YOU CAN'T GO BARGING IN THERE-- HE'S GOT FIVE HUNDRED HOSTAGES!
SORRY, MANOLIS. YOU KNOW I'D NEVER JEOPARDIZE INNOCENT LIVES. JONATHAN POWERS PAID HIS DEBT TO SOCIETY AND WAS SET FREE FOR A SECOND CHANCE, BUT HE FORFEITED THAT CHANCE ON HIS FIRST DAY OF FREEDOM...
...AND NOT EVEN THE JESTER CAN LAUGH AT THE LAW.
I'M BRINGING HIM TO JUSTICE.

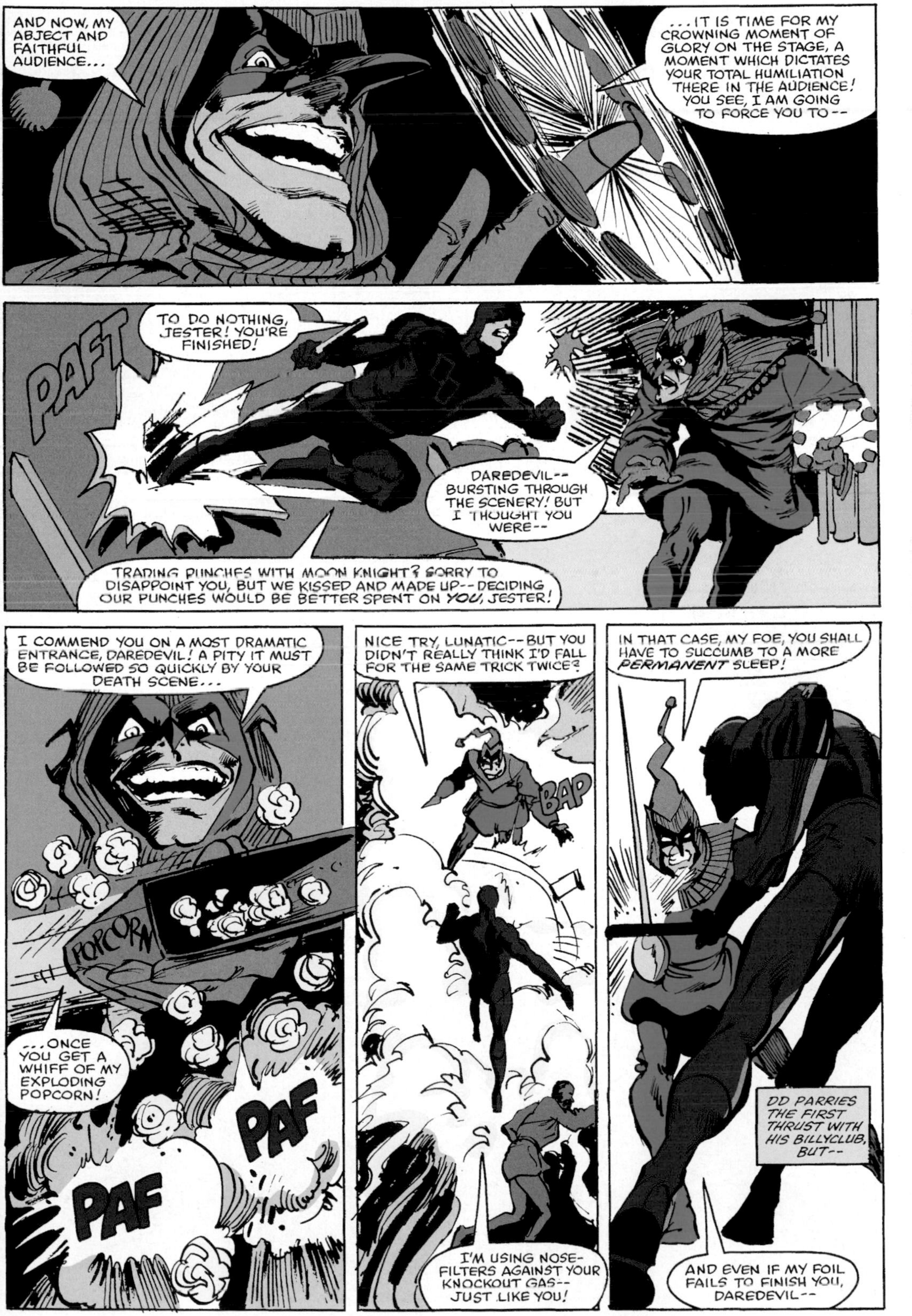
AND NOW, MY ABJECT AND FAITHFUL AUDIENCE...
...IT IS TIME FOR MY CROWNING MOMENT OF GLORY ON THE STAGE, A MOMENT WHICH DICTATES YOUR TOTAL HUMILIATION THERE IN THE AUDIENCE! YOU SEE, I AM GOING TO FORCE YOU TO--
PAFT
TO DO NOTHING, JESTER! YOU'RE FINISHED!
DAREDEVIL--BURSTING THROUGH THE SCENERY! BUT I THOUGHT YOU WERE--
TRADING PUNCHES WITH MOON KNIGHT? SORRY TO DISAPPOINT YOU, BUT WE KISSED AND MADE UP--DECIDING OUR PUNCHES WOULD BE BETTER SPENT ON YOU, JESTER!
I COMMEND YOU ON A MOST DRAMATIC ENTRANCE, DAREDEVIL! A PITY IT MUST BE FOLLOWED SO QUICKLY BY YOUR DEATH SCENE...
POPCORN
...ONCE YOU GET A WHIFF OF MY EXPLODING POPCORN!
PAF
PAF
NICE TRY, LUNATIC--BUT YOU DIDN'T REALLY THINK I'D FALL FOR THE SAME TRICK TWICE?
BAP
I'M USING NOSE-FILTERS AGAINST YOUR KNOCKOUT GAS--JUST LIKE YOU!
IN THAT CASE, MY FOE, YOU SHALL HAVE TO SUCCUMB TO A MORE PERMANENT SLEEP!
DD PARRIES THE FIRST THRUST WITH HIS BILLYCLUB, BUT--
AND EVEN IF MY FOIL FAILS TO FINISH YOU, DAREDEVIL--

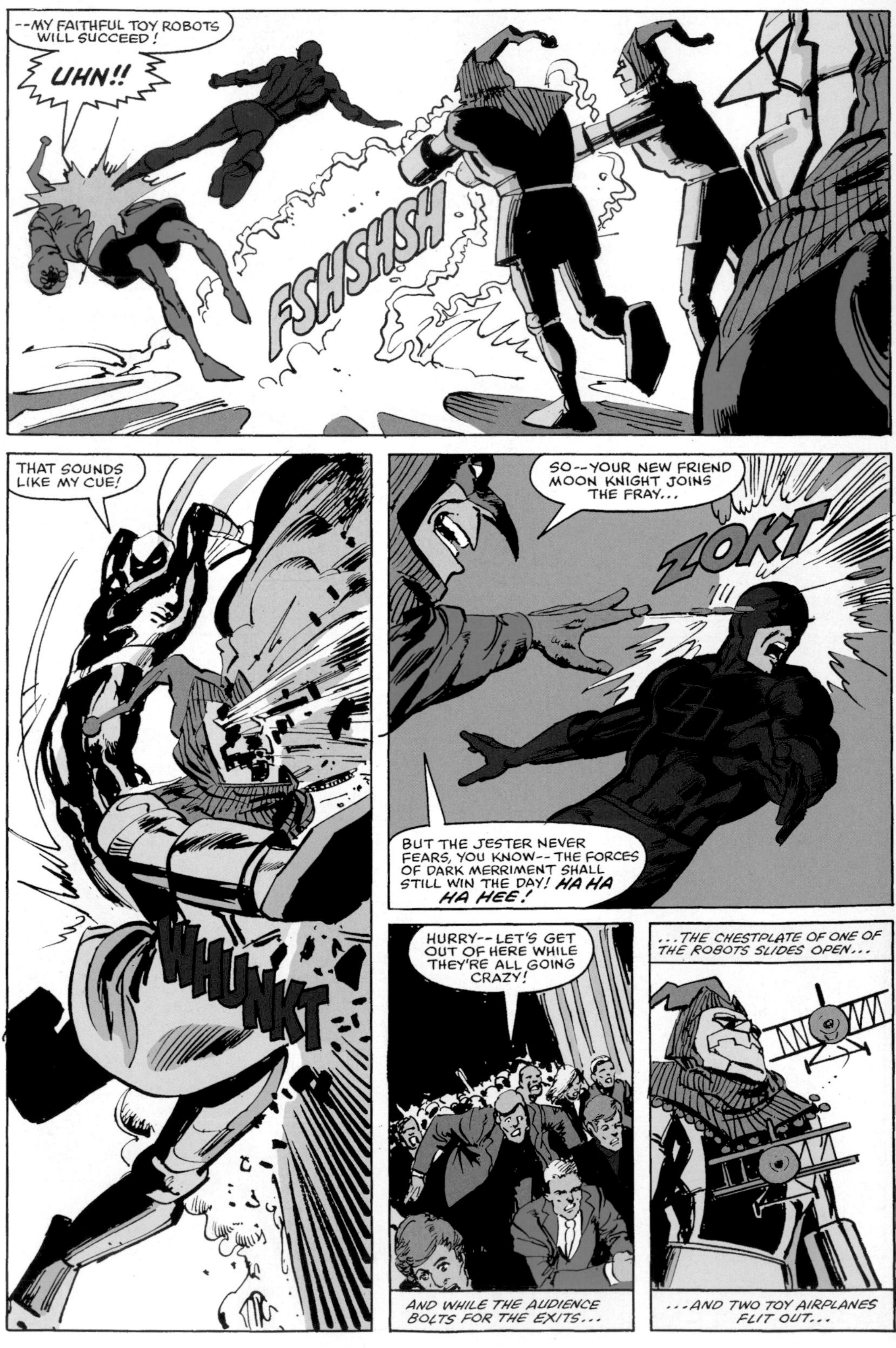
--MY FAITHFUL TOY ROBOTS WILL SUCCEED!
UHN!!
FSHSHSH
THAT SOUNDS LIKE MY CUE!
WHUNKT
SO--YOUR NEW FRIEND MOON KNIGHT JOINS THE FRAY...
ZOKT
BUT THE JESTER NEVER FEARS, YOU KNOW-- THE FORCES OF DARK MERRIMENT SHALL STILL WIN THE DAY! HA HA HA HEE!
HURRY--LET'S GET OUT OF HERE WHILE THEY'RE ALL GOING CRAZY!
AND WHILE THE AUDIENCE BOLTS FOR THE EXITS...
...THE CHESTPLATE OF ONE OF THE ROBOTS SLIDES OPEN...
...AND TWO TOY AIRPLANES FLIT OUT...

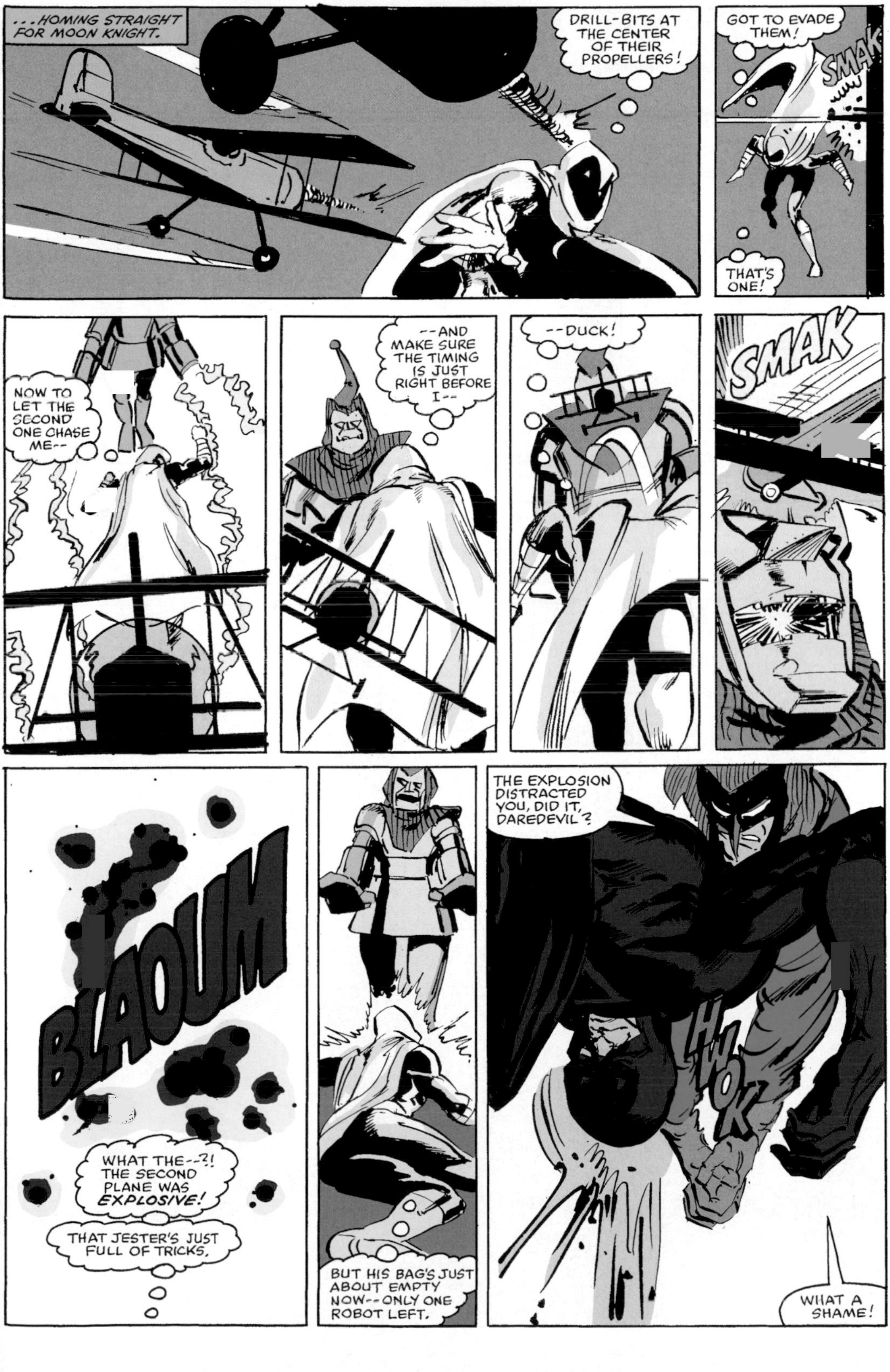

...HOMING STRAIGHT FOR MOON KNIGHT.
DRILL-BITS AT THE CENTER OF THEIR PROPELLERS!
GOT TO EVADE THEM!
SMAK
THAT'S ONE!
NOW TO LET THE SECOND ONE CHASE ME--
--AND MAKE SURE THE TIMING IS JUST RIGHT BEFORE I--
--DUCK!
SMAK
BLAOUM
WHAT THE--?! THE SECOND PLANE WAS EXPLOSIVE!
THAT JESTER'S JUST FULL OF TRICKS.
BUT HIS BAG'S JUST ABOUT EMPTY NOW--ONLY ONE ROBOT LEFT.
THE EXPLOSION DISTRACTED YOU, DID IT, DAREDEVIL?
HWOK
WHAT A SHAME!

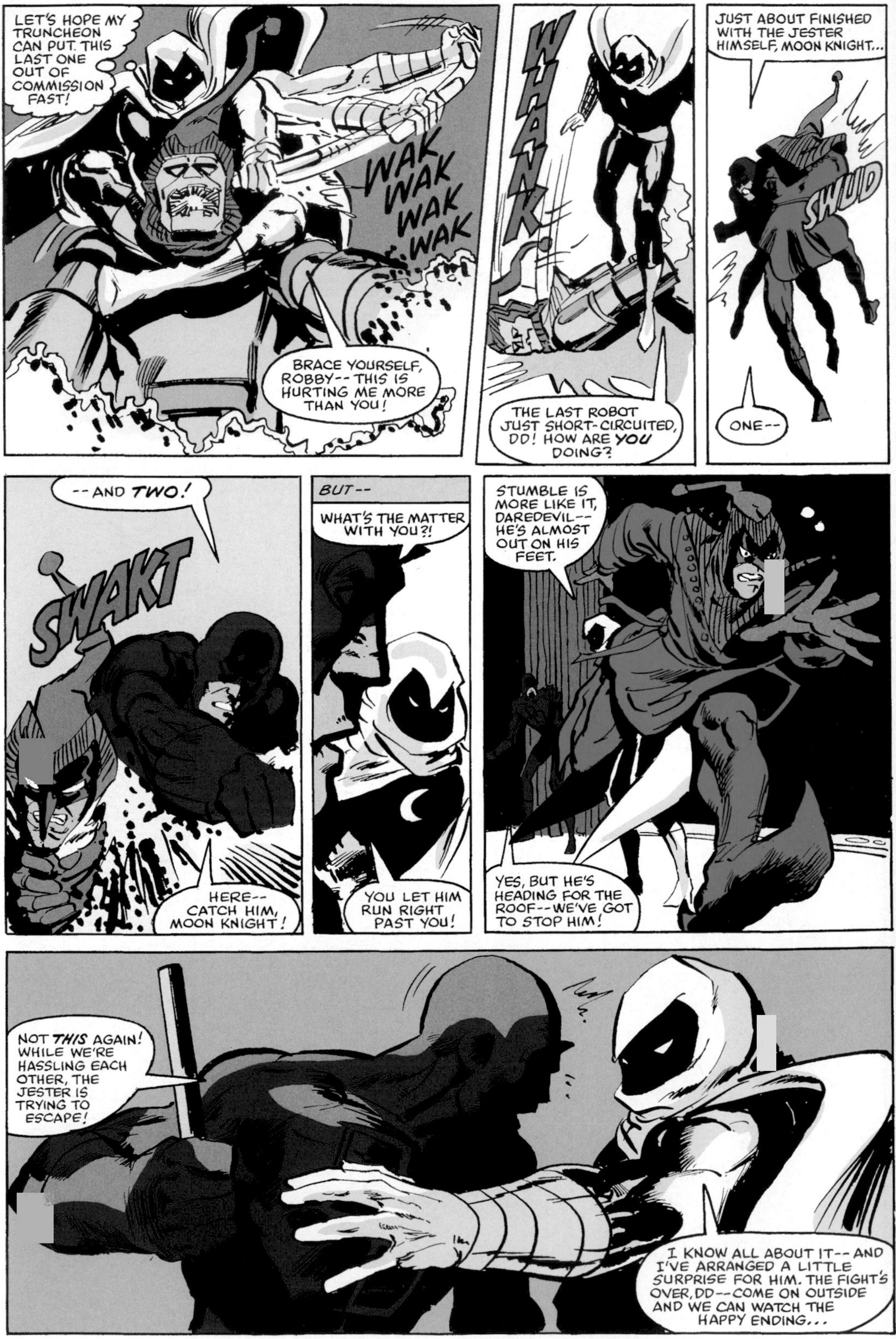
LET'S HOPE MY TRUNCHEON CAN PUT THIS LAST ONE OUT OF COMMISSION FAST!
WAK WAK WAK WAK
BRACE YOURSELF, ROBBY-- THIS IS HURTING ME MORE THAN YOU!
WHANK
THE LAST ROBOT JUST SHORT-CIRCUITED, DD! HOW ARE YOU DOING?
JUST ABOUT FINISHED WITH THE JESTER HIMSELF, MOON KNIGHT...
SWUD
ONE--
--AND TWO!
SWAKT
HERE-- CATCH HIM, MOON KNIGHT!
BUT--
WHAT'S THE MATTER WITH YOU?!
YOU LET HIM RUN RIGHT PAST YOU!
STUMBLE IS MORE LIKE IT, DAREDEVIL-- HE'S ALMOST OUT ON HIS FEET.
YES, BUT HE'S HEADING FOR THE ROOF--WE'VE GOT TO STOP HIM!
NOT THIS AGAIN! WHILE WE'RE HASSLING EACH OTHER, THE JESTER IS TRYING TO ESCAPE!
I KNOW ALL ABOUT IT-- AND I'VE ARRANGED A LITTLE SURPRISE FOR HIM. THE FIGHT'S OVER, DD--COME ON OUTSIDE AND WE CAN WATCH THE HAPPY ENDING...

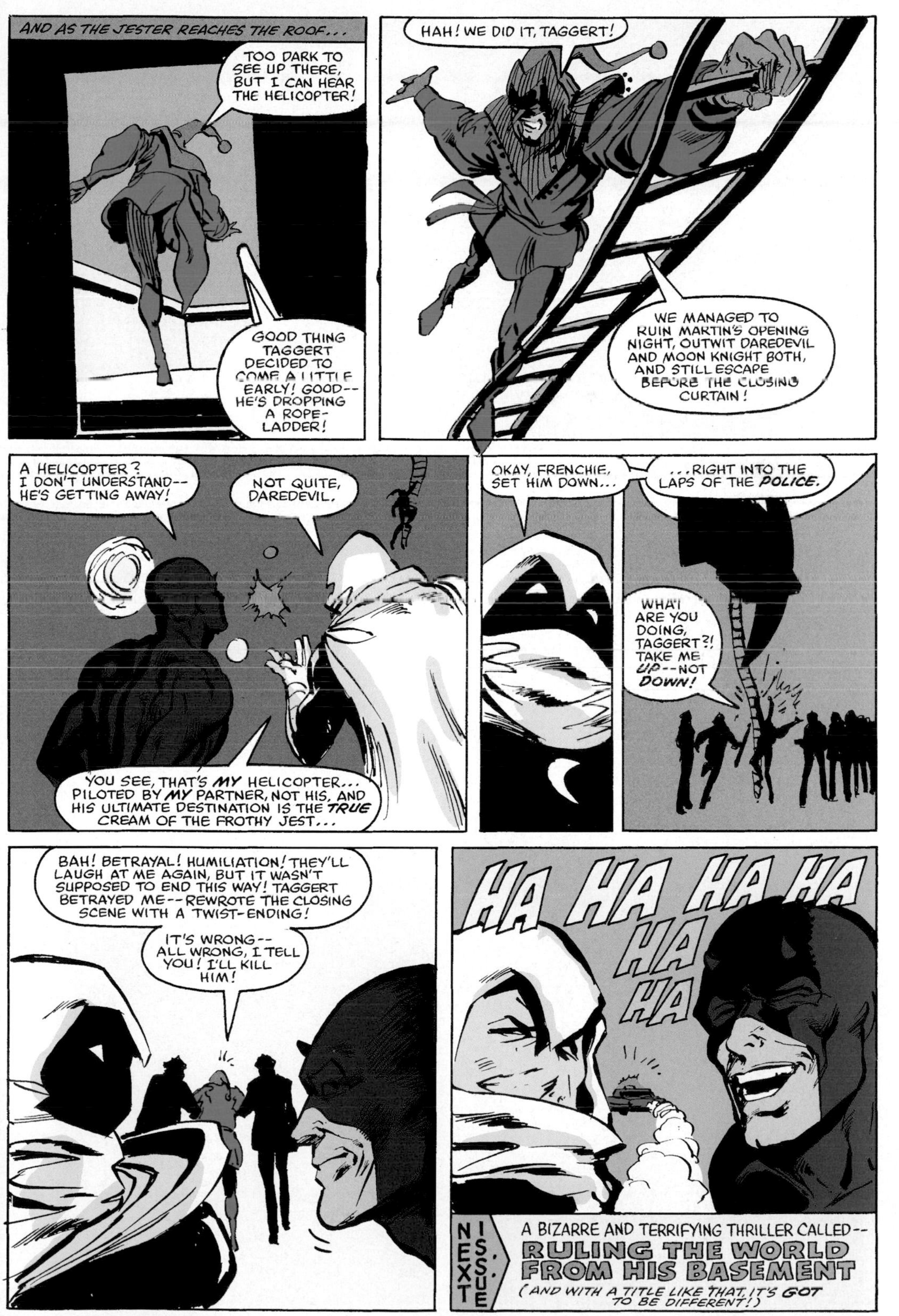
AND AS THE JESTER REACHES THE ROOF...
TOO DARK TO SEE UP THERE, BUT I CAN HEAR THE HELICOPTER!
GOOD THING TAGGERT DECIDED TO COME A LITTLE EARLY! GOOD-- HE'S DROPPING A ROPE-LADDER!
HAH! WE DID IT, TAGGERT!
WE MANAGED TO RUIN MARTIN'S OPENING NIGHT, OUTWIT DAREDEVIL AND MOON KNIGHT BOTH, AND STILL ESCAPE BEFORE THE CLOSING CURTAIN!
A HELICOPTER? I DON'T UNDERSTAND-- HE'S GETTING AWAY!
NOT QUITE, DAREDEVIL.
YOU SEE, THAT'S MY HELICOPTER... PILOTED BY MY PARTNER, NOT HIS, AND HIS ULTIMATE DESTINATION IS THE TRUE CREAM OF THE FROTHY JEST...
OKAY, FRENCHIE, SET HIM DOWN...
...RIGHT INTO THE LAPS OF THE POLICE.
WHAT ARE YOU DOING, TAGGERT?! TAKE ME UP--NOT DOWN!
BAH! BETRAYAL! HUMILIATION! THEY'LL LAUGH AT ME AGAIN, BUT IT WASN'T SUPPOSED TO END THIS WAY! TAGGERT BETRAYED ME--REWROTE THE CLOSING SCENE WITH A TWIST-ENDING!
IT'S WRONG-- ALL WRONG, I TELL YOU! I'LL KILL HIM!
HA HA HA HA HA
HA
HA
NEXT ISSUE
A BIZARRE AND TERRIFYING THRILLER CALLED--
RULING THE WORLD FROM HIS BASEMENT
(AND WITH A TITLE LIKE THAT, IT'S GOT TO BE DIFFERENT!)

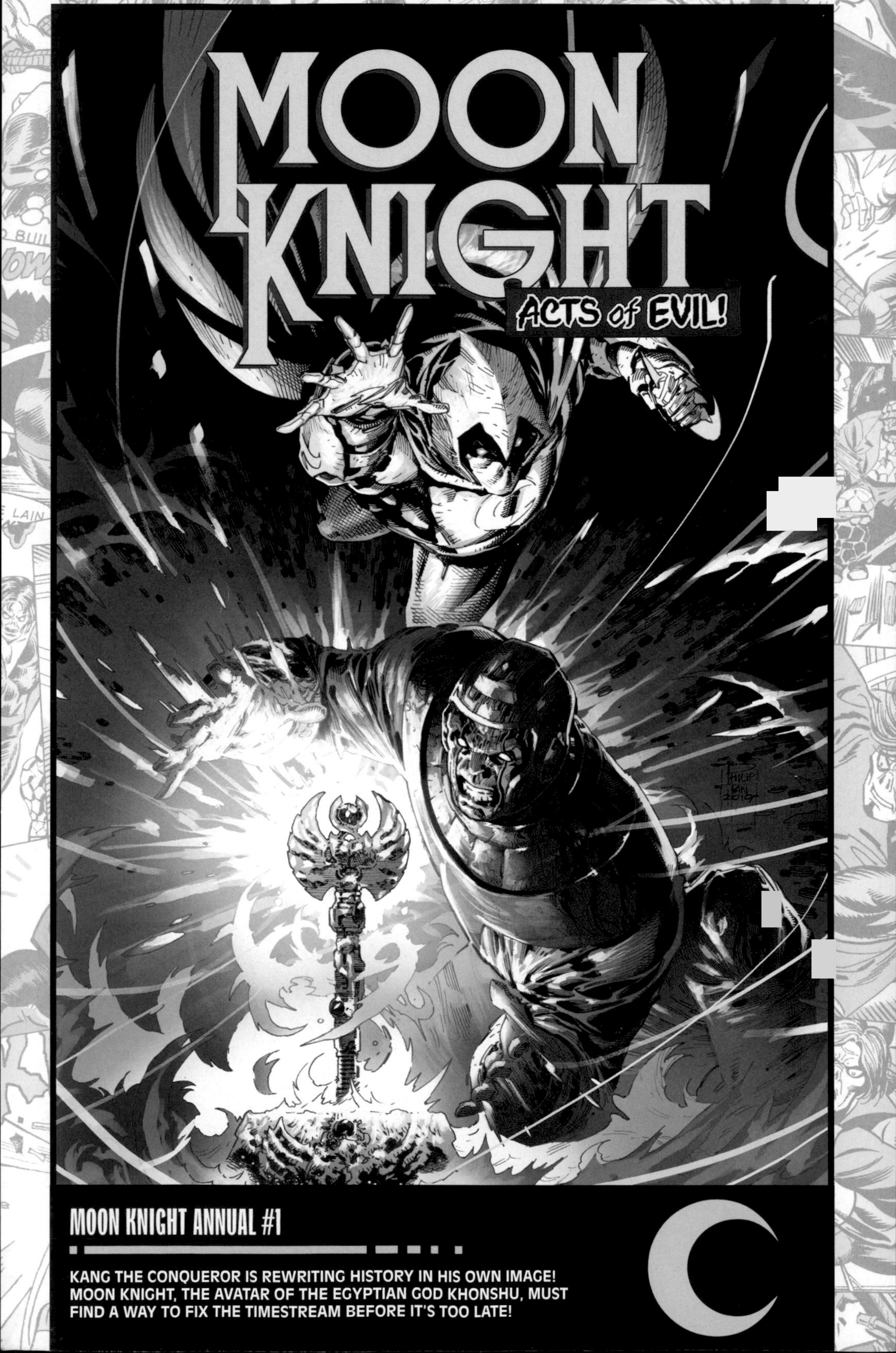
MOON KNIGHT
ACTS of EVIL!

MOON KNIGHT ANNUAL #1

KANG THE CONQUEROR IS REWRITING HISTORY IN HIS OWN IMAGE! MOON KNIGHT, THE AVATAR OF THE EGYPTIAN GOD KHONSHU, MUST FIND A WAY TO FIX THE TIMESTREAM BEFORE IT'S TOO LATE!

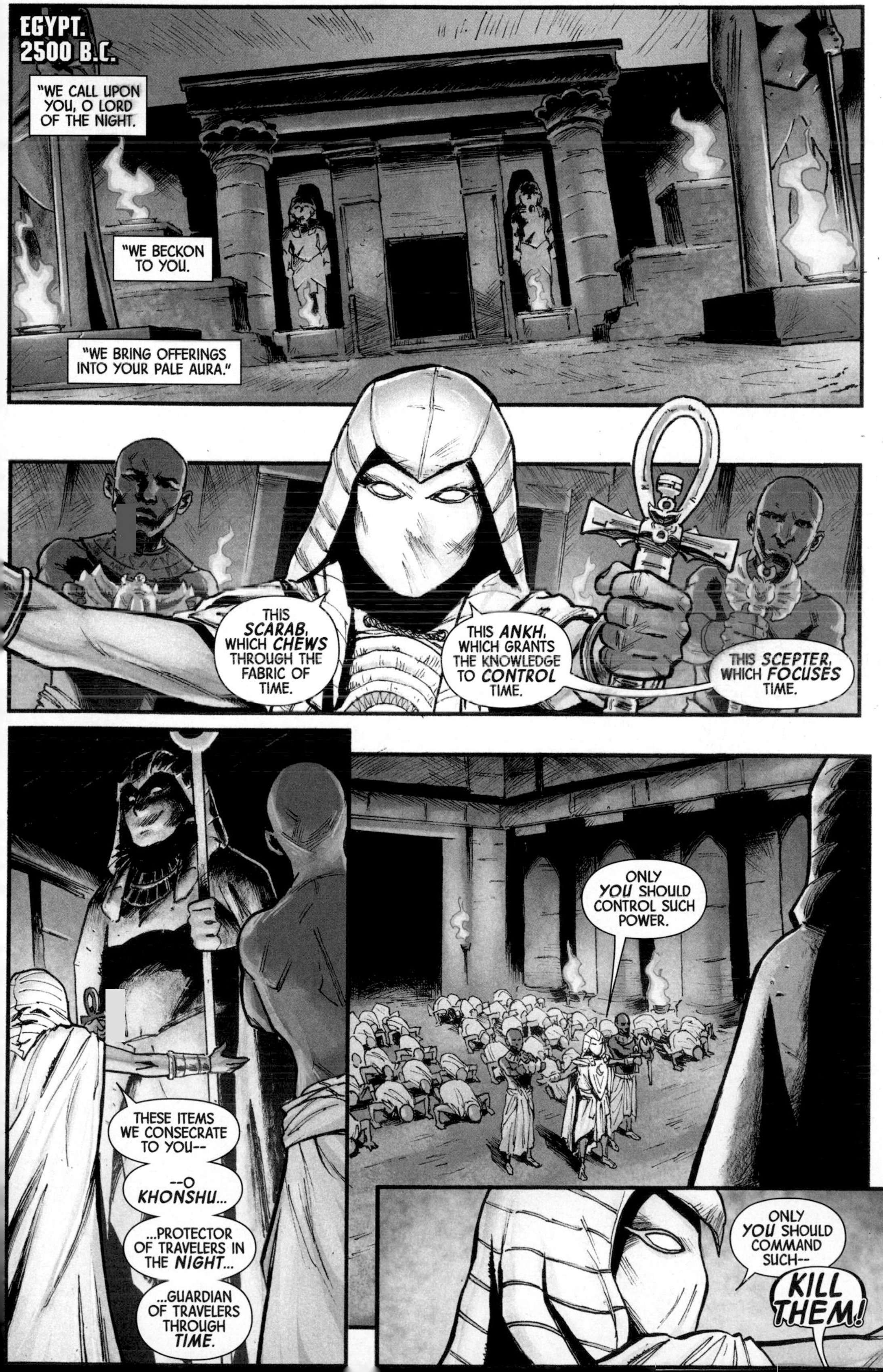
EGYPT. 2500 B.C.
"WE CALL UPON YOU, O LORD OF THE NIGHT.
"WE BECKON TO YOU.
"WE BRING OFFERINGS INTO YOUR PALE AURA."
THIS SCARAB, WHICH CHEWS THROUGH THE FABRIC OF TIME.
THIS ANKH, WHICH GRANTS THE KNOWLEDGE TO CONTROL TIME.
THIS SCEPTER, WHICH FOCUSES TIME.
THESE ITEMS WE CONSECRATE TO YOU--
--O KHONSHU...
...PROTECTOR OF TRAVELERS IN THE NIGHT...
...GUARDIAN OF TRAVELERS THROUGH TIME.
ONLY YOU SHOULD CONTROL SUCH POWER.
ONLY YOU SHOULD COMMAND SUCH--
KILL THEM!

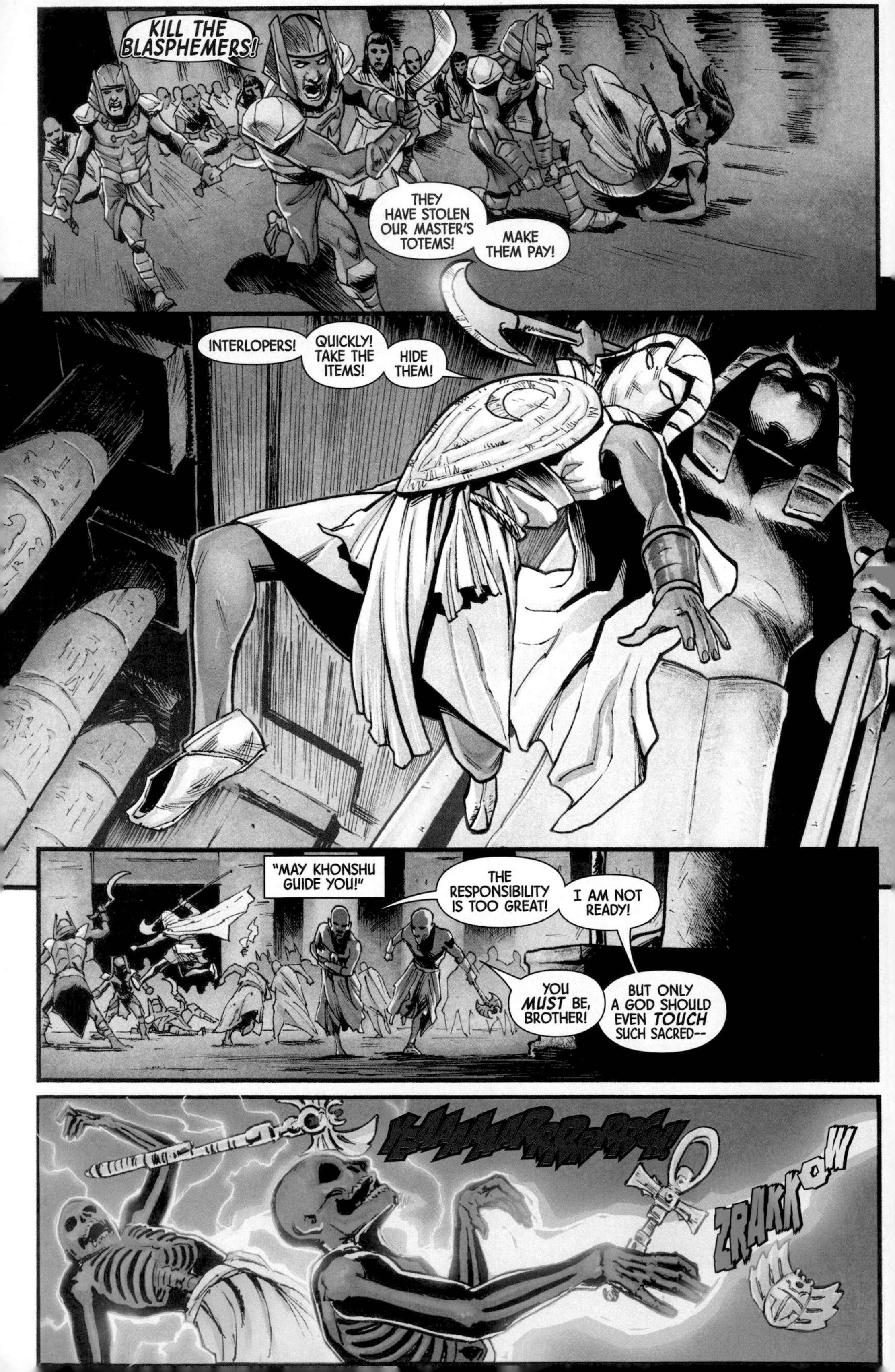
KILL THE BLASPHEMERS!
THEY HAVE STOLEN OUR MASTER'S TOTEMS!
MAKE THEM PAY!
INTERLOPERS!
QUICKLY! TAKE THE ITEMS!
HIDE THEM!
"MAY KHONSHU GUIDE YOU!"
THE RESPONSIBILITY IS TOO GREAT!
I AM NOT READY!
YOU MUST BE, BROTHER!
BUT ONLY A GOD SHOULD EVEN TOUCH SUCH SACRED--
ZRAKKOW

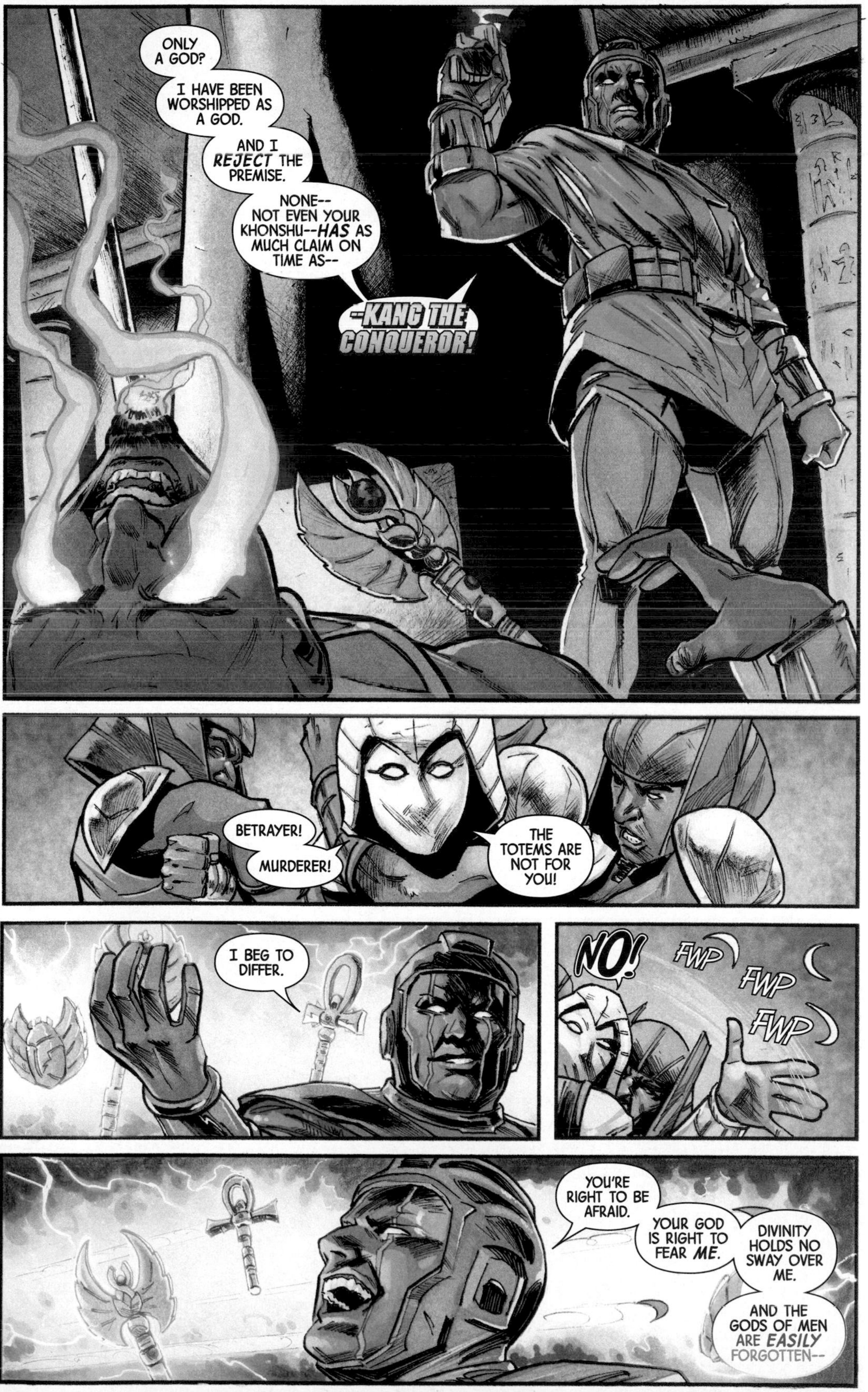
ONLY A GOD?
I HAVE BEEN WORSHIPPED AS A GOD.
AND I REJECT THE PREMISE.
NONE-- NOT EVEN YOUR KHONSHU--HAS AS MUCH CLAIM ON TIME AS--
--KANG THE CONQUEROR!
BETRAYER!
MURDERER!
THE TOTEMS ARE NOT FOR YOU!
I BEG TO DIFFER.
NO!
FWP
FWP
FWP
YOU'RE RIGHT TO BE AFRAID.
YOUR GOD IS RIGHT TO FEAR ME.
DIVINITY HOLDS NO SWAY OVER ME.
AND THE GODS OF MEN ARE EASILY FORGOTTEN--

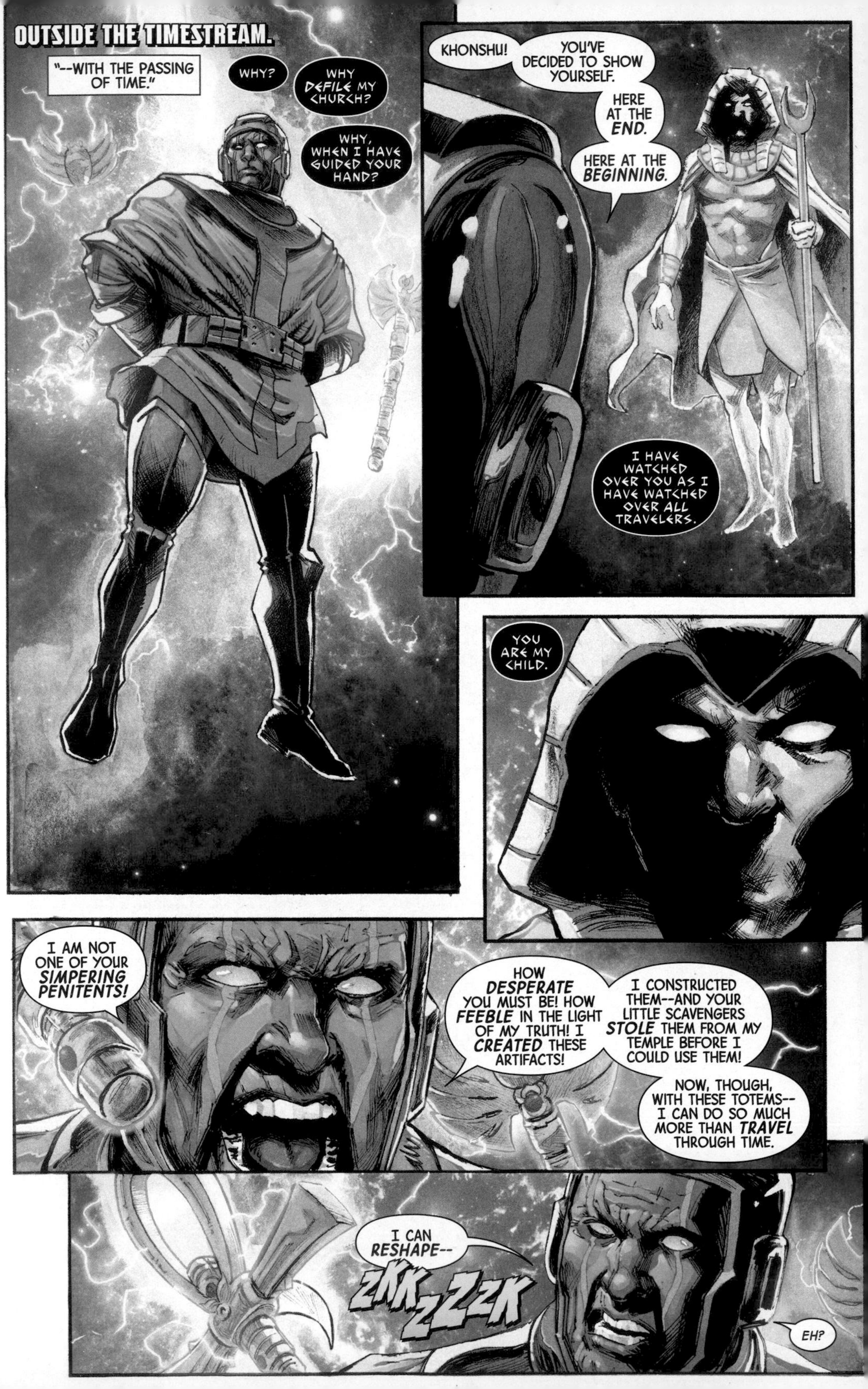
OUTSIDE THE TIMESTREAM.
"--WITH THE PASSING OF TIME."
WHY?
WHY DEFILE MY CHURCH?
WHY, WHEN I HAVE GUIDED YOUR HAND?
KHONSHU!
YOU'VE DECIDED TO SHOW YOURSELF.
HERE AT THE END.
HERE AT THE BEGINNING.
I HAVE WATCHED OVER YOU AS I HAVE WATCHED OVER ALL TRAVELERS.
YOU ARE MY CHILD.
I AM NOT ONE OF YOUR SIMPERING PENITENTS!
HOW DESPERATE YOU MUST BE! HOW FEEBLE IN THE LIGHT OF MY TRUTH! I CREATED THESE ARTIFACTS!
I CONSTRUCTED THEM--AND YOUR LITTLE SCAVENGERS STOLE THEM FROM MY TEMPLE BEFORE I COULD USE THEM!
NOW, THOUGH, WITH THESE TOTEMS-- I CAN DO SO MUCH MORE THAN TRAVEL THROUGH TIME.
I CAN RESHAPE--
ZKKZZZK
EH?

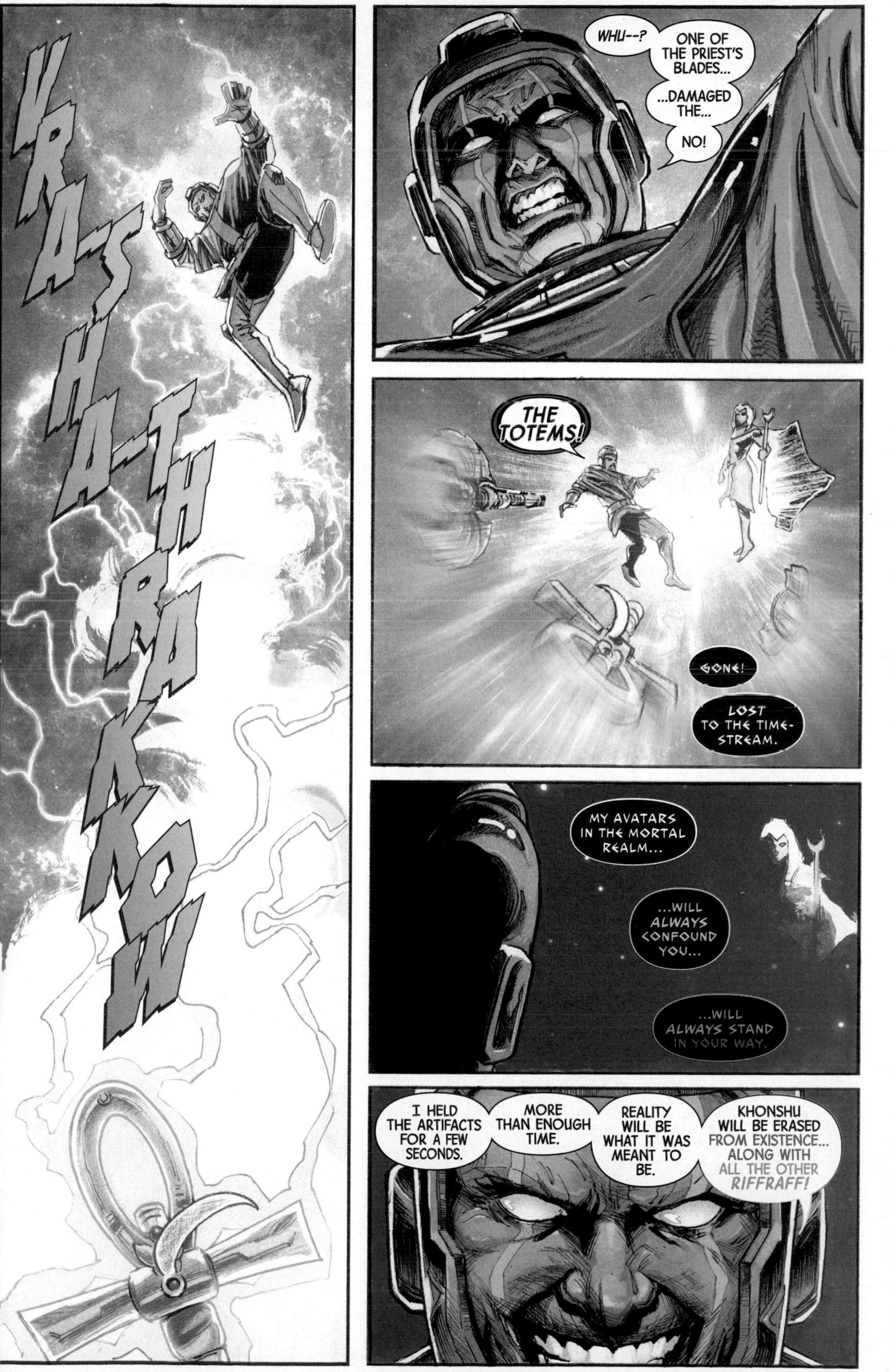
VRA-SHHA-THRAKKOW
WHU--?
ONE OF THE PRIEST'S BLADES...
...DAMAGED THE...
NO!
THE TOTEMS!
GONE!
LOST TO THE TIME-STREAM.
MY AVATARS IN THE MORTAL REALM...
...WILL ALWAYS CONFOUND YOU...
...WILL ALWAYS STAND IN YOUR WAY.
I HELD THE ARTIFACTS FOR A FEW SECONDS.
MORE THAN ENOUGH TIME.
REALITY WILL BE WHAT IT WAS MEANT TO BE.
KHONSHU WILL BE ERASED FROM EXISTENCE... ALONG WITH ALL THE OTHER RIFFRAFF!

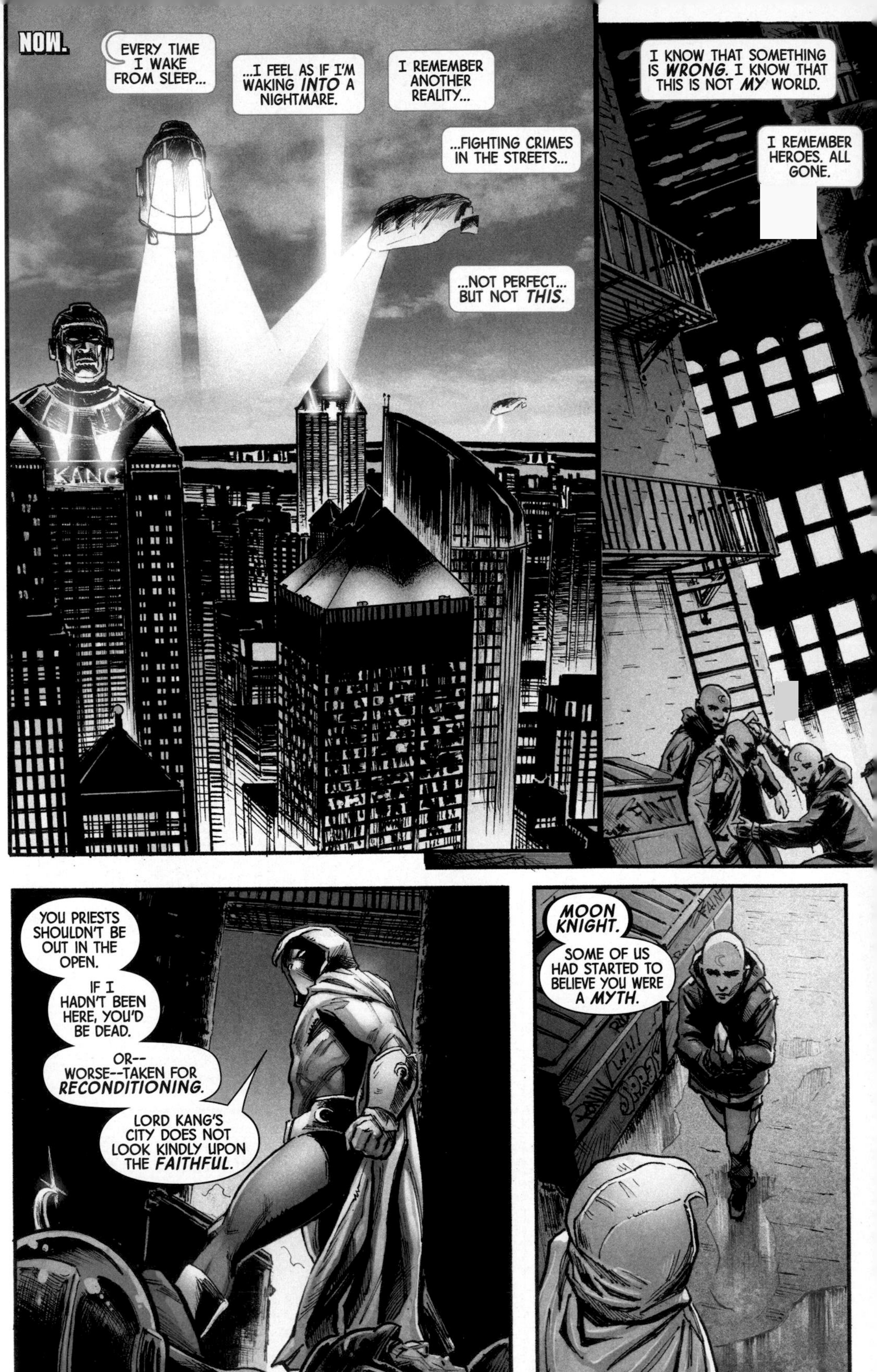
NOW.
EVERY TIME I WAKE FROM SLEEP...
...I FEEL AS IF I'M WAKING INTO A NIGHTMARE.
I REMEMBER ANOTHER REALITY...
...FIGHTING CRIMES IN THE STREETS...
...NOT PERFECT... BUT NOT THIS.
KANG
I KNOW THAT SOMETHING IS WRONG. I KNOW THAT THIS IS NOT MY WORLD.
I REMEMBER HEROES. ALL GONE.
YOU PRIESTS SHOULDN'T BE OUT IN THE OPEN.
IF I HADN'T BEEN HERE, YOU'D BE DEAD.
OR-- WORSE--TAKEN FOR RECONDITIONING.
LORD KANG'S CITY DOES NOT LOOK KINDLY UPON THE FAITHFUL.
MOON KNIGHT.
SOME OF US HAD STARTED TO BELIEVE YOU WERE A MYTH.

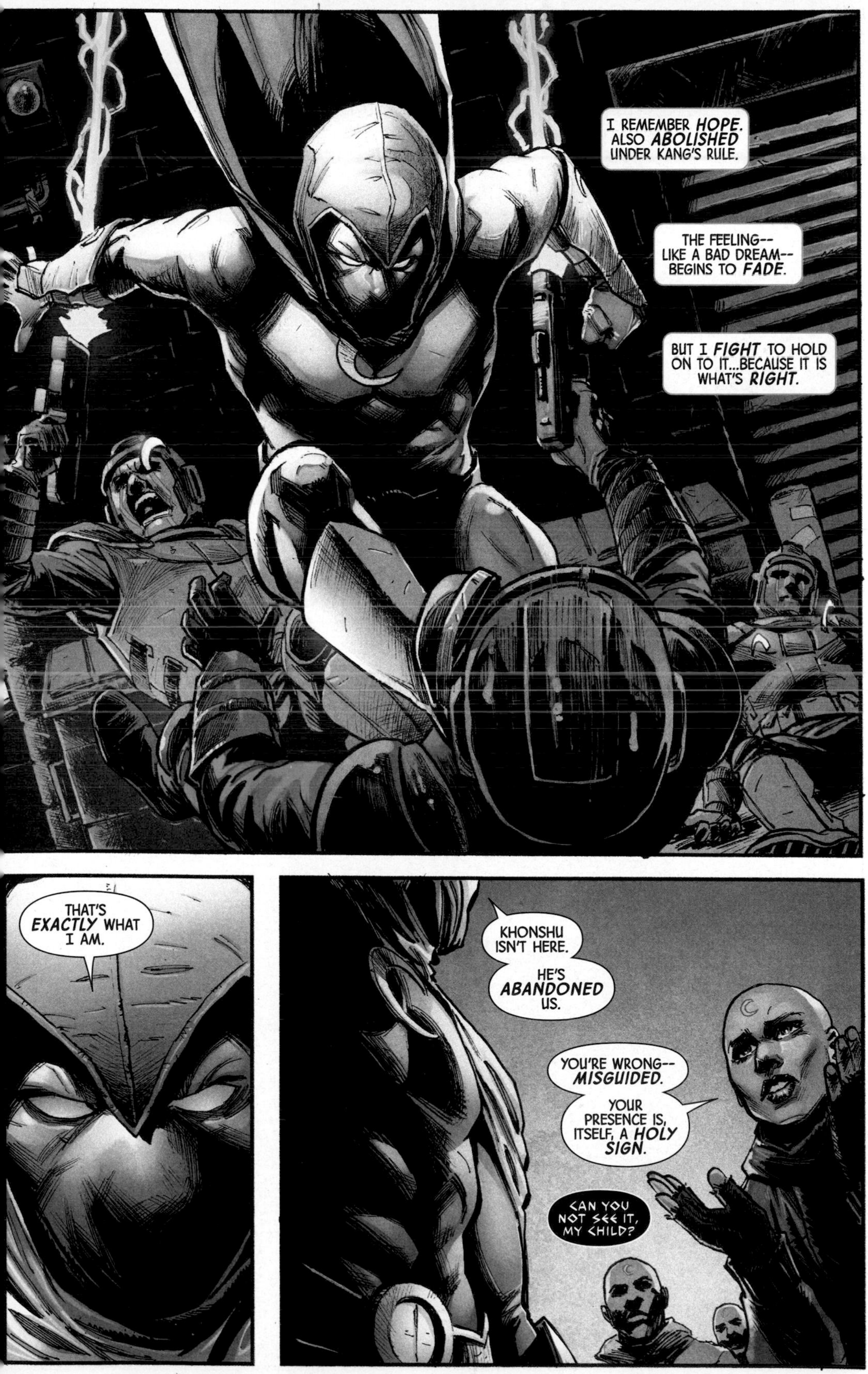
I REMEMBER HOPE. ALSO ABOLISHED UNDER KANG'S RULE.
THE FEELING-- LIKE A BAD DREAM-- BEGINS TO FADE.
BUT I FIGHT TO HOLD ON TO IT...BECAUSE IT IS WHAT'S RIGHT.
THAT'S EXACTLY WHAT I AM.
KHONSHU ISN'T HERE.
HE'S ABANDONED US.
YOU'RE WRONG-- MISGUIDED.
YOUR PRESENCE IS, ITSELF, A HOLY SIGN.
CAN YOU NOT SEE IT, MY CHILD?

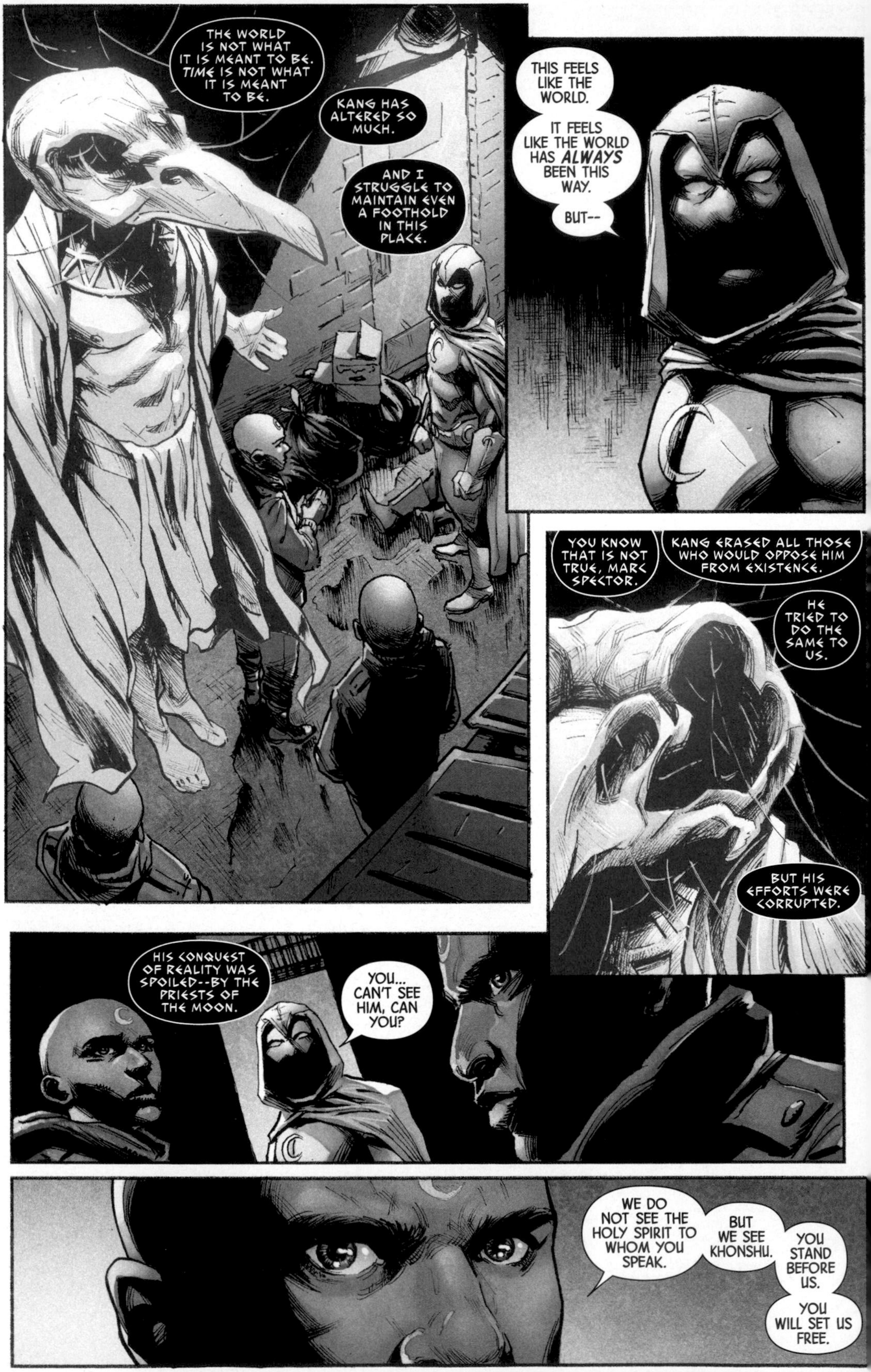
THE WORLD IS NOT WHAT IT IS MEANT TO BE. TIME IS NOT WHAT IT IS MEANT TO BE.
KANG HAS ALTERED SO MUCH.
AND I STRUGGLE TO MAINTAIN EVEN A FOOTHOLD IN THIS PLACE.
THIS FEELS LIKE THE WORLD.
IT FEELS LIKE THE WORLD HAS ALWAYS BEEN THIS WAY.
BUT--
YOU KNOW THAT IS NOT TRUE, MARC SPECTOR.
KANG ERASED ALL THOSE WHO WOULD OPPOSE HIM FROM EXISTENCE.
HE TRIED TO DO THE SAME TO US.
BUT HIS EFFORTS WERE CORRUPTED.
HIS CONQUEST OF REALITY WAS SPOILED--BY THE PRIESTS OF THE MOON.
YOU... CAN'T SEE HIM, CAN YOU?
WE DO NOT SEE THE HOLY SPIRIT TO WHOM YOU SPEAK.
BUT WE SEE KHONSHU.
YOU STAND BEFORE US.
YOU WILL SET US FREE.

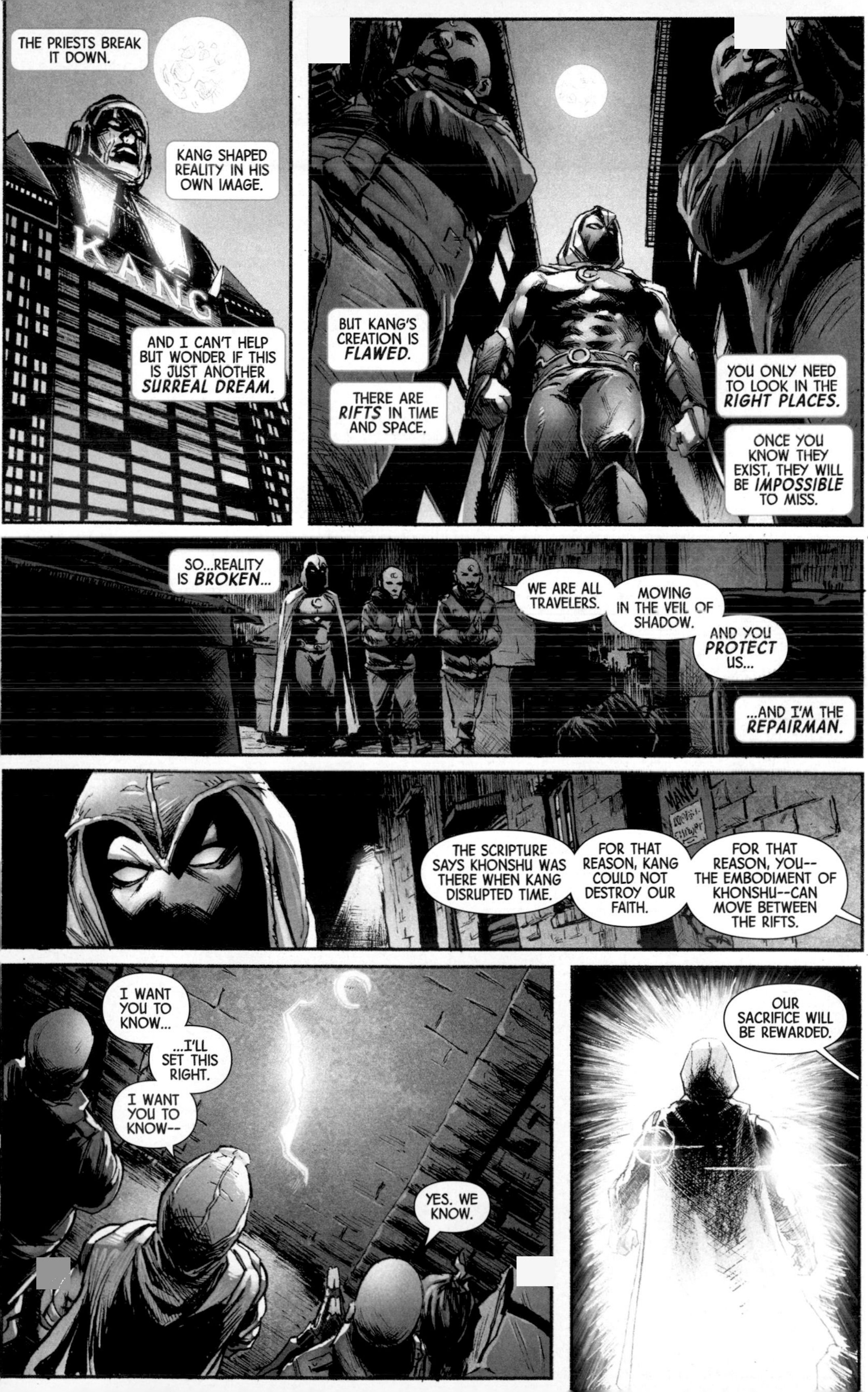
THE PRIESTS BREAK IT DOWN.
KANG SHAPED REALITY IN HIS OWN IMAGE.
KANG
AND I CAN'T HELP BUT WONDER IF THIS IS JUST ANOTHER SURREAL DREAM.
BUT KANG'S CREATION IS FLAWED.
THERE ARE RIFTS IN TIME AND SPACE.
YOU ONLY NEED TO LOOK IN THE RIGHT PLACES.
ONCE YOU KNOW THEY EXIST, THEY WILL BE IMPOSSIBLE TO MISS.
SO...REALITY IS BROKEN...
WE ARE ALL TRAVELERS.
MOVING IN THE VEIL OF SHADOW.
AND YOU PROTECT US...
...AND I'M THE REPAIRMAN.
THE SCRIPTURE SAYS KHONSHU WAS THERE WHEN KANG DISRUPTED TIME.
FOR THAT REASON, KANG COULD NOT DESTROY OUR FAITH.
FOR THAT REASON, YOU-- THE EMBODIMENT OF KHONSHU--CAN MOVE BETWEEN THE RIFTS.
I WANT YOU TO KNOW...
...I'LL SET THIS RIGHT.
I WANT YOU TO KNOW--
YES. WE KNOW.
OUR SACRIFICE WILL BE REWARDED.

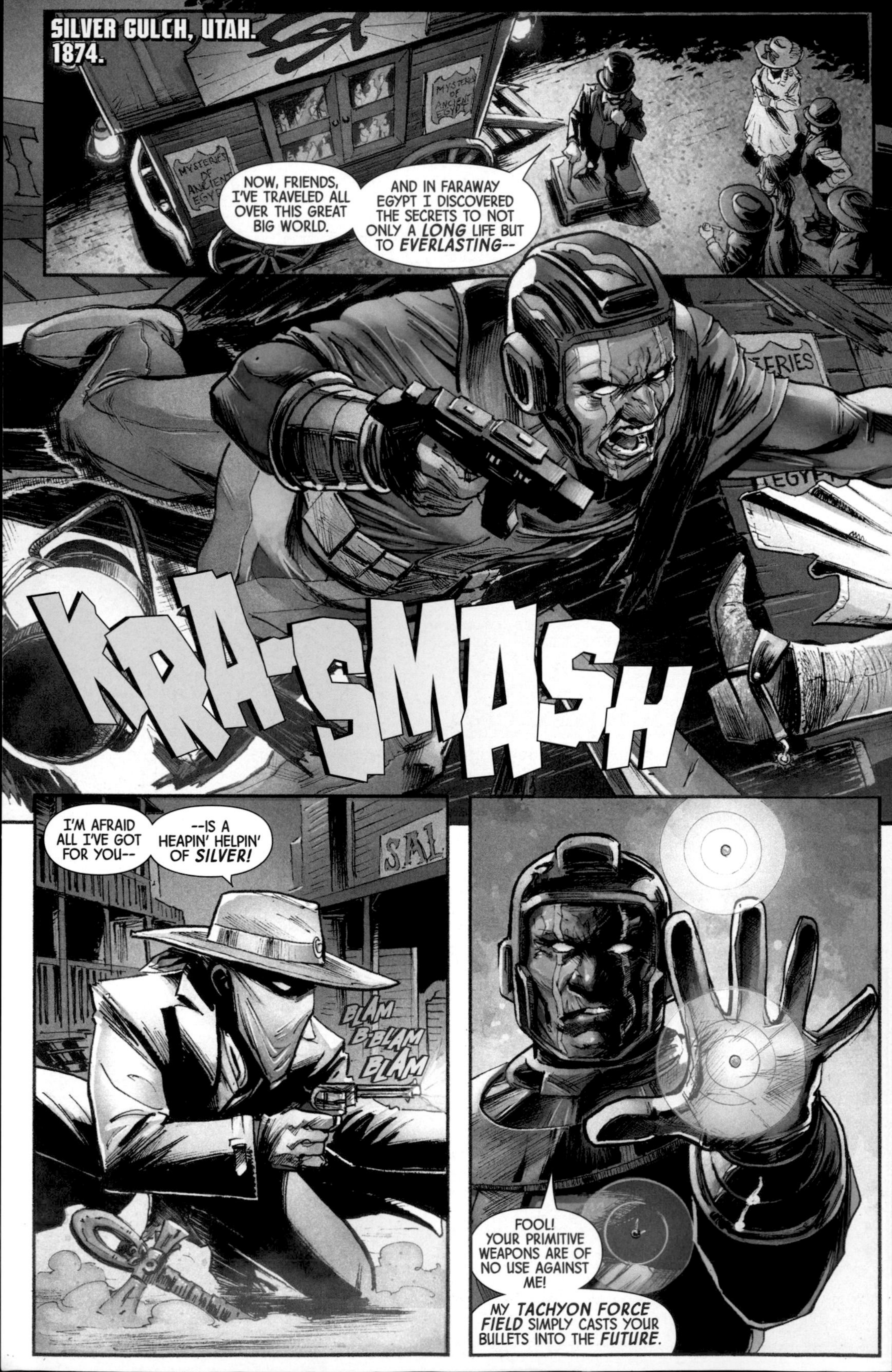
SILVER GULCH, UTAH. 1874.
MYSTERIES OF ANCIENT EGYPT
NOW, FRIENDS, I'VE TRAVELED ALL OVER THIS GREAT BIG WORLD.
AND IN FARAWAY EGYPT I DISCOVERED THE SECRETS TO NOT ONLY A LONG LIFE BUT TO EVERLASTING--
KRA-SMASH
I'M AFRAID ALL I'VE GOT FOR YOU--
--IS A HEAPIN' HELPIN' OF SILVER!
BLAM B-BLAM BLAM
FOOL! YOUR PRIMITIVE WEAPONS ARE OF NO USE AGAINST ME!
MY TACHYON FORCE FIELD SIMPLY CASTS YOUR BULLETS INTO THE FUTURE.

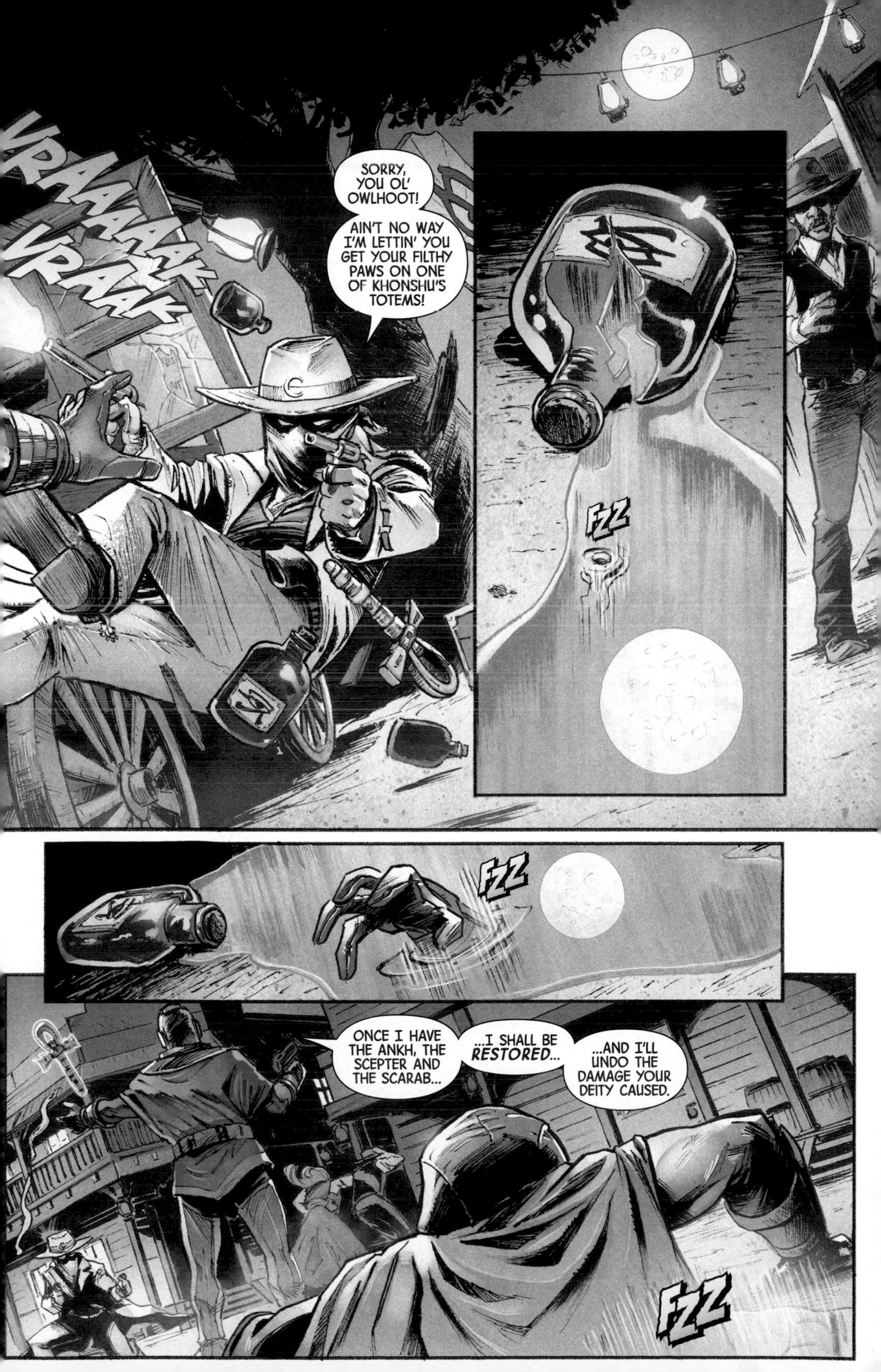
VRAAAAAK VRAAK VRAAK
SORRY, YOU OL' OWLHOOT!
AIN'T NO WAY I'M LETTIN' YOU GET YOUR FILTHY PAWS ON ONE OF KHONSHU'S TOTEMS!
FZZ
FZZ
ONCE I HAVE THE ANKH, THE SCEPTER AND THE SCARAB...
...I SHALL BE *RESTORED*...
...AND I'LL UNDO THE DAMAGE YOUR DEITY CAUSED.
FZZ

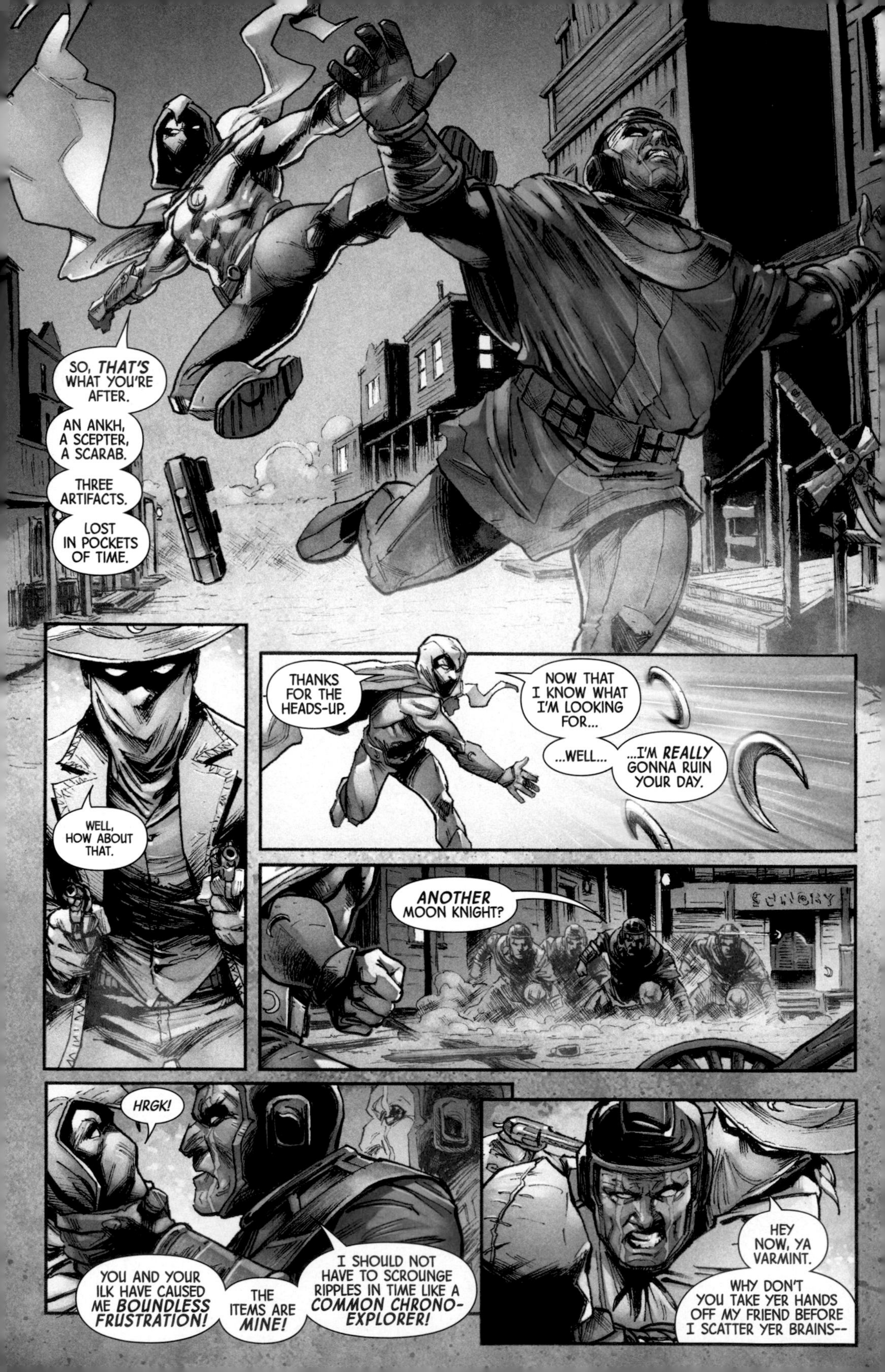
SO, *THAT'S* WHAT YOU'RE AFTER.
AN ANKH, A SCEPTER, A SCARAB.
THREE ARTIFACTS.
LOST IN POCKETS OF TIME.
WELL, HOW ABOUT THAT.
THANKS FOR THE HEADS-UP.
NOW THAT I KNOW WHAT I'M LOOKING FOR...
...WELL...
...I'M *REALLY* GONNA RUIN YOUR DAY.
ANOTHER MOON KNIGHT?
HRGK!
YOU AND YOUR ILK HAVE CAUSED ME *BOUNDLESS FRUSTRATION!*
THE ITEMS ARE *MINE!*
I SHOULD NOT HAVE TO SCROUNGE RIPPLES IN TIME LIKE A *COMMON CHRONO-EXPLORER!*
HEY NOW, YA VARMINT.
WHY DON'T YOU TAKE YER HANDS OFF MY FRIEND BEFORE I SCATTER YER BRAINS--

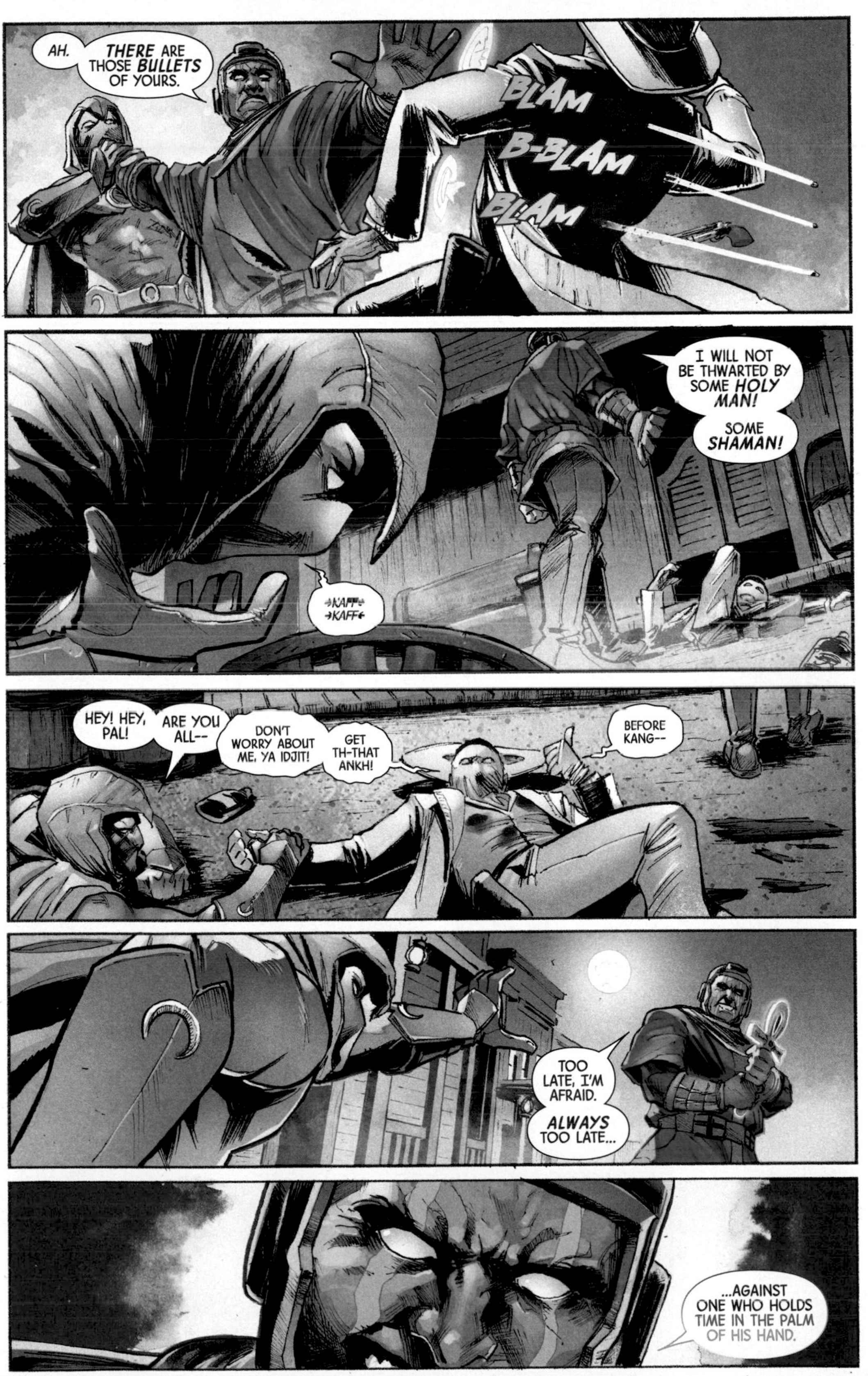
AH.
THERE ARE THOSE BULLETS OF YOURS.
BLAM
B-BLAM
BLAM
I WILL NOT BE THWARTED BY SOME HOLY MAN!
SOME SHAMAN!
KAFF KAFF
HEY! HEY, PAL!
ARE YOU ALL--
DON'T WORRY ABOUT ME, YA IDJIT!
GET TH-THAT ANKH!
BEFORE KANG--
TOO LATE, I'M AFRAID.
ALWAYS TOO LATE...
...AGAINST ONE WHO HOLDS TIME IN THE PALM OF HIS HAND.

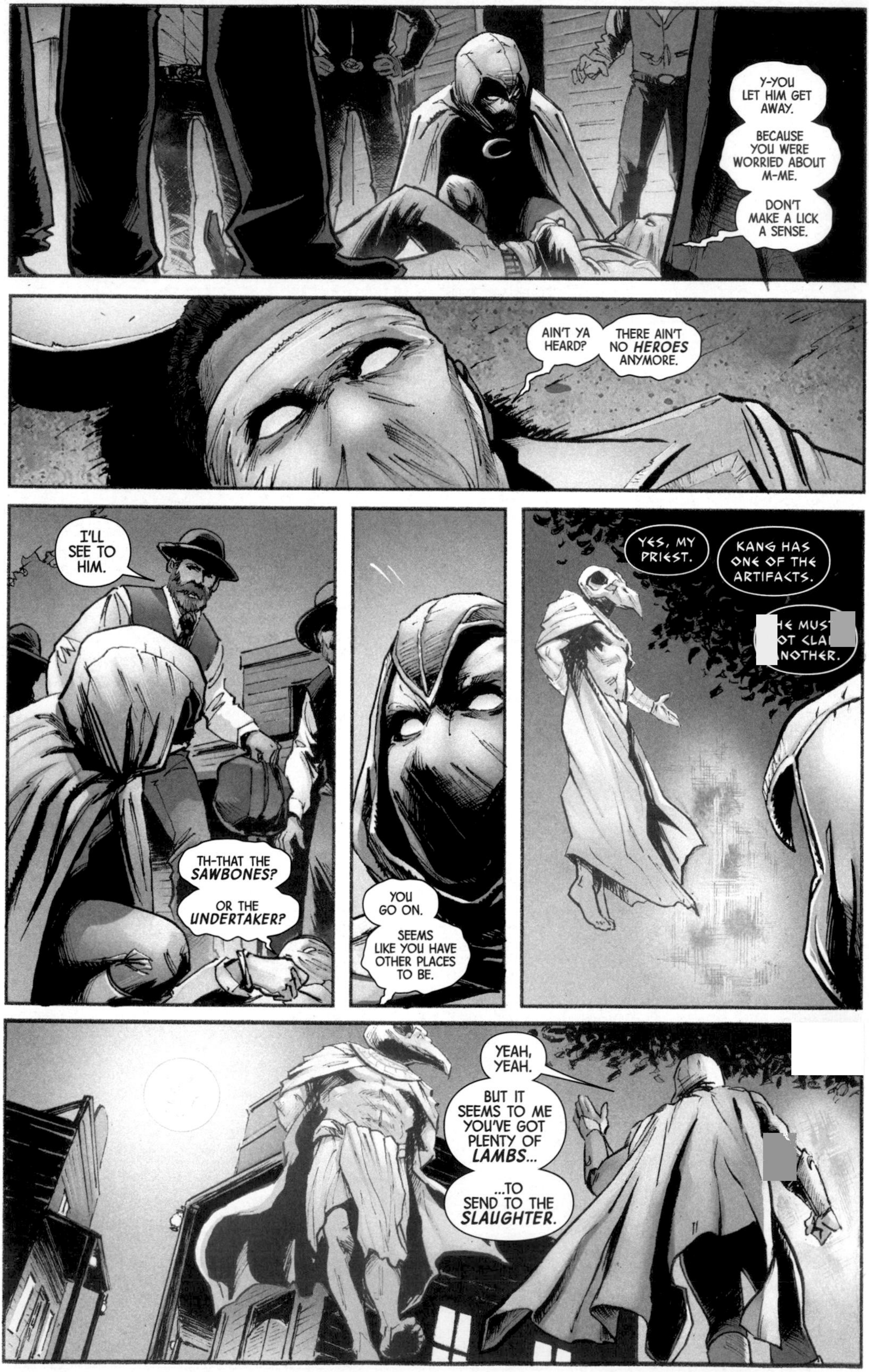
Y-YOU LET HIM GET AWAY.
BECAUSE YOU WERE WORRIED ABOUT M-ME.
DON'T MAKE A LICK A SENSE.
AIN'T YA HEARD?
THERE AIN'T NO HEROES ANYMORE.
I'LL SEE TO HIM.
TH-THAT THE SAWBONES?
OR THE UNDERTAKER?
YOU GO ON.
SEEMS LIKE YOU HAVE OTHER PLACES TO BE.
YES, MY PRIEST.
KANG HAS ONE OF THE ARTIFACTS.
HE MUST
OT CLA
NOTHER.
YEAH, YEAH.
BUT IT SEEMS TO ME YOU'VE GOT PLENTY OF LAMBS...
...TO SEND TO THE SLAUGHTER.

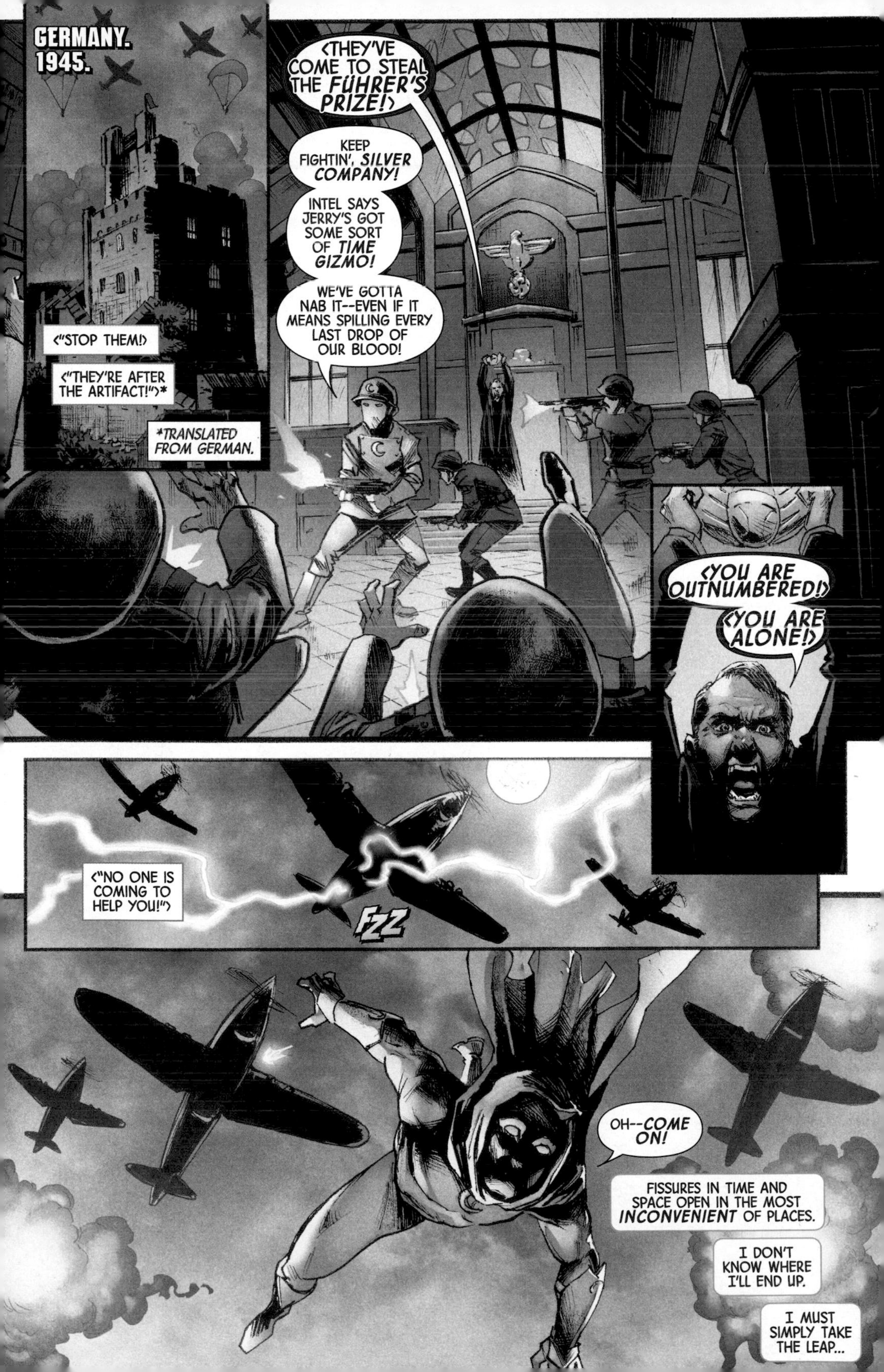
GERMANY. 1945.
<THEY'VE COME TO STEAL THE FÜHRER'S PRIZE!>
KEEP FIGHTIN', SILVER COMPANY!
INTEL SAYS JERRY'S GOT SOME SORT OF TIME GIZMO!
WE'VE GOTTA NAB IT--EVEN IF IT MEANS SPILLING EVERY LAST DROP OF OUR BLOOD!
<"STOP THEM!>
<"THEY'RE AFTER THE ARTIFACT!">*
*TRANSLATED FROM GERMAN.
<YOU ARE OUTNUMBERED!>
<YOU ARE ALONE!>
<"NO ONE IS COMING TO HELP YOU!">
FZZ
OH--COME ON!
FISSURES IN TIME AND SPACE OPEN IN THE MOST INCONVENIENT OF PLACES.
I DON'T KNOW WHERE I'LL END UP.
I MUST SIMPLY TAKE THE LEAP...

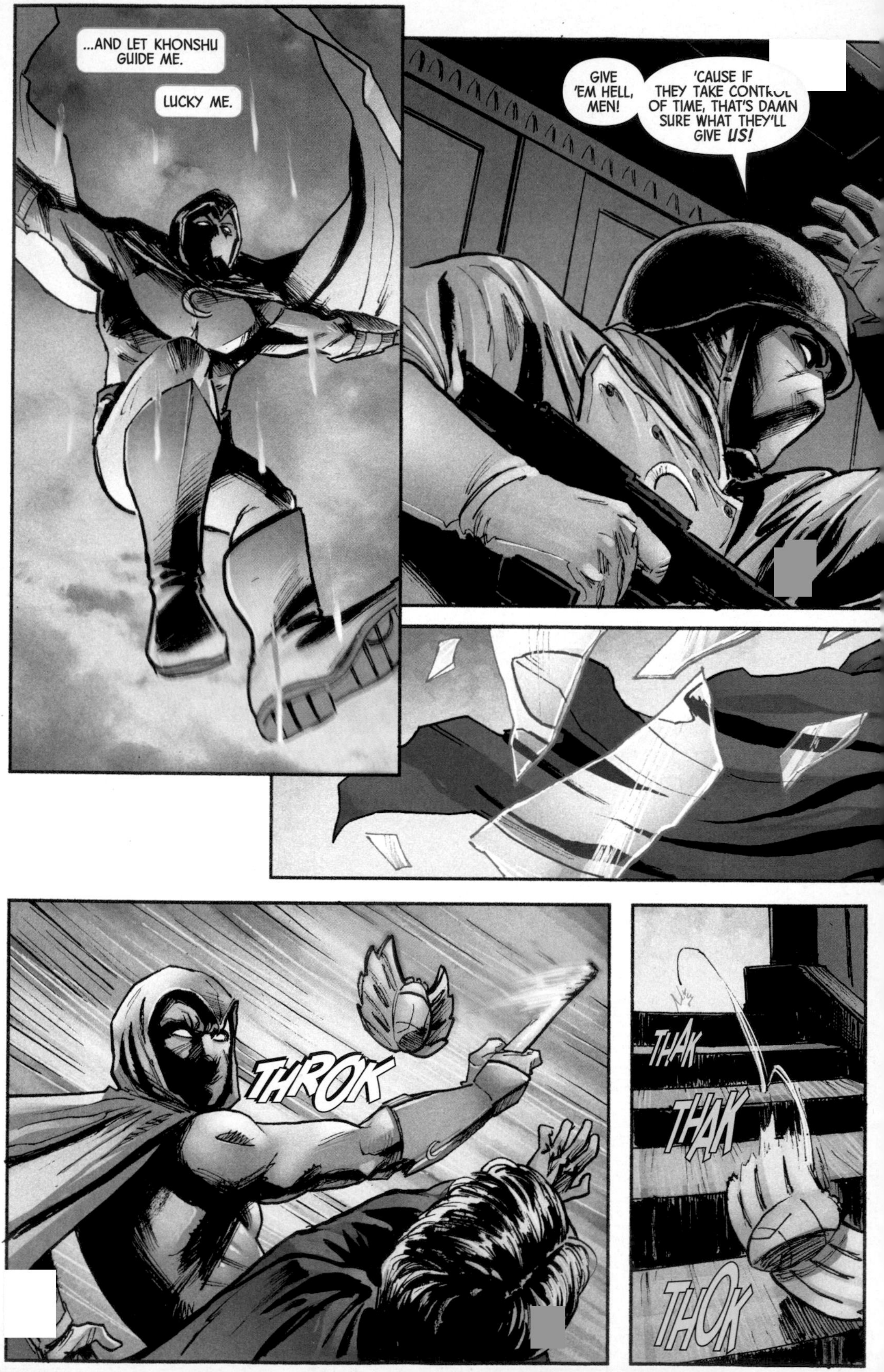
...AND LET KHONSHU GUIDE ME.
LUCKY ME.
GIVE 'EM HELL, MEN!
'CAUSE IF THEY TAKE CONTROL OF TIME, THAT'S DAMN SURE WHAT THEY'LL GIVE US!
THROK
THAK
THAK
THOK

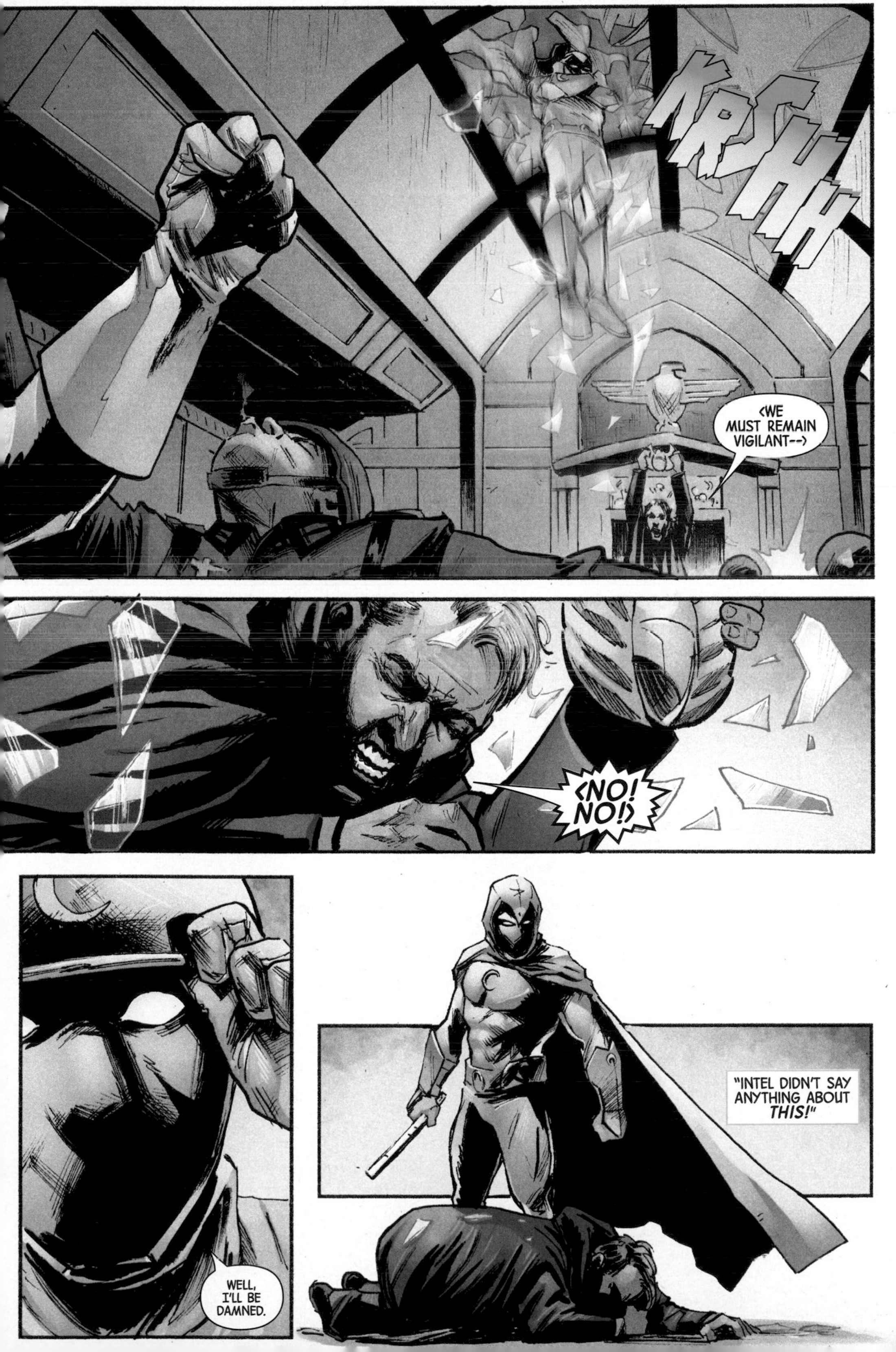

KRSHH
<WE MUST REMAIN VIGILANT-->
<NO! NO!>
WELL, I'LL BE DAMNED.
"INTEL DIDN'T SAY ANYTHING ABOUT *THIS!*"

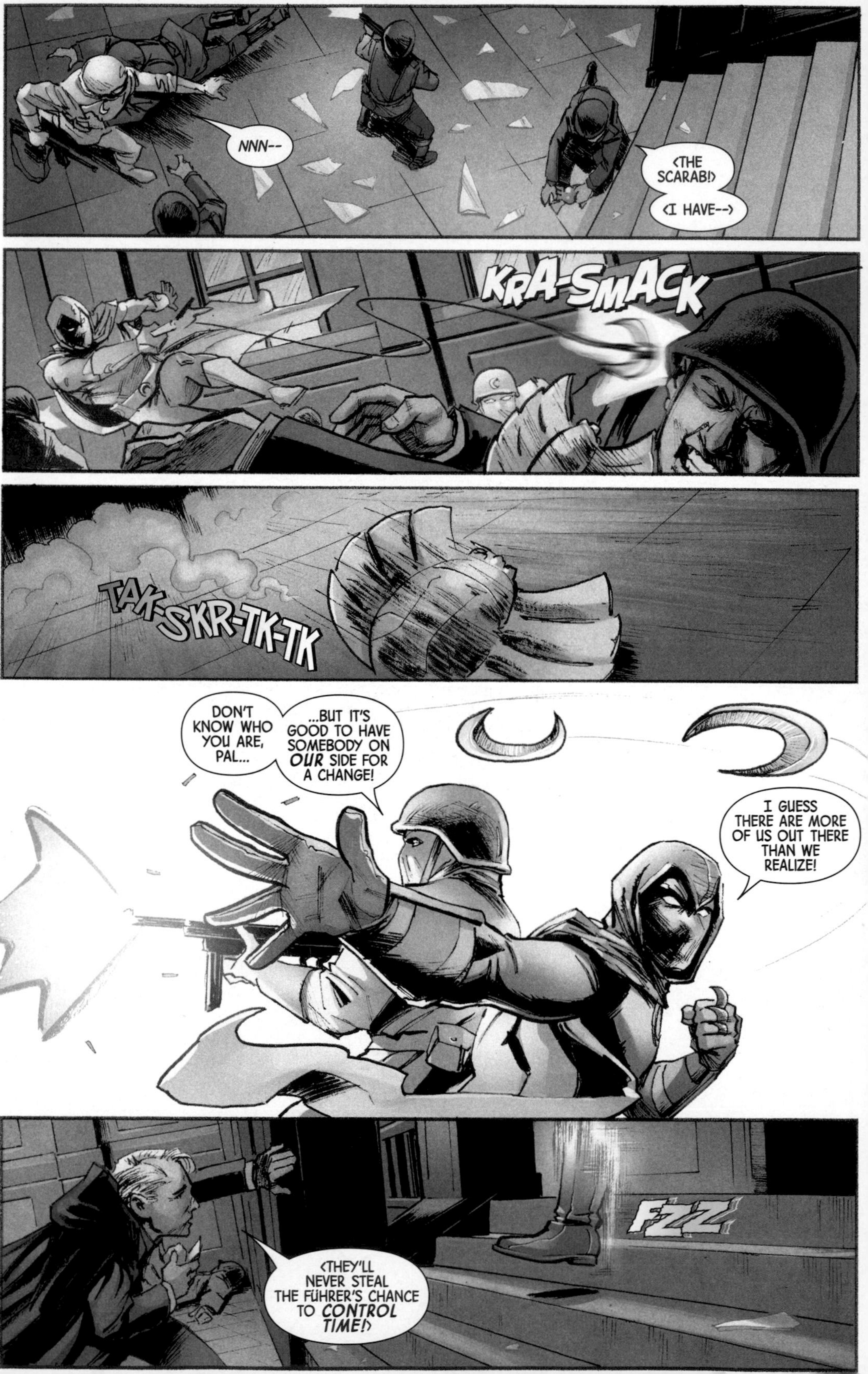
NNN--
‹THE SCARAB!›
‹I HAVE--›
KRA-SMACK
TAK-SKR-TK-TK
DON'T KNOW WHO YOU ARE, PAL...
...BUT IT'S GOOD TO HAVE SOMEBODY ON OUR SIDE FOR A CHANGE!
I GUESS THERE ARE MORE OF US OUT THERE THAN WE REALIZE!
FZZ
‹THEY'LL NEVER STEAL THE FÜHRER'S CHANCE TO CONTROL TIME!›

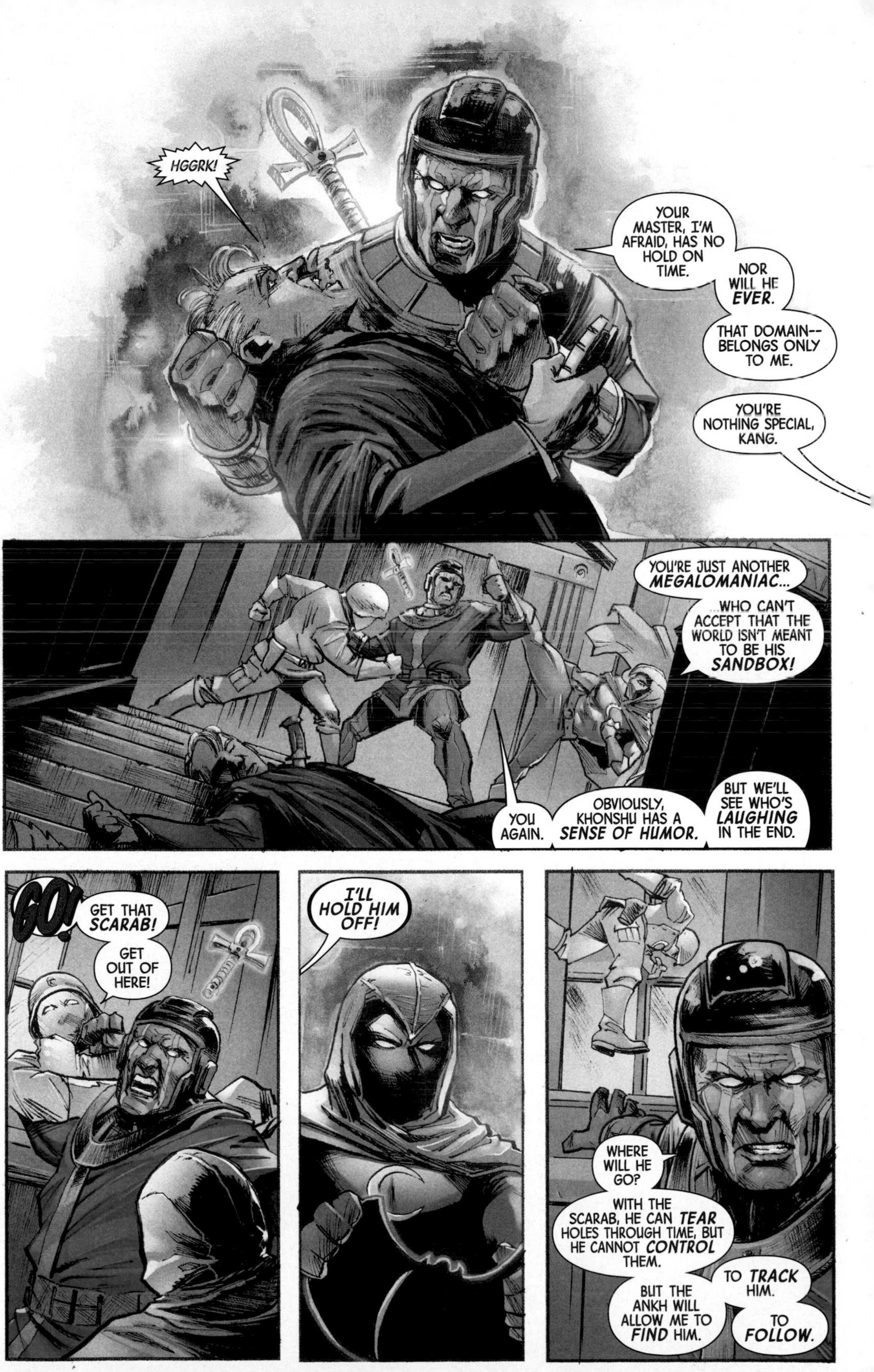
HGGRK!
YOUR MASTER, I'M AFRAID, HAS NO HOLD ON TIME.
NOR WILL HE EVER.
THAT DOMAIN-- BELONGS ONLY TO ME.
YOU'RE NOTHING SPECIAL, KANG.
YOU'RE JUST ANOTHER MEGALOMANIAC...
...WHO CAN'T ACCEPT THAT THE WORLD ISN'T MEANT TO BE HIS SANDBOX!
YOU AGAIN.
OBVIOUSLY, KHONSHU HAS A SENSE OF HUMOR.
BUT WE'LL SEE WHO'S LAUGHING IN THE END.
GO!
GET THAT SCARAB!
GET OUT OF HERE!
I'LL HOLD HIM OFF!
WHERE WILL HE GO?
WITH THE SCARAB, HE CAN TEAR HOLES THROUGH TIME, BUT HE CANNOT CONTROL THEM.
BUT THE ANKH WILL ALLOW ME TO FIND HIM.
TO TRACK HIM.
TO FOLLOW.

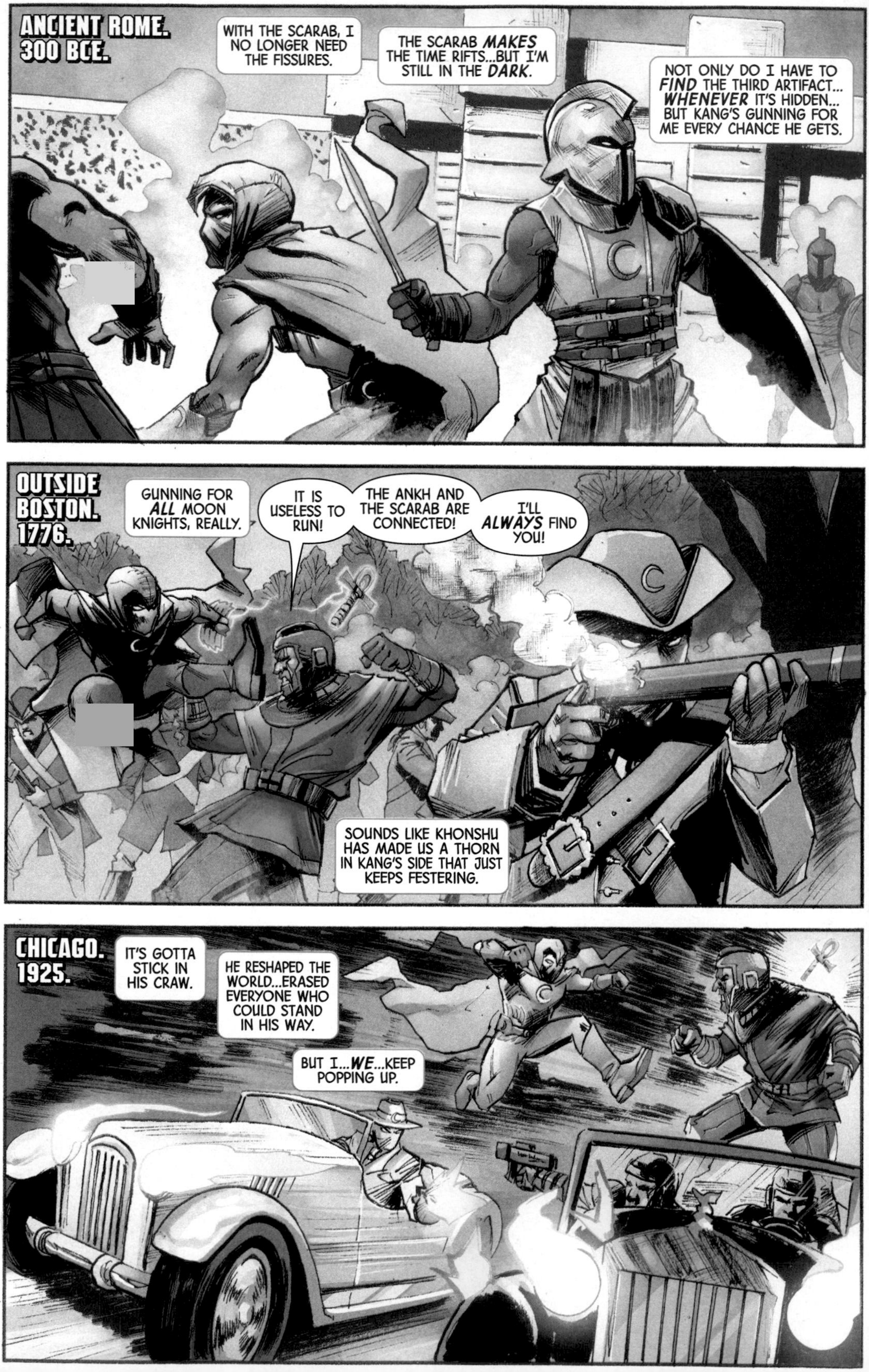
ANCIENT ROME.
300 BCE.
WITH THE SCARAB, I NO LONGER NEED THE FISSURES.
THE SCARAB MAKES THE TIME RIFTS...BUT I'M STILL IN THE DARK.
NOT ONLY DO I HAVE TO FIND THE THIRD ARTIFACT... WHENEVER IT'S HIDDEN... BUT KANG'S GUNNING FOR ME EVERY CHANCE HE GETS.
OUTSIDE BOSTON.
1776.
GUNNING FOR ALL MOON KNIGHTS, REALLY.
IT IS USELESS TO RUN!
THE ANKH AND THE SCARAB ARE CONNECTED!
I'LL ALWAYS FIND YOU!
SOUNDS LIKE KHONSHU HAS MADE US A THORN IN KANG'S SIDE THAT JUST KEEPS FESTERING.
CHICAGO.
1925.
IT'S GOTTA STICK IN HIS CRAW.
HE RESHAPED THE WORLD...ERASED EVERYONE WHO COULD STAND IN HIS WAY.
BUT I...WE...KEEP POPPING UP.

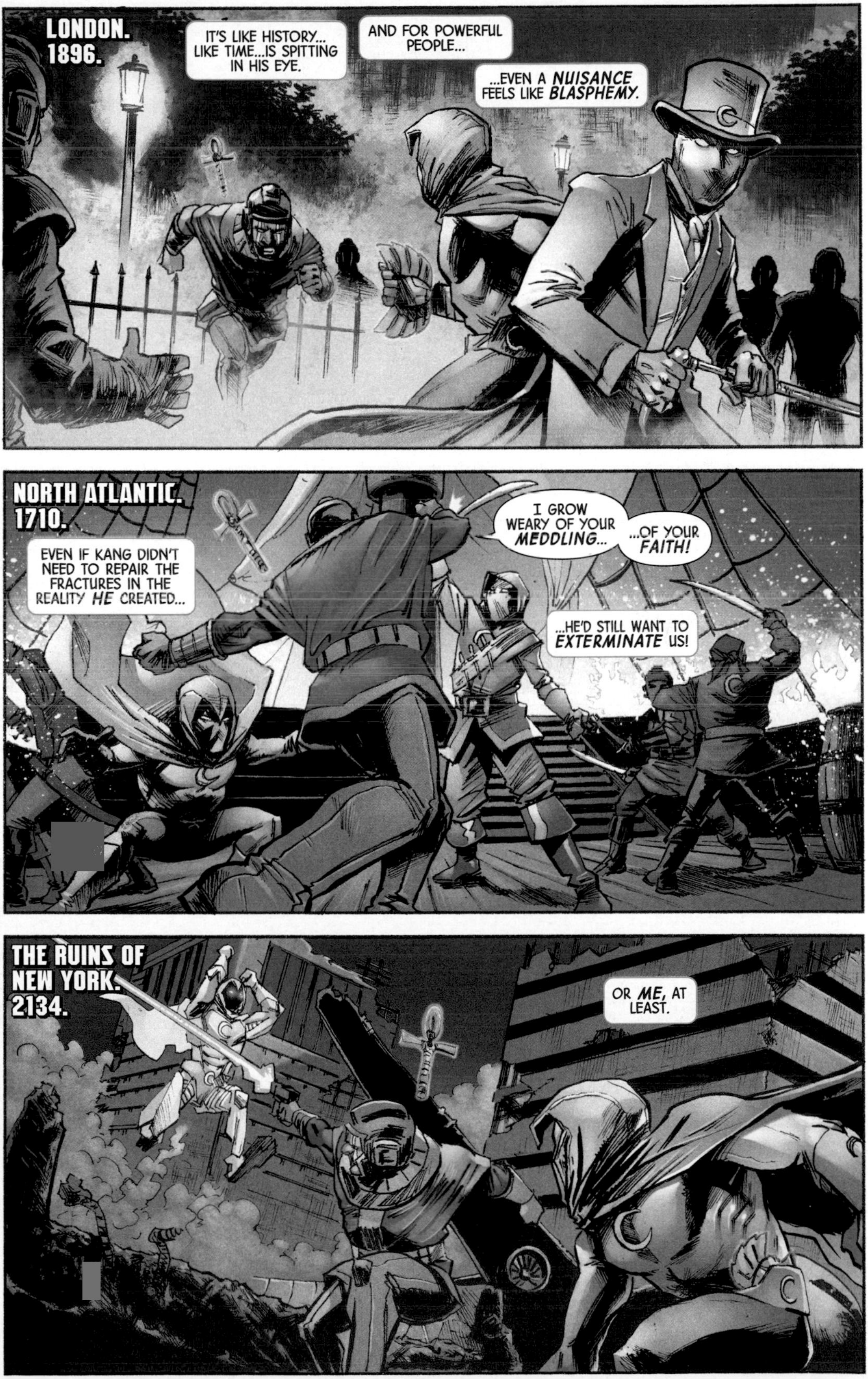
LONDON.
1896.
IT'S LIKE HISTORY... LIKE TIME...IS SPITTING IN HIS EYE.
AND FOR POWERFUL PEOPLE...
...EVEN A NUISANCE FEELS LIKE BLASPHEMY.
NORTH ATLANTIC.
1710.
EVEN IF KANG DIDN'T NEED TO REPAIR THE FRACTURES IN THE REALITY HE CREATED...
I GROW WEARY OF YOUR MEDDLING...
...OF YOUR FAITH!
...HE'D STILL WANT TO EXTERMINATE US!
THE RUINS OF
NEW YORK.
2134.
OR ME, AT LEAST.

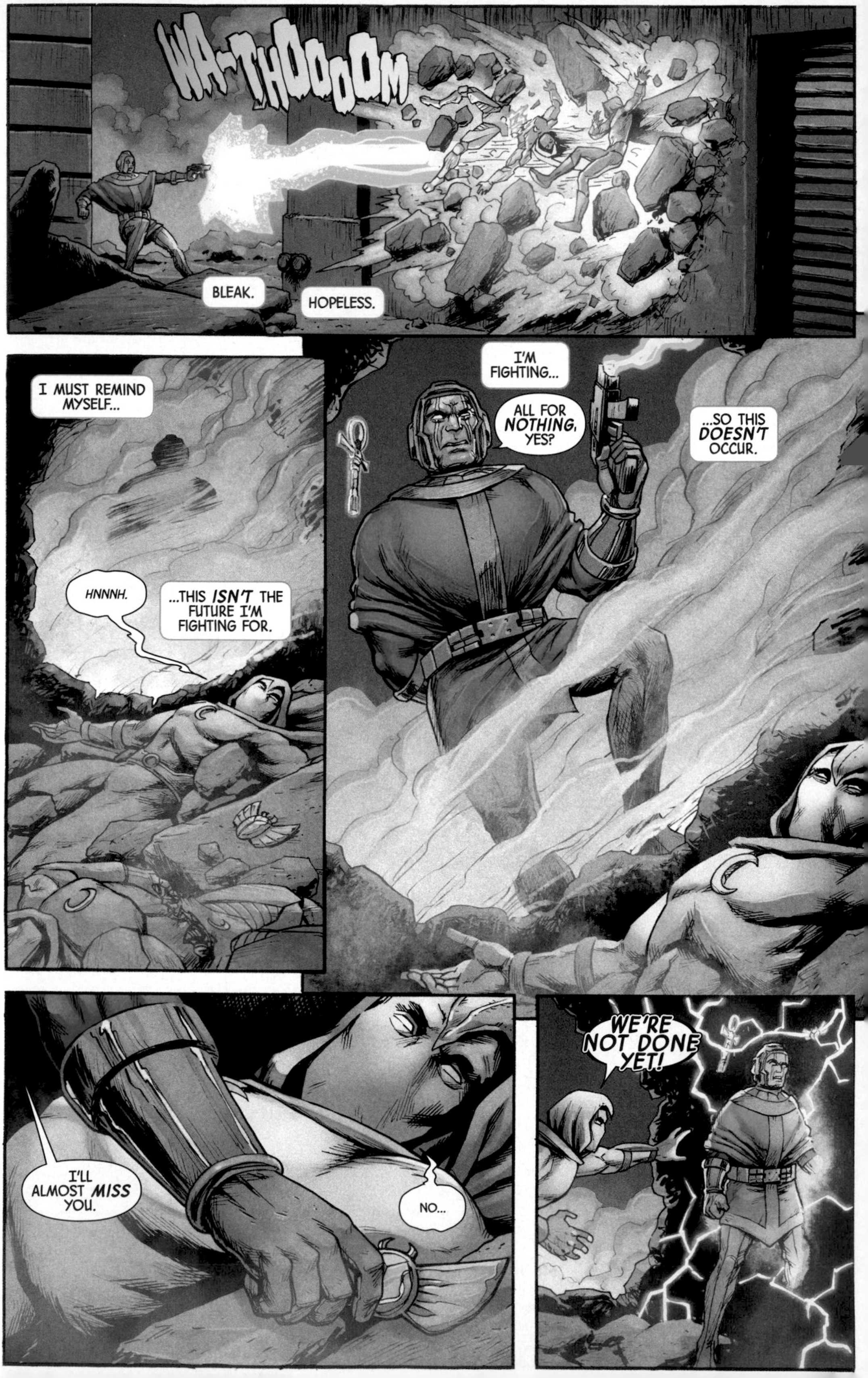
WA-THOOOOOM
BLEAK.
HOPELESS.
I MUST REMIND MYSELF...
HNNNH.
...THIS ISN'T THE FUTURE I'M FIGHTING FOR.
I'M FIGHTING...
ALL FOR NOTHING, YES?
...SO THIS DOESN'T OCCUR.
I'LL ALMOST MISS YOU.
NO...
WE'RE NOT DONE YET!

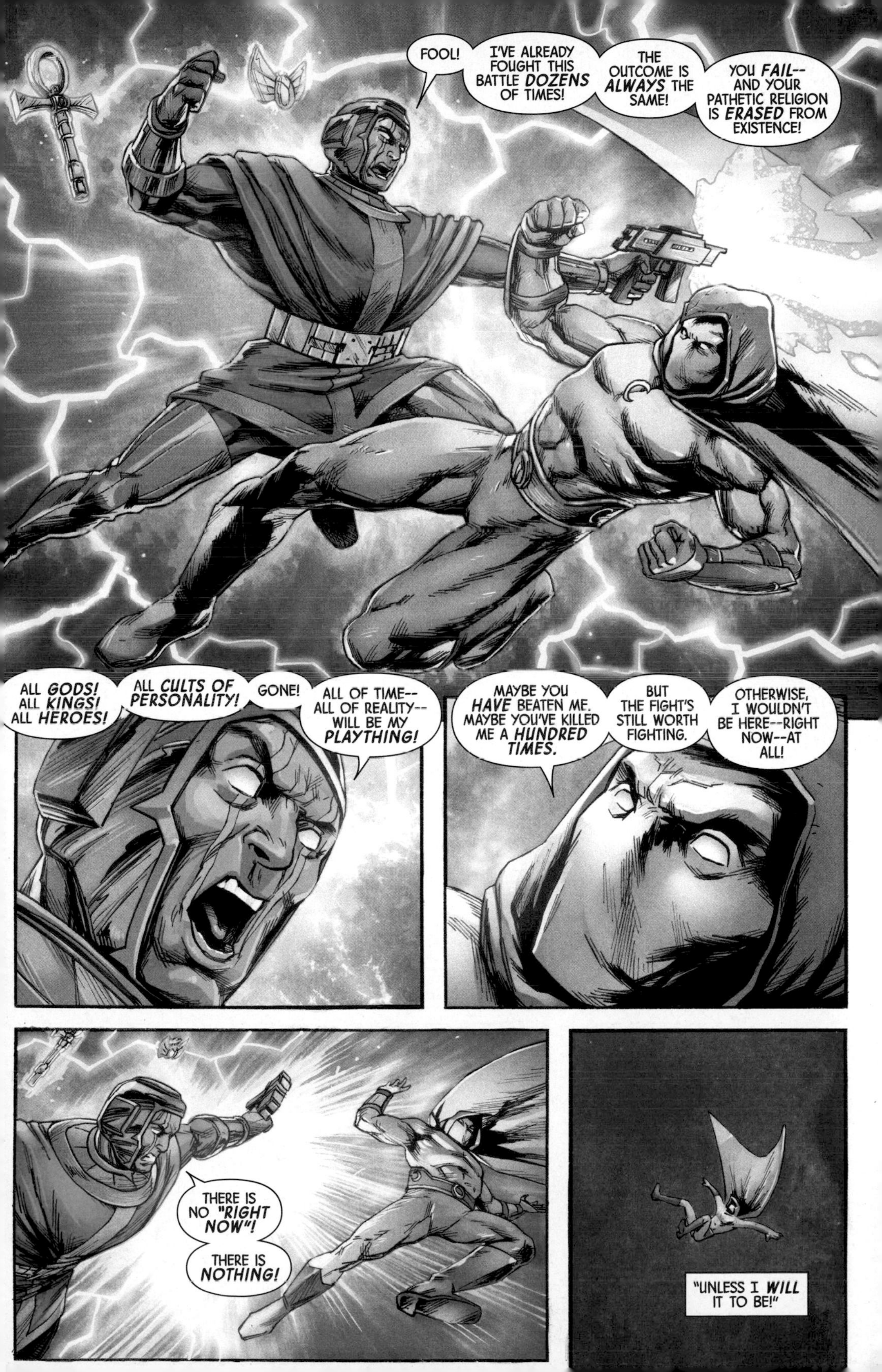
FOOL!
I'VE ALREADY FOUGHT THIS BATTLE DOZENS OF TIMES!
THE OUTCOME IS ALWAYS THE SAME!
YOU FAIL-- AND YOUR PATHETIC RELIGION IS ERASED FROM EXISTENCE!
ALL GODS! ALL KINGS! ALL HEROES!
ALL CULTS OF PERSONALITY!
GONE!
ALL OF TIME-- ALL OF REALITY-- WILL BE MY PLAYTHING!
MAYBE YOU HAVE BEATEN ME. MAYBE YOU'VE KILLED ME A HUNDRED TIMES.
BUT THE FIGHT'S STILL WORTH FIGHTING.
OTHERWISE, I WOULDN'T BE HERE--RIGHT NOW--AT ALL!
THERE IS NO "RIGHT NOW"!
THERE IS NOTHING!
"UNLESS I WILL IT TO BE!"

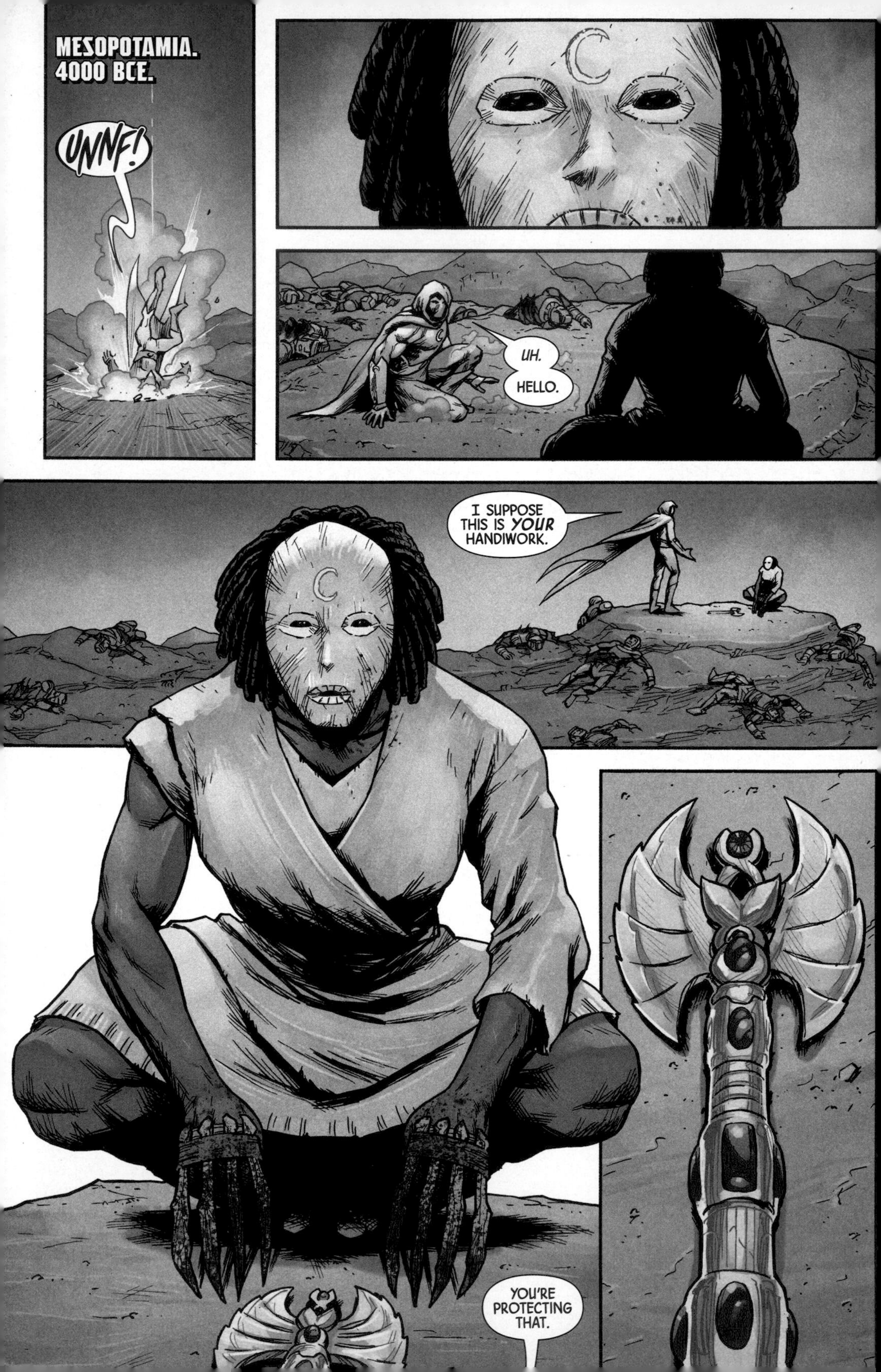
MESOPOTAMIA.
4000 BCE.
UNNF!
UH.
HELLO.
I SUPPOSE THIS IS *YOUR* HANDIWORK.
YOU'RE PROTECTING THAT.

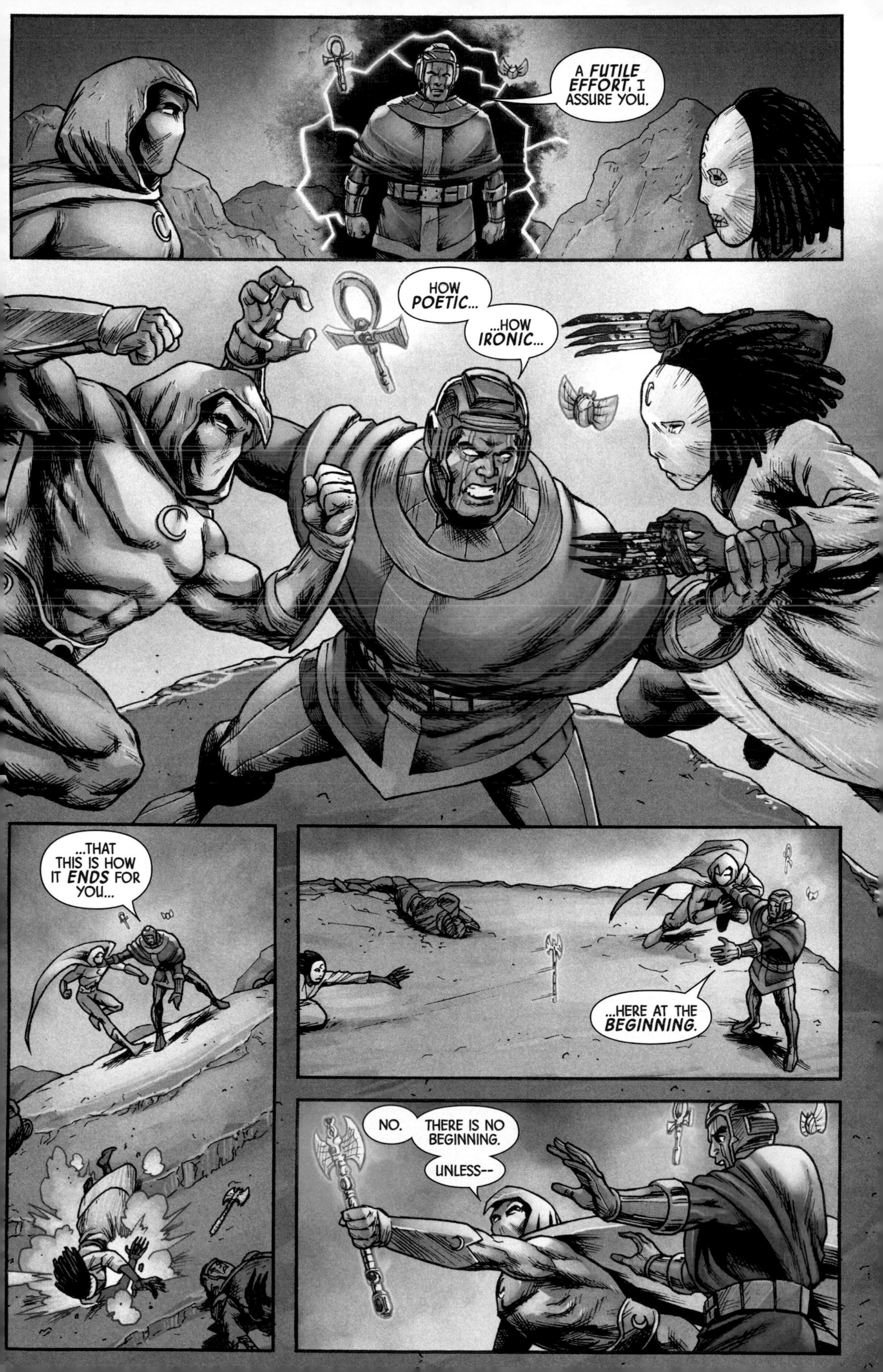

A FUTILE EFFORT, I ASSURE YOU.
HOW POETIC...
...HOW IRONIC...
...THAT THIS IS HOW IT ENDS FOR YOU...
...HERE AT THE BEGINNING.
NO.
THERE IS NO BEGINNING.
UNLESS--

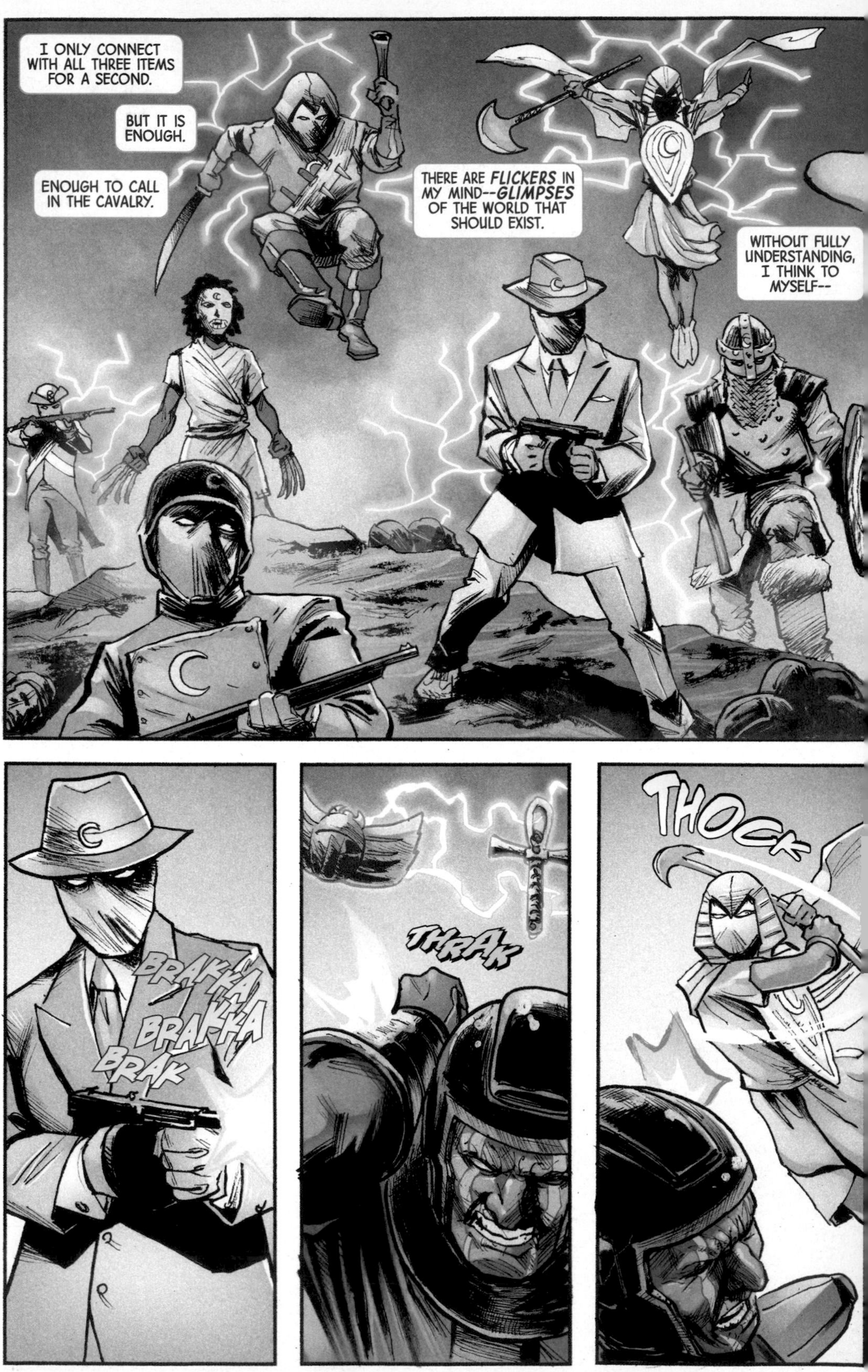

I ONLY CONNECT WITH ALL THREE ITEMS FOR A SECOND.
BUT IT IS ENOUGH.
ENOUGH TO CALL IN THE CAVALRY.
THERE ARE FLICKERS IN MY MIND--GLIMPSES OF THE WORLD THAT SHOULD EXIST.
WITHOUT FULLY UNDERSTANDING, I THINK TO MYSELF--
BRAKKA
BRAKKA
BRAK
THRAK
THOCK

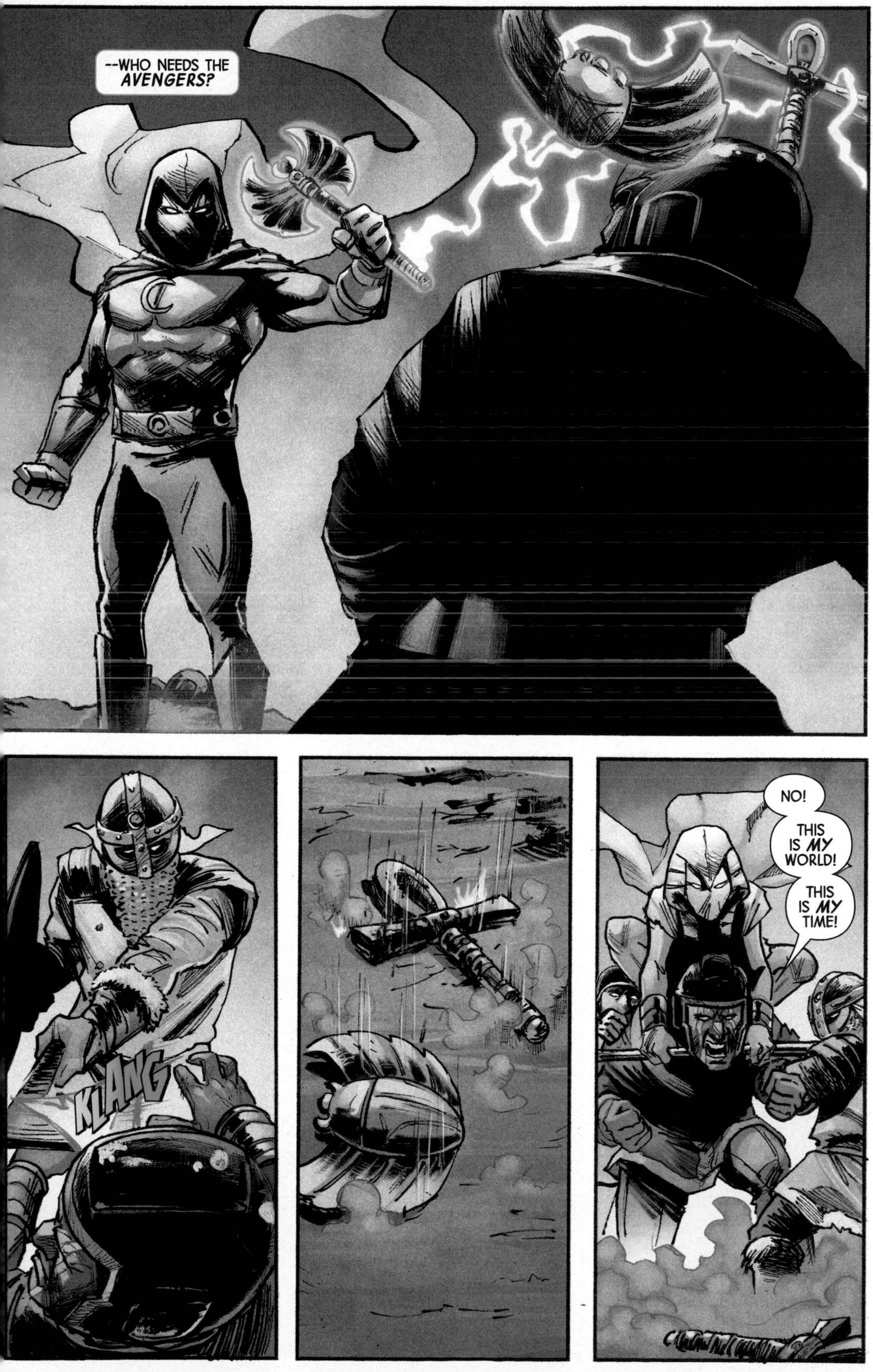
--WHO NEEDS THE AVENGERS?
KLANG
NO!
THIS IS MY WORLD!
THIS IS MY TIME!

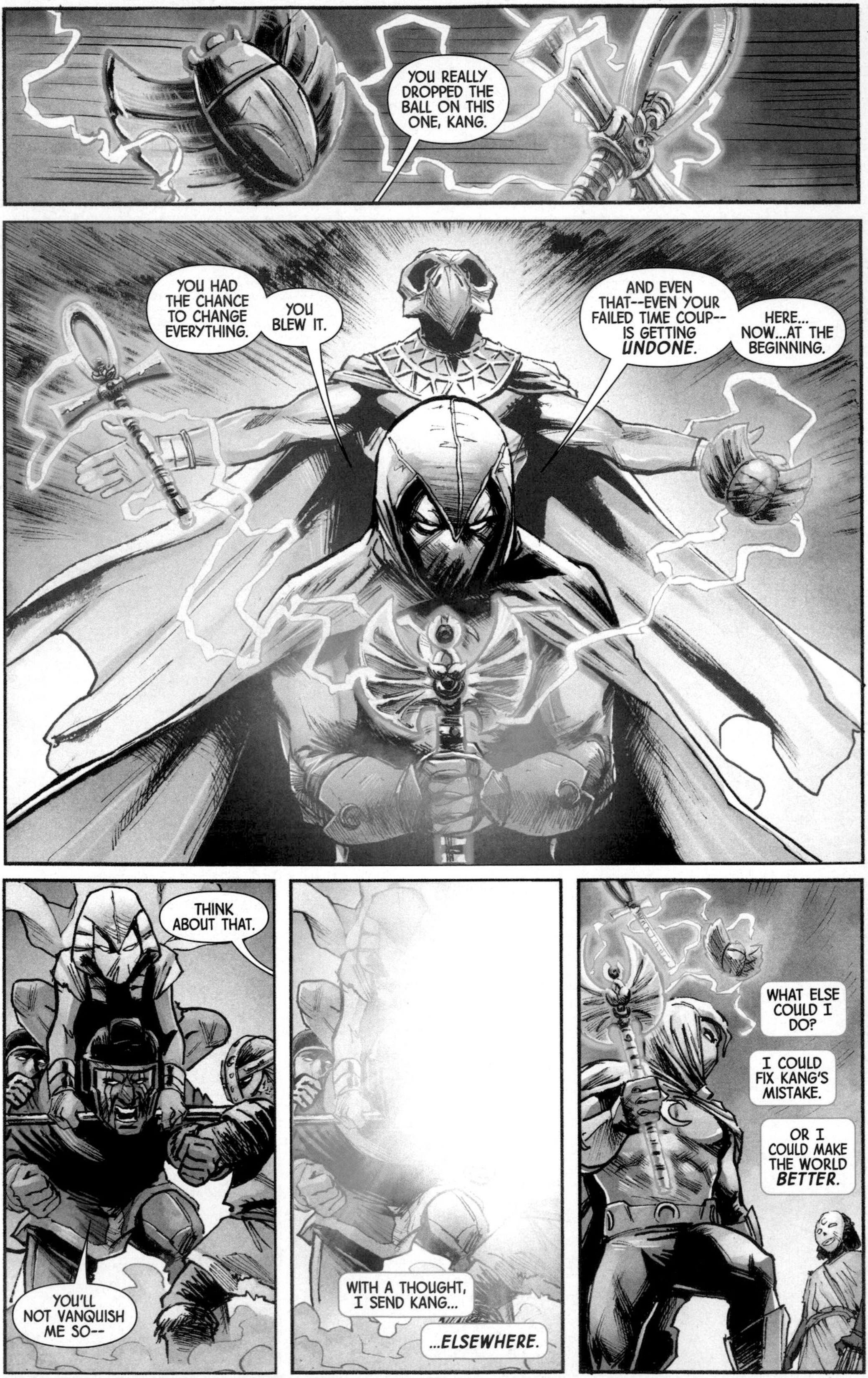
YOU REALLY DROPPED THE BALL ON THIS ONE, KANG.
YOU HAD THE CHANCE TO CHANGE EVERYTHING.
YOU BLEW IT.
AND EVEN THAT--EVEN YOUR FAILED TIME COUP--IS GETTING *UNDONE*.
HERE... NOW...AT THE BEGINNING.
THINK ABOUT THAT.
YOU'LL NOT VANQUISH ME SO--
WITH A THOUGHT, I SEND KANG...
...*ELSEWHERE*.
WHAT ELSE COULD I DO?
I COULD FIX KANG'S MISTAKE.
OR I COULD MAKE THE WORLD *BETTER*.

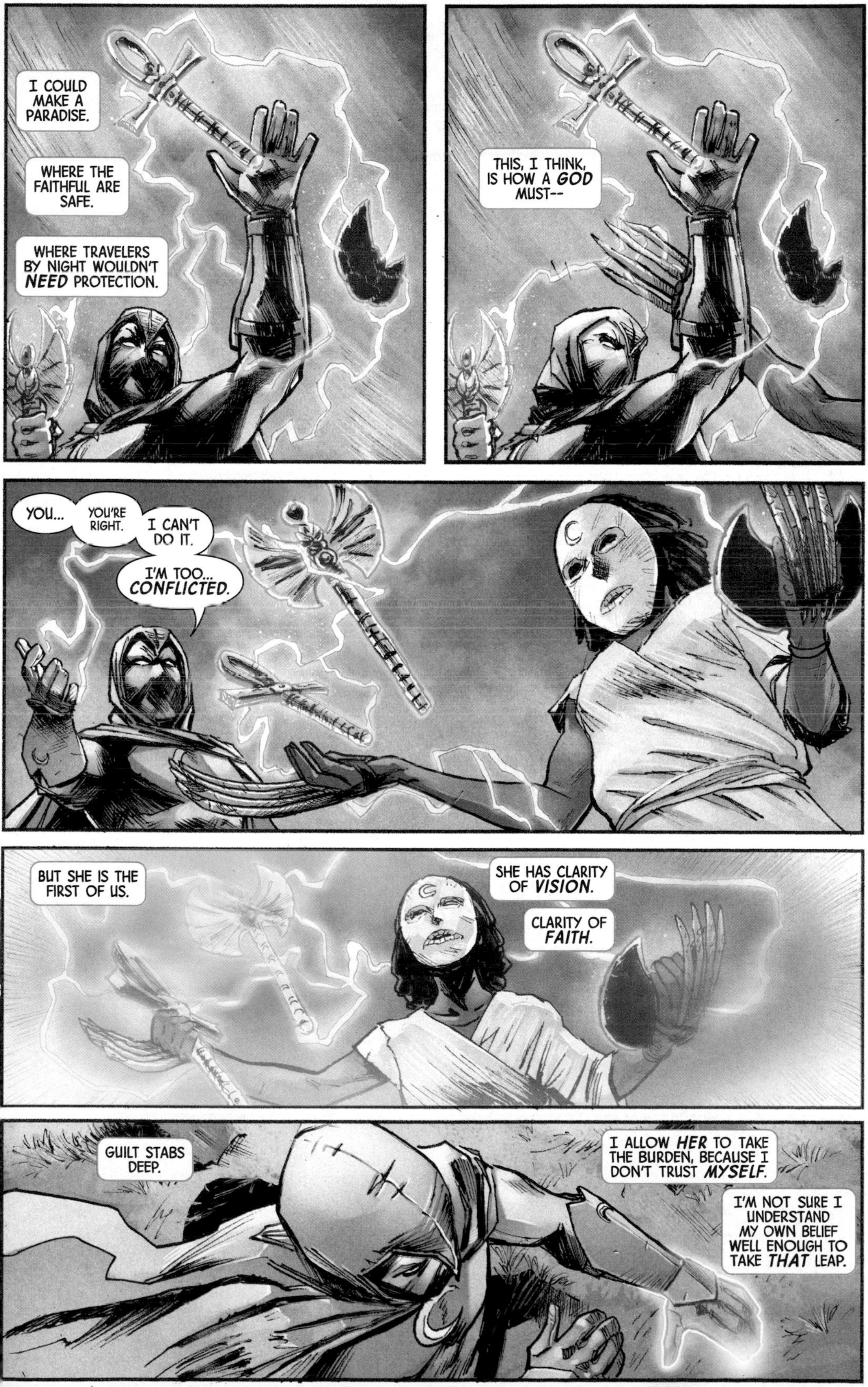

I COULD MAKE A PARADISE.
WHERE THE FAITHFUL ARE SAFE.
WHERE TRAVELERS BY NIGHT WOULDN'T NEED PROTECTION.
THIS, I THINK, IS HOW A GOD MUST--
YOU...
YOU'RE RIGHT.
I CAN'T DO IT.
I'M TOO... CONFLICTED.
BUT SHE IS THE FIRST OF US.
SHE HAS CLARITY OF VISION.
CLARITY OF FAITH.
GUILT STABS DEEP.
I ALLOW HER TO TAKE THE BURDEN, BECAUSE I DON'T TRUST MYSELF.
I'M NOT SURE I UNDERSTAND MY OWN BELIEF WELL ENOUGH TO TAKE THAT LEAP.

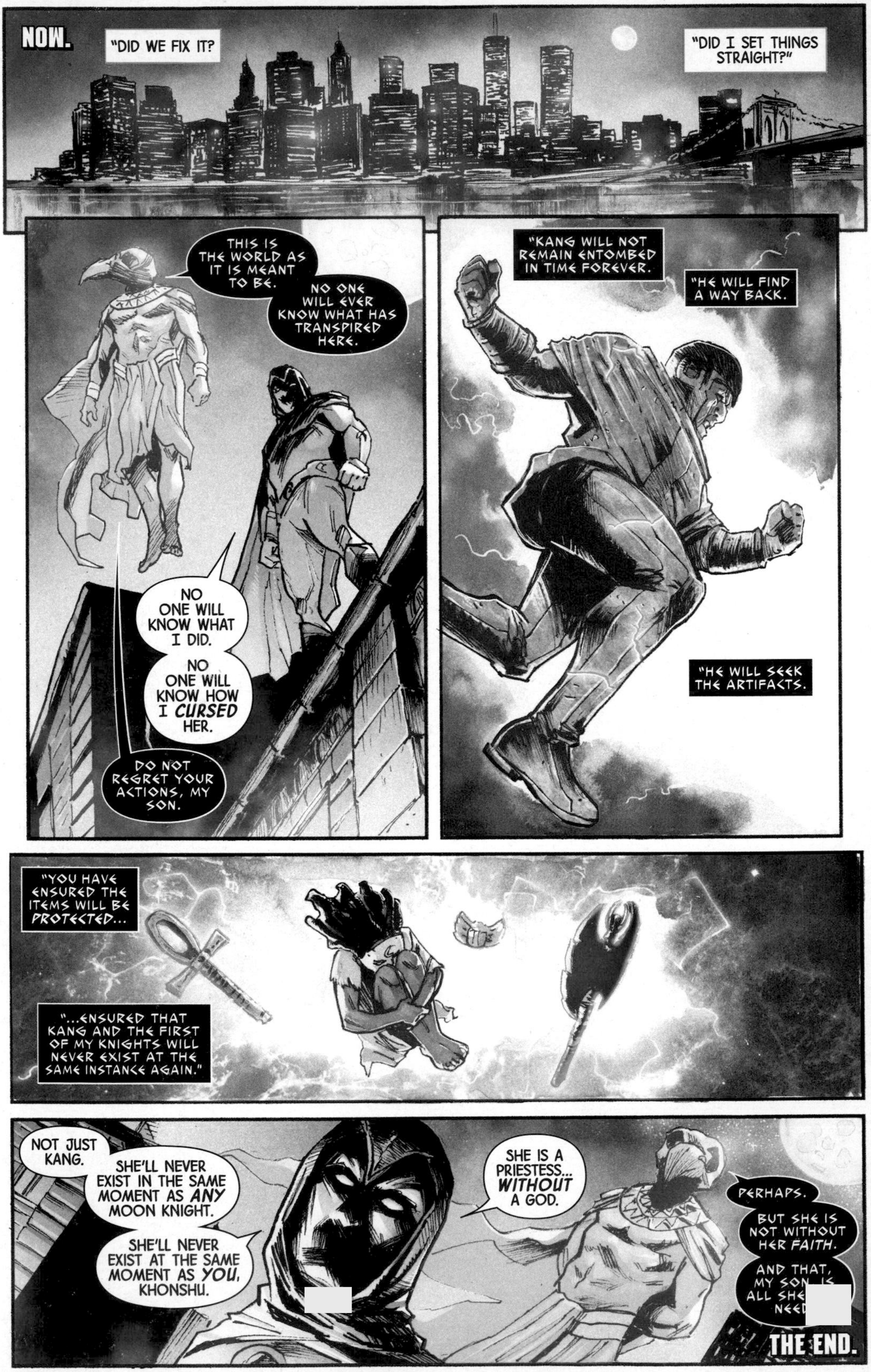
NOW.
"DID WE FIX IT?
"DID I SET THINGS STRAIGHT?"
THIS IS THE WORLD AS IT IS MEANT TO BE.
NO ONE WILL EVER KNOW WHAT HAS TRANSPIRED HERE.
NO ONE WILL KNOW WHAT I DID.
NO ONE WILL KNOW HOW I *CURSED* HER.
DO NOT REGRET YOUR ACTIONS, MY SON.
"KANG WILL NOT REMAIN ENTOMBED IN TIME FOREVER.
"HE WILL FIND A WAY BACK.
"HE WILL SEEK THE ARTIFACTS.
"YOU HAVE ENSURED THE ITEMS WILL BE *PROTECTED*...
"...ENSURED THAT KANG AND THE FIRST OF MY KNIGHTS WILL NEVER EXIST AT THE SAME INSTANCE AGAIN."
NOT JUST KANG.
SHE'LL NEVER EXIST IN THE SAME MOMENT AS *ANY* MOON KNIGHT.
SHE'LL NEVER EXIST AT THE SAME MOMENT AS *YOU*, KHONSHU.
SHE IS A PRIESTESS... *WITHOUT* A GOD.
PERHAPS.
BUT SHE IS NOT WITHOUT HER *FAITH*.
AND THAT, MY SON, IS ALL SHE NEED
THE END.